I May Pre......

Not to know you
But will I ever not love you

A George

Book with own Playlist

A GEORGE

Dear Reader

Thank you for choosing to read I May Pretend, a book with its own playlist, in the same way a film has a soundtrack, this book includes a list in the form of the songs owed & listened to when writing. My writing began in 1978 at 13yrs of age. This story was my third & completed in 1980, the songs listed are songs played throughout the 50s 60s 70s & 80s. The soundtrack of my teens includes songs purchased by my parents because weather we admit to it or not, we all hear what our elders listened to.

Hope you enjoy. Please note many songs have been recorded by more than one artist & only the song name is listed for copyright reasons. I don't want to get into trouble, but hope these songs gain new listeners

The chapters include numbers to indicate what I was listening to when writing & the song list can be found in the same number order at the back of this book. Please enjoy.

Something for the young at heart A gift to you from me because words & music can help our well-being & improve our mental health.

As the self publishing author I would like to say I have not taken any money or reward from anyone & include what were the songs in my family record collection, purely because I see it to be a nice idea & have always mixed my love of music with my fighting with words to help create a fiction filled story. Song 1 is the first song I ever bought for around 35p in the 1970s.

Copyright © 1980 A George
All rights reserved

Author A George asserts the right to be identified as the Writer/Author of *I May Pretend* Not to know you, but will I never not Love you. Thank you for respecting this work.

I May Pretend Not to know you, but will I never not Love you. Is sold subject to the condition that it shall not be lent, resold, hired out or shared or otherwise circulated without the permissions.

I May Pretend Not to know you, but will I never not Love you. Is a work of fiction & as such any resemblance between the characters & persons alive or dead is purely coincidental.

WARNING

A book based on all the firsts experienced in teenage adolescence. Exploring the fun times, difficulties & mistakes experienced on the life journey into adulthood. This book contains language & descriptive text which will offend someone, somewhere. Born in UK Author wrote this book when 14yrs & recommends it for mature readers of 15yrs plus along with adults who are young at heart.

Book with own Playlist
Containing a list of songs around at time of writing
Why not download the list & listen whilst you read

A GEORGE

♪ 1 ♪

*In memory of the family who made me,
my Mum, Dad, Nan & Granddad
To my Aunty Ann & Uncle Alan
Always just a breath away
Gone now, but only until we get there.*

Dedication

Remembering what is youth
My first everything
first friend, first boyfriend
To my first party & the first poster, I hung
To the first song I purchased & played to death
To the first time I tasted what is sweet & sour
First crush, first love & first ever kiss
Remembering my first holiday
The first time your feet sink into soft golden sand
To the first taste of a breeze filled with salt from the sea
To the excitement of a holiday romance
To the first time I was asked to dance
To the heartbreak of each and every goodbye
To all of the many experiences which made us laugh or caused us to cry
If you remember all the first times
this is dedicated to your memories too

A GEORGE

INTRODUCTION

Fifteen & not yet kissed, Fifteen years of age and not yet included on anyones party list, never permitted to go where everyone else goes, her parents wouldn't approve. How was one to learn about the world if she was never allowed to go out and experience what was in it? Fifteen, a mature teenager, being fifteen years old meant she would be sixteen soon.

♪2♪

A maturing female? A girl becoming a woman, loved but alone, looked after while having to learn to look out for oneself, there are times when childhood friends feel more like fleeting acquaintances and parents become prison guards. Adults call it growing up, a time when all senses are heightened and emotions can't be controlled. She saw those around her falling behind as she embraced the urge to race ahead, ready to shake up and change what was. *'Confused?'* Why was it all the things she wanted were all the things others wouldn't allow her to have? *'Teenage hormones?'* A body undergoing a natural transformation; meant a girl feeling anxious about going to sleep for fear of seeing what she would wake up to find? *'A time when each new morning brings a new you.'* New items in the underwear draw, the appearance of what was necessary; indicated the fact what was pure and innocent was slipping away. Strange how changing and becoming stronger can cause one to feel weak, when taking on the pressures of maturing from a child into an adolescent before becoming entangled within the responsibilities of an adult life where it can become difficult to breath.

A besotted teenager? A daydreamer, what else was there for someone like her to do? Television viewing was controlled by her father switching the channel so not to miss what he called vital news. Inflicted by what one finds monotonous results in one becoming bored. A head filled with facts was a mind crying out for something which would entertain and create sensations other than expectance and pressure.

How did they not see her? She wasn't invisible, but neither did she stand out in the crowd.*'Yes Sir & No Miss.'* That which caused her to feel unhappy, was something she had to do, to please those she respected. They were her family and family came first. Lost alone inside a persona created to please all but herself, Jade Jennifer Barris believed she was living proof to the fact people only see what they want to see. Being seen by others as someone who isn't you, results in it becoming impossible to be who you are.

Can love be bought? Provided with everything she was told she would need and surrounded by what was seen to be the best money could buy. Her wealthy parents' spared no expense; when having no time to share because neither had time to spare. Taken to the local cinema to watch all the latest films seen appropriate for their age group and sent to after-school classes to learn the skills seen to be what would be needed in what was their individually planned futures. They were given what was seen to be the latest must have, with each and every passing birthday adding multiple items to the growing mound of things neither would ever need. Possession rich, neither Jade or her brother Jeremy ever went on the expensive far off holidays taken when Mama and Papa left to relax and unwind.

Fact or fantasy? Learning only from books helped nothing and no one. *'Emotionless?'* Jade wasn't sure how or even if she should react to what was a social occasion. A rose in amongst the thorns there to protect her, all she wanted to do was to break free from what was beginning to suffocate. The Princess locked within her castle, if her father was a King, her mother was his pet dragon and her brother the joker whose loyalty switched dependant on who he needed to impress.

Music & Magazines? Lyrics and what was said to be the true life problems experienced by others, pictures and words. *'Attraction & Desire?'* A want to experience what others put on display and a need to be wanted. How can one survive where it feels impossible to fit in? Was it really too much to ask to be like everyone else, did she not breath the same air and attend the same school? Jade spoke the same language and was made of skin and bone like everyone else, yet others refused to accept her being only human. Just a girl, she admired other girls and accepted whatever others preferred, she respected the choices people made, but rarely had she been awarded the acceptance or respect she offered. *'Never nasty or loud.'* Much too quiet and timid to be noticed by boys. Aged fifteen, Jade was struggling to stop her fascination with the opposite sex. Unlike what she heard and saw; Jade had yet to experience any of the firsts; associated with being in her middle teens. First crush, first kiss and first love. *'What would be her first, first?'* Would anything ever come her way? How could it, when no one and nothing was permitted to get close? If they made it through the high security gates and down the long driveway, the staff would discourage and turn them away from the locked door. *'Would she forever be the princess watching the world and everyone in it passing her by from her bedroom within her locked castle?'*

A GEORGE

I MAY PRETEND

Inner Cover
In Memory
© Copyright
Dedication
Letter
Introduction
content List

CHAPTERS

Prologue
Diary Introduction
1: Leader
2: Education
3: Don't Stop
4: Substitute
5: A Little Love
6: Dream Believer
7: Perfect
8: D.I.S.C.O
9: Wild World
10: Live & Die
11: Runaway
12: Once bitten
13: Tomorrow
14: Dreams
15: Far
16: Again
17: Home
18: Young Hearts
Playlist

A GEORGE

PROLOGUE

Told by her father never to give up on her dream, she wasn't sure she'd ever known what her dream was? Different, but never ashamed of those she knew loved her, how could someone so young have regrets? How could she be where she was, about to do what she was doing; after everything she'd done? *'Young & naive?'* Everyone makes mistakes, had she made more than most? Like she was and would always be, her mistakes were different, not the norm, not the mistakes she wanted to make. No one sets out to get things wrong and destroy ones own life, but sometimes it is impossible to prevent others and circumstance from getting in the way. Sometimes one becoming derailed from life's track, is impossible to avoid. *'Where had it all gone wrong?'* Did she only have herself to blame?

Miss. Jemima Jade Denton, sorry for all the trouble she caused, sorry for not being content with the life she was born into and sorry those to have found; have saved her from what she planned so to change her fate. *'Sad & lonely?'* Picked upon and ridiculed for not living in the right area and not speaking proper. *'Home was a flat, not a house.'* Laughed at for not wearing the correct uniform and frowned upon because nothing she owned carried a designers' tag or fashion label. Intelligent, her parents wouldn't stand in the way of what was her high intellectual advances. Supportive to a fault, they weren't to blame. They didn't know any better, what they'd done they did because they saw it as being for the best. *'Loved while being laughed at?'* They said they had every faith in her being able to succeed, but she felt like she was failing. *'She couldn't stop them from laughing.'* No longer responding to those unable to understand, stopping one thing led to her listening to the words of those who never had anything good say. *'Not worthy?'* Some said she had no right to be where her kind didn't belong. A sponsored invitation to be the best she could be, outside what she was there to learn, she couldn't settle, she didn't belong. Not permitted to fit in, she would never be so lucky as to be in the right place at the right time. Not when where she was felt wrong. A teenager living in the halls of residence when her home was only a bus ride away, her attempt to be like everyone else wasn't working. Able to answer what her tutors asked, she could never tell those who should know; what it was she was really thinking. *'A painted smile.'* Friends were nothing more than acquaintances made because they were people in the same place at the same time. Intelligent in the classroom, the words failed to come when she needed to complete what was needed to achieve her social goals. *'Letting everyone down.'* Her father was working two jobs and her mother was telling the neighbours how proud she was of her eldest child. *'Gifted?'*

Why wasn't she more like her sister? Brought up together, given all the same chances and sharing some of the same clothes. The two slept in the same bedroom and joked about liking the same boys, Jemima and her younger sister Jennifer couldn't be more different. The same ends of a magnet, if Jennifer was a rock, Jemima was sand and if Jemima was the rain, her younger sister was snow. Stronger and able to be around for longer, stable and there to help. While her sister did all she could to find her way. Jemima was struggling to help herself and continue in the direction she was pointed.

Her parents' pride and joy, while Jemima was held on a pedestal, Jennifer was the one doing everything she could to survive. *'Happy go lucky?'* Jennifer rarely complained about the things she didn't have, because unlike her elder, Jennifer could always make-do. Her mother and her father, she knew if needed; even her sister would be there, they were there waiting for her to explain why she attempted to do what she wished she'd done. Time away from the family, a safe place to be and space to think. *'Gained qualifications in business studies.'* Institutionalised because professionals said she needed to be kept safe. *'A danger to herself?'* It wasn't her saying the things to have become confused inside her head; but it was she who had to learn how to stop listening to what was causing her to want to end what was difficult. *'Worthless?'* The first boy she loved had dumped her, but not before saying how his being with her had all been a dare. His chance to experience a bit of rough, before being matched with someone of his own kind. *'Not good enough?'* Jennifer would have laughed it off? No, the truth was; Jennifer would have seen through the pretence and recognised deceit from the start. Where Jemima was academic her younger sister was streetwise. Blessed with an intellectual mind, Jemima often found herself wishing she had just a tenth of her sisters' logic and common sense. *'Prepared to give her life to escape wheat was her mind.'*

Sorry, she would always regret not succeeding when attempting what she had. Looked after, nursed and supported back to health. Taken good care of and loved, her reintegration into what was everyday life, turned out to be a longer journey than anyone expected. Institutionalised from the age of fifteen to twenty, saved. Jemima would forever be sorry, because she wouldn't ever be the same as she once was. Grateful, Miss Jemima Jade Denton would be forever in debt to those to have given her the time, respect and inspiration she needed, alongside the medication to have pulled her up from the depth of despair and proven she was able to stand on her own two feet. *'Given a second chance.'*

A lover of her own life, a female with purpose and a career in-which she was able to thrive. Her second female, male relationship resulted in her taking for herself a husband. *'When inside Jemima had a girlfriend.'* Back out in the world, she found a man able to provide all the things which when younger she felt she missed out on, a man who adored her. *'Sorry?'* Jemima would forever be sorry for what she saw to be her biggest ever mistake. Thankful for her life, Miss Denton was sorry that on the day she would never forget, she lost something which could never be returned. *'Sorry?'* Jemima was so very sorry; she would never be able to say the word five letter word ever again. Having almost lost herself and her everything, the strong willed female vowed she would never risk losing anything, not ever again. So not to lose, one must continue to win, never allowing emotions, or others to distract, or hold back what must forever stride forward. *'Strong willed & independent?'* The one who had once felt a need to surrender and give up on everything, wouldn't form attachments she had no need for ever again.

In love, he was older and the first time their eyes met she had been dressed in a hospital gown. Rushing by the foot of her bed with his parents; all eager to know what had happened? *'Sad & vulnerable?'* She noticed how their hasty entrance was followed by an exit which was slow. *'Defeated?'* When next the two met, he was wearing a suit and she was in heels, how could they not ask if they knew one another? How could the two not get along? *'In love?'* Yes, he fell for her, and his being able to answer all of her questions was what led to her learning how to love him. The wedding was the type every girlie girl dreamt of. A struggle, being a wife was a dream whilst becoming a housewife wasn't something she relished. Afraid of surrendering her independence, when her husband made a mistake, she forgave his indiscretion because her turning a blind eye was easier than walking away from the wealth which took them from one class up into another. *'Rich?'* In love, she blamed the other; not her man and never herself. *'Happy?'* A family, she would retain everything she saw as being what she fought hard and worked tirelessly to achieve. From a council estate to a stately home, from tenant to home owner. Content, so long as her secrets were never discovered.

THE DIARY INTRODUCTIONS

♪3♪

Told by her grandfather never to give up on her dream, she wasn't sure what her dream was? Different, but never ashamed, how could someone so young have regrets? *'Young & naive?'* How was she to learn about all the things her parents' protected her from?

Age Nine:

March 4th
Today we said goodbye to gramps, known to his friends as Lonny, the illness to have ravaged his bones grabbed and took hold of his internal organs. Doctors tried, but no one succeeded in persuading cancer to let go of what it clung onto until the end. In the early hours of this morning gramps succumb to the never ending sleep which is death. He hated being bed ridden, he loved life, too young to die. The last thing he said was that I wasn't to cry. "Don't cry because one day we will be back together." Gramps said he wasn't leaving, just moving over to make space for someone else to be given the chance of life. Right now I can't stop crying because I'll never know that someone else, right now; all I want is my Gramps back. I'll never stop wanting the hero I'm struggling to see how I will live without. A strange day, Mama disagreed; but she gave in to grannie wanting all of us to attend the funeral. Saying goodbye is said to help when grieving.

♪4♪

March 13th
Everyone was dressed in black, Mama hid beneath a large black hat and aunt Jennifer joined grannie in wearing a short veil to disguise their tears. Sad, it was raining in a way I've never seen it rain before; grannie

said the rain was caused by the angels crying because the person to have been taken had been taken too soon. Grannie said a sun filled funeral means the one saying goodbye is at peace and happy to go on to the next place. A rainbow is sent by the deceased as a gift to brighten the day of those feeling sad. A dull grey day means the deceased had unfinished business and a thunderstorm indicates a dispute at the gates leading into the next world. I wonder if a thunderstorm means the person isn't really dead and able to come back? If yes, I wish the rain clouds had banged together, I don't want gramps to be gone and I hope grannie will be okay without him. Grandma Loti; our grannie believes in a lot of things, but she doesn't believe in hell and assures me everyone who dies gets into what is their own vision of heaven. Prayers? Why were people thanking the almighty for making gramps ill and taking him away? Songs and poems? Why were people talking to gramps when he wasn't there to hear? Gramps would have told everyone to shut up, to turn the music down and to get to the pub to down a pint on him. Too common for Mama and Papa, Mr. Lonny Lea Denton would have invited everyone back to his local for a pork pie and a pint, the wake was held at a top hotel with five star restaurant. "Posh nosh and bubbles up your nose." Gramps always told me to treat others how I wanted to be treated, he said respect must be given to be gained and told me Mama and Papa's stuffy snobbery was fooling no one. Gramps said no amount of cash ever made a person rich, because ones personal wealth included happiness, belonging, self worth and health. Cancer and ill health took my gramps away, but he said he wouldn't change his being family rich and cash poor for the world.'I hope the next world is good to him.'He loved us and adored his wife, gramps hated champagne and I'm sure I saw grannie feeding hers' to more than one of the pot plants in the hotel reception. Wonder if she knew the plants were all artificial? It made me smile because I knew what she was doing would make gramps laugh. Today I saw a large wooden box people said contained the body of my hero stood covered in flowers. People seem to have forgotten Mr. Lonny Lea Denton was a hay-fever sufferer. 'I would give anything to hear him sneeze again.' Standing inside a room made to look like a church; I watched gramps in his box disappear behind a curtain. Gone? How can someone be here one day and the next be gone? Gramps was here and then he was nowhere. I'll never stop wanting him back. I told grannie I could still hear all the things he said to me and I knew what he would be saying if he was still with us. Grannie told me it was okay, because its our way of never forgetting those who help make us the people we are. I'll never stop loving my gramps, he loved me unconditionally.

♪5♪

Age ten:

<u>*May* 21st</u>
My first birthday without him, I miss his bear like hugs and grumpy sarcasm, gramps would have something to say about what I was wearing and he would see more than the funny side of the fact Mama and Papa arranged a clown to entertain those they invited. A donkey for us to ride on, Mama will explode when she realises it ate her flowerbeds when she wasn't looking and watered her lawn in places which are bound to show. Poor Trevor will have his work cutout to put things right; but he won't complain. Gramps liked Trevor, old school, the two always found something to talk about when walking off to have a crafty cigarette and nip of whiskey. 'Treat others how you want to be treated.' Unlike Mama, gramps would never have others doing for him what he could do for himself, if here; gramps would help Trevor put everything back how it should be. Grannie says her tears are now tears of joy and for all the happy memories. My tears are because I want gramps to be here. Today I am ten, I've

reached double figures and I hate everyone who will have their gramps for longer than I had mine. Not really. I know others can't change what is happening anymore than I can change what happened. Today I am ten. Happy Birthday to me.

♪6♪

<u>Age Eleven:</u>

<u>**September 4th**</u>
New school, new uniform and new shoes, not that my feet have grown, Mama never misses an excuse to go shopping. Designer, she'd have me dressed head to foot in Prada, smelling of Chanel and displaying everything Tiffany like a primed peacock, or over stated advertisement board if school allowed. Mavis sewed my name tags over the labels so others won't see, Mama will never notice because Mama never does the laundry, Mama wouldn't know which dry cleaners we use, keeping mine and Mavis's secret safe forever. Different, it's not easy being someone seen to be different; going somewhere new. <u>Secondary School?</u> *The next step up the ladder of compulsory education. Larger and more imposing, a maze of corridors leading into and in-between classrooms the size of what use to be the primary schools' hall. New rules, keeping to the right, or the left dependant on which direction one is heading, changing classroom for each lesson will take some getting use to and carrying a heavy bag on my shoulder until I reach the year where a personal locker is provided; won't always be easy, especially on the days I have baking, art and gym.*

<u>**October 23rd**</u>
Too much stuff and way too many people. Secondary school brings ten or more primary schools together under one roof, mixing people from different towns, it's my friends' and me who are seen to be the odd ones out. All things shinny and new doesn't mean those known to thrive on being dominate will change. Glad to

have my friends' with me, we were shocked to meet up with those who enjoy seeing and treating us different to how they see and treat everyone else. New teachers and classmates, new timetables and exercise books to take home and cover.<u>I find tin foil looks best and lasts longest.</u> At least it's what Mavis shown me to work, that and a sticky label to write my name on. Baking, I'm ridiculed enough without looking silly, Mavis and me practise the recipes before I have to go into the classroom to bake, she also shows me shortcuts which impress the teachers. Maybe I deserve the names swot and teachers pet? Is being disliked better than failing in what Mama and Papa say will matter most? <u>My education?</u> Is being disliked and succeeding, better than making myself look incapable just so I fit in? I think secondary school is going to be harder, not because the workload and learning is increasing. My first term at my new school is complete and I hate it. <u>I hate being me.</u>

♪7♪

<u>Age twelve:</u>

<u>December 19th</u>
Mugs of cream topped hot chocolate and nights spent roasting marshmallows on an open fire under the stars. Cold never feels so bad when being warmed by the love of those around you. Sam isn't gramps because no one could ever take the place of the man who I will forever call my hero. Sam is a good man, easy to talk to and fun to be around. Sam loves Loti and seeing grannie happy means everything to me, seeing grannie smile makes me smile. Another world, the miles between us mean visits aren't as frequent as we hoped, the distance makes my time with grannie more precious and always too short. I wish I could stay here with her forever, but then I wish I could stay anywhere which isn't where I live.

A GEORGE

<u>*December 25th*</u>
Christmas with grannie and Sam was good, it was busy with everyone coming together and having fun. I say everyone. Mama and Papa left to meet up with friends at the local ski resort. Looking at a map was proof enough to show there is nothing local in Canada. Mama and Papa left Jeremy and me with Loti and Sam while they went on holiday and spent yet another Christmas with those they call friends instead of family.

♪8♪

<u>Age thirteen:</u>

<u>Birthday Party</u>
Family and friends, the best champagne money could buy and restaurant standard steaks on the barbecue, too old for a bouncy castle and donkey rides, clowns are so last year and magicians prefer to entertain at weddings. Grannie and Sam came all the way from Canada, but they're only staying a few days. Aunt Jennifer and uncle Kevin are here for the weekend, the only time I can stand being in my house is when it's full; Mama says crowded, but eight bedrooms and a two bed annex is more than enough space for thirteen people. Grannie and Gramps Barris are here with Uncle Julian, aunty Victoria and baby Elsa. I thought Elsa was a lions' name, but then I guess her cries do sound like a roar. Cute, she's a baby so she doesn't do anything but sleep, eat and smell funny. Cute, I've seen Papa sneak the odd cuddle and I've also seen how quick Mama passed Elsa to Papa when aunt Victoria asked her to help. <u>Thirteen:</u> Today I become a teenager, my friends' are here with their families and I was told to invite a select few from school. <u>Who would want to come?</u> The only others anywhere near my age are here with their parents' because their parents' are people invited by Mama and Papa. It's the same as it always is, told off for spending time with the staff and their children; here to help me celebrate, but only permitted into certain areas. Here to help the caterers if old

enough, here to make it look like I know more people than I ever will, all told <u>If seen they shouldn't be heard.</u> It's my thirteenth birthday party and no one wants to hear what I have to say. I've been up in my room for over an hour and no ones noticed I'm missing from my own celebration.

"One two three, it's only me, coming in ready or not." *Okay, one person saw me leave.* "What happened to the birthday girl?"

Jimmy. Master James Kingston, son of Trevor and a regular around the garden come the school holidays. My friends' think he's cute, he's someone I've known all my life and so to me, Jimmy is like an elder brother, not quite so annoying cos I get to send him home. Jimmy and Jeremy, neither should, but both are caring, considerate and kind. A birthday celebration minus the birthday girl, a children's party without any party games, the cake was made special and the trifle contains sherry. I hope Mama enjoys her day? My birthday wish is to spend more time with grannie and aunt Jennifer before they go home. What I want and wish for never matters. Playing boardgames on my bed with Jimmy, when he arrived; we welcomed my younger brother who joined us too.

<u>Age fourteen:</u>

<u>July 4th:</u>
The 4th anniversary of the day gramps died, I'm about to complain about not seeing those I watch from afar; when I'm never going to see gramps again. Am I selfish to want something, when I have no clue what the something I want is? Is this what adults mean by growing pains? Not aches, or sharp twinges, the pain I'm feeling isn't easy to describe, it isn't something which makes me scream out, but it brings tears to my eyes for no reason and causes me to grab my chest because my heart feels like it is moving too fast, is it

breaking? Maybe my heart size is changing, I hope it's getting bigger and not becoming hard and bitter? I hope things settle soon, because I'm not enjoying getting older on my own.

July 24th
The six week holiday start today, its a miracle I made it to the end of term, not academically, I can handle the work and homework, but I'm beginning to wonder for how much longer I will be able to take the sly looks, name calling and being made to feel like I shouldn't exist. It's not that I don't want to be here, well I don't want to be in this house and I definitely don't want to be at that school, but I do want to live. What I want is a life worth living, where do I get one? Maybe next term will be different? School shutting today means I won't be seeing them until next term, me and Jeremy will be spending the summer with Aunt Jennifer, which means I won't know if any of them visit, or ride by. Them, my friends' Tamara Tilly Tombrink and Gretchen Gloria Garlock. Them? The boys who ride motorbikes. Them? When written between the crisp white pages of my diary, them is everyone I see more clearly now I am a teenager. Them, means those I see passing during the long hours spent sitting at my bedroom window and those I watch when looking out from my classroom. A dreamer? Gramps said I should never give up on my dreams. I watch through the window of Papas car and sometimes I can see what is happening outside the study. Them and they, are the people I see allowing me a glimpse into life outside my confinement. I will miss what happens at school, but I don't want to have to go back. Routine and being out of the house, I miss not being able to see what I should be experiencing. Why am I different?

Rojay rode by early this morning, he was riding a new motorbike, bright red and silver. The others were with him like always and Lizzie Clarke is flavour of the month. Lizzie is still the one wrapping her arms around his leather clad torso and holding onto him wherever he goes. Rojay, Mr. Roland Jackson is someone I mention more than most, someone I keep within the pages locked between the hard covers kept private. Rojay and the girls he dates. If dating is dating when it only lasts a few short days; the girls mentioned are the girls who over the months and years have dated Rojay. The boys who ride motorbikes everywhere they go are always accompanied by girls. Is it a crush? On the motorbike, maybe? The two wheeled, engine powered machines and the freedom they portray is what I crave. The freedom and excitement of behaving like a teenager is a mystery to me. Not the type of girl to be invited to ride.

♪9♪

August 12th
Summer with aunt Jennifer and uncle Kevin. The train journey is always worth what waits at the end. Taken to the station by Mavis and Trevor, our handyman, gardener and full time housekeeper sometimes nanny, the two are always where we need them to be. Not our parents' Mama and Papa don't trouble themselves, too busy providing for our future, there is always an excuse, none of which we haven't heard before. Our household employees' don't have to give us hugs and wave us off, but they insist they do. Always there to wave goodbye, wish us all the best and greet us hello. Mavis always supplies one of her warming smiles, freshly baked cakes and a hot cup of whatever we fancy, always ready to help where and however he can, Trevor never refuses, or complains whatever duty Mama and Papa ask him to perform. We, Jeremy and me agree it wouldn't be the same should our parents' ever interfere in what's become routine. Good people, not a couple, both Mrs. Mavis Martin and Mr. Trevor Kingston have families of their own, living local enough to be there when needed, both do more than each is contracted to do under the terms and conditions

of their employment. Employees, our parents call staff, to Jeremy and me they are family. <u>Fifteen?</u> When I return I'll enter my last year of compulsory education. <u>Six form or college?</u> Should I take a gap year, or go to university? I don't know why I'm questioning what Mama and Papa will have decided. I ask the questions because they are the questions others my age are asking. <u>I may pretend:</u> I'll never be like everyone else.

Fun in the sun, arriving at the station and being greeted by aunt Jennifer and uncle Kevin brings a smile to my face which feels impossible to remove until they stand where they are standing to wave us goodbye and send us back to all the things and places I don't want. Fun in the sun, time for me to assist my aunt while Jeremy goes searching rock pools. <u>Fifteen:</u> A special birthday tea of fish and chips followed by a slice of homemade cake. When upset gramps would tell me it was nothing a little growing up wouldn't cure, but I don't want to grow up before having the chance to experience being a teen. Fifteen and never kissed, not that there's anyone I want to be kissed by, none of my friends' have boyfriends, but both tell me they have experienced holiday romance.

<u>**August 29th**</u>
Going back is never the same as arriving, no excitement, going back to what is mundane and routined isn't a feeling to relish. Unlike the sun drenched beach and flower filled village, the place Mama calls home is dreary and dull, Jemima lives in a house which is clinical, aunt Jennifer lives in a place which is welcoming and homely. Going back means returning to school, one more year, exams to pass and decisions to make. I don't want to go home, but Mavis and Trevor will be waiting. Maybe I'll come back and stay forever one day. Maybe school will be different this year? And perhaps someone will say something to me which isn't a dare, or meant as a joke. The long hot

summer school break, six weeks never felt so short, how could forty-two days have come and gone so quick? No holiday romance <u>Fifteen & still never kissed.</u> Still the name missed off everybody's party invitation list. Older, I hear my elders doubting my becoming any wiser in the ways of the world. Will I ever experience true teenage life? Loved and protected, aunt Jennifer defended the life mapped out for me by her elder sister; calling Jemima a protective mother. If being protective means avoiding any and everything a parent should do, aunt Jennifer couldn't be more right.

The scribbled words of a maturing female, the hardback books locked with a key, which held much more than her thoughts and feelings. The only problem was, she didn't want to be the one she was writing about. Not who she wanted to be. How could one change what was seen to be her fate? Not the type to play up and become a rebel, brought up to think things through. Caring and considerate of others, she wasn't a bad person, the trouble began when Miss Jade Jennifer Barris found herself maturing into an adolescent and growing into a person she didn't want to be. There was nothing wrong with the life her parents' wanted for her, except the fact it was as far removed from actual life and what she saw being experienced and enjoyed by others around her as it could be.

♪10♪

A GEORGE

1: LEADER

♪11♪

Lay listening to the ageing vinyl record collection discovered hidden in the loft, when lay across her spacious pillow filled queen size bed and flicking through another soppy teenage magazine smuggled in by a member of staff. The one to have recently returned from visiting her aunt and uncle felt nervous about returning to school. *'Shy.'* Not being like everyone else meant Miss Barris standing in the shadows and watching others who basked in the adventure filled sunshine of teenage life. "You're shy." Her elders said. *'Shy?'* Even the problem pages inside the magazines she read in secret, referred to her strange uneasy feelings as shyness. "You'll grow out of it." Over the years, the maturing female had grown out of her clothes and her shoes, she'd out grown her toys and the pink fluffy cloud wallpaper still adorning her bedroom walls. *'Maturing into a young woman.'* Growing up fast, Miss Jade Jennifer Barris had grown out of most things; but was showing no sign of growing out of the uneasy sensations causing her to stumble and stutter whenever she wanted to portray herself as being confident and calm. *'A mess?'* Aged fifteen years and entering her final year of compulsory education; Jade felt no different to the way she felt the last year or the year before. Growing into her first bra, her not feeling any different hadn't stopped her looking like someone she no longer recognised when glancing into a mirror. *'Mature.'* Wider hips, a smaller waist and the need for upper body support, her being blessed with good skin and glowing cheeks saved the embarrassment of spots, but keeping her long flowing hair from looking like she'd spent the night sleeping in an oil slick was proving to be a constant battle. *'Different?'* Returning to school at the age of fifteen meant the shy teen not only worrying about her being brought up different, now she looked different too. *'Not the same as everyone else?'* An intelligent student, she hoped others had also matured in appearance. *'Helped by her aunt.'* Aunt Jennifer turned what was her first bra fitting into a fun day out. Unlike Mama, the younger of the Denton sister's never failed to make time to be there, always ready and willing to give direction and show understanding. *'Life would be so much easier if Jade could live with her favourite aunt.'*

Preparing to return to school after the long summer break was like preparing to enter a chamber of torture, an outcast long before her body decided she should look more woman than girl, there were times when school felt like a spaceship filled with aliens. *'A place with few friends.'* A place where she didn't belong, where everything felt wrong and where being clever in the classroom meant having to sit in the shadows when venturing out onto the playground. *'Forever in hiding.'* No one willingly put themselves in the firing line, no one enjoyed being ridiculed. *'Bullied?'* The term being bullied seemed harsh for what had never included physical contact. *'Comical?'* There were times when what others said about her and her friends' caused them to laugh, not that they could laugh in front of those who saw themselves to be superior, wiser, more experienced and much more important. *'Upsetting?'* Jade felt the few tears shed because of what others said were tears being shed due to confusion and frustration. When in the company of those happy to show their dislike; Miss Jade Jennifer Barris felt more anger than pain. *'Being bullied or being weak?'* Why was the classroom a mix of bright and brighter while the playground a constant revolving stage of good against evil? Why couldn't those who didn't care for others; leave those others alone? *'Would the bullying turn physical?'* Would she ever find her pack leader to fall for? Alone, in her room, the teenager to have never experienced the highs and lows of ones first crush; asked a thousand questions about what would, could and should be? *'Why was she so shy?'* Why was she no longer content with her life? Afraid of life because she was encouraged to avoid what others talked about, participated in and appeared to enjoyed. Not like everyone else because she came from a wealthy family where the only other child was her younger brat of a brother, Master Jeremy Jon Barris aged thirteen. *'Different?'* Alongside wealth; many saw the Barris youngsters to have an inbred snobbery which warranted the two being labelled as posh, spoilt and rich. *'Unapproachable?'* Protected by wealthy hardworking parents, as the elite, Jeremy and Jade were seen to be easy targets for anyone intent on inflicting harsh words and mockery. *'Bullied?'* There were times when they found themselves mocked, picked on and ridiculed by those calling them the wrong sort to attend public school. *'Why were they where they were, when no one wanted them there & they wanted to be anywhere else?'*

Quiet and timid with a tender and caring nature, having one parent with a highly paid demanding career in law and another who local's referred to as a lady who lunches, Jade and her brother were seen as coming from the ranks of the privately educated. *'Local?'* Mr. and Mrs. Barris saw them sending their offspring into the public learning system as giving them a chance to gain insight into what each referred to as an ordinary life. *'Local?'* The fact neither parent attended private education and the locality of the best public school in the area meant Jeremy and Jade remaining where the two had been placed by local authorities since becoming of age to learn. *'Outcasts?'* While learning alongside everyone else; neither was encouraged to become involved with anyone not seen to be university material. *'Snobs?'* Many kept their distance. *'Look but don't touch.'* The siblings were encouraged to observe what was life outside the confinement of their home, but not to get involved. Jeremy and Jade Barris were being brought up proper and the last thing either should do was to disrespect, or disobey the authority of their Mama and

Papa. Neither should ever let themselves or their parents' down. *'A lady who lunches?'* The truth was, the female seen by many to be chasing her youth; was the silent business partner of many a salon. A self made millionaire. With shares in the thriving beauty industry at every turn, Mrs. Jemima Jade Barris was a manager seen by outsiders to manage nothing but herself, someone who was never seen out without her designer handbags and high shoes, it was said her natural moody pout was a result of sore, aching feet. *'Unconventional?'* Mrs. Barris never looked, acted or reacted like a mother should. *'Not like other mothers.'* Privileged, Jade and her brother having high earning parents' led to them spending much of their time on their own. *'Allowed to do whatever they wanted to.'* So long as they didn't venture outside the strict boundaries set by a Papa busy fighting for what was right and a Mama increasing her overinflated bank balance by acquainting herself with the highest of high classes. A Mama who would do anything; so long as anything, didn't mean her having to spend time with her children.

Courteous and immaculately groomed, aware of right and wrong, the brother and sister were never naughty. Watched over and looked after by those paid to tend to their every need, from birth to becoming teenagers; Jeremy and Jade were kept safe and secure within the large, luxurious surroundings of the detached house their parents called home and visitors referred to as a palace. *'A maze of rooms?'* A palace where space and privacy was never an issue, where company and having someone to turn to, was rarely found. *'Lonely?'* The two who only ever truly had one another; sometimes broke the rule which stated a brother and sister should never be friends. *'Good children?'* Mama and Papa called them unique. *'Intelligent?'* Jeremy was showing promise in the sciences and his sister a **_'Grade A.'_** Student. Wise with words, what was documented to be their above average intelligence came from books. *'What else did they have* *to do?'* Days of reading and hours of studying the many reference and encyclopaedia's purchased as good behaviour gifts and kept up to date so neither became bored. *'Different?'* How could the two not be confused, when real teenage life was nothing like what was portrayed within accredited literature and the text filled books each was encouraged to turn to and consult should they have a question in need of answering? While other boys kicked footballs and rode bikes; Jeremy hid inside his basement laboratory and called his many magic tricks, his hidden pleasure. Chess was his sport of choice because Master Barris was a gentleman in the making. *'Different?'* While other girls played with dolls and pushed prams, Jade was encouraged to read, listen to language tapes and write essays. Her hidden pleasure was listening to music and her chosen sport if she had to pick, was dance. *'Different?'* Neither engaged in rough sports or ventured out after dark because that wasn't the type of life their parents' planned. *'Look, don't touch?'* In the same way others kept their distance from them, they were warned to keep a safe space between them, others and what was teenage life.

Intellectual and intelligent, clever and on track to complete her studies at a top university. On track to become a lawyer or anything she wanted to be. Miss Barris would thrive in the world of smart suits and briefcases because the only thing she didn't know about, was the mystery which was life. *'Who was she & who would she become?'* When it came to what went on outside the classroom and beyond the walls of the grand property in-which she lived; the maturing teenager had no idea about anything. Real life, rough sports, skirts worn above the knee and being on the streets after dark, for one of such breeding and high standing; true teen antics were neither permitted nor seen to be necessary. It was by mistake she stumbled across the forgotten single and album collection and it was without her parent's knowledge or consent; she asked their housekeeper/cook

Mavis to purchase the weekly magazines she examined in hope of discovering what it was others her age were doing. When alone, Jade read the words and listened to the songs which spoke of current affairs whilst describing feelings and emotions she had yet to encounter. Reading facts advertised as being actual and stories described as true life, the elder sister and only daughter living within the rich and protected Barris household questioned what was her life? *'Jade went nowhere & did nothing she wasn't told she could or should do.'* Why did teachers treat her like she was a precious jewel? Jade may be amongst the brightest of students, like the many hundreds of other pupils attending school, Miss Barris was only human. *'Confused?'* Many suspected Mama and Papa Barris of making financial contributions no headteacher could refuse.

At home, it was her and her brother Jeremy, in school there were two who the maturing teen called friends. Both female and aged fifteen, from pre school to nursery, through primary and into secondary education the band of three; Jade, Gretchen and Tamara had been put and so remained together. Meeting at their weekly horse ridding lessons when three years of age, their children having fun in the hay bales brought together three mothers who wanted what was best for their girls. Owned by Gretchen's mother Gwen, Galloping Glory Stables housed the best ridding school money could pay for. *'A hobby for someone with much & time on her hands.'* Miss Gretchen Gloria Garlock was the middle daughter of plastic surgeon Dr. Ethan Garlock and his ex catwalk model turned horsewoman wife Gwen. *'Clever & pretty.'* Gretchen favoured her mother much more than she was like her father. *'Clever?'* Gretchen would pass her chosen exams; safe in the knowledge she was under no pressure to achieve her academic goals, because she would work beside and eventually takeover her mothers' thriving business. *'Set for life.'*

I MAY PRETEND

The parents of Tamara Tombrink were GP's with their own private medical clinic. Dr. Tyrone Tombrink and his older wife Tessa; referred to only daughter Gretchen as being their miracle, making no secret of the fact she could do and be whatever she wanted, the proud hard working parents vowed always to be there and provide their precious princess with whatever her heart desired. Believing they'd never be blessed with a child of their own, Tessa and Tyrone encouraged their daughter to do her best, whilst making certain she was aware they were there to catch her should she fall. *'Good people?'* Wealthy and well to do persons of importance, while being sent to public school as a matter of connivance, each girl was told never to stray from their own. *'Female friends only.'* Gretchen and Tamara lived by similar rules to Jade. *'Posh & polite.'* Educated by books, brought up by nannies and able to ride horses. *'Why was Jade not permitted to go anywhere but school? Why couldn't she choose her own friends?'* Why since turning fifteen hadn't she been able to stop asking questions? Three friends, each was sent to the local school because it was seen to be an invaluable experience, each was provided with extra tuition because they couldn't be seen to fail and each was permitted to look, but never encouraged to touch or be touched by everyday life.

Sat with her dreams and thoughts of what it would be like to be one of the girls in the magazine stories, or the one who groups and singers sang about in their songs. *'Sat dreaming about being loved & in love?'* In the absence of any comparisons; Jade wondered what it would feel like to go out. To attend a youth club, to get down at the disco or go see a film at the cinema minus a chaperone? *'Being out alone wasn't encouraged.'* When sat in extra lessons, reading books or writing essays; Jade found herself wondering what others her age were doing? Glancing at the new, washed and freshly pressed uniform hanging on the outside of her dressing room door; Jade questioned herself and her ability to survive another year.

♪*12*♪

Dance classes, participating in latin and ballroom, modern and interpretive dance, while others her age attended youth clubs and parties able to meet someone and allow strangers become friends, Jade smiled politely and thanked her allocated partner. *'Sometimes male, sometimes female?'* There were never enough opposites to allow all couples to be mixed and being in amongst friends who numbered three meant someone being left out. *'She didn't mind.'* Not really, not about being the one who got to dance with a variety of partners; allowing her the opportunity to lead and follow. *'Dancing felt like life.'* Smiling and saying thank you, those Jade saw as being friendly and attractive would have their girl and boyfriends' waiting for them outside class. *'Rich boys didn't like shy girls.'* Jade was beginning to believe no boy would ever like her. *'Dance lessons?'* While others were out laughing and joking with friends old and new, Jade was left dancing on her own. Horse riding while others rode bikes, when other teenagers met inside the local shopping centres, Jade took tennis lessons and was instructed on how to walk and talk right. While those her own age gathered to catch up on whatever was going on in the world, Jade was escorted to the library by someone her parents' saw as responsible. Exercising, while other teenage girls were out running around with boys; Jade was swimming in the privacy of her own pool or taking a yoga class alongside Mama with personal instructor Star. *'Time spent together.'* Them not needing to communicate left Jade with plenty of time to think about what was forever on her mind. Recently, she'd started wondering about boys? *'The opposite sex?'* Why did the word sex cause many of a certain age to giggle and turn red? Having researched the biology of the three letter word, a fifteen year old Miss Barris didn't see much to laugh about, having never experienced what was described as flirting, Jade had no clue as to what there was to be embarrassed about.

♪*13*♪

Moving across to the padded, cushion filled window seat as the next tune dropped to play inside the box style record player, Jade glanced out, down and across the extensive grounds to encircled the large building her parents' called home. *'A mansion?'* Locals referred to the extensive detached, as being the local palace. *'A stately home.'* Rebuilt by those to own it and enclosed by rows of trees standing either side of a twelve foot stone wall, what was grand, was only accessible through high security gates leading from the main road into a long driveway. *'Her tower?'* Looking down, out and across what surrounded her, Jade's eyes scanned the deserted street beyond. *'Safe & sound?'* While her elders called what separated them from others; security, she saw it as being all part of her segregation, her private prison, the only thing missing from her windows were the bars. Watching the few cars to pass on what was the main road, she knew how that morning would see everything change. *'School days were different.'* Tomorrow there would be people walking along the pavements as those who had no other choice made their way to school on foot. People who Jade could describe individually would embark upon what in term time they did at least twice a day. *'Never permitted to make her own way.'* Watching people who wouldn't know her name, few classmates and school colleagues had ever taken the time to ask. Snob? *'Rarely did anyone use her name?'* Snob, Posh and Miss Prim, Jade chose to remember the more polite references made by others describing how they perceived her. *'No one knew.'* Not like she knew them, able to say something about each, her personal and natural observation skills were second to none. *'A people watcher?'* Jade Jennifer Barris felt she knew everybody, while to them she was no more relevant than everything else they saw to be invisible.

♪14♪
Sat looking out through the window, she could see them all, the girl with the ponytail and bubblegum, forever chewing, forever chatting, giggling and gossiping. The ponytail bubblegum girl had friends' of varying shapes and size, all with different colour and length of hair, all attempted to clone the one seen to be the leader by wearing the exact shoes and same uniform, making identifying them as a group; easy because each carried the exact bag. *'Factory workers?'* Jade believed people in need of gang membership would find themselves forever working alongside others. Institutionalised, from birth to marriage, people willing to keep to life's natural map by happily following one another to get to where ever they could reach, before heading back again. Jade saw the bubblegum girls becoming the types of females to marry and start their families young, because being married and having children would fit in with the routine of holding down a mundane job.' *Marriage?'* What was wrong with being like everyone else? Why was what they wanted seen by people like her and her parents' as being wrong? Jade believed everyone should be allowed to do whatever made them happy.

The boy on the racing bike, the one who she nicknamed Grasshopper; because that was the creature she saw when seeing him crouched over his low, curved handlebars. Wearing a small green protective helmet on his perfectly rounded head, the matching gloves of white and green covered long, firm, strong fingers which only ever revealed themselves should he see reason to pull on the brakes. With his music supply hooked onto his thick leather belt, Jade felt sure the tunes being played through his headphones would contain a loud, powerful, bouncy beat. During the milder summer months, Grasshopper would pass wearing shorts and thin sports shirt. *'His chosen mode of transport keeping him at the peak of physical condition.'* On school days and during cooler, colder periods of the year, he covered what was lean and toned along with his uniform; beneath a deep green tracksuit, giving his elongated form a bulkier appearance and causing his powerful legs to look even leaner as he peddled. *'A professional sportsman?'* His devotion and commitment to his hobby was relentless. *'He was different.'* But his not being like everyone else didn't seem to matter, because he whose real name was Sawyer Willson, had a purpose. Grasshopper had found his directions and was doing all he could to remain on track. *'Grasshopper had his cycle & his bicycle gave him entry into a cycling club.'* Grasshopper was one of the few odd ones out; to have found his place to belong.

Older girls, six formers walked like models, blushing and giggling at, yet thriving on the constant horn blowing and wolf whistles directed at them because of the way they wore their tops tight and their short school skirts hitched so high; they were only barely kept within the line of decency. Six form girls smoked because they believed it made them look sophisticated. Proud to be seen to wear padded bras and makeup requiring a ton of cleanser to remove. Older, but not old enough, for those who enhanced and flaunted what nature was in the process of developing, them maturing into adulthood couldn't come fast enough. Having began to develop what her younger brother called her curves, Jade couldn't understand the rush. Other girls, females in love with more than themselves would travel to their place of education inside customised cars and vans, happily hanging from off the arms of those who owned and drove the individually redesigned and personalised motorised machines. Courting couples, boys and their girlfriends, girls and their girlfriends, boys and their boyfriends, not husband's and housewives in the making. *'Some were couples in secret.'* Out and proud, or quiet and secretive? Jade saw young couples as being people in need of belonging, girls wanting to be liked and boys in need of proving their manhood. Couples flaunting the fact neither was alone, twosomes, there was rumours that within certain groups, it wasn't unheard of for two to become three and three to be many more. *'Each to their own.'* Discovering what they liked and what they didn't, trying before buying, for someone looking in, it seemed there were some with a need to experience much, before settling for what they wanted.

When watching those who went by on their way to school, Jade saw how everyone seemed happy, like peacocks displaying their tail feathers, many a six former would parade the passion wagons purchased and enhanced to impress and attract a partner, there for all to see, many attempted to out do rivals as those of age to drive, drove their customised wheels to, from and around school with pride. Older, there was no escaping the fact being older and popular was much cooler than being wise. From her window she watched the boys whose ties were never straight, whose shirts were never tucked in and whose hair missed a comb. Boys who swore like troopers, kicked tin cans, spat on the pavement and mischievously caused the neighbourhood dogs to bark. Rebels, refusing to comply within the boundaries of social acceptability, these were the boys who were maturing badly, quickly turning into people who would do what they saw to be the right thing, the types of boys who would continue to fight the system forever by doing whatever they wanted to do. *'Good, or bad?'* Boys being boys, the types Mr. Jerald Barris said never grow-up, the type Papa warned his son to steer clear of; unless he wanted to join them behind bars. The types who would use and break a girls heart. The type who would one day call upon Mr. Barris for his professional services. *'Law breakers?'* Joyriders, thugs and thieves. Boys and some girls making their way through life the only way they could, because they lacked the intelligence to know better.

More boys and the odd girl, next came those who rode motorbike. *'The biker boys, not an official biker gang, some were gang members of the future.'* Some entering the final year of compulsory education, others had remained to complete what was extra, older, none were adult enough to be true members of official motorcycle clubs. Encouraged to repeat what they failed to pass, or staying for six form, the biker boys came from the bottom middle and top of the final school years. The biker boys were the group who each and every morning would ride their powerful bikes full steam by her house. Mainly male, the boys with motorbikes were the boys Jade watched and studied most closely. Sometimes from her bedroom window and sometimes from the rear seat of her father's car, the bikers were the boys she noticed more than any others. Those sitting astride long smooth leather seats were the ones little Miss Barris felt most drawn to. Exciting, reckless and free, Jade watched from afar because she couldn't approach those who like all others wouldn't know her or her name. To those she attended school alongside; Miss Jade Jennifer Barris was invisible. *'Strangers?'* Unless necessary; members of the individual groups never mixed and Jade didn't belong to, or with any. *'Alone?'* Jade didn't want to go back to school. *'A sad, pathetic group of three.'* There wasn't anyone else to blame; but neither was there anything she could do to change how people saw her, older, wiser and ready to experience life like everyone else. Jade was one of the schools' snobs. *'A teacher in the making?'* Her parents would never settle for her gaining employment within what each referred to as a low paid career with few prospects and next to no longevity.

♪15♪

A GEORGE

2: EDUCATION

♪16♪

Climbing into the back seat of her fathers' car, she could barely believe the day had arrived so quickly. *'Where had six weeks gone?'* With everything in her school bag shiny and new, she sat and waited for her brother with his freshly polished shoes, straight tie, starched shirt and new brown leather briefcase; to get in via the opposite rear door. Neither was permitted to ride up front. *'Not the done thing?'* Children should not be heard, remain polite and always look perfect. Mavis had wished them a good day and Trevor tipped his flat cap when watching them drive by. There to wave, Mama was eager to have her offspring out from under her feet. Waiting, Papa was becoming impatient. Mr. Barris always had something to do and somewhere to be.

"Are you ready." He inquired in his usual superior manner, both Jeremy and Jade nodding in agreement as he rolled the silver jaguar down to the bottom of the lengthy driveway, waiting to pull out onto the main round via the high, automatic iron gates. *'Papa, not a chauffeur?'* Mr. and Mrs. Barris weren't averse to paying professionals to do the jobs they couldn't, or didn't want to do. *'His fatherly duty?'* Jerald Barris insisted on being there for his son and daughter whenever he could, driving them to and from school was something he could do on his way to and from the office.

♪17♪

Aware of the unmistakeable roar of those approaching astride their powerful engine propelled modes of transport; her father allowing them to pass before pulling out onto the road, meant them becoming enveloped within the deafening hum left behind. *'Five, perhaps seven?'* Some single riders, some carried two astride smooth black leather seats. Sat in silence, Jade watched, confident none would notice her interest, inside she swooned and her heart skipped a beat, watching like she watched so many times before; a young Miss Barris wondered what it would be like, her arms wrapped around the wearer of one of those smooth, thick leather jackets, her legs astride one of those soft yet firm, long, narrow leather seats and the wind in her hair? Regaining its' natural rhythm, her heart had fluttered with excitement, beating faster with the anticipation of every slight speed increase. *'Oh to ride with biker boys'* Could? Would she ever become a bikers' girl? *'Was that what she wanted?'*

"You are no way raunchy enough for them." Jeremy whispered. Him being the only one to see where his sister's attentions drifted; the mischievous thirteen year old couldn't resist teasing. "They'll never notice you." He continued. Jade hitting his leg and afflicting the sly dig in a way only siblings knew how. Despite his discomfort, Jeremy continued to tease his smitten sister throughout the remainder of the short journey. *'What else was there for a younger brat of a brother to do?'* Seeing herself as the more mature, Jade did all she could to ignore his mocking, but was unable to prevent what revealed her embarrassment. *'Blushing'*

Relieved to exit the car and feeling less than overjoyed to be back at school, when met by Gretchen and Tamara, Jade joined in with their eagerness to show off their new designer school bags and top named shoes. *'Good breeding.'* A friendship born of circumstance, the three remaining close continued because neither could cope with what they endured; alone.

"Good morning girls." Mr. Barris smiled as the twosome made their way over to where he parked.

"Morning Mr. Barris" Both giggled in unison.

"Have a good day."

"Yes. Have a good day dears." Jeremy continued to mock with a wink. Smirking through the reflection of the rear view mirror as he and his father pulled away. Jeremy's lower year classrooms being situated across the large school playing fields inside the second of five

I MAY PRETEND

historical school buildings; meant him being first to be picked up and second to be dropped. *'Bye brother dear.'* How Jade wished she could say what she was thinking out loud? Hoping her brother wouldn't tell anyone about what he saw. *'How could she have been so careless as to allow him to see what she was thinking?'* Would he be the only one to notice how her maturing mind had begun wandering?

"Did we all enjoy the holidays?" Choosing the conversation topic, Gretchen commented on how great they all looked. "Haven't we grown?" She smiled as the three made their way up and into where they needed to be, all heading for the corridor located lockers; each wanted to stay ahead of the rush. "Did you go anywhere nice? Dada took us to France." The only one to have spoken, continued her chatting.

"Really."Tamara gasped. Eager to hear all about what the bragging female was keen to tell. "Was it as exciting as it looks? Did you visit Paris?" Continuing, Gretchen happily gave her in-depth reply.

♪18♪

Jade's attention drifting once more. *'What was she doing?'* Unlocking the door to her locker, Jade caught sight of one of the biker boys. Standing just down the hall and entering a locker not far from her own, someone she'd noticed before. Stood placing his helmet inside the security of his personal locker, Jade watched, her eyes transfixed on one Mr. Roland Jackson. Rojay, all who rode his own motorbike had a nickname. Tall and strong, beneath the dark visor headwear he almost always wore; his hair was fair and his eyes an enchanting shade of blue. Resembling a fairytale Prince, the handsome Romeo who was never short of female admirers couldn't be less charming, not a true Prince. *'Should such an idealistic character ever exist?'* Rojay was rough and ready, a thoroughbred male whose life was filled with misdirection, disadvantages, obstacles and misadventure. Jade didn't know him, not really. Her accelerated intelligent meant sitting in on a couple of his classes; but the two had never spoken. Popular, the type of boy, girls could be seen throwing themselves at the feet of. This term was the turn of Miss Stacey Sutton to do the throwing. *'Why not?'* Jade and everyone in school was aware of the fact Stacey had worked her way through every other eligible male in the area. A regular with the biker boys, no one was surprised to witness the schools' serial seductress approach and plant her lips firmly upon Rojay's bemused, nevertheless flattered face. As a couple the two were well matched, as friends they appeared not to fit. *'Loud & flirty?'* While she enjoyed the attention and thrived on gossip; he led with a firm yet calm and direct hand. *'They say opposites attract?'* None were more opposite than Rojay and Jade. *'Rojay plus Jade?'* What was she thinking and why was she thinking about the boy her eyes were able to see?

"What did you do, Jade?" Gretchen eventually stopped talking about herself and made inquiries as to what her friends' had been doing during the summer break. "Jade?" She repeated impatiently when noticing where her friends' attention had drifted?

"Sorry." The mesmerised teen floated back to reality. "Sorry, what did you say?" She asked. Closing and securing her locker before turning to talk to those waiting on her reply. "Jeremy and I went to aunt Jennifer's." She revealed.

"I was asking about where you went on holiday?" Gretchen clarified the information she required.

"We went to stay with aunt Jennifer and uncle Kevin." The bemused female confirmed how she and her brother had spent four weeks of the school summer break visiting their closest relatives.

"Four weeks?" Tamara gasped. Her astounded tone indicating disapproval. "You were abandoned for four weeks." Shaking her head, the only daughter to busy doctors displayed her disgust at the way Mr. and Mrs. Barris handed their parental responsibilities over to others at every given opportunity. Struggling to believe

Jade and her younger brother had been sent to stay with relatives for four of the six week break; Tamara revealed how she didn't get along with her own aunts and uncles, the truth being; she barely knew those her professional parents' had moved away from; for work.

"How was the beach?" Gretchen inquired. Jade smiling and revealing how the Devonshire coast had been hot and crowded. *'A place others went to holiday?'*

"Time with my aunt and uncle is always fun." She said, the look she gave Tamara, a clear indication of her not appreciating her and her life being judged.

Fun filled and relaxing. *'Who was she kidding?'* When at her aunt and uncles' home situated in a small village by the sea, Miss Barris always had the best of times. When away from over protective, forever fussing parents, Jeremy and Jade took on the role of friends. Forgetting how in reality they were destined to be argumentative siblings for all eternity, when presented with freedom and opportunities; the two relished new experiences and forgot all about being waring brother and sister. "It was great." Jade didn't have one single memory including her aunt which didn't cause her to smile. Away from the big house; Jeremy escaped his geeky shell. *'A geek but not geeky, young Jeremy Jon Barris was handsome.'*

Handsome and flirty, thriving on his ability to meet and get to know those his own age who visited the quaint seaside village and holidayed at the neighbouring campsites, Jade's younger brother proved to be a true socialite when let loose from the restraints of his home and confinement of the classroom. Destined to do great things in the world of science; young Jeremy was a fast learner; quick to develop his interpersonal social skills when becoming aware of how to use his wealth and inherited status to impress and influence. When staying with his aunt and uncle, Jeremy flounced around becoming king of his own castle; while Jade was happiest helping out and working alongside her mothers' only sister inside the post office come newsagents and small village shop. *'Helpful?'* Jade enjoyed hearing the local gossip when catching up with those who over the years she'd gotten to know. *'A second family?'* There were times she wished some things in her life could be reversed.

♪*19*♪

Socialising for the eldest Barris child meant spending time with her long term acquaintance and good friend Miss Shannon Brown, the local who was now seventeen and only daughter to ageing parents and owners of the village café stood opposite the post office. *'Fun & relaxing.'* Time spent with aunt Jennifer and uncle Kevin was more than okay. *'Jennifer was Jade's favourite relative & bestfriend.'* When away from the confinement of her strict home; Jade smiled more yet continued to fail in her quest to learn about life. *'A teenager?'* Jade was older but much more introvert and shyer than her younger offspring. *'Less trusting?'* Knowing much meant understanding the importance of working things out for oneself. *'Never trust what one sees without listening.'* People and things are not always what they seem. No matter where she was; Miss Barris couldn't escape the person her parents wanted her to be. Whilst not knowing what it was she wanted, Jade was certain of what she didn't want and she didn't want to be the one others saw her to be. *'Different & unapproachable?'* Unless it was to ridicule, few gave Jade and her friends the time of day. Never approached, or spoken to unless there was an ulterior motive, normal everyday people didn't associate with people like them for anything other than teasing and torment. *'A joke?'* Her reluctance to mix, mingle and explore; was because she didn't want those she met when at aunt Jennifer's treating and seeing her in the same way she was seen and treated by the majority of people at school.

"New blouse? Nice frills!" When attempting to gain entry into the first class of the new term, those to have remained a group of three were stopped by the one Roland Jackson was calling his girl, Stacey Sutton and friends were retaking the final year to improve grades reported to have been disgraceful. Older, but no wiser, each having celebrated their sixteenth birthday hadn't made either more adult and none were subtle when making comment about others. Holding nothing back, when the opportunity to ridicule Jade and her friends for what they were and the way they dressed presented, those able to talk the talk, yet were incapable of writing the words, gathered to make their attack. Having left the side of her current beau; when joined by her admiring female peers, the one intent on displaying her unauthorised authority saw fit to invade the personal space of others. *'Why?'* The only answer was because she could. *'Why not?'* Those use to being bullied had long since realised bullies rarely had valid reason or motive for what they did. Preventing the three from being where they should be, together with five of her allies, Stacey stood between Jade, Gretchen, Tamara and the classroom door.

"I bet Gretchen is wearing navy knickers." Claire Dime attempted her display of dominance by belittling those chosen to be humiliated. "Had your curlers in, have you Tamara?" *'Deserving of the stick each attracted?'* Clean and smart, well presented, articulate and intelligent both in and outside the classroom, those others saw as being different, knew not to take cash, or anything of any value into school. *'Not anymore?'* Ridiculed for who they were and the lives they led. *'What would Stacey know or understand about what it was like to be them?'* More suited to private education. *'Spoilt Princesses.'* What gave others the right to make comment about what they didn't understand?

Dry cleaned everything, navy knickers were part of the uniform and Tamara's flaming red hair was naturally curly. Chauffeured around in top of the range air conditioned cars, only the best nannies were hired to cater for their every need and no expense was spared when purchasing what each required. *'Nothing is ever as it seems.'* Each saw how outsiders mistook what they saw to be their privileged lives as being perfect. *'Looks were deceptive.'* For Jade, her many expensive privileges felt like nooses around her neck. Older and wiser, Jade saw who she was and what she had as being to blame for creating the obstacles to be overcome. *'Privileges?'* When outside the protective security of her large house, the one others called a snob, found herself without a defence. *'Defenceless & vulnerable, pearls in with black beads.'* The girls to have started out and stayed together from pre school to secondary education; were expected to gain entry into college and university with ease, but only one of them knew she had no choice but to achieve all of her goals. Smart uniforms, designer shoes and branded bags, while some saw them as having better, the truth was, each came from households where nothing was ever good enough unless it was the best. *'Having the best of things didn't equal living the best life.'* Never permitted out after dark and escorted to and from the places she wanted, or needed to be. Fed the finest of food, she wore the most expensive of designer clothes, but like everything else in her materialistic life; everything Jade owned was chosen for, never by her. What others referred to as shyness, Jade realised was her feeling trapped. *'Caged in.'* Like a wild animal unable to roam, like a bird without wings, Jade Jennifer Barris felt there was something not right and couldn't believe it had taken almost sixteen years for her to realise somethings were just wrong. Trying as best they could not to react to those intent on making them a laughing stock, only when the teacher arrived; did everyone get to go into class.

Sat alongside Gretchen and Tamara, like all returning to school after any length of time, Jade was beginning to settle into the daily routine. Maths, Gym and English, lunches were far removed from being the finest cuisine; but the three refused to allow more suitable meals to be sent in. *'Packed lunches sent on demand.'* While her friends' failed to share her disappointment and sense of being restricted, them being the odd ones out; meant each coming to terms with the fact they would carry the labels of snob, stuck up bitches, brainy cows and ugly sows around with them when inside the school gates. *'Snobs?'* Misunderstood by others who didn't share their background. *'Posh?'* Because each spoke proper and was interested in learning, pupils making the most of their education. *'Intellectual?'* In the same way they were misunderstood, Jade, Gretchen and Tamara struggled to understand the lives' of those they saw to be rough round the edges and rude. *'Why did people have to be so rude?'*

♪20♪

"I never! I never did anything, they're lying!"

"You're a tart, we're finished." Two weeks into a new school term and already Stacey was staging one of her loud, often distressing, always public lovers tiffs out on the school steps. Feeling the end of another school day couldn't come fast enough, in the absence of any after school club; Jade wanted to get out of the noise filled institution as quickly as she could, dropping instead of emptying the contents of her school bag into her locker. *'Alone?'* She was running late, Gretchen and Tamara having gone on ahead, aware Papa would be waiting; she was in a rush. *'Unaware?'* Jade hadn't seen what was happening as she made her way out of school towards the steps. *'Shouting?'* There was always someone shouting? *'A crowd?'* The female leaving in haste had often wondered why so many chose to gather in an area designed for people to step up and walk down. *'Not a seat, steps.'* At the end of her school day, her wanting to leave made Jade oblivious to those around her.

"Rojay please, please you have to believe me." She begged him to listen when it was clear he was the only one not hearing what she had to say.

"Get off of me!" Pushing Stacey and her desperate advances away; she moved back, stepping back and flinging her arms out in a desperate attempt to steady her sudden stumble, the female to lose her footing as she lost her balance; moved into the path of another. Stepping back, her instability, caused Stacey to knock into the one who at that moment was innocently making her way down to join Papa and Jeremy waiting by the car. *'What happened?'* Descending steps descended a thousand times before, her intention was to join those there to collect her following another tiering day. *'How hadn't she seen what others stood watching?'* Focussed on nothing but leaving, the one few noticed was use to allowing what went on around her, pass her by. *'What was happening?'* From walking and standing upright; why was she falling? Failing to stop herself, she stumbled and tumbled, falling. *'Top to the bottom.'* Crashing to the hard stone floor like she was a boulder freed from its' precarious position. *'What?'* Unable to control her descent. *'Where was she going?'*

"Jade!" Hearing her brothers' gasp of horror, she saw nothing. Rushing over to the foot of the steps where she landed with a thud. *'Her head, her back, her arms & her legs.'* Certain something would be broken and aware there was nothing they could do to prevent what they and others witnessed, both Barris men were appalled by what each foresaw as having caused their family member to sustain what could be substantial injury. *'Where was she?'* Shocked, stunned and confused. *'What happened?'* Falling from the top to the bottom of twenty or more steep, stone steps. *'Unable to save herself.'* It seemed impossible she would survive without needing urgent medical attention. *'Had anyone rushed away to telephone for an ambulance?'* Watching on helplessly Mr. Barris saw his defenceless little girl being knocked off balance; before tumbling down and over what was steep and constructed from hard, cold sharp stone. *'A terrifying accident?'* No one could survive the horror many sensed to be watching in slow motion .An accident? For Jade it was sudden. *'Over in a flash?'* The uncontrollable stumbled felt like it was happening in double time. *'No!'* Why her and why in front of everyone? *'How?'* Lay like a rag doll, her passing when she did; saved Stacey from falling. *'Rojay grabbed & saved his girl?'* How? Jade being pushed down, kept her enemy upright. Walking before falling, stunned and disoriented, being asked if she was hurt? Able to hear and see, she struggled to remember anything.

"What do you think you're doing?" His tone caused both Rojay and Stacey to stop and watch as Mr. Barris advised his bewildered and dazed daughter not to move. *'No one was to touch her.'* Jeremy was to keep watch. "Where are your teachers? Why is there no supervision on these steps?" The male wanting answers made his demands as having heard the commotion, the school head, Mr. Albert Lowe appeared, to investigate, his arrival causing many a lingering pupil to walk away.

"Mr. Lowe."

"Mr. Barris?" The suited, shirt and tie wearing gentlemen acknowledged one another's presence. "Mr. Barris, What is going on here?" The head inquired.

"Help me up." Jade asked her brother to assist as she struggled to get herself back onto her feet.

"You shouldn't." Jeremy said; but nevertheless gave his strength and support to a sister insisting she needed to get to the car.

"Help me." She asked and he agreed. Keeping one eye on Papa as he ascended the steps to approach the schools' headmaster standing at the top.

"My daughter was very nearly killed." Unimpressed to see his children making their way to his car, Jerald told Mr. Lowe he would be taking his daughter directly to the hospital. "That girl knocked Jade from the top to the bottom of these steps." He continued to express his disappointment in having observed the lack of discipline and supervision which enabled such a thing to happen.

"I see." It was difficult for anyone not to see when the evidence was in front of them. Dazed, bruised, scratched and bleeding, Jade wished the ground would open up and swallow her whole. *'Wishing Papa wouldn't fuss.'* The embarrassed female climbed into the rear seat of the family car. Hurt, her suffering was nothing compared to what it would be, Stacey wouldn't allow this to rest should she be punished. *'If she ever recalled what had taken place?'* Jade would be in for it from her all time bully.

"I never touched her." Pleading her innocence was inevitable."I never." Stacey protested when questioned about what she was doing? "She's just clumsy." The guilty teen attempted to switch blame. "The posh Princess should watch where she's going."
"Mr. Barris, I," It was clear Mr. Lowe didn't know what to say.
"You do know who I am?" The man use to representing what was the law of the land, questioned the male struggling to display his authority.
"Of course Sir." The less senior male nodded. Jeremy whispering as he told his sister the newly appointed headmaster had no clue who Papa was. *'A name on the parents register.'* What the head of the school didn't know was what Mr. Jerald Barris did for a living, if someone needed friends' in high places, the one who was father to Jade and Jeremy had acquired the highest.
"Papa will want answers." He said, both continuing to watch what was happening from inside the car.
"I trust the culprits will be dealt with accordingly."
"Of course." Lowe agreed."Immediately." He said before requesting the presence of both Stacey and Rojay in his office. "Shall I fetch the school nurse?" He offered but Mr. Barris was adamant his daughter needed the assistance of a more qualified professional, reminding the inexperienced educator of how bad it would look for him and his school, should the matter go to court.
"Papa's going to sue the school." Jeremy smiled. "And our Mr. Lowe is going direct to his filing cabinet to see what Papa does for a living." He laughed, quickly

closing the window as he sat beside his sister. *'Sniggering.'* What Jeremy found funny, Jade believed would take a lifetime to live down. *'What a fool?'* Her being the least popular would mean it being her fault; her innocences wouldn't matter to those who would now accuse her of causing trouble for Stacey. *'What had she done?'* Jade couldn't remember. *'Had she slipped?'* Her bruised face was proof Stacey's flying arms had made contact. *'How had they not fallen together?'* Having regained her balance, Miss Sutton had grabbed hold of Rojay, who in turn assisted her to steady herself before removing her hands from his jacket and straightening himself and his attire. *'Had anyone attempted to help Jade?'* Her brothers' had been the face looking down on her. *'Had Rojay reacted?'* Why would he and why did what he did and didn't do, matter?

"I am taking you out of that school." Not how are you or asking if she needed help? Papa was annoyed as he climbed into the drivers seat.

"Will that be before, or after we take her to the hospital?" Jeremy questioned.

"I don't need to go to hospital." Jade said.

"You're bruised and bleeding." Her brother fussed, Papa passing the cars first aid kit and telling them not to get blood on the cream leather seats.

"You're leaving that school." The adult continued. "It's obvious the experience we hoped you'd gain could result in you being killed." He complained as their journey got underway.

"No," Jade shook her head. "I only have half a term to do." She said the end of her education was near.

"Half a term is a whole six months, you could be dead in six months." Being a man who spent his working hours dealing with law breakers and delinquents, the head of the Barris family was well aware of how quickly bad situations turned worse.

"I've got exams." His daughter reminded him. "My plan is to take what exams they will let me from the end of year and through into sixth form."

"She's right Paps, she'll never pass anything if she changes schools now." Jeremy defended his elder. All be it mockingly; sometimes her brat of a brother could be quite loveable and appear almost human.

"Have you stopped bleeding? Do you think anything could be broken?" Papa asked.

"No," Still in shock, Jade admitted to feeling numb.

"Do you need stitches?" Having assisted and watched his sister wipe what was bleeding, Jeremy agreed when she said she didn't need to go to hospital. Despite his having helped and managing to change Papas' mind, Jade could never break the unwritten law which states how rival siblings, brothers and sisters, sisters and sisters, brothers and brothers whatever? Whoever, siblings should never, not ever say. *'Thank you.'* No gratitude and no apologies, siblings were never to reveal what everyone else knew, the fact they would always be there for one another and never let one another down. "I think she'll survive." He agreed when Jade insisted they be taken back to the house.

"You should have taken her to the hospital." Overseeing what came natural to their housekeeper, when watching Mavis bathed and dressed for Jade her wounds, Jemima insisted her husband call Dr. Tombrink and get Dr. Judd to make a house call. "Our little girl could be brain damaged." Dismissing her husbands' insistence and not hearing him tell her how both the GP and psychiatrist would be working, Jemima told Jerald if he wasn't prepared to take Jade to the hospital, he needed to insist the medical professionals call to see her.

"A full physical and mental assessment."Aware of his sisters' embarrassment, Jeremy agreed when instructed to remain with her and Mavis in the study to have become a medical room. *'Chief bandage folder.'* Unlike his parents' Jeremy didn't mind being there to help, unlike Mavis, the young male couldn't resist mocking what all saw to be unnecessary and over the top.

"You two shouldn't laugh." The mature housekeeper said, herself struggling not to comment on what she saw to be extreme. "Though if you're able to laugh, you mustn't be feeling too bad." She rubbed Jade's arm as a sign of affection and caring. *'More compassionate than her own parents.'* More understanding and always there for them, Mavis was more than a family employee. A sergeant grandmother, even Loti agreed the level headed, hard working and loyal female made an excellent stand in for the times she couldn't be with her grandchildren. Bathing and dressing what was bruised, scratched, cut and swollen, the woman Jade and Jeremy wondered what they and their parents' would do without, told the injured teen she was sure she would mend. "Rest and a warm drink." Having assured all to ask that she didn't feel sick and was able to move all her limbs, Jade nodded when Mavis pointed out it was her pride to have been hurt most. *'Stupid?'* Unsure how she would face those to have seen what Stacey was calling her clumsy stumble. "Things will work themselves out." The woman to have been with the Barris family for over twelve years; assured the one who was upset and embarrassed, people would soon find someone and something else to gossip about. *'Accidents happen.'* Jade wished this accident hadn't happened to her. "Up to bed with you." Mavis said she would make a milky sweet drink to help wash down a couple of painkillers. "Will you be able to manage?" Unsteady and sore; Jade said she would be fine. One wobbly leg in front of the other, never before had she relied so heavily on what was the solid wood banister, never had she climbed the wide, elegant staircase so very slowly. *'Could she manage?'* Jade would never admit she couldn't and knew to fall or stumble again would result in the calling of an ambulance. Never normally noticed by her mother, she intended to pass without disturbing those whose voices were being raised. *'Often heard shouting.'* Feared that them arguing was being caused by her fall, Jade knew other people would be talking about her in the playground if nowhere else. With no clue as to how she could avoid what would be the wraith of Stacey Sutton. *'What a fool?'* What an idiot, how stupid was she not to have seen what was happening. *'Why her?'* Making her way to her room; Jade hoped the incident observed by many, would soon be forgotten by all.

Unable to shower due to the fresh bandages, when up in her room, she washed her face, cleaned her teeth and changed into a comfortable pair of pj's. *'Why her?'* Mavis was right when saying it was her pride which hurt most. *'You could have been killed.'* When Papa shown concern, her brother said it would take more than a flight of concrete steps to break his sister and even though he joked about her having a hard, empty head, Jeremy told Jade to promise she would let him know if she felt dizzy or got a headache? *'Carin & handsome?'* Her brother would make someone a wonderful wife one day.

"Are you really okay?" Bringing her the hot drink recommended and made by Mavis, Jeremy joined Jade inside her room. "Don't cry." Placing the mug of hot chocolate onto the bedside table, he picked up the box of tissues and joined her on her large bed. Passing what he saw being needed, Jeremy assured her everything would be fine. "Don't cry." He said.

"It's the shock." She hadn't meant to cause concern. "I'll be okay." Taking the offered tissue, she sat herself up as best she was able and dried her eyes. "Was it bad?" She needed to know how it had looked. *'Had she exposed her underwear?'* "It's all a big blur." She admitted to not remembering. *'Had she rolled, or tumbled?'*

"Lucky you wear a full and not one of those micro skirts." Jeremy assured her; he hadn't seen anything he shouldn't. *'Not that he looked.'* "You moved like an elegant rag doll." He smiled.

"There is nothing elegant about falling down steep stone steps." Jade said there was no easy, or right way to fall, when falling was unexpected. "Was everyone laughing?" She asked. She'd seen sniggering and she was aware onlookers had been told to move on, but in amongst the confusion, Jade had heard nothing. *'For a second she'd thought she'd gone deaf.'* For an instant she'd thought she was dead. People were bound to have laughed. *'From school snob, to the school joke.'*

"Mavis is right." Mavis was rarely wrong. "There will be something else to talk about tomorrow." Trying to assure her, Jeremy reminded his sister; how he'd helped her into the car as fast as he could. "Mama would have brought the drink, but." He said when passing the mug.

"She was busy." Jade completed for her sibling the sentence each had heard and repeated a thousand times.

"I can give you a hug, if you like." Jeremy offered with open arms, lifting and pushing one of her many scatter cushion into his hands, Jade told him to behave and hug a pillow.

"Can I keep it?" How could a thirteen year old know what to say and how to help, when parents refused to say anything?

"It's yours." A siblings' way of saying the two words which should never be exchanged; was to agree, to give and to accept, saying what each wanted to hear without words. Jeremy said the soft fluffy pink cushion would help him sleep.

"Just my colour."He joked."Dr. Tombrink can't make it, but he's on standby should you take a turn for the worse in the night. Dr. Judd on the other hand, she is on her way." Moving off the bed, the joking male told his sister she was going to have a visitor.

"I'm tired." Injured and upset, Jade had, had enough of people for one day.

"Don't pretend to be sleeping, Dr. Dizzy will think you're dead." Bidding her goodnight, Jeremy said to holla if she needed him; as glancing to her bedside telephone, she said she would call and he gave her the thumbs up. Skipping as he left with his fluffy pink pillow under his arm. *'Sometimes having a brother made Jade smile.'*

♫21♫

Psychotherapy and physiotherapy Dr. Tombrink advised a few days of rest, which following negotiations resulted in Jade having to do four hours school work over seven days, while convalescing between inside her room and the study. Arriving unannounced, aunt Jennifer and uncle Kevin brought flowers, a get well card and chocolates. Saying they could stay as long as they were needed, when asking why Jade was in studying instead of being in bed, Jemima insisted her sister and brother-in-law go.

"Thank you, but we can manage." Jemima told the family members willing to help, she had everything under control, accusing them and their easy going attitude of distracting and hindering her daughters' recovery. *'Jade hated when Mama fought with her aunt.'* Sisters, Jade and Jeremy hoped with all hope, them and their sibling rivalry wouldn't continue into adulthood. A letter and extra telephone calls from grannie. *'Jade hated being injured while enjoying the extra attention from the family members she missed.'* Family members she wished lived closer. *'Jade didn't want her aunt & uncle to leave.'* Having agreed to a one night stop over, Mama and Papa insisted they go.

♫22♫

Two weeks, one week off school and another avoiding all physical and strenuous activities. Under the watchful eye of Dr. Tyrone Tombrink, Jade continued to experience soreness and muscle twinges, along with aches and pain which at times hindered her movement. Hurting and unsure, under the guidance of Dr. Daisy Judd it was agreed she could and the relief on her parents' faces' was evidence she must, when all agreed her returning to her place of education would no longer harm. *'Glad to have her out from under their feet.'*

Having handed her parental responsibilities to Mavis, Jemima made no secret of hating the inconvenience caused by concerned family members constantly enquiring for updates. *'Busy.'* While Jade savoured every moment, Mama disliked the fact Papa saw it his duty to spend his evening with the one unable to leave the house. *'If she could, Jemima would have taken Jade back to school herself.'* The lady of the Barris house was overheard on more than the odd occasion; stating how she believed her children should be sent to boarding school. *'Out of sight?'* Jemima said seeing too much of her children drove her out of her mind. Not a natural mother, unless required, Jade and Jeremy were instructed not to get in their mother's way.

Two weeks, rejoining Gretchen and Tamara for the weekly after school dance class to learn Ballroom and Latin alongside Salsa and Line dancing, Jade was instructed to sit and watch. *'Ease oneself back in.'* There wasn't anyone who hadn't heard about what happened and everyone had been instructed by Mr. Lowe to look out for and take care of the daughter of the man ready to destroy the school and everyone in it, should she not be treated right. *'Dance lessons?'*

"All young ladies and gentlemen need to know how to take to the dance floor." Mr. and Mrs. Barris insisted their children sign up for anything and everything seen to provide the necessary life skills required by the well to do. Drama was questionable, but horse riding, tennis, yoga, elocution lessons, piano and singing classes were none negotiable. *'Glad to be out of the house.'* Even her having to sit and watch, was better than being home.

"I could take you home if you like dear." Gretchen's mother offered, when Mr. Barris failed to arrive.

"I'm sure Papa won't be long, he'll worry if I'm not here waiting." Jade insisted she should wait.

"If you're sure?" Promising to telephone home if still waiting in ten minutes. *'Had he forgotten?'* With no sign of her brother, it was obvious Papa had collected Jeremy but failed to return. *'It hadn't happened before.'* There was a first time for everything and Jerald having his routine disrupted was bound to have had an effect. *'Had Papa forgotten?'* Ten minutes turned to thirty and thirty into thirty-five. Why was she waiting and why hadn't she agreed to Mrs. Garlock taking her home?

Sat waiting at the foot of the school steps, Jade shook her head, not wanting to recall how she fell from the top to the bottom, maybe it was a blessing she couldn't remember the event to have taken place between her locking her locker and insisting her brother help her up off the ground. Allowing herself to do what she believed shouldn't be done, Jade used the wall to the side of the steps to sit. *'Stupid'* Back in the classroom for little over a week, she was still waiting for Stacey to do, or say something. Feeling more numb than ever before, the pupil living in fear of what others had planed, struggled to think straight as she wondered what she should do? *'Why was she waiting where she was vulnerable?'* Had everyone else left to go home?

♪23♪

"Jade isn't it." Stunned and wondering who knew her name, she was aware the voice to have spoken was male. *'Who?'* Standing, she found herself joined by the one she called Grasshopper. *'What did he want?'* "Is everything all right, school's shut." He glanced at what was being locked up for the night.

"I was." Jade stuttered.

"Waiting for your dad?" The male completed her statement before asking if she would like him to walk her home. Glancing at his low handled bicycle, he told her he could push it. *'How kind.'* She hadn't realised he knew her name. *'How sweet of him.'* Revealing how he knew who she was and where she lived, he repeated his offer to help. "I pass your house." He told her. "Sort of." His eyes indicated his ability to recall how far back from the main road her actual residence was situated.

"I best wait." She thanked him; before repeating what she said to Mrs. Garlock. Papa would worry if she wasn't where she should be. *'If he arrived?'* Getting onto his bike, the one to have noticed her, said she should take care. *'How thoughtful?'* She never noticed Grasshopper talking to anyone before, not anyone outside those who were members of the cycle club he championed. How different he sounded, not like she imagined. *'Had someone dared him to approach her?'* The young man had sounded sincere. *'Late leaving?'* Like herself, Grasshopper often remained behind for the extra out of school activities. *'Had she thanked him?'* Jade hoped she thanked him for being so thoughtful and kind.

Unsure how long she waited before deciding to walk, ignoring her own advise, Jade set off to embark upon something never done before. *'Fifteen & never walked home from school.'* Never had the one who was fast approaching her sixteenth birthday attempted to cover the distance between her house and her school on foot. It wasn't far and she knew the way. Six roads, the final one being the main road which ran long and straight; all the way to and by the large gates which opened onto the driveway leading up to her house. *'How could she go wrong?'* Sure she could do what she planned, Jade checked one last time for any sign of Papa. *'Was he was all right?'* Out the school gates and left to the church, before crossing the road and taking the next left to the bottom of the street. Right and straight to the Wild Tree Inn where she needed to cross the road and turn right again. *'What could happen?'* Late afternoon wouldn't turn to night in the time it would take to walk what sounded far, but seemed no distance. Cross the road at the Inn and continue, this road was winding and changed to another by Galloping Glory Stables and ridding school, the entrance of which she would pass before coming to the main road which would lead her to her house. *'She could call in on Gretchen if she felt unable *to make it.'* Upon reaching the main road, Jade would turn right and continue walking. It sounded far; but each change of direction was visible from the one before. To drive the distance took less than ten minutes and she estimated the walk would take around twenty-five. *'Half hour tops'* Convinced Papa would see if he drove by; the lone female set out to do something she always wanted to do. How could her doing what everyone else did; be wrong? Smiling; the air felt surprisingly warm and fresh as she began what felt like her first ever adventure. Streets looked different when not being observed through the glare of a car window and being out in the open smelt fresh. *'Freedom?'* Nothing felt, or smelt like being free, when inside a car the air felt stuffy because her being cooled by actual fresh air bore little to no resemblance to the air which entered in through ventilation systems designed to be directional. Streets didn't smell like freshly polished leather and real trees bore little resemblance to regularly waxed wood. While her fathers' top of the range Jaguar, Range Rover, Aston Martin and Mercedes were equipped with every mod con and add on luxury his money could buy, nothing manmade, or artificial could simulate what was natural and real. Free, feeling the afternoon sun radiating through the soft cloud cover; having placed her coat inside her school bag, she removed her school sweater and hung it over her shoulders before continuing on route. Savouring every sight, sound and smell which late September had to offer. Pleased the country in-which she lived was experiencing what meteorologists referred to as being an extended Indian summer. *'Unusual but appreciated.'* Hitting her bare skin with a gentle firmness; the one out on her own relished the cooling sensation caused by the slight breeze stroking her face before running through her hair and exploring her senses like a thousand fingertips.

♫24♫

I MAY PRETEND

Like a caged animal finally released, Jade was powerless to prevent the sweet smile of relief printing itself across her face and running like unfolding paper across her lips. Absorbed in the feeling of complete release; the lone female failed to hear what silently pulled up beside her.

"You decided to walk?" Grasshopper? She thought he'd headed home ages ago, but then she should have realised how he never went directly home without first completing his daily training programme. "Mind if I walk with you." *'Why would she mind?'* Why did he want to? Believing the only way of discovering the answer was to talk to him, she smiled and nodded as he began to walk by her side. *'What would she say?'* She wasn't normally chatty. *'What would he say?'* Pushing his cycle with his right hand, as they walked, she allowed him to talk. "I'm hoping this weather doesn't break anytime soon, it's great not to have to wear my wet gear when riding." He smiled.

"It's good to be able to be outdoors." Jade agreed. "I don't get out enough." She sighed.

"You should get yourself a bike." Was Master Wilson chatting her up? Was this flirting? *'How would she know?'* She knew to ask outright what it was he wanted, would be rude.

"Maybe." She shrugged. Not that she would be permitted to ride it outside the grounds surrounding where she lived. *'Maybe?'* The truth was, she owned more than one bicycle already, Jade had a number of things with seats and wheels sat somewhere collecting dust. Spoilt, she and her brother were gifted any and everything to have been a fad; soon forgotten.

Bikes, scooters, roller skates and skateboards, between them Jade and Jeremy had all things seen to be what all children must have. *'Impatient?'* While Jeremy took to everything with wheels; Jade struggled with her balance, meaning Papa gave up on her, leaving Trevor and his son Jimmy to show her how to ride what eventually she mastered with difficulty. *'No enthusiasm?'* A straight line on the skateboard, on roller skates she eventually manage everything including steps, whilst the scooter was the easiest, her tricycle and bicycle had been the most exciting. *'Exciting & adventurous?'* Enjoyed and enjoyable; right up to the time when Jimmy rode out the gates, staying back; she wasn't permitted to exit the grounds within which she lived, not without adult supervision. Left behind, she remembered not knowing if she should smile or cry? Cycling was exciting until she realised the large grounds around her house weren't large enough for her to experience what it was truly like to ride.

Walking with Sawyer, Jade couldn't help wonder if the two were being watched? Walking alongside a boy of the same age; the young female felt her heart sink and her fear raise as she noticed one of Papas' cars coming towards them, switching lanes and parking up as close as it could get. *'Here it came.'* Expecting Papa to jump out of the drivers side ready to tell her she shouldn't be walking the streets and demanding to know who she was with? Jade felt shocked when it was the passenger side door to open and Jimmy who jumped out to ask if she was all right? *'Not Papa?'* Jimmy said he and his father had been looking for her. *'Sent to find her?'* Trevors' son apologised for not noticing she hadn't arrived home with her brother. *'Had Papa collected Jeremy?'* Sat waiting behind the steering wheel, upon seeing Trevor, Jade realised her families long time employee could be the one to have failed in his extra duties. *'She wouldn't tell if he didn't.'* Sat watching his son explain how it was Mavis who noticed she was missing. Trevor shook his head at the way Jade's expression changed upon being told how Mr. Barris had consumed his favourite tipple once home. *'Papa wouldn't drink & drive.'* No one should, but his having to sentence those who had, meant he couldn't.

"Sorry." Jade said no one should apologise on her fathers' behalf. Another caring and considerate male, it seemed she was surrounded by nice guys. *'The way Jimmy & Sawyer looked at each other caused her to realise just how nice.'* Jimmy she knew about, but Grasshopper?

"Hello, I'm Sawyer." The way her companion greeted Jimmy answered more than a few questions. "I go to school with Jade, I'm sixteen." Dumbfounded, but most definitely interested, Jade told Sawyer the male to have caught his eyes was Jimmy, nineteen and recently back from travelling. Mr. James Kingston was hoping to become an interior designer, while his proud father was steering him towards becoming a landscape gardener. *'Good with flowers.'* She and his family had known what was Jimmy's sexual preference long before he began to question anything. *'Happy?'* Accepted and loved. Jimmy hadn't yet had a proper boyfriend, but it was only a matter of time. *'Coincidence, or planned?'* When she next got Sawyer on his own, she would be asking if he used her to meet the one he was failing to tare his eyes away from.

"Nice to meet you. We should get you back Jade."An obvious attraction. *'Shouldn't they exchange telephone numbers, or arrange to meet?'*

"Bye Sawyer."Walking with Jimmy who opened the rear door of the car and encouraged her to get inside, Jade told the one watching with his mouth open, she would see him in school.

"In you get." Jimmy was talking to her, but he was looking at him. *'This was flirting.'* Why weren't they telling one another what everyone else could see?

"Looks like you may have to play cupid." Trevor also asked Jade if she was all right, as she sat herself behind him, both watching because both sensed the sexual tension between those speaking to one another with their eyes.

"Thank you?" She told Trevor she was grateful as upon getting back into the front passenger seat; Jimmy turned and asked how well she knew Sawyer?

"I've seen him loads, but I never spoke with him until today." Swerving questions from both Jade and his father, upon arriving at her house and being greeted by a somewhat anxious Mavis, it was clear the staff and neither of her parents' had panicked about her absence. "Thank you." She smiled. Expecting Jimmy to prevent her from going inside so he could ask more, she told him, if he was interested in Sawyer, he would need to get on his bike. *'Confused?'* Jimmy asked if she would tell her friend he would like them to meet and she said she would see what she could do.

"Cupid."Trevor repeated in a whisper.

Back, safe and sound, dinner was unusually quiet, Jeremy telling his sister, Mama and Papa had been arguing. *'About what?'* The two rarely communicated enough to form a conversation, while both seemed to becoming experts in disagreeing. *'What could be wrong?'*

"Does this mean movie night is cancelled?" The answer to her question was No. Another family get together which saw each member doing his, or her own thing while sitting in the same room? All to attend the weekly event knew there must be a logical explanation for it, but none truly understood what each entered into with the intention of leaving as soon as possible. Thursday night in the Barris household was movie night, each got their turn to choose which video they hired, but only the one whose choice it was, actually paid enough attention to watch. Taking place in the room they called the family den, a square room tucked in-between others, a library. The windowless space was fitted with ceiling high bookcases, in the centre of which three large sofas formed a horseshoe around a large television connected to a video recorder and external speakers. Mama would sit at the desk behind the centre sofa, facing, but rarely watching the television, sat doing her paperwork by the light of a dim desk lamp. Papa would take the seat in front of her to enable his reading through one of his many case files. *'Together but not there for one another?'*

I MAY PRETEND

There were times when Papa's movie choice didn't turn out to be anything like what it said on the box. *'Lemon popsicle?'* A movie about teenagers, but not about the kind of teenagers he wanted his children to be, not about the things he wanted his children to see. Sex and all the things not to do, everything which could go wrong, did. A sad tale of getting it wrong and not being careful. *'Of course Papa switched it off & yes Jeremy, Jade & Jimmy snook back to watch it, before Trevor returned it to the hire shop.'*

Busy parents, when Jimmy joined them, the Barris children took chances neither would ever take alone. Told they had nothing to complain about, Jimmy said they should see themselves as lucky to be protected from what he called the wraith of the world. A good friend, Master James Kingston was treasured by his parents' because he was their last, not their youngest. Mr. Trevor Kingston and his wife Carol were parents to four children, twins Jake and Juliet had died before their first birthday. Cot death, it hadn't struck twice, that which few understood struck on the same night in the one place and took two, the twins died together; while TJ Kingston had been born with a condition to have awarded him a life which lasted only three years. Four children, when thinking about what Jimmy's family had been through, Jade agreed her and her brother had nothing to complain about. *'A hard worker.'* Mr. Trevor Kingston said he didn't mind his wife not going out to work, because to him he felt blessed for everyday she was there. *'A good man.'* Trevor had no problem accepting his sons' sexuality, because him having a child was what was important. A loving and loyal family, people who looked at the world differently, because the world hadn't looked at, or treated them like everyone else. *'Loyal employees?'*

Mavis and not Mama, their housekeeper had noticed what no one else did, like they so often were; Mama and Papa had been caught up in themselves and much too busy doing their own thing. Married with a grown up daughter and two grandchildren she rarely saw because they lived in the city. *'Not the closest city.'* Mavis's daughter Rose moved from north to south before moving to settle in the city of another country, Rose her husband Edmond and their children Grace and Gavin had made themselves comfortable in the city of Edinburgh. *'Happy?'* Mrs. Mavis Martin was married to Tim. A supermarket manager Mr. Martin was loving and supportive, often arriving to escort his wife home should she have need to work late, or the time of year bring darkness before it was time for her to leave. Driver of a dark green Allegro, Mama was heard telling Tim he should park around the back when needing to stay for more than a moment. *'Down to earth & rebellious.'* Tim made sure everyone saw what he was driving, often honking on his cars horn to be sure the woman he called old spiky pants, was aware her picture perfect driveway was being polluted by him and his old faithful. *'Loyal, loving & kind?'* All got along with both employees who often found their sanity in one another; especially should times became unbearable, or each find themselves struggling to hold their tongues. *'Good employees?'* They often disagree with what they heard and observed, but neither could afford to lose what helped paid their household bills.

A mother much too busy with her paperwork, invoices and orders, there was always somewhere Jemima had to be and things she needed to do. *'A self made millionaire.'* No one would take from her, what was her astonishing achievement. *'Unable to give her family her time?'* Suppliers to meet, contracts to sign over lunch, clients to dine with at dinner and products to test, interviews and surprise visits to make on those she insisted promote her and her brands her way. While having concurred the beauty market for the upperclass, there was always something new to be introduced and forever a need to remain one step ahead of the competition. A mother incapable of mothering and a father who ruled with a rod of iron, or his gavel, a decider of fates, who failed when it came to deciding what was best for his own children. Responsible for the decisions he made when in the courtroom, his offspring hadn't arrived baring individual case files, because it was with him they should be making their history, a little more attentive than his wife, at least Mr. Barris had emotions, even if his main one was anger.

Where was he? Standing at the bottom of the school steps, Jade told herself she wouldn't wait for as long as she waited the last time he failed to remember his fatherly duty. Why was he being so forgetful? *'She could walk.'* She had done it before. *'What was keeping him?'* Wondering why the responsible adult was failing in what was his usual routine; she remembered his never admitting to having forgotten the last time. Seven days on and another dance class completed, this time her having joined in meant Jade feeling tired. *'She would be okay.'* The weather wasn't quite so warm, but she had her coat. *'Mavis said she should never leave without her coat through from October to May.'* Dull and dismal, it wasn't raining and the wind had dropped. Zipping herself into what was lined and had a hood, she jumped when Grasshopper rang the bell on his bike to gain her attention.

"Hello again." He said. Stopping and preventing her from leaving. "You okay?" He asked, as regaining her composure; she attempted to hide her shock by nodding and asking him how he was? "Good," He smiled. Seven days on from the first time their eyes met, Swayer and Jimmy were an item. *'Dating?'* Happy for them, she understood the two keeping what was a blossoming relationship to themselves.

"Hope he isn't hindering your training." Having heard her good friends' joyfulness and excitement at having his first real relationship, she hoped that like Jimmy, Sawyer was happy too.

A GEORGE

"By that I take it you've seen him ride a bike." Sawyer grinned. His nod telling her, he was liking the time he was spending with his new found friend.

"I'm sure you can fix his bad habits." She said causing him to blush as he admitted to finding some of his bad habits entertaining.

"Need someone to walk you home." He offered. Jade telling him she would be fine. She didn't want to hold him back. Aware of how his time was being divided between more than his education, his cycle club and his training, the smiling female insisted he go enjoy the film he and Jimmy had planned. "Take care." He hadn't used her to get to her friend, the day the two laid eyes' to have become transfixed, had been the first time they met. *'Love at first sight.'* A true example of one good turn being rewarded with another, each was the others first real boyfriend and both were excited by the prospect of having found someone they could talk to, be with and share everything alongside. Happy for them, Jade was still smiling at the thought of being cupid. Not that she'd had to do much, she understood the two putting someone in the middle to soften the blow should the reply to their questions not be what they hoped. *'Lucky?'* Both were hoping the exact same. *'Fun loving, intelligent & adventurous?'* They made a good couple. *'Handsome.'* Once news got out, there would be many a heartbroken female to have been carrying a torch for one, or the other, because in appearance, none was different to the other, both strong, the two kept themselves in good shape. *'Polite, helpful & caring?'* Who didn't want a partner who shared what was everything a person should be. *'Understanding, non-judgmental, forgiving & kind?'* When seeing how Jimmy had found his man. Jade wondered if she would ever find hers? *'Did she want a boyfriend?'* If she was honest, she didn't know what she wanted?

Smiling, as she continued on the route she knew would take thirty minutes, she soon became lost in her own thoughts. Daydreaming, as she entered a world of her own making; she neither heard nor noticed the approaching motorbike which pulled up by her side.

"Jade!" Stopping and turning to see who called her name, feeling both shocked and surprised to discover Roland Jackson sitting astride his motor powered cycle as it purred by the side of the road. *'Had he called her?'* She wasn't sure .*'Was she dreaming?'* Had she fallen asleep while waiting? "Hi there," He announced with a wave, removing his helmet so to make himself heard and understood. *'What was he doing?'* Looking around; she believed he must be talking to someone else? Checking the road and pavements, she felt sure he'd mistaken her for another. "Jade," He repeated.

"Hello." Replying nervously, she looked to see if they were being watched. *'What did he want?'*

"Hi," He smiled. "Off home?" He inquired and she nodded. Unsure whether to remain, or continue, the shy female hovered as Rojay manoeuvred himself and his motorbike closer to where she stood. "I spotted you and I just wanted to say I was sorry."

"Sorry?" She didn't understand. *'Why was he sorry?'*

"I know it was sometime ago, but I can never get you on your own." *'Had he tried?'* Jade hadn't noticed him attempting to gain her attention, she would willingly have given the young and somewhat handsome Mr. Jackson her undivided attention if she'd known he wanted it. *'What did he want?'* "I hope you weren't badly injured." He was right, the accident, or incident had happened sometime ago, over four weeks ago and she was rarely on her own, but she was okay. The teasing encountered upon her return to school had been worse than the actual injuries. *'Stacey hadn't said anything, but Stacey had a lot of friends ready to speak up for her & against the one seen to have damaged her reputation.'* It being a while ago meant time had moved on and the gossips were searching for another subject.

"I'm fine." She told him. Her mind racing. *'Was this not what she wanted?'* Hadn't she dreamt of talking to a boy, *'To this boy?'* If so, why did she feel the urge to run?

"Your injuries kept you away from your after school activities." *'Was this a trick?'* Jade failed to see what else it could be, how did someone like Rojay know so much about someone like her? She hadn't realised there was anyone who knew anything about her and what she did. *'This had to be someone's idea of a prank.'* His kind didn't mix with girls like her, biker boys didn't associate themselves with good girls. *'Was this Grasshopper playing cupid?'* Why was she thinking what she knew sounded stupid?

"I had some bruising." She rambled.

"Everything all right now?" He asked. Continuing to seek reassurance about her wellbeing. *'Maybe he was checking she wasn't going to sue?'*

"Ye," Yes, she was all right, almost back to full fitness, give, or take the odd twinge, light bruising and fading redness surrounding a scabby scratched knees, unattractive, irritating and sore, but she was over the worst of what resulted in the multitude of minor irritations her mother called sever injuries and Dr. Judd noted as being traumatic.

"I'm glad." Was he? *'Why?'* Calming herself, the girl not use to being around boys; hoped she wasn't blushing, because she sure felt hot.

"It was an accident, I hope Mr. Lowe wasn't hard on you." She eventually found her voice.

"Nothing I couldn't handle."

"No," She agreed there wasn't much the hardcore biker couldn't handle. From his motorbike to his many admirers, Jade couldn't think of anything he would struggle with. *'Help with his homework?'*

"Would you like a ride?" What she wouldn't give to be able to say yes, to ride would be a dream come true. Looking down at the fine piece of machinery standing beside her, her knees fell weak in anticipation of fulfilling her recurring fantasy, but knowing exactly what Papa's reaction would be, she reluctantly declined and admitted to enjoying the walk. "No daddy tonight? Doesn't he normally pick you up in one of his swish, all singing all dancing motors?" Why was Rojay continuing the conversation? Switching off and wheeling his motorbike alongside them, the inquisitive male asked if she was late, as for the third time since joining her, she checked her watch."Daddy is normally prompt."

"Normally," Embarrassed by not being streetwise and ashamed of her lack of independence. *'Papa's little girl?'*

"Not tonight?" Her follower questioned what she was questioning? *'Papas' pampered Princess?'*

"Probably held up at work."If she was honest, she was growing concerned about the missing parent who forgot return for her. *'Called back to work?'* Drinking again? Both Jade and her brother felt there was something upsetting the household. Why hadn't he sent one of his employees? Sometimes he and not Mavis would send Trevor. *'Why had he forgotten her?'* Aware she should be questioning what had happened to her attentive Papa, the truth was, she was enjoying being free.

"So, what is it he does, your dad?" Rojay asked. His question making it clear he wanted to fill in the gaps and discover what he didn't know. "Is he a barrister?" He asked. *'Did Mr. Jackson require representation?'* "A judge?" Why was he asking what he was? Was he in trouble? "A good job would explain the flash motors and large house." He said. "It really is a large house." He observed as the two reached the high, double iron gates fronting the long paved driveway leading up to the substantial property.

"Yes," Jade agreed. Stopping and turning to face the one she only ever dreamt of being so close to, the one to have escorted her without being asked to. *'Without asking if she wanted him to.'*

"Home." He smiled.

"My house," She nodded. Secretly wishing she lived further. Six roads, it was on the final stretch Rojay started walking alongside her. *'Why?'*

"Glad you weren't badly hurt." Having accompanied her to her destination, the one seen to be the next leader of the biker boys appeared reluctant to go.

"Fine." She assured him. Nervous when being with someone she secretly admired.

"Stacey is such a loud mouth." He said.

"Yes," Preventing him from saying anything more against the one meant to be his girl. "No one is going to sue." She assured him.

"Sue?" He questioned.

"Papas' bark can be more vicious than his bite, but everything is fine. Thank you for escorting me." She looked to the building in-which she lived, indicating she should get herself inside. *'Not wanting her parents' to see.'* "I enjoyed the walk." She smiled.

"Me too," Her companion mirrored her delight before climbing onto his motorbike and stating he would see her around. Before she had time to reply, Rojay left. *'Was she dreaming?'* Standing and watching him ride away. *'What was that about?'* Making her way up and into her house, Jade struggled to take in what had happened. Entering her house, Jade wondered what Roland Jackson wanted?

♪25♪

3: DON'T STOP
♪26♪

Dinner in the Barris household brought the family of four into the only other area within the large building they shared their time. *'Breakfast, dinner & Thursday movie night in the den.'* The early evening meal was a time to reflect on one's day, time to enjoy good food and embark upon family conversation.

"He forgot again didn't he." Jeremy whispered as opening the evening's topic for discussion, Papa said there were going to be changes. *'More work & longer unsocial hours.'* Her brother nodded when she surmised it being Papas new job commitments; he and Mama had argued about.

"I'll not be available to collect you in the afternoon." Informing his family of how his chauffeur duties would be restricted for the foreseeable, Jade bravely admitted to having enjoyed the walk home. Aware neither over protective parent would approve, or give consent to her doing the same again, Jeremy told his sister she was on her own.

"You walked?" Appalled by the idea of having to walk the streets. "Have Papa and I not taught you anything? The streets are no place for a young lady alone, they're dangerous." Jemima stated.

"I was fine." Jade believed she never felt finer. It wasn't like it was the first time. *'The time when staff & not family realised she was missing.'* Her first time appeared to have gotten overlooked.

"You were stupid." Scolding her for being foolish and irresponsible; Jemima looked to her husband for support.

"I'll supply the two of you with enough extra money to cover the cost a taxi." Mr.Barris offered. Shaking her head in protest, the younger female at the table said spending money in such a way was a waste.

"I've no need to get a cab; the walk takes thirty minutes tops." She attempted to convince those listening how the route to and from school was easy. "Its' healthy to walk." She justified her reasoning.

"I'm not walking." Jeremy disagreed. "I hate walking."

"Trevor can use one of the cars." Jemima suggested the part time handyman, full time gardener, sometimes butler; be given yet another role by becoming the one responsible for making sure the Barris offspring arrived at and returned from school safely. "Him, or his son." She revealed hearing how their employees' graduate son was home from traveling and in-between jobs.

"No," Jade shook her head. *'She didn't want to take Jimmy away from spending time with Sawyer.'*

"Yes," Jeremy nodded. "We shouldn't deprive a young man of the opportunity and experience of paid employment." He told his sister she was being selfish.

"We don't need a driver for a ten minute journey." Throwing her brother a glare which warned him to cooperate; Jade continued to plead her case. "We can walk, I want to walk." She said. *'A friend employee?'*

"You will do as you are told young lady." Interrupting his daughters' protest Papa's tone indicated his being far from pleased. "Mama is right, the streets are no place for a young lady on her own. Do you not read the newspapers? Do you want me to show you what I see and other people have to deal with everyday."

"But Papa," Jade sulked. *'Hoping to gain the support of her male parent.'* Like every teenage girl knew she could, little Miss Barris attempted to wrap Papa around her little finger. "Papa," She pleaded.

"You heard." The strict male remained determined.

"I'm almost sixteen." The teen being stubborn continued her protest, her intention being to have her elder recognise her developing maturity and independent capabilities by awarding her, his trust.

"If you refuse to use a taxi, I will have no choice but to hire a chauffeur." As expected, neither Papa, or Mama was going to give in. Jade wasn't ever going to get her own way, or make her voice heard.

"No," She nevertheless continued to disagree. Shaking her head, inside she winced at the thought of the attention her arriving to school in a taxi would create. *'Couldn't her parents' see her torment?'*

"Taxi cabs are common." Jeremy said he preferred the idea of a chauffeur. "Much more exclusive and up market." He smiled a smile which indicated he'd won.

"We don't need either." Jade had her say before being asked why she was being difficult?

"What's gotten into you?" Mama inquired.

"You wouldn't understand." Of that, the struggling teenager was certain. Mrs. Barris never understood anything about being young and different, because Jemima never saw a problem with being rich and pampered. *'Not born into money.'* Self made and not born into her exclusive life; Jemima now thrived on having wealth and status.

"Maybe we won't." The older female agreed. "But we'll understand even less if you don't explain." Like always; Papa agreed in attempt to be fair.

"Do you really want to know?" Jade took a deep breath as her parents' asked she tell them. *'Why not?'* With a shrug of her shoulders, she guessed she had nothing to lose. Perhaps they would understand? *'They were young once?'* "I have too few friends." She began. All, including her brother; turning to listen to her heart felt words. "Everyone believes I'm a snob and they call me a stuck up bitch."

"Mind your language." Jemima stated firmly.

"Mama, I'm trying to explain what it feels like to be me."

"People are just jealous princess, take no notice." Papa explained the thoughtless antics of others. "This is why Mama and I do all we can to protect you." He said, explaining how everything done by him and his wife was done with the best of intentions.

"So I'm to sit back and take it." The deflated youngster sulked. "I have no choice but to remain a spoilt bitch for the rest of my life." She sighed. Jemima again warning her about the use of unsuitable language at the dinning table. "I'm sick of it." Jade complained.

"Right young lady, that is enough." Papa announced as in a sulk, his daughter admitted defeat, telling those sitting at the table; she knew they wouldn't understand. "There is nothing to understand." Mr. Barris insisted. "If you refuse a chauffeur, you will have to give up your after school activities." The head of the family threatened to stop paying for anything and everything which took place outside of official learning.

"No," Seeing such a compromise as unfair, Jade insisted she needed her after school classes.

"Then you will do as we say." She was told.

"I can't." Defiant, for the first time ever, she was answering back because she couldn't give up what little freedom she'd gained.

"Why can't you?" Mama inquired. In the absence of a reply Jade was told her insolence wouldn't be tolerated and requested to go to her room. *'What had she expected?'* Agreeing. *'Go to your room.'*

'Go to your room.' Where else was there for her to go? She wasn't allowed anywhere else, having spent hours locked away with her books and her music, day after day for most of the day when absent from school and everyday after her lessons, there wasn't anywhere else for her to be, but her room. Alone with her few happy memories and many daydreams. Jade had probably spent half her life, sat within the heavily decorated walls and trapped within the place known to all living under the same roof as her room. Turning the key so to avoid any unwanted intrusion, she put on one of the long playing albums.

♫26♫

Sitting herself by her large picture window and sinking into the deep padded seat, she picked up her private diary, unlocked it and lifted her pen.

Oct, 11th
She drives me mad, she makes me crazy, what is wrong with her? Mama, My mother, Mrs. Jemima Jade Barris is cold. She is so cold, to call her an ice maiden would be too warm a name. What did I ever do to her? Maybe she never wanted to be a parent? Why have two children? Why have Jeremy and me when it's clear we're an inconvenience? All I did was walk home from school. Sometimes I look at her and see a stranger, she is always here, but we are never alone, we've never been close and when there are things to say; it is Papa who speaks. When there are chores to be done, it is a member of staff who does them. I admire Mavis and not only because she is more caring than Mama could ever be. What does Mama want me to do? Why doesn't she want me?

Lifting her pen from off the paper, Jade stopped to think. All too easy to rant and complain, especially when there was so much she could say about the woman she failed to understand. Miss Jade Jennifer Barris didn't like putting others down, or dwelling on faults. *'What made a good parent?'* Not Jemima, not parent maternal; she wasn't all bad either

Oct, 11th continued
Lunching with clients and testing the merchandise, Mama is kept busy, the gifts are good, I appreciate she chooses well, but I don't remember her ever asking me what I want. I don't recall her ever holding me. Jemima is often here, but she is never near and I feel like I don't know her, I fear she doesn't want to know me. I watch her with Jeremy; Papa says it's because he is a boy and I am a girl, aren't we both children? No kisses, no cuddles, no praise. I doubt she will ever be proud of me. Her struggle to know what to say means

we rarely says anything. I hope I don't grow up to be like her. All I did was walk home from school.

Jade hoped when she was an adult, she would be more like her grannie Loti. Mrs. Loti Louise Denton-Stableford was Mamas' mother. *'Her hyphenated surname was because she remarried.'* Warm, loving, caring and kind. A woman to have lived an experience filled life, Loti loved, accepted and stood by her family unconditionally. Being wrapped in grannie's arms was like being enveloped in a giant protective quilt. Like having a special blanket. Unlike her eldest daughter; Loti was welcoming and spoke direct from her great big heart. *'A good listener with time for everyone.'* There were times Jade wished she could run away and go live the rest of her life with the ageing lady who cared without having to prove to the world how much. *'Understanding & non judgmental?'* Loti never criticised without her criticism being accompanied by a plausible explanation and a heap of actual facts to back her up. Mama was emotionally distant and Jade hated how the physical distance between her and grannie, equalled the thousands of miles she felt separated her and Mama

A lover of life and everyone in it, at the age of fifty-seven, the widowed Mrs. Loti Louise Denton remarried and left her homeland to start a new life with her new husband Sam. Mr. Samuel Fernando Stableford was younger; a step-grandad. *'Cancer took the man who held the place reserved for the eldest male & head of the family.'* Mr. Lonny Lea Denton was also fifty-seven when he left his family, not that he wanted to go. Lonny's departure hadn't been by choice and for him there would be no one visiting, or any chance of him making a return trip home. *'It all happened so fast.'* Losing gramps hurt like nothing Jade ever wanted to feel again; but like everyone; she knew the tear filled, heart shattering experience would be repeated. *'We all live & so each of us will one day die.'* Loti losing her life long friend and loving, loyal life partner proved difficult for the woman to have met her soulmate in the school playground. Together since the age of fourteen, Loti and Lonny had rarely spent a day apart since what each described as being that fateful day. *'Their spacial day?'*

A day back when the school playground was a place divided into areas where pupils played real games, back when the school yard was for gossip and its' field for football, the sudden thunder clap and burst raincloud sent everyone running for shelter. *'A sudden storm.'* The bicycle sheds were full and all covered porches bursting at the seams. *'Rain, thunder & lightening.'* No one wanted to be outside, but all had to wait for the teachers to unlock what was kept bolted when those there to learn went outdoors to play. Taking his raincoat out of his school bag, the young male who would soon be leaving full time education to pursue a career beside his father in the cotton mill, asked a soaked Loti Louise Green if she wanted to share what he held outstretched so to keep his head and shoulders dry. *'Get wet or stand close to a boy she didn't know?'* Loti agreed to join Lonny. *'Saved from the storm.'* The way her grandparents' met was seen by some to be romantic; while being described by them as fate, because neither believed they would ever have seen the other had they not been forced together through circumstance and necessary. *'Love at first sight?'* Each shook their head; but them standing together under the raincoat in the playground led to Lonny asking Loti if he could see her again. Agreeing, the two had seen one another almost everyday since. *'Till death did them part.'* Jade's grandparents were the type of couple other couples thrived to be. *'Happy & in love.'* It wasn't easy when Loti found herself on her own. *'Sometimes it's wrong for two to become one.'* Spending the first three months with her youngest daughter Jennifer, a widowed Loti moved into the Barris household in time to spend Christmas with her grandchildren. Invited to stay for as long as she wanted, Jemima and Jerald saw the bonus of free childcare giving them the opportunity to partake in many more childfree holidays. A Christmas ski trip with influential friends. Mr. and Mrs. Barris spent four weeks in the snow; while their children spent time with the grieving grandparent who met and fell for the charms of a young and very handsome Mr. Stableford.

Younger, the male working for the large landscaping company hired by Mr. Barris to secure all boundaries and take the garden from playground to sophisticated space dedicated to grown-up entertainment; was always smiling. Paid to transform areas built for play, the instruction was to create both covered and open areas to dine and relax. February was cold and Loti continuously taking hot mugs of tea, along with her homemade soups and freshly baked scones out to those working hard, led to her having the one all called a cheeky chappy, eating out of her hand. *'Friends?'* Younger than gramps, Sam was seen by some to be too young, but he helped Loti smile, smiling and laughing. *'Not loving gramps less.'* From the cold chill of February, through to the warmer month of May, some said she'd experienced her second love at first sight encounter, fifty-six and forty-three. She was a widow and grandparent to two, he was hardworking and a long way from home. Some said he mended her heart, others were heard whispering about how he'd gotten his hands on her purse and many said it was too soon. *'Some people aren't meant to be on their own.'* Loti didn't have money, forced to leave her council run property because it had been in her husbands name. Jade's maternal grandparents' weren't and never had been wealthy.

Mr. Stableford enjoyed his work, but the born and bred Canadian; hated the British seasons, his wealth not grannie's, that and him being homesick was what took them across the seas to a place where he was able to combine his green fingers and eye for design with his love of the open waters and boats. Moving himself and his new bride from England to his homeland, Sam and Loti left the United Kingdom to maintain and manage a large country park and campsite by the edge of a lake; Jade said looked and felt like the sea. *'Marrying one year after meeting.'* Refusing all offers to remain within the Barris household, Mrs. Loti Louise Denton-Stableford made her permanent residence and a new life with her new husband in his country of origin. *'Old & out of her mind.'* Jemima never agreed with what her mother was doing. *'An exciting fresh start.'* Aunt Jennifer supported the decision, believing all including her own mother deserve to be happy. Sam promised he would look after his wife forever. Assuring her grandchildren there would be visits, four years past quickly and Canada hadn't gotten any closer; with no amount of telephone calls filling the gap left when all a granddaughter wanted was someone older, someone wiser, an ear to listen and a firm shoulder to cry upon. When all Jade wished for was her grannie to hug and to be hugged by, there was nothing which would compensate. Loti leaving her family to live so far away sometimes caused Jade to feel abandoned. Maybe it was people leaving; which caused her to feel alone.

Like Loti, aunt Jennifer had spent time living within the Barris household, occupying a guest bedroom she turned into her own self contained space. From the day Jade had been born; Jemima's younger sister had been around. Told it was the result of a family falling out which caused the youngest, unmarried Denton sister to become homeless, Jade struggled to recall a childhood memory which didn't include her favourite aunt. *'Young & foolish.'* Official or not, aunt Jennifer had been the Barris's first live-in nanny until Mr. Kevin Karl Perron came calling to whisk her off her feet and move her from the busy town to a seaside village, where she became his wife and local post mistress. Not as far as grannie, but too far to see everyday. The new Mr. and Mrs. Perron taking over what had for generations been a family run business; meant Jennifer leaving what she knew, to take up what was seen to be an important position within a thriving village community .Jade understood how things and people have to move on, aware nothing and no one stays the same, her seeing everyone happy; made her happy too.*'Pleased.'* A maturing Miss Jade Jennifer Barris hated feeling like she was the one being left behind and abandoned by those she loved.*'Those she knew she was loved by, seemed so far away.'*

Lifting her pen, having turned to a clean page, there was much which she wanted to write, yet felt unsure where to begin? No matter what she wrote, or how she wrote it, she knew she would never, not ever forget this day and the sense of freedom felt while walking along the local streets. Jade would never forget her first, or her second and very probably her last ever walk home.

Oct, 11th
Today Grasshopper was full of smiles, he and Jimmy are really happy. Today I wondered if Grasshopper was out to play cupid for me like I did for him. Today I got my second taste of freedom and I know I want more. I want to feel the fresh air causing my skin to feel like it's being kissed as it sweeps over every inch of me. I want the breeze to move my hair in and out of my eyes, and I want my eyes to see what is actual. I want to touch the grass and smell the flowers. Today I spoke to Rojay and I hope we get to talk again. I'm not sure what it was he wanted? He said he was checking I was well following my stumble. He asked about what Papa did to earn so much money? Maybe he's planning to rob the house? Strange; I never expected him to be so calm and collective. Nice, we shared a pleasant stroll, even if he didn't ask permission to walk me home. If all boys are like Rojay, boys are nothing like those described in books, or portrayed in films, but what do I know? The only members of the opposite sex I have contact with are my brother and Jimmy. Do girls see

my brother the way I see Rojay? How do I see Rojay? What is it I'm thinking and why? Do all girls think about boys?

Always, Jade would write the words which best expressed her thoughts and allowed her inner feelings to escape, writing, in her continuous attempt to record events and describe how she coped, she left no topic unexplored, the teen use to being on her own; described how she felt and wrote about what was going on inside her head. The book which lay before her as she bent over its' open pages contained all details of her year thus far. The book she wrote inside was one in the growing collection which over the years she had bought, or been given. At the young and tender age of seven years, Jade Jennifer Barris owned a personal and private collection of her everyday, a record of what was her life events and every thought she ever had. *'Her diary'* What else was there for such a lonely, intelligent young girl, young lady and maturing young woman to do?

Oct, 11th
Rojay and I? Me and Rojay, all he did was talk to me and push his motorbike alongside us. Rojay and Stacey are a couple so I guess he was checking I wasn't going to land his girlfriend in any more trouble. Stacey and her friends' hate me more than before and yes; Mama and Papa wanted to sue, but sue who? Whatever money won would come from the school. I don't want any more trouble, but I would like to see Rojay again.

Despite having managed to write over five pages of descriptive text when sitting by her window and while lay in her bed, Jade didn't tell a sole about the day she would never forget. Perhaps it was because she knew her friends' wouldn't understand, or maybe it was because she didn't understand. Especially when upon leaving her next after school dance class; she found herself in the company of Mr. Roland Jackson once more. *'What did he want?'*

"Alone again?" The approaching male had a bright, warm and friendly smile on his face.

"So it would seem." She agreed. Having waved goodbye to Gretchen and Tamara, she hoped her shock wasn't obvious when the one joining her; pulled up at the foot of the school steps she descended. "And I managed to walk from the top to the bottom, all by myself." She smiled as he lowered and shook his head.

"Clever you." He said. "Daddy working late again?" Despite knowing she shouldn't, Jade had decided not to use the money in her pocket for a cab. *'Jimmy was to be instated as their full time chauffeur, but he had his advanced driving test to pass first.'* Jade's intention was to risk the short walk home for a third time. *'What her parents' didn't know wouldn't hurt them.'*

Pushing his motorbike alongside her as she started to walk, the male she hadn't expected; appeared eager to engage in conversation again.

"I never see you out and about." He said.

"No, I don't go out and about." Admitting what was her life, Rojay questioned why? "The truth?" She asked.

"Of course the truth." The one listening nodded.

"My parents' don't allow it." Embarrassing, the truth was, she had prison warders for parents.

"But aren't you?"

"Fifteen almost sixteen." She completed the young males statement. "Try telling them." The lonely female stuttered, stopping herself when realising she was beginning to rant. "Sorry." She apologised.

"So what do you do?" Her pursuer inquired. "When not at school?" He asked.

"I go to after school classes. I do my homework, I read books and I listen to music sat in my bedroom." The list of activities wasn't a long one, she could write what she did on a postage stamp, meaning that should she have a penpal, she would only ever require postcards to keep them updated. "Interesting isn't it?" She shrugged. Turning the questions on him."What do you do?" She wanted to know.

"Hang out, ride my bike. All the usual stuff." Jade wished she knew what all the usual stuff was? Whatever, it sounded like fun, because whatever it was, it had to be better than being a prisoner in your own house. Walking slowly so to prolong the conversation, like previously, Jade found herself wishing she lived further away.

"Do you ever go out?" He asked.

"Not really."She shook her head. Struggling to think of a time she'd been permitted out of the house without she was going to an appointment, or class. Never permitted to be outside her boundaried life without adult supervision, the answer to his question was no.

"Jade?" Stopping, the excited teenager looked into the eyes of her companion. Stopping, she looked to see if she could workout what it was he wanted? "Would you like that ride?" He asked. Only barely hearing his words; she saw how the leather clad biker boy was different when outside school. Handsome, Roland Jackson was even more good looking when being caring and kind, sweet and understanding. *'What girl could resist?'*

"Pardon." Her heart skipped a beat. She heard what he said, not clearly, but correctly. Jade knew what he'd asked and wanted him to repeat his offer; needing those vital seconds to make up her mind.

"Would you like a ride?" He repeated.

"When?" She gasped

"No time like the present." He offered.

"You mean now?"

"Why not?" He shrugged. Seeing no reason to be refused and turned away for a second time, the male eager to show off his bike and ridding skills offered his spare helmet.

"I've got to get back, Mama will be worrying." The one out doing what she shouldn't, wanted; but she was unable to say yes.

"I'll take you." He assured her she would be all right. Aware her concerned expression was covering her restrained excitement; Rojay assured Jade he and his bike were safe. "I promise not to speed." He smiled. *'How could she resist?'* Placing her schoolbag across her shoulders, her struggling to fasten the somewhat alien, hard headwear thrust into her hands caused her to feel clumsy, not easy. Managing with a little assistance to secure what was necessary before climbing up astride the long, narrow, black leather seat, she climbed behind her new found friend. *'What was she doing?'*

This was it, this was her dream come true, wanting to scream with delight, needing to shout and tell the world she was doing what she believed she would only ever dream of doing. This was it, wild! More wonderful and than she imagined. Sitting bolt upright, shy, she was no way confidant enough to hold on around her rider's leather clad torso. Resting her bare hands lightly onto the tops of her own thighs, balancing with ease, she used her feet to grip and hold her body in place. Inside; her heart beat faster. *'Jade wanted to go faster.'* Like he promised, Rojay didn't speed.

"Thank you." She smiled. How could she not be smiling when handing back the helmet? How could she not thank him for making her dream come true? *'Wow!'*

"You enjoyed it?" He asked. Was it not written all over her face? Yes, of course she enjoyed it, magical! Jade had been a passenger on his motorbike. How she wished she could shake the uncertainty she felt and understand his motive? If only she understood what was happening? Could she call this her perfect day, or would there be a sting in the air to have run through her entirety? Unsure, Jade was struggling to understand why the one set to be the next leader of the biker boys was mixing and risking being seen with the school snob? Happy to have experienced her brief moment of wildness, Jade felt her concern growing. What did he want? *'Stacey would be furious.'*

"Would you like to come and see a film?" He asked.

"Why?" Believing she was entitled to an explanation for his sudden interest she questioned his motive? *'With Stacey?'*

"Because I'd like to take you out" He smiled.

"It wouldn't be possible, no." She shook her head.

"You don't want to go out with me?" Not accustomed to rejection, the biker boy lost his smile.

"My parents' are really strict." How could she expect him to understand? Jade didn't always understand and she didn't know why the school hunk was asking her out? Was this a joke? *'A bet?'* Maybe it was a dare? Feeling the need to be careful, Jade felt she should act cool to protect herself from hurt, upset and whatever else he and his friends' had planed. Her parents' wouldn't allow her to befriend a boy like him.

"Thanks for the ride." She smiled.

"You're welcome." Replacing his helmet he rode away. *'Welcome?'* Without saying goodbye, Rojay left Jade to walk her driveway alone. Rich bitch! Snob! Spoilt cow! Silly sow, *'She could hear them.'* All the sly comments, all the remarks made when he returned to tell his biker pals and their girls about how she rejected him and his offer of friendship. Rejected? His friends' were bound to jump to his defence when told about what happened between Mr. Jackson and Miss Barris.

Sitting in her usual place; back by her bedroom window, the lone and somewhat lonely female wondered how much she was worth? A bet? What if her judgment was wrong? Could she have ruined everything? *'Why fret?'* Did she like him? Was her first motorbike ride going to be her last? Picking up her pen and diary, the teen still feeling the tingle of excitement running through her bones; couldn't wait to put into words how her first ever motorbike ride made her feel.

"Jade! Jade there is a telephone call for you." Her brother unintentionally interrupted her thoughts as she stretched across her bed to pick up the receiver of her bedside telephone expecting to hear the voice of either Gretchen, or Tamara.

"I've got it Jeremy." Listening for the click to indicated her brother had put down the receiver on other line and was no longer listening only when she was sure he was gone did she say. "Hello."

"Hi."The reply and voice was unexpected. "Jade?" The one on the line inquired as she almost dropped the cream and gold handset from her grasp. Straightening her body into a sitting position. *'Reacting like the person on the other end was able to see her.'* Her throat felt suddenly dry. "Jade, it's Rojay." Yes, she'd figured that. "Hope you don't mind me calling?" He continued.

"No."Though her parents' would feel differently should they find out? *'How had he got her number?'*

"Are you on your own?" He asked.

"My parents and brother are downstairs." Why ask? Was his plan to rob her house, she would take whatever he wanted and gladly give it to him? *'If her possessions were what he wanted, he could have them all.'*

"I'm calling to ask you out." Revealing his intention, he repeated his earlier invitation.

"I said. I can't." She couldn't, could she?

"Your parents?" He questioned.

"My parents." The privileged teenager confirmed.

"Are they the only reason?" He asked. Continuing before the one listening had chance to reply. "Jade can we meet?"

"Meet? When?" Surprised by his insistence, she needed more information

"Now."He suggested.

"I couldn't." Leaving her house without good reason was impossible. *'Guarded within what was more secure than a prison.'* "Sorry," She apologised.

"Tomorrow?" He pleaded. "I need to see you. I have to talk to you." He said. "Meet me after school by the steps." He said and she agreed to try. "You will be there?" He urged. "Tell your parents it's an after school

I MAY PRETEND

class." Sounding like he had everything planned, it became clear Rojay was much more accustomed to deception than she was at behaving like a teenager. *'Friday was one of her only free nights.'* Could, should she deceive those she lived with to meet with a boy she barely knew? How does anyone get to know anyone if they never meet?

"Okay." She agreed.

"Great, Bye."What had she done? Never had she felt the need or had reason to deceive Mama and Papa. *'Why agree?'* Remaining across her bed, with her music continuing to play out from the single speaker on her old style record player; Jade felt both confused and excited. *'Why?'* What was it he wanted to talk about? Was it her naturally suspicious mind telling her, she was best to think and expect the worse? Unable to understand Rojay's sudden and eager interest, perhaps she was being gullible in believing he was genuinely concerned about her injuries, confused by his actions. From where had he gotten her telephone number? What could someone like him want with someone like her?

♪27♪

<u>Oct, 18th</u>
I cant stop thinking about the telephone call. I can't get the sound of his voice out of my head. I never asked him about Stacey? Surely they can't still be together if he's asking me out on a date. Nothing like I imagined, he doesn't shout or demand anything, polite, he listens. He asks questions. What is it he wants? He made my dream come true. I wasn't scared, I was terrified. He promised he wouldn't speed but I wish he'd gone faster. I wish our journey had been longer. I sat astride the long leather seat of a motorbike. I thought I would slip at every turn, I felt the heat of the exhaust warming my ankle and sensed the purring of the engine throughout my entirety. From tension to relaxation, from fear to freedom. If I never get to be a passenger on another motorbike, at least I got to do

what I always wanted to do, once. Why does Rojay want to meet with me?

"Jeremy tells me you received a telephone." Jemima opened the breakfast conversation as all including Mavis looked to Jade for a reply.

"Maybe?" The younger female defended her privacy.

"Did you receive a call?" Nodding, Jade agreed she had. "From a boy?" Her elder continued.

"Yes, it was." Her brother interrupted. Happy to squeal and glad to land his sister in strife.

"No, it wasn't. It was a girl from school, a friend." Lying, Jade aimed at Jeremy the evil, hateful daggers all brothers and sisters, sisters and sisters, brothers and brothers have at one time or another had cause to exchange.

"Sounded male to me" The deflated sibling shrugged.

"Well, she wasn't, she isn't. You should get your ears checked." She told him with a second death stare.

"Who was it?" Mama asked.

"Rose." Jade thought quickly. Inspired by the view of the flower filled garden outside. Noticing the large single red rose swaying by the dinning area window, Mavis struggled to keep her knowing smile to herself.

"Where's Rose from?" Mama sought the information all parents require when discovering their offspring to have found a new friend and Mavis muttered the words *'The garden.'* Under her breath

"School, she was ringing to ask if I was interested in joining an after school class, today." Seeing, Jade took the given opportunity. "I'm going to be late. I said I would check it out." She had done it, she'd lied.

"What class?" Papa questioned what else there could be for his daughter to do? "And how much will it cost?"

"Creative writing" Aware the school ran one, the babbling teen hoped she'd gotten the correct day. "The first class is a free taster." She forced a smile.

"And how do you intend getting home?"

"May I have some money for a cab please Papa?"

"Of course." Jerald smiled. Taking a crisp new twenty pound note from his wallet and passing it over. "Keep the change, Mama always does." He teased, before rushing everyone along, insisting it would soon be time to leave. "The school has my details; should you decide to sign up to become the worlds next best selling author." Shocked at how easy it had been to deceive. *'What had she done?'*

Neither Jade nor her brother received regular pocket money, their parents' being wealthy meant them having savings, money was safely invested for when they were older, for now the two received money as and when money was needed, often being given much too much for their needs. So much, more; over the years Jade managed to put hundreds of pounds in kept change into her personal piggybank. Money she chose to keep and kept hidden away for emergencies. *'Her money?'* Perhaps Rojay wanted money? He'd made a big deal about her living in a large house. *'Whatever?'* The end of school couldn't come soon enough.

"Creative writing?" Tamara gasped when Jade repeated her line and retold her lie to her friends.
"Why do you want to do that?" Gretchen questioned?
"Why not?" Informing those listening how it could be interesting; Jade said she could become a famous novelist, or train to be a journalist? Telling her friends they should give themselves options and using the line. *'A certificate was never a wasted piece of paper.'* Jade secretly hoped neither would be interested in what she attempted to sound enthusiastic about.
"I don't fancy it." Tamara admitted to having to do enough writing in essays and exams, a fact Gretchen was in complete agreement with. Relieved and more than happy to hear their disinterest; having checked and gotten confirmation her chosen subject was available at the time she needed it to be, Jade struggled to disguise the relief felt by knowing neither of her friends would

discover, or disclose her deceit. Friday was a busy night at the stables and for Tamara; Friday was pamper night for her and her mum. *'Too busy with prior engagements & on going commitments.'* When her friends said they were sorry, Jade told them it was okay. *'She would be fine.'* The truth being, Jade needed to do what she was doing, on her own.

Watching from the classroom window, when on her own she made certain all who knew her and more importantly; all who knew her parents had left before making her way into the girls changing room to replace her school uniform with jeans, trainers and the embroidered designer top hidden inside her schoolbag. Out of her dreary school clothes; Rojay had to double take before recognising the girl he arranged to meet. His reaction only adding to her nervousness as he passed, before returning to where she stood. Smiling, words weren't exchanged as the biker handed over his spare helmet and she secured it in place before climbing astride his motorbike behind him. *'Her second ride.'* Avoiding the main roads and busier streets, the two rode off the beaten track. Still not confident enough to hold onto the rider in the way she dreamt she would; Jade nevertheless enjoyed a much longer and more varied journey. Becoming more comfortable and feeling a little more at ease with the mix of exciting and stimulating sensation, out on the unrestricted roads where Rojay increased his speed to the limit; Jade felt her heart race and her everything wanting more. Whether the two were traveling down a street, around a narrow lane, or speeding up a large main road, with Rojay, Jade felt safe. *'Where were they going?'* Cutting across the local sports field by the sports hall and going beyond the community centre, what started outside school had taken more than a little detour to end by the side of the local railway track. *'What was he doing?'* The railway was a place where the two would be alone. *'What did he want?'*

"Okay?" Watching as his passenger dismounted his mean machine; Rojay checked she wasn't worried.

"Fine." She smiled as she removed her helmet. "That was great." She praised his skill.

"Is here okay?" He asked and she inquired as to what he was referring. "Is here okay for us to talk?" He repeated. "Is here private enough for you not to be seen." He told his companion he understood how them being together would have to be kept low key. "Your parents don't have a dog they walk this way do they?" He asked.

"Like they'd walk their own dog." Jade shrugged. Assuring him the Barris household was a pet free zone and her parents' rarely walked anywhere. "Here is fine." She said. Wishing he would get to the point? Whilst flattered by the attention, there was no hiding the fact she was growing tired of the small talk. "Why?" She asked as he repeated his need to talk. "Then talk." Not her usual restrained self. *'Impatient & anxious?'* Jade needed to understand what was going on? *'Was she in danger?'*

"Do you like me?" He asked as she admitted to barely knowing him. She knew his name, she was aware of his age and his place of education. Jade knew some of Rojay's likes and dislikes and saw he was handsome, but she didn't know the male who was Roland Jackson. "We could change that." He smiled as she inquired as to why they'd want to? "Because I like you." He said. His words causing an uncomfortable silence as Jade struggled to know what to say. Reaching out and gently moving her hair from her face, Rojay said he liked her. *'Sinister more than seductive.'* What did he want? Would he push her under the next train if she refused his advances?

"I don't understand." Confused by what she was feeling, Jade pulled away. "You don't know anything about me." She stated.

"Why agree to meet?" He questioned. With more than one answer running through her mind, Jade could tell him it was because she was interested, or simply because he'd asked. Taking a deep breath; the female who was out of her comfort zone, toyed with the idea of saying she'd agreed to meet him because she wanted to know what he wanted, because she had nothing else to do and because she wanted to ride on his motorbike.

"Because I was curious." She sighed. Wondering what would happen next? "Is this a bet?" She asked.

"A bet?" Rojay repeated.

"How much do you stand to gain if I become your girlfriend?" She wanted to know. "Who dared you to approach the rich bitch?" She asked. Her companion shaking his head and informing her, she'd got it wrong. *'No one told Rojay what to do.'*

"I like you." He revealed. Assuring her, she wasn't another name to add to his ever increasing list of conquests? *'Was going out with a rich girl on his list of things to do before he died?'* Before he left school? Jade couldn't bring herself to believe his interest in her was genuine and without motive. *'Was she being naive?'* Was she being overly cautious? *'What had she expected?'* How could she expect anything, when she knew nothing about teenage life? *'Stacey's revenge?'* He said he never really noticed her before the day she fell down the steps and said since meeting, he couldn't get her out of his head.

Glancing at his blonde hair and clear complexion, studying his strong muscular physique, for the first time; Jade saw what his many female admirers must see. For the first time, she saw passed his motorbike, through leather jacket and around the tough exterior of the rough and ready biker boy. Yes, she dreamt of being with him because he was a boy and she was a girl. Jade also dreamt about going to America, who didn't dream about what they found attractive? Having read about the attraction able to lead who knew where? Jade couldn't allow anything to happen, her parents would never approve. When with him, Jade realised Rojay was a good person, but maybe he wasn't the right person for her, she wasn't his kind. Visiting America was a possibility while her being with a bad boy would never be accepted.

"Why me?" She asked

"Why not you?" He threw the question back.

"I'm not."

"My usual type."He completed the statement he believed she was about to make. "Perhaps it's you being different that attracts me." His words did nothing to stop her confusion.

"This is what you wanted to talk about?" She sought confirmation.

"You're not interested." More accustomed to getting his own way, Rojay took her inquiry to mean more rejection.

"I'm confused." She admitted.

"When I say I like you. I mean I want us to be a couple. I want you to be my girlfriend." He said.

"Your girlfriend?" She repeated. *'Had he ran out of options?'* Was he not on and off with Stacey Sutton? "How are we meant to be any kind of friends, when I'm not permitted out?" She asked. Wondering whether or not he had listened to anything she told him?

"You're out now." He said and she agreed.

"Friends."She smiled.

"Not my girlfriend?" He questioned. Again touching her face and moving his head towards hers as he spoke, she wanted him to kiss her, Jade wanted to kiss and to be kissed, but moved away before their lips touched. *'Was someone watching?'* Unable to risk this being a dare set up to cause humiliation? Jade had never kissed, or been kissed before. *'What was she doing?'* Pushing away his advances with her hand, Rojay taking her hand into his; sent a tingling sensation up and down the length of her spine as he whispered the words, trust me. *'More sinister than seductive?'* Maybe she was reading him wrong and maybe he was saying what he wanted to say in the wrong way?

A GEORGE

"I." She attempted to explain her inexperience. *'How could she say she never had a boyfriend?'* Fifteen, almost sixteen and never kissed. *'Why agree to meet him?'* Hadn't her father warned her about putting herself in situations like this, what was thinking, what was she doing? "I should go." She felt the need to leave.

"Wait." Still holding her hand, as she turned to go, his gentle yet firm grip caused her to turn back and face him. "I can take you." The more mature and worldly wise male said he wouldn't allow her to go home alone. "I never meant to offend." He apologised for not realising she wasn't interested.

"It would be difficult." She couldn't see how them being together would work. *'Different?'* She wasn't his usual type of girl and the only other boy she'd befriended was Jimmy. The son of Trevor and Carol was more a brother, never a boyfriend and not the type to be interested in her. *'Rojay's boyfriend?'* Flattered. *'Was she dreaming?'* Sure she would wake up to find herself at home in her bed sedated by painkillers and waiting for the doctor to give the all clear to return to school.

"We can take it slow." No one would approve. He sounded like he knew what he was doing and promised he wouldn't do anything she didn't want him to do. *'Their secret?'* They agreed not to tell anyone until both were ready to let the world know they were a couple.

♪28♪

Whilst her being dropped back at her house proved easy, them meeting proved more difficult to organise and even harder to maintain. It was a miracle no one noticed the longing, sometimes loving glances being exchanged whenever they came within sight of one another and it was amazing how no one saw the way they touched, all be it only slightly and sometimes by accident; whenever the two passed they did any and everything to maintain contact for as long as each could prolong every brief encounter. *'Their secret?'* Each would give the other a sign. *'Her finger touching the palm of his hand.'* His smile caused her heart to skip a beat and each and every time she heard his distinctive voice within the vicinity; her stomach filled with a fluttering she was powerless to control. Sure those around her were able to sense her excitement. *'When she dropped her pencil case he ran over to pick it up & pass it back.'* Blaming her blushes on being allergic to the schools heating system, Jade found no excuse for the way her pulse soured each and every time he brushed by. *'Exciting?'* When possible she climbed onto the back of his motorbike to enjoy his being able to take her home. Friday was their day and every Friday after school the two would ride, walk and talk. When away from everyone else, Miss Barris and Mr. Jackson got to know one another more.

"What did he want?" Jeremy asked when noticing the way the biker boy rode away?

"Who?" Sure she was fooling no one but herself, Jade denied having noticed. "The bikers are always hanging around." She shrugged. *'Jade liked Rojay hanging around.'* Sometimes Tuesday, always Friday, anything else was a bonus. One day, two, but never more than three, their days were when the two would visit what each called their special place. *'Alone time?'* When able, Jade invented fictitious trips to the library, her doctors and even the dentist in a bid to spend time with the boy she was growing fond of. *'Her boyfriend?'* Unlike she suspected, he never once asked for money, nor did he want her to do his homework. All be it discreetly, Rojay ignored other girls and as for the bet? Like her friends' and family, his were oblivious to the time they shared. *'A secret friendship?'* When spending time together they held hands, sat side by side, walked and talked. Days turning into weeks, before they knew it, the two were celebrating their one months anniversary. *'One month together.'* Almost sixteen; Jade Jennifer Barris had her first boyfriend, but still hadn't experienced her first kiss. *'One month?'* On the eighteenth day of November, Rojay handed her a pocket size teddybear holding a rose and she gave him new gloves to wear when riding. Black leather and expensive, the two read one another perfectly. *'New experiences?'* She enjoyed the time they spent alone. *'Happy when on their own together.'*

"Thank you." Pushing her hair back and moving his head towards hers as he spoke, she wanted him to kiss her. *'Why hadn't he kissed her?'* Placing his hand on her face, he looked into her eyes and she nodded, this time she wouldn't push him away. Placing his lips upon her lips. *'What was the sweet sensation sweeping over her entirety?'* As Rojay wrapped his arms around her, she didn't want to resist his advances, with his lips pressed against her lips, she felt safe, warm and protected. Comfortable within his grasp; despite his obvious strength, Rojay had a touch which was gentle. "I really like you." He said. *'What was happening?'* Her first kiss. *'Was this love?'* Wrapped within his strong arms; her heart skipped a beat, feeling sure she would melt, she placed her arms up around his broad masculine shoulders and held onto him like she never wanted to let go. "You make me so happy." He smiled. Delivering kiss after kiss, it seemed once it started, there was no knowing when their kissing would stop. Aware of how his previous relationships were renowned for being short lived. Jade didn't ever want to be his ex. Certain that with her, he was different, she knew he was a boy and all boys his age like to brag. *'Gossip.'* She could hear him telling his motorbike pals how he kissed a girl who had never been kissed. *'Had she done it right?'* "I'd never hurt you." He promised his intentions were honourable and said she was his best ever girl.

Weeks, one month, before they knew it, their second month anniversary was looming. *'Two months together?'* October, when her parents hosted their masked halloween ball, Jade pretended to be ill. Leaving the house under the cover of darkness and joining her boyfriend, wearing a skeleton mask, gloves and long black leather jacket to disguise her identity. On the night said by some to be dedicated to the dead, no one questioned the plausible story Rojay told. His cousin visiting from France, he said his cousin didn't speak much english and no one asked whether the one in the skeleton costume was a girl, or a boy? Ridding together, when alone they held hands and on the strike of midnight, back by the large metal gates to her house, they kissed goodnight. *'Exciting?'* Sometimes it felt like there was nothing Rojay couldn't or wouldn't do so the two could be together. *'Would they tell their friends?'* November, When most stood watching those hired to let off the annual firework display put on for staff and their families as way of thanking from Mama and Papa, Jade stood with the one wearing his scarf around his mouth and woollen hat pulled down tight. Jimmy's friend, should anyone ask. Jimmy, Jade, Sawyer and Rojay. On November the fifth; Jade's boyfriend became Jimmy and Sawyers good friend Ray. Appointed the position of family chauffeur; young Mr. Kingston hadn't meant to discover her secret the way he did. There to collect her from school, he assured his employers' daughter he wouldn't tell anyone what he knew. *'Friends?'* Rojay hadn't liked the way the male who was almost twenty smiled and winked when agreeing to turn a blind eye so long as Jade never told Papa how he and Sawyer sometimes borrowed one of his cars. *'Older & wiser?'* Jimmy was there when needed and despite his not always liking the biker boys attitude, he promised Jade he would never betray her trust.

December, it was cold, but as yet there was no snow, icy in the morning, the afternoon saw roads clearing of frost and she heard Rojay promising he would be more careful. *'His bike rarely got put to bed.'* A true biker, when some changed two wheels for four, he simply wore more layers and told Jade to hold tighter.

"Where have you been?" Mrs. Barris inquired as her daughter arrived home giving her normal reply of *'Creative writing.'* "No."Jemima disagreed. Revealing the fact she telephoned the school and discovered her lie.

"Where have you been going?" The angry parent wanted to know why she was being lied to. *'What could Jade say?'* The month was December and the effect of the coldness on her glowing complexion was a clear give away sign she hadn't been indoors. "Jade?" Mama questioned. The school not taking payment for her new after school class had rose suspicion. *'Fun while it lasted.'*

"I was with a friend." She admitted, but her strict and protective parent wanted to know more.

"Who and where?"

"Just a friend, we went for a walk." Jade insisted before being sent to her room with a warning she would go without dinner if she continued to withhold information. December the sixth, Jade hoped she would be able to meet up with her boyfriend for their three month anniversary. A name tag, the type worn by those in the army, along with a voucher for him to choose the inscription, gun metal titanium. Jade believed he and their three months together was worth the expense and more. December, she hoped her chance to give Rojay what she purchased when out shopping with Jimmy wouldn't end up being handed over in secret, she wanted to see his face, she liked when she made him smile and enjoyed when the two were together alone.

Aware Papa would arrive with a sermon about the do's and don'ts when it came to being his daughter, she waited for what she knew wouldn't be an easy conversation. *'Unable to admit to having a boyfriend.'*

"You should never have to lie to us. What if you had an accident? What would happen if you got yourself lost and we didn't know where to look?" Apologising before repeating what she told Mama, Papa asked if the friend was male, or female? More use to questioning, Mr. Barris often resorted to the use of his expertise when wanting to extract withheld information.

"Does it matter?" Fully aware it was the only thing which mattered to those who said it was their job to keep her safe, Jade shrugged her shoulders.

"Jeremy tells us you have been seeing a boy." Her male parent revealed his source. *'Sweet Jeremy?'* She should have known she could count on her brother to spoil her fun. "If what he tells us is true, I forbid any further communication. You're to stop seeing whoever this friend is effective immediately." What had she expected? Awash with luxuries and showered with expensive gifts, money to do with whatever she wished, Jade wasn't permitted to have fun. *'Loved, perhaps?'* When it came to her parents' she wasn't ever trusted.

"I am almost sixteen." She pleaded her case.

"In which case you should act your age." Papa advised but she didn't know how someone her age should act. "Teenagers don't lie and deceive their parents." Jerald said he and Mama were disappointed.

"Teenagers go out and have friends. Teenagers have fun." Jade revealed what she'd learned.

"Teenagers living under my roof do as they are told." That wasn't what her magazine said. Always doing what was expected, happy to do whatever she was told to do, Jade wouldn't stop seeing Rojay. *'Secret meetings becoming more secret.'*

♪29♪

School break time was spent wherever the three friends felt safest, somewhere out of the way; where each could assist with getting extra work sorted.

"Jade!" Turning; she felt shocked to see him heading towards her. It was lunch break, they were still in school and people were watching, others were listening. Tamara and Gretchen were sitting by her side. *'What was he doing?'* Mr. Super cool, the leather jacket wearing biker boy was approaching a table reserved for outcastes and weirdo's. Rojay had said Jades name where he could be heard. "We need to talk." He requested she join him out of earshot of their eager audience and with a nod she agreed. Placing his hand on her arm to encourage her to stay close, Rojay said her brother had, had a word.

"What?" Unable to believe her ears, Jade struggled not to laugh. Her little brother telling the tough and rough biker boy to stay away didn't seem read? "What's he going to do, shoot you with his spud gun?" Whilst admiring his bravery, Jeremy's sister couldn't foresee how he would intervene if his intervention was warranted. *'Sweet.'*

"I don't want to stop seeing you." Rojay told her and she admitted to feeling the same. Nudging one another, Tamara and Gretchen watched Jade and Rojay touch before kissing and revealing the fact they were a couple.

"Everyone will see." She blushed. Remaining by her side, Rojay admitted to no longer caring about who knew. If unable to see one another outside school, the two would meet inside. *'Was this happening?'*

♪30♪

It was out, the hottest gossip of the week was the scandalous story of the shy and quiet, little rich girl being with the big bad, mad biker boy. Miss Jade Jennifer Barris and Mr. Roland Jackson found themselves more popular than an ice cream on a summers day. Mentioned in every conversation taking place within the playground and school walls, the two smiled when together and laughed when hearing the whispers. *'It will never last.'* Together they shrugged off the disapproving glares, shaking heads and comments revealing the fact no one believed them being together would work. *'Rojay's new girlfriend?'* Rojay and Jade? Stacey was far from happy.

"Creative writing?" Gretchen commented.

"You'll get a reputation." Tamara warned. Both females revealing how they were far from impressed by what they discovered. "What do you think you're doing?" Jade's friends made it apparent the arguments weren't to be confined to disapproving family members. "Why him?" Tamara wanted to know, asking what it was Jade saw in Roland Jackson, maybe the question should be what he saw in her? Shrugging her shoulders at those who shook their heads; Jade said she and Rojay were happy. Happy, unlike others, once the news of their relationship became public knowledge, the hate mail began to arrive. Being the targets of sly looks and hurtful remarks, the holier than though attitudes shown by her closest friends soon became the least of Jades' problems; with anyone who was anyone, telling her to go back to her own kind. *'Different wasn't welcome in the world of the norm.'*

Heading out to meet Rojay by the steps following her weekly dance class, having made arrangements for Jimmy to collect her from the community centre within the hour, Jade felt shocked to discover Stacey stood waiting with back-up. *'Such girls were rarely alone.'*

"He's not coming." She announced. "They warned him off." Stacey told Jade her waiting was pointless. "They warned him and now I'm warning you." The one not afraid to speak her mind but not brave enough to make her stand alone continued to release her words. Nervous and confused; Jade didn't answer as she attempted to make sense of what was going on. *'A fight?'* What was she being warned about? Shocked to see Rojay's arrival, Jade had felt upset to hear Stacey and her friends insisting he didn't care. Looking to him for an explanation, it seemed Miss Sutton wasn't being entirely honest. Turning from Jade to look at Rojay stopping and removing his helmet before dismounting his motorbike and demanding to know what was going on? Stacey said she was glad to see him, while her face told a different story.

"Are you okay?" Ignoring the flirtations smiles and welcoming words from the one there making a play for his attention, it was Jade the arriving male expressed his concern for. *'Okay with him there.'* "Stacey?" He questioned his ex's presence.

"I was passing." She lied. Disappointed to have her plan interrupted. *'She hadn't expected him.'*

"What was she telling you?" Glancing from one face to another, despite knowing Rojay would protect her, Jade's confusion lead to her shrugging her shoulders and saying."Nothing."

"We didn't think you'd show." Not ready to leave; Stacey revealed what Jade couldn't. "We spoke to Spike." She admitted. Spike being one of Rojay's closest friends. "He said it's the rich bitch, or the club, you can't keep both." She repeated what Rojay had heard before. Glancing from Rojay to Jade and back to Rojay, Stacey's smirk indicated believing she knew something they didn't. "His friends will drop him if he continues seeing you." She warned.

"Let's go." Taking Jade by the hand and leading her to his motorbike, they left others with no option but to watch them ride away. *'What was happening?'*

"What have you done?" Jade's concern was obvious. The local park and not the railway. *'Jimmy would be at the community centre.'* "I have to go." She panicked. *'She couldn't be late.'*

"Stacey said something." Realising they were going nowhere until he had the information he required, Jade removed her helmet to talk. "She warned you off?" He correctly assumed. "That bitch." He muttered.

"Are we breaking up?" She asked. "Spike is important isn't he?" She sought confirmation?

"Our leader, Spike is the link between us and our being accepted into a proper club. Some call him the patch man, if he refuses a reference, we never get to wear any." The loyal biker's tone fell as he replied her question. "We have fun don't we?" He asked.

"I understand." She knew she could never compete with a whole club. Rojay's motorbike was his life and him getting into a real bikers' club his life ambition. *'A family tradition.'* Rojay's dad and brother were fully fledged members awaiting him to make them proud. Having made his pledge and proven his loyalty, the club he wanted to be a part of was preparing to take him into their brotherhood. *'Was this why he rarely kept a girlfriend?'* Them being together had lasted almost three months. *'Good going for him?'* She understood his commitments, she knew he liked her and accepted the fact she would never come first. His motorbikes, bikers and the bikers' club would still be there when she wasn't. *'He had to go with what gave him a future.'*

"I chose you." He said. Standing beside and pulling her into his arms, kissing the person he said he was proud to call his girl. *'Boyfriend & girlfriend?'* Jade was flattered and agreed she would stand by him whatever. *'Not understanding what whatever could be?'* Certain Spike would change his mind, it wasn't Jade, who she was, or where she came from making her the wrong type to be a bikers' old lady. "The problem is your dad." No biker should be involved, or related to anyone who worked for or within any agencies awarded with the legal right to enforce the law. "So long as you're not planning on following him into the courtroom." Jade assured Rojay she had never so much as considered a profession in law, not even a secretary. When ask what it was she wanted to do, Jade had to admit to not knowing, her parents plan was for her to remain within the institution of education for as long as possible.

"An accountant."Rojay agreed his club would accept someone good with numbers, so long as the numbers remained on their side. "Of course." She agreed, Jade could do loyal.

Apologising for not thinking about the consequences of her not being where she was meant to be, she was late. Jimmy had waited and waited, but when they arrived at the community centre, he was gone. Sorry? She agreed to him taking her home. A longer ride, with the weather becoming colder and the roads getting slippery, she said yes when Rojay said she would need better protective biker wear. Gloves, boots, a jacket and trousers, thick and padded to protect from the chill, she would need waterproof everything if she was to continue ridding with her biker boy. *'Black, silver, white or grey.'* He said colours had to be kept within what was accepted by the club to which he belonged and the one awaiting his entry. Shivering, Jade agreed a shopping trip sounding like fun.

"Where have you been?" Her body almost lost its' skin as upon dismounting the motorbike she was confronted by her angry parent."Well?" Mr. Barris awaited an explanation as removing his helmet; Rojay made ready to jump to her defence.

"Papa."Jade gasped. Her eyes seeing a somewhat sheepish Jimmy standing by Jerald's side. *'Backup, or punishment?'* The look she sent in Rojays direction said she was sorry.

"Where?" Papa repeated

"With Rojay."She admitted.

"Rojay?" Mr. Barris questioned. Turning his attention to the male accompanying his daughter

"Roland Jackson Sir."The younger man used his official name when introducing himself and offering his hand was the rights and proper thing to do but his hand was instantly dismissed.

"Jade, who is this?"Papa insisted she explain.

"He told you, this is Roland."She hoped her elder would be kind.

"So Mr. Jackson Explain yourself?" Jerald demanded.

"We went for a ride Sir."

"You took my daughter out on that contraption?" Examining the motorcycle with eyes, scanning both the male and his machine, Jerald allowed Rojay time to collect his thoughts as he assured his elder; he was a careful. "I don't care how careful you think you are son, my little girl isn't to go on that machine of yours ever again and I'd be grateful if you kept your distance." Remaining stern and displaying his authority Mr. Barris instructed Jade to go inside.

"Rojay is my friend." She protested.

"Not anymore," Taking the helmet held by his daughter and throwing it back to its' owner Jade's Papa told Rojay to leave, instructing a reluctant and embarrassed Jade to go inside he refused to listen.

"I'm sorry." The upset teen apologised when forced to enter in through the gates with the parent demanding Jimmy have their unwanted visitor leave.

"Is he always like that?" Rojay asked as a somewhat nervous Jimmy continued to stand where he stood.

"Protective."He nodded.

"Will she be all right?" Resisting the temptation to rescue the one he saw being held captive, Rojay was assured Jerald loved and would never harm his princess.

"Old school." Jimmy defended the actions of the one he now worked for, informing Rojay of how it wouldn't matter who he was. If Papa didn't know him, he would never be seen as acceptable.

"You know them better than me." Rojay sighed.

"I'm meant to be chasing you off."

"Thank you." Rojay winked.

"For what?" Jimmy didn't understand.

"Being more civil than he who believes he is superior." Before ridding away; Rojay wished Jimmy luck working for the man he saw to be unreasonable, arrogant and a bully. "Tell Jade I'll see her in school." Jimmy said he would try.

♪31♪

A GEORGE

4: SUBSTITUTE

♪32♪

Dear Miss Sweetness & light, you think you shine as bright as a Christmas tree but you can't keep the only gift I need. The dance is soon, so I am writing to tell you Roland will be taking me. This is getting beyond the joke it was intended to be. Time to give up. Surely you see he is only with you because you happen to be the last half decent virgin in school. I want him back, so unless you want your body separating from your limbs, you best leave him alone.
Stacey:

Jade
You heartless, selfish bitch: You can have your choice of anyone you want. We all know daddy will pay to give his princess whatever her heart desires. You have something belonging to me. Rojay is mine, hands off or die.
Stacey:

To Jade
Turn up to the dance with Rojay & you will never walk again. Stacey:

Jade
I am begging you to stop seeing Rojay. I can't live without him, I love him more than life. I know deep down he loves me. We are meant to be together. He likes you for your money. I can't compete with riches. Please stop my heart from breaking before I stop breathing. If you don't see me at the dance, my death will by on your head. I am no longer able to live with the uncertainty and need you to tell him to come back to me before it is too late. I need my Rojay back by my side, without him I am no one. If you don't see me at the dance, my friends will make sure you are never seen again.
Stacey:

♪33♪

Questioning what he was looking at, Rojay finished reading the words scribbled on scraps of paper. A mix of threats and warnings Jade saw to be the sad ramblings of someone suffering heartbreak, confusion and loss.

"She's jealous." *'Stacey & half the school.'* Since them being a couple became public knowledge; there had been hate male, nasty messages, threats and more name calling than ever before. *'Protective friends?'* Unsure why she kept the notes to herself; Jade said she was showing him because his ex was threatening to hurt herself.

"She's saying she can't live without you. What if she does something?"

"She won't." Watching as he folded and placed the scraps of paper back into the pocket of her school bag; Jade's companion assured her, he knew Stacey.

"You don't think we should tell someone?" Leaning up against the heavily engraved trunk of the large tree as he approached; Jade felt her breath being taken long before the kiss he delivered actually took it away. *'Was this love?'*

"Her english teacher, maybe."He signed.

"You think she needs help?" Jade asked.

"I think fiction like that could see her becoming a best selling author." Rojay shrugged. "We should add our pledge." Looking to the inscriptions carved into the large trunk of the ageing oak; Rojay said they should add their names to what for generations had been known as the love tree. *'Were they in love?'* Standing together within what was the picnic area of the local national park, not secluded, not out of sight like when down by the railway. *'Together?'* Looking at and reading what others inscribed, Jade stopped Rojay from using the penknife he took from his pocket to make his mark.

"No," She shook her head. "You did read what Stacey wrote?" She questioned what appeared to be his lack of understanding. "She's threatening to hurt herself, or worse." Jade told Rojay they shouldn't ignore what she saw to be a cry for help. "Maybe you should talk to her." She suggested.

"Why?" Angered by having what he saw to be his romantic gesture dismissed, Rojay turned and stepped away from both Jade and the tree.

"The girl is threatening to hurt herself." Following the male to have walked over to and sat himself down on the nearby picnic bench; Jade needed him to take responsibility. "She could hurt herself." She said, sitting opposite and watching as he played with the sharp knife he looked proud to be in charge of.

"Or you." The disinterested male reminded her how the threats hadn't only blackmailed, Stacey's words had also threatened Jade. "People who say they will harm themselves rarely do." Unable to take her eyes off the small, sharp shard of metal as it reflected in the fading winter sun, concerned by the way her frustrated companion was poking the tip of the blade into the wood of the table before twisting and turning it, she wanted to tell him to stop. *'Did she like, or hate when Rojay played tough?'* Why was he not concerned? "She's threatening you." He said.

"Will you protect me?" She asked. The boy she felt sure she was falling for; moving his free hand across the table towards her caused her to smile in anticipation of hearing the positive reply required.

"If only the rest of the world would leave us alone." He said as she placed her hand into his. "Maybe we should declare our commitment in blood?" Holding and turning her palm upwards, Jade flinched when seeing him raise the hand holding his knife.

"No!" Retrieving what she didn't want him to cut. "No, why would you do that?" She asked. Watching as he again moved from where he was to another location. Moving away Rojay accused Jade of being a princess and told her, she needed to get over herself. "Did you want to cut me?" She asked. Watching as he made his way back to the love tree.

"Look." He said .Aware she was behind him. "Look at the tree and show me where it says Rojay and Stacey forever." He insisted. Looking at the many inscriptions, Jade failed to see the name Rojay plus anyone. "It doesn't." He confirmed. Again raising the penknife to make its' mark in the ageing bark.

"No."She said. "Don't." She shook her head."Not yet." Stepping between Rojay and the tree he intended to slice into; she only barely avoided the blade making contact with her face."Not yet." She repeated as he lowered what would have scared. "Would you have cut me?" She needed to know and he told her. No, "Did, Do you love Stacey?" She asked and he turned away. Sitting on the ground and stabbing his knife into the earth before him.

"It's your name I was going to put with mine." Shaking his head, he said he couldn't believe what he was hearing.

"Do you think she's lying about not being able to live without you?" Sitting beside him, Jade had questions.

"I know it's difficult to believe, but I think she'll survive." He mocked. "Stacey is a big girl who can look after herself." He sighed.

"Did she tell you she loved you?" Searching for an explanation for his sudden mood change, Jade sensed there was something wrong. "Did you love her?"

"What kind of a question is that?" She saw it as being a straight forward one, Rojay's defensiveness causing her to think that despite his never declaring his feelings on the trunk of the love tree; he had something to hide. "Why keep those notes?" He asked and she admitted her intention was to add them to her diary. "You keep a diary." He laughed. The thought of someone composing a book of thought filled words amusing him as Rojay inquired whether he got a mention?

"Maybe" Jade blushed. Again questioning him about his feelings for Stacey?

"I've never loved anyone." He admitted. "Not any of the tarts from school." Angered, despite his attempt to reassure her such a reference didn't include her; Rojay failed to sound sincere. "You're different." He said. "She's jealous. Stacey isn't like you. Being a jealous, possessive girlfriend isn't your style." Telling Jade she should stop stressing about what neither of them could do anything about, Rojay reminded her of the fact Stacey had friends' to turn to. *'A clan to protect her.'* Jade being a girlfriend for the first time meant she didn't know her style? Jade Jennifer Barris having lost so many people from her life meant it only natural for her to be overly possessive; but she didn't know whether or not she was jealous, because jealousy wasn't something she'd experienced. Perhaps she was obsessing over Stacey because there was something more difficult she had to discuss. Maybe they were both being edgy because both were on the edge of discussing something neither wanted to talk about

"Take her to the dance." She suggested.

"What?" Rojay shook his head. "I'm with you." He reminded her. "I was joking. You know I'll protect you." He promised. "Stacey won't do anything, not while I'm with you."

"Stacey doesn't matter." Jade sighed.

"What?" He asked. "The dance?" He realised. "Daddy won't let you go." He assumed. "You want me to take Stacey so I won't be on my own." He said. "No," He said they would find a way. "We can meet there."

"I wouldn't be on my own." Jade lowered her head. Unsure as to how she was going to say what she knew she had to, she took a deep breath. "I will be at the dance." Taking another deep breath; the one unsure of the reaction she would get; continued. "But I won't be there with you." She gulped. "Papa's arranged for me to be escorted by the son of a friend." She knew he couldn't; but she hoped Rojay would understand.

"You agreed?" She didn't blame him questioning her loyalty.

"I can either agree, or stay home." She explained her options. "I would rather be with you." She assured him.

"Do I know him?" He inquired. Suggesting he have a word with her arranged date, Jade said he shouldn't, threatening violence was never a good idea and it would only confirm how Papa saw him. *'A thug?'* If her date didn't go running to her parents, Gretchen and Tamara were bound to inform the appropriate adults, either or both resulting in Rojay being blamed and seen as the one in the wrong

"I don't like it anymore than you do." She said.

"Let him bring you and join me." He said he would wait outside the school instead of picking her up from her house, but she told him it wouldn't work, she would have to stay with her friends.

"The girls would have Papa collect me before we said hello." She agreed to thinking the exact thing; explaining how there was nothing which wouldn't result in her being picked up and taken home.

"Okay." Disappointed. "No worries." He forced a smile before planting a kiss on her cheek and assuring her everything would workout. "We can deal with this." He said he would save her a dance.

♫34♫

Gucci; Jimmy choo or Prarda? What other decisions did girls like Gretchen, Tamara and Jade have to make when dressing for something as important as the school dance. Adding the final touches to makeup applied by beauticians and hair styled by professionals brought in from one of Mamas' top salons, Jade's friends advised her on what they believed she should wear. Having spent most of the day being pampered by those working for Jemima, all agreed they couldn't look better. New hairstyles, perfect manicures, pedicures and freshly buffed skin. Jade knew she should feel on top of the world, but the truth was she didn't care how she was looking. Jade wasn't happy making any kind of effort when she wasn't going to be the girl on Roland Jackson's arm. Unfair, why couldn't she and Rojay be together, they weren't doing anyone any harm and what she was about to attend was meant to be something Jade would never forget.

The Christmas ball, the end of year dance was the saying farewell to one year because it would be the next when those attending school again came together. It wasn't snowing, but it was cold, the annual Christmas celebrations took place in the final week of the year and were split over three days, the lower school got a traditional party with party games, party hats, turkey and table crackers along with a visit from Santa, middle school pupils attended the local theatre to watch a pantomime followed by Christmas dinner provided by the theatres' canteen. A Christmas Ball, the most sophisticated and glamour filled celebration awaited the attendance of those in upper school. *'15yrs to 21yrs'* Food, drink and music from a DJ and local band. *'Adults & those on the brink.'* The end of year Christmas Ball gave those attending their final year; the chance to mix with those continuing into sixth form and beyond. All events were ticketed to raise funds for the school and chosen charity, but only the Christmas Ball was open to guests. Jade sometimes wondered whether Mama and Papa had purchased her and her guest their tickets when she first entered the secondary education she would soon have to think about leaving. *'Set up?'* Feeling and acting more like a sulky teenager than her Papa's pampered, primed and proper princess, Jade went through the motions of the day with little input. *'Beautiful?'* Tamara chose dark blue, a backless, full length dress of pure lace underlaid with skin toned satin, the smart royal block of colour suited her olive complexion and deep red hair, straightened and cut into a shoulder length bob. *'Stunning.'* Gretchen settled for a silver grey cocktail number with a floating fishtail skirt which stroked the ground as she walked. *'Beautiful?'* Jades' choice was black. *'Something to capture her mood.'* Her friends were far from impressed by what they saw to be dreary and so; last season, at least it was designer.

Disappointed by her lack of creative imagination and enthusiasm, the *'A line.'* Off the shoulder with attached sheer wrap to be worn around the waist or arms had a scattering of diamanté which those in their teens said made it old fashioned, not right for someone her age. Jade wasn't listening to those checking her wardrobe for something else.

"They won't recognise us." Tamara announced. Checking her own and the refection of her friends as all stood before the full length dress mirror.

"We look stunning." Gretchen smiled. Each checking and rechecking one another's chosen outfit, makeup, hair and shoes. While Tamara had a simple but stylish bob, Gretchen allowed her mousy brown locks to fall in long spiral curls pinned up at either side to reveal her silver rose earrings. *'Happy?'* Jades' dark hair was styled in a way which caused it to appear longer, layered and wavy. *'Different?'* That which she normally tied back; was free flowing. Her friends' said her dark look reminded them of a gypsy, or witch. *'Plain?'* Jade wasn't in the mood to be anything but dull and uninteresting.

"Great clothes and great dates." Both Tamara and Gretchen struggled to contain their excitement while Jade continued to go with the flow. *'Friends of friends?'* It was what their type were encouraged to do. *'Stick with their own.'* Arranged dates were meant to lead to relationships and relationships within the circles which their families moved, were much more about creating, or continuing status than they were about feelings and emotions.

"Will you be seeing Roland?" Gretchen asked.

"You'll never get astride his motorbike wearing that." Tamara pointed out the complication her long length gown would cause when turning the conversation to the subject Jade expected to be broach sooner. Not holding back, her companions said she should concentrate on getting her life back on track. *'Too cold & slippery to be out on a bike.'* Jade wouldn't expect them to understand the excitement, or see Rojay the way she saw him.

"I don't know what you see in him?" Gretchen shrugged.

"Such a creep."Tamara winced. Both saying she should dump the rebel and be with her father's choice. Master Bartholomew Robert Hallas. Known to family and friends as Bobby, the son of her father's friend was eighteen, handsome, healthy, wealthy and said to be wise, a strapping young man. Bobby was everything Mr. Barris wanted for his little girl, everything Rojay wasn't.

Respectable, clean cut, intelligent and talented, recent conversations within the Barris household were filled with nothing but praise and admiration for the boy who was to be Jade's date for the Christmas Ball.

"We'd have fun, me with Tarquin, Gretchen with Greyson and you with Bobby." Tamara was more than happy to say how she saw and believed things should be.

"You know staying with our own kind makes sense." Gretchen pointed out the plus side of such a prospect, but Jade barely knew Bobby, a stranger. Of course she understood how a relationship with someone her parents' and friends' approved of would be less complicated, but she had a boyfriend, and despite the difficulties; Jade saw Rojay as being the right boy for her, the rough and ready biker boy made her happy.

"Who will he be taking?" Tamara shown an interest as Jade shook her head. Rojay said he wouldn't take anyone, the truth being, he was free to take anyone.

"Jade!" Papa's call indicated the arrival of those there to collect them as Tamara and Gretchen giggled, hugging one another with excitement upon making ready to leave.

For Miss Gretchen Gloria Garlock there was Mr. Greyson Gaylord Pettson. Almost nineteen and studying law at the local university, like many from a well to do family, Greyson didn't encourage or appreciate having his name shortened to Grey. With the prospect of a career where suits, shirts and ties would be plenty, a young Mr. Pettson was investing heavily in the finest threads money could buy. Smart and ambitious, Gretchen's parents' approved. *'Tick the perfect match box.'* For Tamara Tilly Tombrink, Mr. Tarquin Trent Tailor was waiting to be her escort. Nineteen, Tarquin was an animal lover; working his way through five years of medical school. With parents in the same business, his aim was to become the manager of his own practise. A vet and a solicitor, Jade saw the two respectable males as being the ideal partners for her equally unambitious friends. A country businessman and high flying law enforcer, suited and booted, handsome and smart. Jade was happy for those who's smiles indicated the fact each approved of what had been arranged. *'Sweet?'* The male waiting to escort her was Bobby, not Rob, Robbie or Robert. Mr. Bartholomew Robert Hallas was named after his great, great grandfather and as an up and coming sportsman, he was following his namesakes' career path too. *'Easier to remember?'* Bobby was his chosen shortened name because a more common name made him more approachable. With his natural born talent in football, Bobby Hallas had been spotted early; with papers for him to turn professional ready and waiting to be signed. Not born into money, Bobby's father sold cars and his mother was a seamstress specialising in wedding and prom dresses, making both self made. Jade and the others saw how out of place and uncomfortable Bobby looked when stood waiting. Shy, Tamara pointed out how Jade's chosen escort could turn out to be more her type, given the fact his father had reunited with his old school friend when calling upon Papa for his professional services inside the courtroom. *'A posh boy from rough & ready stock?'* Tamara told

I MAY PRETEND

Jade, she and young Mr. Hallas could be a match made in the ghetto?

"A little rough around the edges." Gretchen observed.

"Just how she likes em." Tamara smiled.

"Handsome."While Tamara and Gretchen greeted their chosen partners with eager excitement, Jade felt her accompanying Bobby to be a betrayal. Aware it wasn't his fault, unwilling to make his plight an easy one. Following her friends' as all walked down into the entrance hall, Jade wasn't, surprised when Mama requested she join her in the front reception lounge.

"Black?" Mrs. Barris questioned her daughters' choice. "Where did you get a black dress?" She wanted to know? Black being a colour she would never dress a teenage girl in. *'Not yet sophisticated, Jade was much too young to be seen as sexy.'*

"Aunt Jennifer was throwing it out."

"Best thing for it." Jemima expressed her discussed.

"She said black is sexy." Jade's hope was that Mama would prevent her from venturing out in the outfit meeting her disapproval. A ploy, the reluctant teen decided she shouldn't attend the dance and planned to go out of her way to be stopped.

"It's too late for you to change now." Sighing, it was left to Jade to suggest she shouldn't go, not if she was going to cause embarrassment. "Bobby is waiting." Jemima reminded Jade of what she saw to be her commitment, reluctantly admitting the speckled diamanté and silver wrap helped the hideous outfit look seasonal. Disappointed, Jemima told Jade she must go to the dance because it was rude to let Bobby down.

♪35♪

Walking into the highly decorated school hall, the girls couldn't help but feel the loud powerful beats being played out through numerous loud speakers hit them with a force which almost knocked them off their feet. *'Unaccustomed to heels.'* The ball was traditional, a disco with live band, the normally cold plaster and wood panelled walls were disguised with lace drapes and fairy light curtains. *'Warm & welcoming.'* Covered with a mix of fine tablecloths; the many round dinning tables fitted in with what was the glitzy theme of red, silver and gold. *'Wow!'* Arranged so the centre of the grand hall became a dance floor, tables were accompanied by four, six, eight and ten gold with red padding chairs. *'Different?'* It felt odd arriving at the large and imposing place of education after its official opening times ended. Shocked by the vast amount of people already enjoying the party atmosphere, Jade scanned the area in searched of Rojay, while Bobby offered to fetch drinks. Leaving the group to take their places at a table large enough to accommodate their number.

"This is nice." Tamara smiled. Tarquin pulling out and then pushing in what she chose to be her seat. "I could get use to this."S he said and Gretchen agreed. Aware their friend was looking around the busy hall, both encouraged Jade to stop standing and sit with them.

"Bobby is nice." Tamara smiled. Her attempt to regain attention which was everywhere but with those she was with; failing. *'Where was he?'* When her friends sat together, Jades' eyes looked for Rojay.

"The hall looks good." Nudging the one distracted from what she believed mattered most; Gretchen told Jade to forget him and enjoy the night.

"Nice school building." Tarquin admitted to having gone to an old stuffy establishment for boys only. "We didn't do Balls." He said he was looking forward to what for him was a new experience.

The bar was behind where they sat and the stage in front, closest to the dance floor; Jade felt lost in amongst the sea of people constantly moving around.

"Three pineapple juices and three cokes." Bobby gave the barman his order, looking around as he waited. Telling him her drink choice had been the most Jade had said since the two met at her house.

"Is it you?" Turning to reply the strange inquiry and expecting to be greeted by an avid football fan, Bobby was met by a somewhat intoxicated Mr. Jackson. "Glad to see you're not planning on getting yourself drunk." He stuttered. "She's underage." The drunken male continued. Making no secret of the fact he was drinking. *'Beer from a can.'* Rojay smiled broadly between slurred word.

"Yes, Thank you."Bobby replied the barman's request as to whether or not his drinks required ice, taking the given opportunity to turn his back on his unwanted, unknown admirer, Mr. Hallas believed the drunken male must have mistaken him to be someone else.

"A college boy," Rojay stated. Making it clear he wasn't about to leave. "Rich daddy?" He asked. His raised voice causing others to look, some scanning the area for approaching adults to prevent whatever would be.

"Can I help you?" Bobby replied the continuous coaxing. "Do I know you?" He asked.

"She is my girl." Rojay revealed his problem. "Did you hear me?" He asked. Raising his voice louder and gaining even more attention from those around. "Jade is my girl." He stated as both Greyson and Tarquin took it upon themselves to assist Bobby with the drinks and anything else he needed assisting with.

"There he is." Tamara commented.

"You must be so proud." Gretchen smirked. Both finding what they saw to be most entertaining, those who had never spoken to Rojay saw the big bad biker boy displaying what all expected from someone like him. "He's drunk." Gretchen stated the obvious.

"And look who he is with." Tamara observed. Pink, tight and strapless, her chosen dress was a short silk slip beneath a triple net tutu style over skirt which reminded Jade of something worn by a Barbie doll, shorter at the front and full length at the back. High clear plastic heeled shoes and a fluffy fake designer handbag bearing a gold crown. *'Stacey?'* Who else? *'Who would stand by Rojay no matter what?'* "Sad."Tamara sighed and

Gretchen called it tragic; watching as the girl more accustomed to being the bully, took Rojay by the arm and encouraged him to leave. Advising he stopped drawing attention to himself, Stacey hushed a ranting Rojay by placing her finger on his lips.

"My girl!" He warned. Pushing Stacey aside "She should be here with me." He said, not listening when Stacey said she was there with him. *'There for him?'* Allowing his female companion to lead him away, Stacey led Rojay by Jade and onto the dance floor.

"What did you expect?" Tamara shrugged. Watching what was happening; Jade felt numb, emotionless, abandoned and lonely. Watching Rojay with another girl wrapped in his arms; Jade felt her heart sink to the very pit of her stomach, causing her to feel both sad and sick. *'What was he doing?'* Sitting himself by her side as he returned; Bobby passed to Jade her juice, his eyes glancing to the brooch he'd presented before leaving. A beautiful and unusual diamanté cluster Mama said helped brighten her dress. With a deep disappointing sigh, Bobby told his companion he had no idea.

"I'll return it." She offered. Aware of his glare and feeling more than a flush of guilt.

"Your boyfriend?" Looking for confirmation, Jade turned to watch Rojay dancing with Stacey.

♪36♪

"Be sure to save me a dance." Those had been his words when last they were together. *'We will get through it.'* He promised. Why was he dancing with someone else? *"I understand."* He said she should do her father's bidding. How could she expect a drunk to remember and act in a way he assured her, he would? With his arms wrapped around his chosen partner, even if their closeness was in part due to his requiring support to remain upright; she saw how comfortable both were in one another's embraced. A couple, companions, two people who were right for one another, there was no denying Rojay and Stacey enjoyed one another's company. Singing, swaying and dancing, hands holding

hands and arms wrapped around one another, there was no escaping the fact the two had done what they were doing a million times. Friends, girlfriend and boyfriend, laughing and joking, whispering and then, there it was. The action which indicated Rojay and Stacey being on a date. *'The kiss?'* If honest, it was something she expected to see. *'They kissed?'* Lips meeting lips caused upset and shock. *'A kiss?'* It was long and it was lingering, as Rojay placed his lips onto Stacey's receptive pout, he did so with passion. As the dance floor fell into almost darkness, in amongst other couples Rojay and Stacey blended perfectly. She wanted to scream, she wanted to hit out, Jade wanted to tell Stacey Sutton to get off and leave her boy alone, she wanted to hit out at Rojay for behaving like he was. Seeing what she saw; Jade wanted to hurt them like they and their public display of affection was hurting her. *'Why do that?'* Realising the boy who called her, his girlfriend hadn't so much as said hello, Jade wanted to call it a night and say goodbye? *'How could he?'* Having sat watching him with another, Jade wanted to run away. *'Watching?'* Unaware, she heard little of what was going on around her. *'Why would he?'* The others at her table made conversation and drank while she nodded and smiled, all the time failing to join in. Jade had done nothing but watch Rojay with Stacey.

"I thought you were his girl." Bobby said.

"Yeah," She sighed. Agreeing when her companion asked if she wanted to dance? Placing her hands around Bobby's neck, Jade apologised for her behaviour.

Bartholomew Robert Hallas, dark and handsome, his chosen career kept him in peak physical condition. *'Handsome, strong, caring & kind'* Losing herself momentarily in the magic of the music; Jade allowed the one everyone called Bobby to lead her around the dance floor, permitting herself a moment in which she believed her parents could be a better judge of character than she was. Like most girls and women would, Jade compared the two she found herself in the middle of. Rojay,

A GEORGE

Roland Jackson and his motorbike were exciting and different, Bobby was healthy and polite, when held within his muscle bound arms, Jade realised Bobby and his open top sports car could be fun. *'More mature?'* Without knowing him; she didn't see Bobby being someone who played games. Did he like her? She wouldn't blame him if not. Bobby was where he was because his parents' and hers arranged him to be. Deceitful and disrespectful, aware her behaviour and attitude had been unforgivable, Jade would accept him telling her to leave him alone if that was what he wanted.

"You and him?" She didn't blame him being confused. *'Confused & hurting.'* Jade was confused.

"No," Sure she no longer wanted to be with the person who didn't deserve her trust. No, she told the one holding her, she was no longer Roland Jackson's girl. *'Back with Stacey.'* Once the shock wore off, Jade felt sure she would get over her short lived relationship with the school thug. *'Wrong?'* Why had Rojay been nice to her? *'Naive?'* In same way everyone does, she would learn by her mistakes. *'Fun while it lasted.'* Deep down she'd known a day like this would come. *'Head up & best foot forward.'* Despite feeling like she was bound to fall over; Jade could hear her gramps urging her to stand up for herself and be brave. *'Was she playing games?'* Or was Jade just young, she felt young. A teenager on the brink of discovering what teenage life was all about. A young woman attempting to learn the true meaning of life and untangle the interwoven web which was ones first everything. *'Did she love Rojay?'*

♪37♪

Placing her head onto Bobby's strong shoulder, her eyes met the approving smiles on the faces of both Tamara and Gretchen before being turned around and falling upon the disapproving, angry and shocked glare which Rojay threw in her direction. Like a child getting her own way, Jade wanted to pull out her tongue and shout *'ner ner nan ner ner.'* Instead, she chose the more mature option of smiling and allowing Bobby to take her hand as he led her off the dance floor back to her seat.

As the music stopped and the main lights came on, the hall which had been mood lit, was illuminated so people could see what were the annual presentations. Top girl and boy, Jade won overall top student for academic excellence, something she wasn't expecting, most in the grand hall looked in disgust at Stacey who booed what others cheered and clapped. While neither Tamara and Gretchen received anything, both congratulated their friend for doing her parents proud. Something she doubted she could ever do. A good night for most, Tamara asked if Jade would have chosen a different outfit if knowing she would be called up on to the stage. When Jade said she couldn't change anything, Bobby told her there wasn't anything she needed to make different.

Gathering their belongings as each prepared to leave they found their attention again being distracted due to raised voices. *'Another argument.'* Gretchen said that at least this time they weren't going to knock anyone down the school steps, her reference to how this had all began causing Jade to wonder if she was doing the right thing?
"No!" All heard Stacey scream out in attempt to keep Rojay by her side, encouraging him to join her outside and insisting he escort her home, the distressed female took and kept a tight hold on her companions arm; making it clear; her having her man back meant her not being prepared to let him go. "You are here with me." She insisted. *'What was happening?'* Remembering how kind, caring, loyal and understanding Rojay could be, Jade's heavy sigh and shrug of her shoulders revealed how everything the two shared was gone, everything he promised meant nothing. *'Was it the drink?'* Just forty-eight hours earlier he agreed to her doing what Papa wanted. Promising he would save her a dance, sneak her a kiss and be her boyfriend whatever, he had convinced

her all would be fine. Two days ago; Rojay told Jade he felt nothing for Stacey. *'Where were they going?'* Everyone including Jade watched as Rojay left with Stacey.

"Someone isn't happy." Tamara commented and Bobby asked if Jade was okay.

"Fine." She assured him.

"I hope this means Mr. Motorbike is history." Tamara said Jade was well rid of the boy causing nothing but trouble. Following them out, watching as the biker boy argued with the doormen and told his companion to stop her fusing; all in Jade's company disapproved of what each called thuggery.

"I understand his upset." Bobby said. Those with him stating how being upset was no excuse to be rude.

"It's getting late." Jade sighed as all continued to leave the school, making their way to the waiting cars.

The cinema, ice skating and the fairground, perhaps even a day by the sea when the weather improved. Listening to the plans being made as all made, Jade found herself agreeing how the six doing things together could be fun. Her being with those her parents' approved of, could create the opportunity for her to experience what could be new and exciting. *'Would Bobby forgive her rudeness?'* Waving as Tarquin took Tamara in his two seater MG, the four to have arrived and so would leave in Bobby's silver convertible, were interrupted. *'Stopped'*

"Jade!" Prevented from climbing into the car via the door being held open, she recognised the one calling her name."Jade can we talk?" He asked. Appearing soba and in control Mr. Jackson approached."Please?" He begged.

"Are you okay?" Bobby checked and she asked if he would wait. "Call if you need me." He nodded. Walking away, Jade reluctantly joined Rojay, the two moving out of earshot of those getting comfortable in the rear seat of the car while Bobby waited where he stood.

"You look nice." Rojay commented as deciding the distance between them and her friends' was adequate Jade stopped. Cautious, she knew she couldn't afford to make more mistakes. "I meant to say earlier, you look amazing." He told her. "You take my breath away." He smiled.

"So much so it prevented you being civil" She reminded him of his unacceptable behaviour.

"I wanted to talk to you. I wanted to dance with you."

"It doesn't matter." She shook and turned her head.

"What's his name?" Glancing by her, he asked about the one who was keeping his eye on them?

"Bobby," She replied.

"Seems nice."

"He is." She agreed and was asked if she liked him?

"What happened to Stacey?" She felt the need to switch the line of questioning.

"Gone home." He gave her the information she required. "We weren't here together, we just arrived at the same time." Making a poor attempt to plead his innocence; Jade believed she'd seen enough to know he didn't care. Noticing his motorbike, the hurt female also realised her not caring, didn't automatically mean she could stop being concerned.

"Your bike?"She questioned. Concerned by the fact he'd been drinking; she didn't want his usual skill filled judgement compromised on the slippery winter roads.

"I'll walk. Join me?" He suggested. Jade's second backward glance indicating she couldn't. "Will you be seeing him again?" He asked.

"I thought you were with Stacey. I saw you kiss her." She pointed out what had given a misleading impression.

"I knew you were coming with someone else. I was stupid. I was jealous." The usually strong and stern male defended his behaviour. Jade telling him what had happened was probably for the best. *'A great couple.'*

"No," Telling her she was wrong. Rojay immediately accused her of being clever. "You sly slut," He called her a tease. "You planned this." He accused her of running back to her own kind. "Daddy got his way." He said and she agreed; he normally did. "It wasn't me tonight, it was."

"The drink?" Jade presumed.

"Amongst other things."Shaking her head, the one learning about teenage life, realised she didn't know Rojay at all. The male she called her boyfriend was a complete stranger. "He's lucky I didn't hit him."Again displaying his anger as she turned to return to those waiting his taking hold of her arm startled and caused her to scream, his grip preventing her from walking away, his immense force almost dragging her to the ground as her only choice was to stop and step back.

"Get off me." She told him. Aware Bobby would come if she called. "Get your hands off me." She insisted.

"It's me who broke this off." He told her. Putting his face close enough to hers to whisper, he warned her not to go spreading gossip. "You make sure you remember. It was me." Without speaking she released herself from his grasp and rushed back to where Bobby stood ready to go to her aid? "I used you!" Rojay called. His tone returning to its earlier drunken, angry tone. "No one believed I could be interested in such a spoilt bitch." He yelled as she reached Bobby. "She's an okay snogger, but you'll never get past first base with that one." The lone male continued his ranting, his threatening manner causing Greyson to exit the car and stand beside Bobby in attempt to urge him to back off. "She's frigid." Not willing to stand back and allow the verbal attacked to continue, Bobby stepped forward ready to defend Jade's honour; Greyson telling him any conflict was pointless.

"He's not worth it." Jade encouraged them to leave Rojay to his own devices as she got into the waiting car, immediately apologising to Gretchen for the delay and agreeing she had, when asked if she'd come to her senses.

Keeping Jade's drop to last, Bobby wanted to talk and so switched off his cars engine.

"Your pin."She remembered her promise.

"Keep it." He admitted to his having forgotten about the trinket which was a traditional gift.

"I'm so sorry." She apologised.

"It's me who should be sorry. I never realised you had a boyfriend."

"I don't." She assured him.

"Gretchen and Tamara said the two of you have been together a while." She should have known she could count on her friends' to fill in the gaps, no doubt throwing in their own disapproving opinions.

"I'm sorry you got dragged into it." She thanked him for being her escort and seeing her safely home before pushing open the car door to head inside.

"I'll walk you." He said, immediately stepping out and escorting her up to the front door where both were greeted by Mr. Barris inviting Bobby in for coffee as Jade bid them goodnight to retire to her room.

Sitting by her bedroom window, having changed into her nightdress, Jade waved when Bobby eventually left, no doubt having had an interesting conversation about her with Papa. Watching as he drove away; she suddenly became aware of the fact the stubborn biker boy may not have kept his promise. *'He & his motorbike could be out on the roads?'* Despite his actions and bad behaviour, she didn't wish Rojay any harm.*'Watching as snow began to fall.'* From having no-one in her life, Jade Jennifer Barris appeared to be attracting the interest of two very different and very handsome young men. Was this how it was supposed to be? *'Was this growing up?'* One minute her life felt empty and meaningless with nowhere to go and nothing to do, the next she was faced with having to make decisions about what to do next, where to go and who to go with? Had what she'd experienced with Rojay been what others refer to as being a brief fling? Three months was a record for the young male known to change his girlfriend more often than he changed his shirt. From October through to December, time passed swiftly and Jade had, had fun, failing to see the point of a relationship to have gone nowhere, Rojay's behaviour was evidence of her having meant nothing. The only thing Jade could believe, was when he told her, he'd never loved any of the tarts from school. *'Was she a tart?'* Feeling something she never felt before. *'Was she about to experience her first broken heart?'*

♪38♪

5: A LITTLE LOVE
♪39♪

Smiling and joking about what had been an enjoyable evening, as she sat eating her lunch with Tamara and Gretchen, Jade felt relaxed, smiling even when joined by Stacey and her followers. *'Having their say.'*

"Nice to see you back playing with your own kind." She understood the scorned female's need to be heard, aware of how in her eyes Stacey had won, Jade expected the gloating. "I told you he wasn't interested." The one seeing herself as superior reminded Jade of the words she'd written.

"Feels good to be right doesn't it." Jade smiled.

"Yeah," Like a peacock with its' tail fanned, proud and triumphant, Stacey agreed. *'The winner?'*

"You should try it when it comes to your exams." Jade confirmed the true meaning of her previous statement, aiming her comment at her unwanted companion's inabilities and away from what she and others saw as her achievements and natural talent. *'Never beaten inside the classroom.'*

"I have no need for qualifications." Miss Sutton stuttered in attempt to remain dominate.

"Good thing, considering you can't even spell the word." Jade retaliated.

"Got a taste for the rough have you Miss Goody two shoes." Penny Queens stated in attempt to jump to her stuttering friend's defence ."Think you're invincible now you've played with a bad boy." She snarled as Tamara stood and those attacking leant back and giggled.

"Jade has a new beau." Her friend boasted.

"Our boys have career prospects." Gretchen bragged.

"Really; good lookers for swats." Stacey revealed her having taken notice of their escorts.

"Rich."Penny commented.

"I think we all got what we wanted." Jade hoped to bring the conversation to an end. With only two days left before the Christmas school holidays, Jade wanted everything to come to an end so she could begin afresh in the new year. *'Her first bout of foolish mistakes.'*

"Rojay seems pleased." Stacey smiled.

"I'm glad." Jade lied. "I can see the two of you being very happy together." Showing her support for the rekindled relationship; Jade wanted the renowned bullies to back off.

"You can count on it." Stacey winked when making sure she got the last word.

♪40♪

Happy, Jade appeared happy and on the outside she looked happy, in truth she felt unsure and as the split became public knowledge, she was most definitely not happy with the way Rojay was spreading untruths about what had been their innocent encounter.

"You didn't?" Gretchen gasped when hearing the whispered rumours echoing around school.

"What do you think?" Interested to hear what her friends' believed, Jade was struggling to believe those who knew her best, needed to ask?

"What would I know? I never believed you would get yourself mixed up with someone like him in the first place." Gretchen pointed out how she no longer knew what Jade would and wouldn't do?

"Tamara?" Jade looked for support.

"No, I don't believe you would be so stupid."

"I wasn't stupid, but I was foolish." What did it matter what Rojay was saying? First Jade and now her friends' knew the truth. *'Everyone was entitled to one mistake?'*

♪41♪

Tight jeans and a chunky sweater, Jade felt sure; for a night which would include ice-skating her choice of clothing was appropriate. With school closed, she hoped her Christmas holiday would be peaceful and fun filled.

"Bobby is here!" Jeremy called. Knocking on her bedroom door as with a final glance in her full length mirror, she began her descent downstairs.

"Here she is." Papa announced. A smile of pride printing itself across his normally stern authoritarian face. "And doesn't she look lovely." He commented.

"Yes, Sir."Bobby agreed. His words causing Jade to blush as like a freshly polished trophy; Papa presented her to her date.

"Hello." With a smile Bobby held out his hand for her to take, assisting her down and off the final few steps of the staircase.

"You kids enjoy yourselves." Kids? Papa's comment sounded even more awkward to hear than it had been for him to say.

"We will and I will have your daughter home early." The young male assured the smiling parent; his princess would be looked after. Leading her out to his waiting car as she picked up her scarf and gloves from the hall stand.

'December most definitely wasn't motorbike weather.'

It felt strange being alone with him, not having the others giggling in the back meant the interior of the car was silent, nice. It felt good to be able to talk without interruption or fear of being overheard, misquoted and talked about. As Bobby opened the conversation, Jade was relieved the two had arranged to meet Gretchen, Tamara, Greyson and Tarquin outside the ice rink.

"Do you go skating often?" Bobby made inquiries as to Jade's skating experience.

"Not really, my aunt use to come down and take me at weekend. Papa is a slopes man and Mama sits in the bar." She attempted to explain how things were. "Papa rarely allows me out of his sight, unless I'm with an adult."

"If I were your father I'd be protective too."

"Do you skate a lot?" She switched the questioning.

"Quite a bit, it's good exercise, helps with balance"

"I thought it would be risky, given your prospects."

"A footballer?" Bobby confirmed the meaning of his companions comment. "I could just as easily damage something walking down the street."

"You're good on skates then?" She assumed.
"I'm fair." He nodded.
"And at football?" She inquired.
"Fairer."He smiled.
"I may fall over." She warned.
"If you do, I promise to pick you up." Bobby nodded when eventually they pulled into the carpark, finding a space beside Tarquin's customised electric blue van, it was clear their companions had arrived together.
"You're late." The boys announced. Banging on the bonnet of Bobby's car as it came to a halt and they opened for Jade her door. *'Happy?'*
"You're early." Bobby insisted. Defending himself and his companions time of arrival. "We are on time." He checked his watch as all headed inside.

♪42♪

"Bobby's good isn't he." Tamara observed as having changed into their skates the three females stood watching from the side of the smooth shinning ice rink. Decorated for Christmas, the place to which the boys had brought their girls on what they were calling their first official date; couldn't be more atmospheric. "The two of you belong together." She smiled.
"Greyson and Tarquin are looking good too." Jade observed the three males displaying their skating ability.
"They are good." Gretchen confirmed.
"Unlike Rojay."Tamara sniggered.
"Unlike Rojay."Jade reluctantly repeated as Tarquin skated up to lead his girl out onto the ice.
"I reckon she's jealous." Gretchen said.
"Jealous."Jade didn't understand.
"Of you and Roland Jackson."Gretchen nodded.
"She hates him."Jade disagreed with what she heard.
"Does she?" Gretchen winked as she too left to join her partner, leaving Jade to wonder what it was she was implying? Could Tamara be jealous? *'Why?'* Watching as she skated hand in hand with Tarquin, Jade felt confidant Gretchen was wrong.

I MAY PRETEND

♪*43*♪

"Need a hand to hold?" Bobby inquired. Bringing Jade back into the realms of reality as he rescued her from her thoughts.

"Yes, yes please."She smiled. "It's been a while." She admitted.

"Hold onto me. I won't let you fall." No, Bobby wasn't the type to allow her to fall, not the type to hurt, or allow her to be hurt. Tamara was right, Bobby was one of the good guys. Leading her slowly out onto the ice; he shown her how best to glide across the hard, frozen water. Twisting and turning, skating around her unsteady form and helping her move over what was smooth and slippery. Jade's partner kept his promise not to let her fall as like her personal bodyguard he positioned his hand on and around her, preventing any unwanted collision between her and the ice as they glided along. Smiling and laughing, with Bobby, Jade was having fun.

♪*44*♪

Stopping for refreshment, the six friends removed their skates and found a table inside the rinks' snack bar.

"What will it be, Jade?" Like the gentleman he was, Bobby saw to his partners' needs first

"Milkshake," She requested. "Strawberry."She stated her preference as her friends' followed suit.

"I bet Rojay never bought you milkshake." Reopening the topic she was struggling to let rest, Miss Tombrink continued her sarcastic remarks and sly comments in reference to the rebel their friend had chosen to be her first boyfriend. "I bet he couldn't afford the milk."

"What is wrong?" Jade asked."What is this fascination you have with Roland Jackson?" She wanted to know.

"I was just wondering." Tamara blushed.

"Wondering what?" Gretchen asked.

"About why anyone would want to have a penniless, good for nothing, for a boyfriend." Tamara stuttered. "I'm curious as to what he had to offer?" She asked. Her tone revealing her lack of honesty.

139

"His body."Jade stated. Smiling at the shocked looks received from both bewildered females. "You should see what he keeps hidden under that leather jacket." She laughed. Gretchen smirking as she was the first to realise what was happening due to the sparkle in Tamara's eyes.

"You fancy him." She accused.

"She fancy's who?" Tarquin inquired, returning to the table with the others.

"You."Jade covered for her blushing friend.

"Really."The mature male beamed.

"Sure, of course I fancy you; I wouldn't be here if I didn't. If it was someone else I fancied, I'd be with them." The one whose cheeks had reddened; threw a look of dismay in the direction of her friends' both sniggering in attempt to hide their mischievousness.

"Milkshake madam."Bobby placed the requested thick, pink, fluffy textured beverage before Jade as the conversation changed to what the six planed to do next.

More days and nights out, being committed to his football training, Bobby made his apologies in advance. *'Sorry.'* He apologised for not being able to commit, while insisting his harsh and somewhat restrictive schedule shouldn't prevent Jade from being included. When dates were proposed and Bobby said he couldn't, Jade said she would very probably be busy too. Eager to know if she'd enjoyed her evening, Bobby asked if she was okay.

"Yes."Parked in the driveway outside her house, the handsome male repeated his apology for being busy assuring her it wasn't an excuse.

"I'll be there whenever I can." He promised.

"Don't worry, I'm busy most evenings." She revealed. "Dancing, drama and horse ridding on the weekend. I sign up for extra classes to get me out of the house." When school resumed, Jade would be rushed off her feet.

"You don't like your house?" Bobby questioned, glancing at the magnificent property stood before them.

"I'm almost sixteen and I think this is the second time I've been permitted to go out after dark without adult supervision." She attempted to explain.

"Most people don't like the dark." Bobby told her and she told him how she craved freedom, constricted by the confinement of the place her family called home; the instant she allowed her true feelings to escape in the form of words; Jade was the one apologising.

"I know I shouldn't complain." She sighed and Bobby asked if he could call her?

"I'd like that." She agreed.

"We could go see a late film." He suggested the type of planned date he could keep.

"That would be nice." She smiled.

"I'll walk you to your door." Opening the car door and escorting her up to the illuminated front porch, Jade found herself liking the fact he was a gentleman in the making. "I guess this is goodnight." He stated.

"Goodnight." She repeated with a smile as he bent forward and she pulled away.

"Sorry." Apologising for having misread the situation, the confused male turned to leave, catching his hand in hers; Jade told him she was sorry. "If you're not interested." He began. "If it's too soon." He assured her he understood, but he was wrong. *'Jade was scared.'*

"I haven't had much experience." She blushed. "Rojay was my first and he was." Taking a deep breath, she told the male whose hand she was holding onto, she'd pulled away because she wasn't sure what to do. *'Did she want him to kiss her?'* Handsome. *'Did she like him?'* There was nothing not to like? The truth was, she didn't want to spoil things. "I like you." She smiled and he agreed to liking her too. "Goodnight." She whispered as with her hand holding onto his; the two touched until the last possible moment, touching until with arms outstretched; each had no option but to let the other go.

How? *'Wow!'* Why was she tingling? *'A fluttering?'* Could what was taking over her everything; be more than what had been the excitement of the night? Like being invaded by something she couldn't describe, she felt powerless to resist the strange sensations engulfing her entirety. *'What was happening to her body?'* Why? How could she be having similar feelings with a second and completely different member of the opposite sex? *'Was she a tart?'* Could it be those who others call tarts, go from one boy to another so to feel what she was feeling, time and time again? *'She understood if they did.'* Jade liked how she was feeling. *'What was she doing?'* Having said goodbye to Rojay and hello to Bobby, when waving Bobby goodbye, Miss Jade Jennifer Barris found herself questioning her morals. *'What was she thinking?'* The truth was she wasn't, for the first time ever, she was allowing what would be, to be. Lingering by the front door, the tingling, swooning and smiling female hadn't wanted to go inside. *'What a night?'* Was this what being a teenager was like? She didn't want this night to end. *'What would happen next?'* Smiling, she recalled all the things she'd enjoyed about being out with Bobby, them holding hands and him protecting and treating her like she was his princess. Happy, she stood savouring every moment they'd shared, from the time he arrived to pick her up, to them not wanting to let one another go. *'They hadn't kissed.'* Smiling, Jade recalled how it felt to be held by Bobby as he prevented her from falling on to the ice. *'The perfect gentleman?'* She wondered if he would call and when?

"You always remember your first love." Overheard by Jemima, Mavis's comment was immediately seen to be about Bobby. *'Watching.'* Mavis was making ready to leave and Mama opening the front door meant it was time for Jade to go in. "Glad you had a good night dear, see you in the morning." Their housekeeper gave a look which wished her luck.

"Night Mavis." Bracing herself for Mama's words; the returning female believed there was nothing anyone could do, or say which would stop her from smiling.

"You did the right thing." Closing the door, Jemima praised her daughter for what Jade felt sure was the first time ever. *'Had she?'* Accepting what her parent said the smiling teen nevertheless wondered what she'd done? "You're first kiss should be special." When Mama smiled; Jade found her thoughts drifting back to when she'd been with Rojay. Being with Bobby was fun; he treated her well and respected her wishes, he was handsome and she knew given the chance he would make her happy. In her head Jade could see herself being with Bobby, but every time someone made a comment about the one they called her Mr. Right, Jade found her thoughts returning to when she'd been with Mr. Wrong. *'Bobby, or Rojay?'* Had she pulled away from Bobby's kiss because he wasn't Rojay, or was it because their first kiss should be spacial? *'Had Rojay been her first true love?'* When questioning her actions, she felt her heart attempting to rule what was inside her head.

♪45♪

Christmas was quiet, being her parents turn to host, her aunt and uncle came and went, along with the few flakes of snow released from the low clouds hovering beneath winter skies. A family meal and telephone call from grannie. Jimmy brought Sawyer when joining in with the watching of seasonal films in the den and the playing of new boardgames with Jade and Jeremy, both telling the happy female they wished they had half her luck when it came to attracting boys. Tranquil fun, Christmas was a time for family and over the Christmas period Jade, Bobby and Rojay spent time with their individual and very different families. An uneventful new year, Mama and Papa were invited to spend the bringing in of another twelve month period with friends while Jade and Jeremy spoke to relatives on the telephone before bidding their housekeeper and her husband goodnight and spending what was the changing of one year into another; up in their rooms. Two weeks, within what felt like no time, it was time to go back to school.

♫46♫

Sitting alone, Jade was shocked to have her lunch and her privacy invaded. *'What did he want?'* Accompanied by Jed, *Jerry Donaldson* Baz, *Barry Winters* and Kez, *Kevin Kerick,* Roland Jackson stormed in through the closed classroom door and walked directly up to the female sat by herself.

"Busy?" He asked. Perching himself on the corner of the desk.Sitting herself upright and putting down her sandwich so to look up from the assignment she'd decided to tackle, Jade wished she'd joined Gretchen and Tamara in the school canteen. "Bet you're missing our fast rides." Her unexpected visitor grinned.

"Did you want something?" She asked.

"Studying to keep up with Mr. College degree?" He observed the fact she was writing. "You and pretty boy doing all the things Papa approves of." He commented. Jade reminding him what he was asking was none of his business. "Isn't she lovely Baz?" He said. "Beautiful." The inquiring male stated. Placing his hand under and lifting her chin in a somewhat rough manner; forcing her to look up at those to have gathered. *'What was he doing?'* Showing her off like she was his to display, Rojay's eyes revealed unhappiness, but why wasn't he happy? *'Where was Stacey?'*

"She is." Baz nodded. "Much more lovely close up." He commented.

"Isn't she just." Rojay sighed. Releasing his grip as feeling relieved, she lowered and shook her head. *'What was he trying to prove?'*

"What do you want Roland?" She repeated.

"It's Rojay." The one who was unexpected and unwanted snapped his words. "I wanted to say hello." He grinned. His voice changing to a softer and more gentle tone as he pushed back her hair with his fingers.

"An old conquest; ah Ro."Baz smirked as Kez and Jed sniggered. Pulling her head away from the one who had wrapped her hair around his finger tips, Jade struggled not to scream when realising he was pulling her hair to keep her attention. *'What did they want?'* Laughing and making inappropriate jokes at her expense, she wished she was anywhere but where she was. Half in fright, half in shame and half because she didn't know what else to do; Jade lent in towards Rojay still holding her hair as he licked her face before releasing and letting her go. *'Why?'* Lowering her head and holding back her tears, Jade wanted her unwelcome company to leave.

"She was some conquest." Like some crazy person, Rojay's mood and tone changed for a third time, he and his friends walking around and mocking.

"I envy you Rojay." Jed commented. Leaning into her as she cringed, her whole being struggled to be calm.

"She was nothing special." Rojay sighed.

"I bet she was different."

"Cleaner."Causing his friends to laugh and his victim to feel physically sick, Jade did all she could to refrain from commenting on his continuing lies. Why was he saying and implying what he was? They'd done nothing wrong. Not believing her ears, she didn't understand why she deserve such a vicious verbal attack. How could he belittle her like he did? How? Why? Why was he telling lies? She hadn't spoken to him since the dance, neither had she commented on the lies he told about her. Jade hadn't said anything because she knew there was nothing she could say.

"I'm available should you wish to try more of the rough stuff." Kez announced. Rojay insisting it was time for them to leave, their childlike laughter echoing throughout the whole of the school as they went. Breathing a heavy sigh of relief, Jade convinced herself, her no longer being with Rojay was for the best.

♪47♪

Replacing the telephone, she smiled at the prospect of spending time with Bobby, but as she lay on her bed Rojay was the one who filled her thoughts.*"You will remember your first kiss."* How could she forget? Sitting by the railway; she shivered, not because she was cold; she was nervous. Roland had a reputation with girls and

A GEORGE

she had never been alone with a boy. *'Shivering?'* October was unexpectedly sunny, but the winter sun wasn't able to project the type of heat removing the need to wear a coat.

"I like you." He told her she was special, his strong, long male fingers feeling soft and gentle, like the fluttering of feathers as they reached out to stroke her face, enveloping her within what felt safe. *'Gentle?'* His lips felt like rose petals as they came down onto hers, as they brushed across and widened the tiniest of gap formed to reveal her teeth. *'Helping her to smile.'* Like leading a dance, he made the first move and she followed. Gentle, considerate and kind. Jade would never forget her first kiss; even if it was obvious the giver remembered nothing. Such a kiss for Roland Jackson must have been his hundredth, perhaps even his thousandth, he'd said she was special, but gone on to make sure she knew she meant less to him than everyone else."Cleaner?" Able to hear his words and mocking laughter clearer when inside her room, seeing the teddybear he bought her and remembering what caused her heart to hurt. *'Her ex?'* Roland Jackson was her Mr. Wrong and even though she was seeing what others warned her about, she didn't feel ready to kiss Mr. Right. Jade didn't want Bobby's lips to rub Rojay's kisses away?

"Cleaner!"

"She was nothing special!" Shaking uncontrollably, she hadn't known whether her shaking was caused by fear or excitement? *'Bobby was reliable, Rojay unpredictable.'* Drifting back in time, she remembered the touch of his rough, yet gentle hands and the feel of his thick, smooth leather jacket as she snuggled up into his broad, manly chest. Closing her eyes, she could smell his smell, feel his touch and taste his taste. *'How?'* What enabled her to remember such things so fondly after what he said? How could she possibly feel anything but contempt towards the beast happily spreading untruths the type of person she was? Why would and how could she continue to have sweet dreams about Mr. Roland Jackson? Why, in her dreams did all thoughts of Bobby disappear? *'With the wrong one?'*

♫48♫

Sitting behind the heavily engraved wood top desk at the back of the otherwise deserted classroom, she looked up in shock and utter dismay as the door swung open. Wiping dry the tears shed after another morning of being teased and called despicable names, Jade stood to greet her unexpected visitor, his arms filled with colourful and fragrant filled flowers, his face wearing the brightest of smiles. Words weren't exchanged because when falling into his strong arms, words weren't needed. The ringing which sounded to interrupt what felt good wasn't the loud chimes of the school, or church bells, but that of her morning alarm. *'A dream?'* It seemed Jade's life had turned full circle again becoming a life dominated by dreaming sweet dreams. Dreaming instead of living?

♫49♫

"Popcorn?" Bobby seemed to be forever feeding and buying her things while she seemed to be forever saying thank you. "Good?" He referred to the film which had been a premiere with everything including the red carpet and guest characters. *'Not famous enough to be photographed by paparazzi.'* Up and coming. Mr. Hallas the sportsman, was seen to be important enough to be given VIP tickets to whatever, wherever, whenever it was happening. Joking about how it would be his face on the front of a newspaper one day, Jade reminded him of the fact good footballers kept their names and face's at the back. *'No scandal.'* She agreed she would, when asked if she'd help keep him on the straight and narrow.

"Yes." She nodded. The cinema seemed to be the only dates the two were able to keep. So long as they were out after dark Bobby was able to escort her to whichever evening show she wanted to see. *'At his beck & call.'* By his side when he asked. There was the odd occasions they managed more than one late night in a row and many a journey home spent explaining what he missed having fallen asleep beside her. *'His head on her shoulder?'* The cinema, bowling and more ice skating, January, February and March. Both got together whenever they could, squeezing in what was precious time in-between his friendly games, important matches and training. Bobby being a football professional in training; meant him and Jade missing out on what the others arranged to do at the weekends.

"Have Greyson and Tarquin told you about the plan to visit the sea this weekend?" She was told something, but she hadn't paid much attention. The times spent with her friends without Bobby were times she wished they allowed her to stay home. "Jade, I don't think I'm going to make it." On just such occasions it seemed he was never able to make it. A good person, she was beginning to feel like she got the booby prize instead of the pick of the bunch. She understood his need to stick to his strict schedule, but four months of coming second to his commitments; left a lot of time to wonder.

♪*50*♪

"He'll join us if he can." Greyson assured her as Jade passed her bag and climbed up into the rear of Tarquins' multi seated van. The van all found to be spacious and comfortable for longer trips was customised to the highest spec. Fitted carpet and cushioned seat covers, arm, head and foot rests. That which its' creator called the beast, was what Tamara referred to as being their get away vehicle. The ideal place to hideout, she winked and giggled when informing her friends' of how some seats reclined to form a double bed.

"We'll keep warm if we get stranded." She joked about there being sleeping bags and covers within where they sat waiting for their final pick up to be ready.

"It's hardly sunbathing weather." She assured Mama the sun hat and sun lotion she was insisting she take wouldn't be necessary; while a somewhat impatient

I MAY PRETEND

Tamara thanked Mrs. Barris for what she was calling a fashion icons must have.

"We should let the youngsters get going Miss. Drive careful." Mavis smiled. Waving as with a sigh of relief Jade got into her assigned seat; watching as the families housekeeper encouraged Mama to go inside. *'Preferring her parent when she didn't show an interest.'* Aware her checking and re-checking everything twice was purely to be sure her daughter didn't mess things up with Bobby; the truth was Jade was growing tired of his forever being absent. A day by the sea in the unpredictable month of April? *'Why had she agreed?'* As the others chatted, laughed, joked and sang together; Jade found being part of what her friends planed and enjoyed, difficult and uncomfortable.

♫*51*♫

The beach, a funfair and the pier, all agreed, no matter what the weather there was lots of somethings for them to see and explore. *'A day spent by the sea?'* Jade wished she could be like those around her, wanting a hand to hold when walking on her own, she longed for someone to help her feel warm when sitting in the shade.

"He'll be here." They repeated, when remembering she was there. Walking, exploring and ridding the rides, what should have been exciting, was no fun alone. *'Bag watcher.'* Jade said it was fine when the others left what needed watching to ride the fast rides. *'Fine.'* She forced her smile having rode what had the capacity to take three or more riders.

♫*52*♫

Sitting on a bench along the side of the pier while the others played on the many games and visited the stalls, she never felt so alone. *'Cold?'* With the fresh breeze running through her loose, free flowing hair like the thousands of soft bristles on a brush, her skin tingled and her core felt like it was turning to ice. Sat looking out across the deserted sand covered beach below; the lone female found her view extending from the land, out into the misty grey blue sea. Unpredictable, April was a mix of heat filled sunbeams and cool breezes fast to turn cold, most definitely not sunbathing weather for. Grateful for the sweater, scarf and hat Mavis said would be useful when slipping them into her bag. *'Alone?'* Sat watching the waves lap the shore, the trickling sound was joined by the echoing of her friend's joyous laughter being carried up and around by the breeze which contained an ice bite like chill as the sunlight began to fade. *'Late, getting later?'*

"Are you cold?"

"A little."Replying without turning, believing the inquiry had come from Greyson or Tarquin, Jade assumed they were checking on her. "Then would you like to take a stroll?" The next inquiry was what caused her to take notice, surely neither of her bestfriends, boyfriends' would be so forward? "I made it." Bobby smiled causing both surprise and relief. Standing to greet him, she agreed to his request, placing hers into his offered hand they began their walk.

"You must be tired." She said as they strolled arm in arm down to the end of the long, brightly decorated, busy and somewhat noisy aroma filled pier, telling the others of their whereabouts as they walked by.

"I'll be fine. I missed you." He told her.

"Missed you too." She admitted and she meant it, she had. If being alone was what she wanted, she could stay home. "Did training go well?" Obliged to inquire. "I do understand it taking up your time, but it's nice when you can be with us." She smiled.

"We could spend more time together." Bobby had a plan."Come watch me train." He suggested. "Come watch me play." He said.

"Why ask now?" Confused.

"I wasn't sure you'd want to." He admitted to not wanting to chase her away or take her for granted. "Not many girls are interested."

"In you; or football?" She questioned

"Both."

"Thousands of girls go for football players."At least that was what the magazines and newspapers reported.

"Rich football players."Bobby agreed some in his chosen sport attracted a certain kind of girl.

"Are you saying you never get girls coming to watch you play?" Jade wouldn't believe him if he said yes.

"Not that I notice." The grin on his face revealed how like most sportsmen, he wasn't entirely blind to the attention he and others like him attracted. "Will you come?" He repeated his invitation.

"Maybe, if only to keep my eye on the competition." Jade smiled as Bobby wrapped his strong, warm, loving arms around her, his touch causing her to giggle mischievously as he squeezed her playfully.

"Got you." Gretchen called. Snapping a photograph as she and the others approached. All continuing to pose for and take photographs before leaving the pier to head back to the noise, excitement and adventure of the near by rides on the funfair.

♫53♫

From the big wheel to the big dipper. From the ghost train to the tunnel of love, together and apart, the six rode, walked through and experienced what the fast rides and sideshows had to offer. Reluctant to join them in the Black Hole, with Bobby's support, gentle persuasion and offered hand to hold, Jade joined in; where she usually stood back to watch. *'Safe & relaxed.'* With Bobby she felt safe, happy and content, enjoying even the most hair-raising and highest of amusements, the one not use to spending time with others her own age, had fun. Late lunch, early dinner was a feast of fresh fish and chips eaten with fingers direct from the traditional newspaper wrap. Huddled together inside one of the many large old fashioned bus shelters along the breezy seafront, the friends savoured the day to have been almost perfect. *'Almost?'* Because nothing is ever absolutely perfect. *'Almost?'* Because if there was such a thing as a perfect day, this day was as near as it got. *'A happy day?'* The smell of salt and vinegary chips lingered and sand got everywhere. With daylight fading, each to have enjoyed the sea, sand and attractions felt happy to call it a day and make their way back to the carpark.

Climbing into his waiting car having waved the others goodbye, Bobby assured Jade it would warm up, passing her the wool picnic blanket kept on the back seat for just such occasions, he switched on the powerful engine and turned up the heater.

"There's something in the glove compartment." He smiled.

"For me?" She questioned. "What?" She asked as the one happy to drive her home got their journey underway.

"Take a look." He urged. Pulling open the compartment door to find a neatly wrapped gift, unsure what to say? "Open it." Her driver insisted. "It won't bite." He said. Carefully, aware Bobby was keeping one eye on the road and the other on her, the fact she recognised the box inside the gift paper as coming from a jewellers; caused her to feel confused. Without looking inside, she knew what it would be, but didn't know how she felt about the boy her parents' saw to be her perfect boyfriend presenting her with a ring.

"Don't worry." He assured her. "It's a friendship ring." Flicking up the hinge lid, her eyes lit up at the sight of the glittering, glistening diamond and sapphire studded band. "We are friends aren't we?" He asked.

"Of course." She smiled. "Of course we're friends, this is beautiful, but if you don't mind, I'll wait until we stop before I put it on."

"Why?" Bobby questioned. His disappointment in her reaction clear to see.

"I'd like you to put it on for me." She'd read about it in her magazines and she liked the idea of the boy who clearly cared for her; placing a ring on her finger. Also; she wasn't entirely sure which finger was her friendship finger? Luckily he agreed to her request.

Parked outside her house, Jade thanked Bobby for his kind and thoughtful gift as he placed it onto her finger, the centre finger of her left hand.

"It's lovely." She complimented his exquisite, no doubt expensive taste. "Really lovely." She smiled, stopping him as he went to lean back into the drivers seat. Looking into one another's eyes, both questioned if the other was sure before agreeing they were. *'A kiss?'* Bobby and Jade held hands, they hugged and sometimes he kissed her on her cheek and forehead. *'Kissing like friends kiss.'* This would be their first real kiss. *'Lips upon lips.'* It was a peck at first, when first Bobby placed his lips upon her lips, he did so in the same way he placed his lips upon her cheek. *'Eyes asking the question to which the answer was yes.'* Placing his lips back upon her lips, she closed her eyes and allowed him to take the lead. *'Different?'* Stronger and more in-depth, sure her spine would melt if he didn't stop soon, she didn't want what had begun to stop too soon. Eyes which said yes asked one another if they were okay when eventually what was their first kiss came to its end. *'Wow!'* It had taken four months, worth the wait. *'Wow!'* Swept off her feet, Jade wasn't sure her weakened knees would be strong enough to hold her weight when it was time for her to stand.

"Will you come watch me play tomorrow?" Unsure who would be first to speak and not knowing what would be said, Bobby's request sounded perfect.

"A match?" She knew his endless training was leading to something and he said play, not train.

"Rumour is there will be a scout in the crowd." He revealed and she realised the sacrifice he'd made.

"You shouldn't have come." She said.

"I wanted to see and spend time with you."

"You should have been home resting." Sounding more like his parent or trainer than his girlfriend. "I will be there." She promised and promised again when the two eventually said goodnight, their lips meeting for a second time. "Yes."She agreed to being his girl. *'How could she resist?'* Walking up to her bedroom, Jade found herself hoping Bobby's kiss had erased all trance of what had been the lingering imprint left by Rojay. How could she know how having experienced what had felt good, she would encounter better?

♪54♪

Following Papa and Bobby's father, Jade took her place at the football stadium, taken up inside the seating area reserved for the family and friends of the players, nothing was how she imagined.

"We meet again." Mr. Hallas smiled upon greeting his dear friend."Little Jade's all grown up; I can't remember when I last saw you lovie, but I hear you and my Bobby are getting along famously."

"Yes Sir," She agreed. Mr. Tyler Robert Hallas wasn't what she imagined, not what anyone pictured when the description was wealthy father of an up and coming professional sportsman. Not someone she saw being a friend of Papas' but they insisted on being best buddies. Wearing a large overcoat around his shoulders and continually transferring his over sized cigar from his mouth to his hand and back again. Tyler was a chirpy chappy, the type of character acquainted with sales; a car salesman who sold secondhand bangers to those down on their luck, while building his wealth from the astronomical interest rates his finance department handled and sometimes handled badly. The truth was, whatever his background, Mr. Hallas was now the man responsible for supplying rich clients with top of the range vehicles for sale and hire along with a chauffeur, bodyguard, or both. Mr. Hallas ran the most prestige car showroom and unique security firm in the country.

"Do you like football?" He inquired.

"I've never watched a game before." She admitted.

"Takes you back don't it Jezza? Your paps and me attended many a Saturday afternoon match back in our youth; not that we dreamt of affording family seats back in those days." Bestfriends, the two mature gentlemen were unlikely companions on the face of what was their individual history. Papa being the son of a bank manager meant his being expected to prosper within the realms of academia, his only choice had been to achieve what was required for him to gain entry into higher and on to further education. School, college and university. His private house being on the outskirts of a large council run housing estate meant him mixing with some who his parents' would have rather he didn't. Jerald and Tyler should never have been, but having met over the garden wall, there was a time when the two were inseparable. Like Papa Mr. Hallas now provided a high standard of living for himself and his family, unlike Mr. Barris, the bulk of Tyler's financial gains may not have come from legitimate means. Unlike either of her own parents' Mr. Hallas had neither forgotten, nor was he ashamed of his roots. Unlike Papa, Bobby's male parent was visibly proud of his family, especially his son. "The boy is one of my finest achievements." He boasted. Cheers ringing loud as the game got underway. Shocked and surprised, Jade became lost within the electrifying atmosphere to surround her and everything within what was a clean and grand stadium.

Excited by the roar of the crowds, her being an absolute novice meant she wasn't sure whether Bobby was playing to his full potential. *'A good game?'* There was no denying he looked good. Handsome, his long hours of intense training moulded his strong muscular stature to almost perfection. *'A God?'* Many a good sportsman found him, or herself worshiped by adoring and enthusiastic fans. Bobby Hallas had never smoked, he rarely drank, he didn't fight and he wouldn't use bad language. *'Not with intent,'* Always polite and courteous, he was charming without having to try and it was clear he was his fathers' pride and joy. When watching his son, Tyler found great pleasure in showing off his boy. Proud to the point of almost exploding, able and happy to explain the many rules of the game called football, Tyler shared what he saw to be his sons success.

"Bobby will be pleased you came." He told her as she struggled to keep track of his on pitch whereabouts. *'How could he move so fast?'* Rarely still and always in the thick of the action. "He's noticed you." She was told when at half time, with his team trailing one goal to nil, Bobby and both teams left the field, most looking to see if they could spot family and friends in the crowds? Two minutes into the second half, the score was miraculously equalised, causing the cheering crowds to turn up the loud and excited volume.

"Yes, Wow! That's my boy!" Tyler jumped into the air as his son placed a second ball into the back of the opposing teams net. "That's my boy!" He repeated. Hugging and lifting Jade off her feet, swinging her around with excitement as with the final score of three goals to one, the ninety minute match came to its end. They'd done it, they'd won and Bobby had scored two of the three winning goals. *'Jade was proud too.'*

Waiting outside the changing room while Papa and Tyler went in to congratulate the boys, uneasy and out of place she looked around.

"That's Bobby's girl.""Hearing what some said. "She hangs out with biker boys." Did she? The whispers didn't help the way she was feeling. *'Shocked!'* Had Bobby said something? If she and Bobby were so well suited, why did she feel out of her depth. *'Bobby's girl?'* Yes, yes she probably was, but how come strangers knew what she was unsure of? *'Rojay?'* So what if she had a previous boyfriend? *'The more girlfriends a boy had the better.'* Rojay had been nice to her, her friend, the two had done nothing wrong. Jade had done nothing to be ashamed of. *'Why did she want to run & hide?'* Answering the snide remarks inside her head, the waiting female wished those talking about her were able to hear, wishing she knew something about them, she realised she couldn't so much as recall the numbers displayed on the back of their shirts.

"You made it?" His welcoming smile shone bright as he kissed her cheek.

"Hi."Boy was she pleased to see him.

"What did you think?" He asked.

"You were great." She said.

"Only great?"

"What do I know?" Jade shrugged.

"He was fantastic, fantastic." Rubbing his sons' freshly washed, neatly combed hair, Tyler again displayed his fatherly pride."Fantastic!" He said.

"He is so proud of you." Jade informed Bobby as their elders took the lead on route to the carpark.

"Yeah, Are you coming back with us?" He asked "There is a celebration at the club." He smiled.

"I best stay with Papa." She told him.

"In that case it looks like the answer is yes." Bobby continued to smile as they followed the chatting males from in, to outside.

"A celebration?" Jade questioned.

"A chance for us boys to let our hair down, a party." Bobby assured her, she looked and would be fine. *'Not dressed to party.'* Seats, or standing? Football was an outdoor sport and for being outside in the unpredictable month of April; Jade wore what was warm and snuggly. Jeans and a jumper under her padded Jacket, a scarf and gloves. Jade asked Bobby if she had time to call home and change?

"Bobby Hallas?" Appearing from nowhere, the male requesting he confirm his identity looked official. "Are you Bobby Hallas?"

"Yes," Confidant his father and couch were within sight and earshot should he need them. Bobby stopped, encouraging Jade to stand beside him, she noted how all around fell silent. *'What were they doing?'* Eager to discover the strangers' intentions, Bobby wasn't the only one wanting to hear what he had to say.

"Yes, Wow Yes:"Bobby answered. "Yes:"He yelled as for the second time that afternoon Jade felt her feet leave the ground. He'd done it, Bobby Hallas was the one. The stranger was the rumoured scout and Bobby the team member he spotted. The one asked, Bobby was the training footballer being offered the opportunity to turn his career around and go professional sooner than was predicted. "Yes, Yes!" His excitement was breathtaking, as too was that of those who suddenly came rushing forward, taking and shaking him by the hand, hugging and lifting him up into the air. Carrying him up on their strong shoulders. Jade stepped back and watched, her eyes and her heart smiling for him as he and his teammates celebrated his good fortune. Yes, she smiled. Yes, she was happy. Happy that was until her heart skipped a beat, almost stopping; sure it was about to exit via her drying mouth, her eyes fell upon eyes to have observed her first. *'What was he doing there?'* No, as the excitement around her and her own feelings of pride, joy and happiness became overshadowed and eclipsed by what she was seeing, she felt her smile fade. *'Who?'* What was he doing in amongst the cheering crowd, he never mentioned being a football fan? No, she struggled to believe her eyes as she saw someone to have seen her first. Someone who was watching and had continued to watch her and her actions for who knew how long? Suddenly and unintentionally; her smiling eyes met the deep blue of Rojay's glare. *'Rojay was watching her.'* Why? Why if he had been her once in a lifetime mistake; did not only the memory; but him, himself continue to enter her thoughts and invade her days. *'Why was he haunting her like a bad dream?'* Why was the male who now referred to her as being a snob and worse, stood watching over and monitoring her every move? When Mr. Hallas and Papa shook hands with the scout requesting to sign Bobby. Jade felt relieved that the large, dark suited males blocked her direct vision of the one she noticed watching her. Blocking her sight and catapulting her trail of thought out of the past and back into the present. Jade came out of her dream and returned to reality. *'Had she imagined his being there?'* A celebration? Leaving where they were, all headed to the party, drinks and dancing.

Meeting up with Mama, Jeremy and Mrs. Suzann Hallas, Jade being more formally introduced to Bobby's family, friends and teammates wasn't as bad as she first imagined. Friendlier and more approachable than first impression led her to believe. *'Gossips, or hypocrites?'* Having proven to be the best of them, those Bobby called his teammates would no longer matter, because he would soon be with a new team. A party, dancing and chatting, pleased to have her brother by her side whenever Bobby was taken to talk to someone about something. Jade was also glad Mama had brought something more appropriate for her to wear and relieved to find the female toilets clean enough to use for changing. Sorting her hair and make-up best she could; Jade smiled when Mama told her she looked fine and they returned to join in with those ready to party.

"They make a lovely couple." Tyler was heard saying his son would be hard pushed to find a better partner when the time was right for him to need a good woman.

"I see he bought her a ring." Jemima expressed her approval; while Jerald said he wasn't sure.

"A friendship ring." His tone revealed what he saw to be the insignificance of what others called a generous token.

"You are right" Tyler nodded. "Bobby will have no time for girls, not with his career to concentrate on."

"A professional." Jerald congratulated his friend for creating himself a sporting genius. "Jemima and Suzann will have them married off if we let them." He warned as both looked to Bobby dancing with Jade.

"A wife, a mortgage and children of his own before he gets a chance to catch his breath." Tyler shook his head.

"No professional can afford such inconveniences hanging around his neck, not at this stage of the game."

"Glad we agree." Jerald smiled. Both men assuring one another of how they would discourage the relationship before it got serious ."Too young to rush into something they'll regret." Mr. Barris said when the time was right, he would be proud to have Bobby join his family, but didn't want to see his princess hurt by what both males foresaw as being difficult times ahead.

"We'll tell them there's no rush." Those with more life experience; knew how time and distance often resulted in a relationship fizzling out.

"If it's meant to be, they'll wait." The chatting men also knew, to tell their children not to do something, would result in them doing everything they didn't want them to do. *'No rush,'* There was nothing rushed about the relationship between Jade and Bobby. *'Happy to spend time together.'* She wore his ring because they were friends, neither had declared their undying love. Two relationships and still the word love hadn't been mentioned. *'Was she doing something wrong?'* Teen magazines had pages crammed with the four letter word, yet it hadn't escaped her own or Bobby's lips once. *'Did she love him?'* With the after match celebrations coming to an end, his kiss goodnight made her feel warm and tingly. How could kisses feel so passionate if not being delivered with love? *'What was it, she was feeling?'*

♫55♫

12th April
Does love truly exist? The after match party was fun, Mama brought me a dress and shoes to change into, so I could remove the boots worn for the terraces. Bobby really knows his footwork, whether wearing his football boots, or his dancing shoes, he never puts a step wrong. Despite him being one of My own kind as Stacey pointed out. He isn't dull or uninteresting. Together we mingled amongst his friends and everyone really likes him. Together we danced, he whirled me across the

dance floor and held me close for all to see. Whenever I'm near he holds me, touches and makes me feel like I'm his princess, he makes me feel special and I enjoy his company. I like going out with him and enjoy being seen with him. It's nice we don't have to hide our relationship, not that I'm completely sure what our relationship is? I don't know if I'm in love with the one I call my boyfriend. I know I like him. I really, really like Bobby a lot.

Stopping her writing and putting down her pen, Jade glanced at the ring on the middle finger of her left hand *'A friendship ring?'* That was what it was, what it stood for and it seemed friends' were what they were? Jade and Bobby were friends. Flicking back through the thin, crisp scribbled on pages of her diary, perhaps it was fate, or maybe it was because she'd read the pages so very many times before; Jade stopped on the date.

<u>*October 3rd*</u>
Freedom; my first ever true taste. To feel the smooth yet hard solid pavement beneath my feet, felt like I was walking on air.

Skipping down the word filled lines and moving on through just a few of the crammed packed pages, she read through the words she'd written. Reading about what had happened, the one to have experienced being a teenager for the very first time, began to feel the feelings felt. Alone in her bedroom, Jade smelt the same smells and thought the thoughts to have entered her head when out on her own.

<u>*October 8th*</u>
It was cold, but it didn't matter, racing from out of the girls locker room and down the steps, I wasn't late, I was just in time and my heart skipped a beat as he pulled up beside me; asking me to climb up onto his powerful, purring machine, it was happening. My true teen adventure was about to begin.

♪56♪

Climbing on, holding on, she already knew the destination, crossing the deserted sports field to a place which was safe, because it was a space few people ventured. Making their way through the narrow pathways not easily accessible by a motorbike, both knew they wouldn't be seen. *'Cold & isolated.'* Not even the most dedicated of runner, or devoted dog walker ventured along what led nowhere when the weather was cold. Arriving and sitting themselves at the top of the railway embankment, confidant their meetings would remain secret.

"Cold?" Rojay asked. Sitting beside her on the thick waterproof sheet always carried beneath the seat of his motorbike.

"No, not now." She admitted. Smiling as he placed his strong, leather covered, protective arm around her.

"Our meetings will be sweeter in the spring." October was mild and November turned cold, Roland bending forward to kiss her meant her not caring about the weather, as his lips met her lips; she believed his kiss could melt snow. Holding his gloved hand, the wink he gave seemed sly yet flattering as he gently pushed her back. Unlike she once imagined, Jade didn't feel threatened by the boy everyone referred to as being a rebel. As his lips pressed against her lips; she felt relaxed. Removing his glove, he stroked her face before moving the same ungloved hand down and sliding it onto her up-stretched neck, kissing her again and again, just as his excitement grew, so too did the strange never before experienced feelings which stirred inside her.

"It's a shame it's so cold." He whispered; as from her head to her toes she tingled, her heartbeat quickening so much she was able to hear its' rhythmic pounding get louder and louder. Her pulse raced and before she knew what was happening Jade felt her whole inner and outer self fighting the narrow line between tension and relaxation. *'What was he doing?'* Moving his strong,

I MAY PRETEND

heavy male hand further and further down, Rojay lay his outspread fingers to rest on her breast, a breast still fastened beneath her coat, a breast which rose; lifting to meet his advances. *'What was she doing?'*

"I'll find us somewhere warmer." He promised. His wondering hand finding her hip and almost reaching the line of her panties before she sprang into a sitting position to halt his advances.

"Are you all right?" He inquired .Surprised, the young and handsome male was clearly not accustom to being rejected, neither ready nor prepared to give her acceptance. *'What had she been thinking?'* A teenager experiencing true teenage adventure for the first time, she wasn't ready to delve into a world she knew nothing about, whether or not she would save herself for marriage she wasn't sure, Jade wasn't afraid and Rojay hadn't threatened, or done anything wrong, but she wanted to go home.

I almost allowed myself to cross the line between tension and relaxation. Rojay agreed when I asked him to bring me home, but I knew he was disappointed. I don't know if he respects me enough to wait until I am ready. How can I tell him how what he sees to be a bit of fun, means much more to me?

Closing her diary, she wondered what would have happened had she chosen relaxation? *'Would she still be with Rojay?'* Would he have taken Stacey to the dance if she and he had done more than kiss? There had been more dates, dates when she found herself in need of excuses. Jade told Rojay she had to get home, she faked appointments and she shivered whenever he spoke about finding a warmer place. Growing closer, for most of the time everything was fine because she believed she'd found love. Her first true love. Before she knew how she was feeling, it was over. *'What would Jade do if Bobby wanted more?'*

♪57♪

A GEORGE

Bobby was dark and Roland fair, Bobby had brown eyes and Roland blue. Both taller, both were older and both physically strong, physically fit, healthy and handsome. Bobby was a devoted sportsman while other than the girls he liked to have around him; Roland's only interest was his bike. Bobby knew commitment and loyalty; he could and would be true and remain devoted. Bobby Hallas worked hard to achieve his goals while Roland Jackson never; and probably never would reveal his true self, his feelings, his hopes and his fears. Different, complete opposites, both were boys to who Jade had found herself attracted because both made her happy, both showing a life she once and for a long time only dreamt of being a part of. *'What was she thinking?'* Bobby Hallas hadn't attempted to touch her breast and Roland Jackson had never whirled her around the dance floor, Rojay had helped her to feel free, but he never made her feel special. With the top down on his car; she was able to feel the wind running through her hair. *'Four wheels weren't as thrilling as two.'* Looking at the differences and all the things she liked and disliked about Rojay and Bobby; looking at the advantages and disadvantages, when thinking about the two boys maturing into two very different young men, Jade questioned whether or not there was such a thing as LOVE?

♫58♫

6: DREAM BELIEVER

♪59♪

A boyfriend, dating, going out, going steady, a pair, a couple, boyfriend and girlfriend, Jade and Bobby?

"You're dating a professional footballer." Impressed by what they saw to be life changing news, her friends' could barely contain their excitement.

"He's still Bobby." She reminded all of how the signing of papers didn't make him a different person. *'He hadn't gone into a telephone box to come out wearing a cloak?'*

"And he asked you to wear his ring." Gretchen said she was lucky while Tamara complained about Tarquin leaving her finger bare.

"I want jewellery." She sighed when looking at the stone studded band shinning from Jade's left hand. "I spend loads more time with Tarquin than you do with Bobby. You're with us more than him." She attempted to justify sounding like a green eyed monster.

"We got together on the same night." Gretchen failed to share Tamara's logic; informing her of the fact they were in relationships, not taking part in a competition.

"He's always training, you don't see one another for days." Jade didn't need reminding. "Guilt gifts." Tamara came to a conclusion which helped her feel better.

"You must be happy for him." Gretchen said she, couldn't wait to congratulate Bobby on his achievement.

"I am." Finding it difficult to prevent her smile, Jade glanced at the ring on her finger, remembering back to the day when it was given as a symbol of friendship. Remembering back to when Bobby scored the winning goals for his team and the day when the scout approached him, when he span her round, lifting her in the air with excitement and saying he was glad she was there, glad to be sharing his good fortune. Smiling; Jade remembered all the times Bobby held her in his arms.

"Yes." She sighed. Yes, she was happy. From fearing he

was the worse of the bunch, having gotten use to his commitments and missed dates, she now smiled when he fell asleep during evening visits to the cinema and saw it as cute when yawned, the perfect gentleman. *'The best.'* Caring and thoughtful, his good prospects were nothing more than an added bonus when it came to the boy who was loyal, understanding and kind. Shaking her head, Jade no longer saw anything to complain about her boyfriend.

"A professional footballer?" Tamara repeated. "No doubt he'll have to travel." She commented. "You'll see even less of one another." Determined to find fault with what she referred to as being a good thing; Tamara's negativity caused Jade to ask how they could possibly see less of one another? *'Not possible?'* She didn't see what difference him travelling would make?

"Doing what he wants to do." She hoped to prove she could put others and their needs before her own, wanting to be supportive; Jade felt prepared for what could be a long distance relationship. "What is it Tarquin wants to do? To be" She inquired.

"A vet," Unimpressed, an everyday veterinary surgeon would be no way glamorous enough a husband for someone as right and proper as Tamara. "What about Greyson?" She turned to Gretchen

"Solicitor," Giggling when able to picture themselves supporting their partners in his chosen career. Tamara could be Tarquin's receptionist, or practise nurse, with her hair neatly tied back and up beneath a hair net worn purely for hygiene reasons. A short, tight pure white uniform, tan tights and white pumps. Tamara admitted to liking the thought of wearing a uniform, but not glasses. Gretchen would be Greyson's secretary. Her hair in a bun, Gretchen would be the one wearing the glasses; perching them on her nose, or hanging them on a gold chain around her neck. Dressed conservatively, her place would be behind her word processor and her note pad would always be to hand should the love of her life require dictation. As her friends foresaw their future roles developing and resulting in each becoming a lady of leisure once their betrothed established their chosen careers, Jade struggled to see where she fit in? His personal cheerleader? The girls laughed and she couldn't blame them. *'His fan?'* With or without her by his side, Bobby wouldn't have to worry about being on his own. *'A professional footballer?'* He would have his teammates and supporters, whether he noticed or not, Bobby Hallas would never be short of admiring fans; meaning Jade would be nothing more than another face in his watching crowd.

♪60♪

With Papa's workload further increased, Jade waited outside school for Jimmy, alone she found her thoughts wandering back to what she and her friends discussed. *'A cheerleader?'* His personal support team. Smiling to herself, she guessed that, that was what she was. Glancing at the golden, jewelled friendship ring and watching it sparkle in the fading afternoon sun, she felt glad the drier, warmer weather was returning.

"Very nice," It was little wonder she didn't hear his motorbike as he exited the school building approaching from behind and walking by where she waited at the foot of the steps. "Very nice," He repeated. Continuing on his way and disappearing in the direction of the bikesheds as Jimmy drove up, parking her fathers' jag by her feet. *'Very nice what?'* What had she expected him to say? *'Hello, How are you?'* It had been five months since they realised they weren't suited, why hadn't his words stopped echoing inside her head. *'Still in her heart?'*

"Still friends?" Jimmy asked. Revealing the fact he noticed who her glance followed. "He is a dish." Being local meant Jimmy knowing who most people were and what they were up to. "Any sign of him wearing his patch yet?" He asked, but she hadn't noticed. "A fully fledged biker, no wonder Papa told you to stay away from the local rebel with nothing but a clutch for a brain." Practical not academic, they say opposites attract.

A GEORGE

"You did a good job warning him off." She reminded her driver of how he was the one to tell Rojay to leave.

"He sounded like he really liked you." Jimmy said his telling the biker boy to go, resulted in the two engaging in conversation. "None of my business what the two of you get up to, but please don't tell me you're cheating on Mr. Super sport." Her loyal friend swooned.

"Never." Her tone scolded the one seen as insolent, her voice rising because she needed to hide the guilt she felt for thinking about one when with another.

"Do you want to talk about it?" His knowing her like he did, meant Jimmy knowing when she had something on her mind? *'What was there to talk about?'* Jade had much too much she needed to say.

"We went out a couple of times, but we didn't do anything." She told the one willing to listen how Rojay hadn't had a civil word to say to her since she told him he was better off with Stacey.

"You sent him back to his ex?" Jimmy asked why she would do that? "The apprentice mechanic, big bad biker set to take over his fathers' ailing business, his shed, I mean garage? Or, super spunk? I mean a sporting hunk set to become a footballing hero with a regular pay packet bigger than his ego?" Jimmy commented on her choice being a difficult one. *'Or not?'*

"Bobby doesn't have an ego." She accused him of making things up.

"And biker boy has no head for business, but my guess is they will both get on in their chosen careers." Watching as Rojay sped by on his motorbike. "A good biker is only ever loyal to those whose badge he gets to wear." Both noticed the addition of a leather waistcoat over his jacket.

"Why are you comparing them?" Jade asked.

"Why are you unable to take your eyes off him?" Continuing the drive back to her house; Jade had to admit she didn't know. She hadn't thought he would ever speak to her again. *'What did he want?'*

♪61♪

Watching, like she always use to when standing by her locker, she saw how he took out his helmet. Fighting the urge to speak. She wanted to say. Hi, but resisted when her thought and line of vision was interrupted by Tamara and Gretchen rushing her along."Very nice." Roland Jackson? Why had Rojay admired and made comment on her ring?

"I bet it's plastic." Stacey Sutton's comments weren't quite so complementary when arriving to invade the space where Jade and her friends' waited to be collected. Lizzie, Penny and Paula, what did they want?

"Careful you don't fall." They teased as Jade stepped down off the final step.

"Rojay reckons your college boy gave you a ring." Penny commented as she and the others positioned themselves in a semi circle around her.

"Are you engaged?" Lizzie asked. "Bit young." She smirked.

"Give us a look." Stacey insisted. Lifting and checking all four of Jade's fingers on her left hand.

"Wow!" Paula gasped. Impressed by the genuine jewels sparkling as they caught the light. "Expensive, he must be rich" She commented.

"He must be mad." Lizzie shook her head.

"Are you engaged?" Stacey like Lizzie mistook the finger upon which the ring had been placed for the one on the same hand which had much more significance.

"No."Jade shook her head.

"Not yet."Gretchen interrupted. Both Tamara and Jade sending her looks which questioned why she said that?

"What's going on?" Noticing the gathering, Rojay pulled up to see what was happening?

"Rojay?" Stacey's surprise was obvious.

"We were admiring the ring." Penny said. Rushing over to greet him with a kiss. Miss Penelope Petal Bolton was Roland Jackson's chosen flavour of the month, her smile showing clearly how she was enjoying his attention. Knowing, Stacey knew; the whole school knew he was again working his way through the available, the rough and the ready, the willing and those playing hard to get. *'He would get back to Stacey eventually.'* Watching; Jade watched and wondered whether or not Stacey could and would wait for him? *'Why wait?'* As Penny climbed up behind him and sat astride his purring machine; in the same way Stacey's face changed, Jade's heart sank to the pit of her stomach. As Penny wrapped her arms around his soft, smooth black leather jacket, scooping them up and under his new waistcoat, Jade felt hurt and rejected. *'Jealous?'* Could Jade be as jealous as Stacey looked?

"He isn't with the queen of sleaze any more then." Tamara referred to Stacey as she and those still with her dispersed, rushing to find themselves a ride home.

"No." Jade sighed. Not knowing who to feel more sorry for, Stacey or herself?

♪62♪

May 21st
My sixteen birthday, can you believe it? Mama actually allowed me to choose my own outfit. Tamara and Gretchen will be here any minute and I know I should feel on top of the world, but I'm not sure how I feel. Maybe I will know better by the end of this evening? When my party is over.

"Downstairs looks great." Gretchen announced. Expected, it was no surprise she and Tamara were the first to arrive. "Wow! And doesn't the birthday girl look great." She gasped. Entering Jade's bedroom as the bedside clock stuck seven. The caterers had been busy all day and Mama was rushing around arranging, organising and rearranging everyone and everything, while Jeremy was under strict instruction to be on his best behaviour. Permitted to have a friend over to stay; both pesky thirteen year olds were warned not to get in anyone's way.

"Congratulations." The friends entered into a three way hug which never looked or felt as comfortable, natural or genuine as it should. "Sixteen?" They agreed to looking forward to a good night. In little over half an hour, or an hour because it was fashionable to be late; other guests would start to arrive. *'Who?'* Jade may have chosen her outfit, like always; Mama chose the food, the drink, the decorations, the entertainment and the guests

"Do I look all right?" Jade asked. Checking her appearance in her long free standing dress mirror. Deep purple lace over black silk with crushed velvet, her maxi length dress was off the shoulder with fitted bodice and flowing skirt, her shoes were sequin covered sandals with a heel just high enough to improve her posture and leg shape, while being low enough to wear all night. Jade wore her hair in long, loose curls.

"Beautiful."

"Perfect." Her companions assured her, each checking and complimenting one another's chosen attire. Gretchen's choice was a full skirted, shin length navy and white, spotted dress with stiff underskirt and Tamara's a Chinese inspired wrap dress, something her father picked up on his travels.

"Perfect." Yes, they all looked perfect. Handing to the birthday girl her gifts, Jade felt no surprise at the vast expense her friends' or their parents' had gone to.

"You're only sixteen once." Being the same excuse given by her parents when presenting her with a gold watch, perfume from Paris and a solid silver pen set.

"You're only sixteen once." Others also spoke about the magic of being sixteen when handing the birthday girl the beautifully wrapped parcels to include *Make-up:*
Under garments of the finest silks:
Gold necklaces:
Bracelets:
Earrings:
Porcelain dolls:

Jewellery boxes and *saving vouchers.* Jade was given everything which any sweet sixteen year old could ever want or wish for, everything one could ever dream of. From Gretchen; extra's included a bumper record collection of sixties and seventies music, while Tamara gave a gold plated hair care set.

Nodding politely and shaking all offered hands, Jade greeted her party guests, relatives, friends' and friends' of her parents. Despite the time of year, uncle Kevin and aunt Jennifer saw such an important occasion was just cause to leave their post office/village shop in the safe hands of neighbours for a day or two, both pleased to be beside the one each called their favourite niece, both ready, willing and more than happy to join in the evening's celebrations. *'Their only niece.'* Fruit punch and fresh salmon, Aunt Jennifer nudged her niece, winking about how her parents wouldn't notice her and her friends participating in the consumption of alcohol while also telling her she knew she would be careful. Trusting and loving? Why wasn't Mama like her sister? Aunt Jennifer was right, there was everything including a bar and barmen to cater for the alcoholic needs of those congregating to celebrate her day. From the reception hall, Mama rushed Jade through the splendour of the spacious dinning room and into the adjoining dark, hard wood and glass, plant filled conservatory; where in amongst the mingling crowds they found Mr. and Mrs. Hallas. Not having noticed them arrive. *'Some said they walked in the back way.'* Jade wasn't surprised to learn Bobby was running late. *'Why should this night be any different?'* Why would her birthday interfere with his schedule?

"He will be here." Suzann assured the birthday girl her son wouldn't let her down on her special night. *'He will be here.'* Everyone assured her, whenever his matches, practice matches or training kept him away, whenever his chosen profession caused him to run late or miss dates, there wasn't anybody who didn't assure Jade, Bobby would be with her when he could.

"It's lovely to meet you again dear."

"You too Mrs. Hallas."Jade smiled.

"Please call me Suzann, Bobby talks about you so much I feel we're already friends." Jade doubted Mama would ever say the same. *'Why was it she bonded with every female except the one said to have given her life?'* Jade and Mama didn't argue, they couldn't, the two didn't talk enough to fall out. Not really; not like a mother and daughter should talk.

"Suzann." Jade smiled.

"Is this the ring?" She admired her sons' taste.

"Yes."Yes, that was the ring, the ring which ever since being placed on her finger attracted more attention, remarks and criticism than anything else. The ring which caused her to answer and be asked more questions than ever before. Yes, that was the friendship ring, the symbol which to Jade had one simple meaning, a meaning which those around her appeared to believe meant much more. Excusing herself, the birthday girl joined Tamara, Gretchen, Greyson and Tarquin to have found themselves a quiet and more private table outside on the paved patio area of the garden. Taking up what they said would be their residence for the night, all insisted they weren't going to give up the table beside the largest patio heater for anyone. May, was warmer, but the unpredictable time of year meant there would soon be a chill in the cooling night air. *'Cosy?'* Jade liked that her friends' looked happy.

"Join us?" All insisted.

"Lovely party."Tarquin complemented the hostess.

"Where is your drink?" Greyson noticed what was missing?

"I haven't had a chance." Jade admitted to not having had time, one hour into the joyous celebrations and she felt she'd been on her feet for days.

A GEORGE

"A birthday girl without a drink, will not do." He continued. Jumping to his feet and leaving to fetch the much needed refreshment.

"You met Bobby's mother." Gretchen stated.

"She's nice." Jade nodded

"Bobby isn't here." Like she always did, Tamara stated the obvious. Agreeing, Jade shook her head only to be told he wouldn't be long.

"Thank you." She smiled when Greyson returned with her drink and a somewhat large tray of food, thrust upon him by Mama as he passed.

"Cheers."

"Happy birthday"

"All the best,"

"Happy birthday."As all raised filled glasses and Jade thanked them for their kindness and company she felt herself blush. Remaining to enjoy their lively and joke filled conversation Jade allowed her party to continue around her. *'Smiling & laughing.'* Glancing momentarily from the brightly illuminated, richly decorated, cheery sounding house, Jade's attention drifted from the conversation to the deep, darkening greenery of the large surrounding garden with the neatly trimmed hedges and thick healthy bushes, bordering weed free flowerbeds and perfectly, evenly mown lawns. Beyond the large brick built barbecue, following the free standing lamp lights which lined the curving brick path. Without moving from her seat Jade's eyes took her back in time, embarking upon a journey of days gone by.

♫*63*♫

Coloured balloons, a high set sun, streamers, party hats and a long table laden with food, drink and snow white paper plates. As the man dressed as a clown chased her giggling friends, she ran for the safety of Papa's side. Sitting on the garden coach swing and being told not to move until the hired photographer had taken the photographs to be hung in pride of place around the house. She recalled her being told to cheer up and reminded to smile. *'Birthday pictures?'* There was the

I MAY PRETEND

one with the balloons, one with friends she didn't know, one with her brother and one with her cake, there was a photograph of her blowing out six flamed candles. *'Six candles?'* Daytime garden parties, Jade realised her being reminded to smile meant she hadn't enjoyed what was happening. From six to sixteen.*'Where had the time gone?'*

"Mind if we join you." Acting like he was somewhere he wasn't meant to be, Jimmy arrived like a whirlwind attempting not to be noticed. Never calm, but always collective and polite, he and Sawyer said hello before thanking those who agreed they should take a seat. The son of a valued employee, Jimmy Kingston was always there, sometimes allowed and sometimes told not to make his presence known. Now employed by the household and reliant upon them in the same way his father was for his weekly wage; Jimmy wasn't sure he should be acting like he was a guests. Invited. *'Top of her list.'* Jimmy and Sawyer had both received personal invitations from the birthday girl herself and she was over the moon to see them.

"Are the two of you friends?" Recognising the Barris employee and the cyclist from school, Tamara and Gretchen spoke the words their questioning expression asked, smiling, Jade believed the two would work it out eventually. Able to hear Mama calling.

"Jade!" Standing, the birthday girl enjoying time with friends was led away to open the front door. *'Wasn't Trevor manning the entrance & exits?'* "Go on, open it." Mama urged and as she did her eyes were met by an array of colour the likes of which she had never seen. *'How could one person hold so many flowers?'*

"Bobby?" She gasped as he presented her with the freshly arranged bouquet, sixteen white roses surrounded by flowers which intermingled sixteen individual colours. "Wow; they're lovely." She smiled. "Beautiful." She gasped. How thoughtful, how very like him to think of something unique and special.

"Stunning."Mama interrupted. Aware she couldn't keep away, Jade knew Jemima had been listening, peeping from behind the door left purposely ajar and waiting for her chance to join them. "Mavis! Mavis put these into water at once." She instructed their housekeeper to be quick.

"Happy birthday."Her final guest whispered kissing her cheek and taking her by the hand as the lady of the Barris household rushed them through into the dinning area and beyond so to introduce the couple to any and everyone she saw to be important. With the background music encouraging people to dance, Jade apologised for the formalities keeping them away from what others in their age group were enjoying.

"Happy birthday Miss Barris."Mavis said she'd placed the floral arrangement in her room.

"Thank you." Unlike Mama, Jade always made a point of being polite to those assisting her and her family in their daily life.

"You're here." Bobby's mother greeted her son.

"Yes, mum I'm here. I take it you had chance to meet Jade properly this time?" He pointed out how the last time the two were in the same room, everyone had been too busy celebrating, to talk.

"You were right about her son, a beautiful young woman if ever I saw one." Suzann smiled. "You shouldn't keep her waiting." She scolded his tardiness.

"No, I know and I'm sorry." He apologised.

"She'll have to get use to waiting if she wants to be the girl of a footballer." His father interrupted. Having spent much of his time at the bar; Bobby's proud father slurred his words as he reminded all listening of how his sons career must come first. "My son won't be home much, not once he signs for his new team." He bragged.

"They've placed you?" Jade asked aware Suzann was attempting to hush her ranting, whisky swigging husband as Bobby escorted her out into the garden, insisting they needed privacy to talk. Greeting the others, they promised to catch up later before continuing to find a quieter spot, Sawyer and Jimmy again being heard to say they wished they had half her luck as Bobby whisked the birthday girl away, their glances and nods being what caused Tamara and Gretchen to realise the kind of friends' the two young males had become.

"Jimmy really likes you." She smiled. "Lucky he found himself a boyfriend, or I'd have competition." She smiled. Watching as her companion's expression remained serious. "They have." She repeated. Reaching the couch swing and taking a seat."They found you a new team." She said.

"I'd hoped to tell you." He sat beside her.

"That's good news ?" She questioned his reluctance.

"Yes."He agreed. His tone convincing no one.

"Isn't this what you work so hard for? What you always wanted."She asked.

"Yes."He nodded.

"Then why the glum face?" She questioned.

"If I sign, it will mean moving miles from here."

"If? Are you saying you're not going?" She didn't understand.

"I want to."

"Then you should." She insisted."But?"

"The team is based down south." He said.

"My aunt and uncle live south, it's a distance, but it isn't a bad place. I adore my holidays down south." Jade smiled.

"It isn't the place that worries me." Bobby shook his head.

"Then what?" Jade asked.

"What's going to happen to us?" He wanted to know.

"We can write." Jade reminded him of how both knew how to use pen, paper and the telephone.

Passing months had seen the two become close, learning much about one another, they agreed to always wanting to remain friends no matter what. *'Friends?'* If it wasn't for the fact they kissed and were recognised as being a couple; good friend was what they were. *'The best of friends?'* If having to describe what they were, Jade would say they were comfortable.

"I didn't want to spoil your birthday." The late comer apologised for not having done the right thing.

"You haven't, your news means we have two reasons to celebrate." Jade continued to smile.

"You're so sweet." He said. Taking her into his strong arms and kissing her, having kissed her many times before, this time felt different. This time Bobby felt different, moving his strong, large hands down from her shoulders and onto her waist, Jade felt her body being drawn into his, moving closer and closer until there was nothing between them but the clothes they were wearing.

"I love you." He told her. Saying it in a whisper. "I love you." He announced. His hand finding a resting place just above his companion's knee.

"I think we best rejoin the party." Jade stood.

"I'm sorry. I didn't mean to. I." Bobby stuttered. "I mean, I wouldn't have done anything. I" He apologised.

"I know." She assured him. Smiling and taking him by the hand as she led him back up to the patio; arriving just in time to see her large, candle filled birthday cake being wheeled out followed by all at her party.

♪64♪

"Make a wish." All to have gathered; encouraged Jade to do what all celebrating a birthday were expected to do. Doing what they asked. HELP! That was what she wished for. As everyone broke out into a chorus of Happy Birthday. HELP was the only thing Jade needed, it was all she wanted, assistance and guidance with sorting her feelings? HELP with understanding teenage emotions. When it came to reaching sixteen, HELP was all Jade could think of wishing for. Hugging and assuring her she would be fine; it was aunt Jennifer who noticed something was wrong.

"I'm here for you." Telling her niece she was there if she needed to talk, Jennifer agreed they could and would

catch up when things got quieter. "Promise." Both knew promises between them were never broken.
♪65♪
Whirling around what had become the dance floor in the dinning area, Jade felt safe. Wrapped in Bobby's strong arms and forming dance chains with her friends, she suddenly realised she had the best of friends in those there to help her celebrate.
♪66♪
Whirling around, dancing, laughing, singing, joking and chatting when surrounded by those she knew.
♪67♪
Dancing with Jimmy and Sawyer made her laugh and feel happier than ever before.
♪68♪
Talking with her friends, unlike past birthdays; Jade realised she was no longer forcing the smile showing how she was enjoying her party. *'Happy?'* Confused, with a head full of questions, there was no doubting the fact her having gained the freedom she saw every teenager as needing; resulted in her feeling happier than she ever remembered feeling before. *'Happy?'*
♪69♪
"I can't ask you to wait." With the party drawing to an end; Jade and Bobby strolled hand in hand around what was the quiet and extensive garden surrounding the Barris's grand house. Alone beneath the moonlight."It wouldn't be fair of me." He continued, but she wasn't listening.

"I use to hate birthday parties." She sighed. "Mama and Paps would arrange it all, the food, the entertainment, even the guest list. After tonight, I think I'm going to miss them." She sighed.

"Your parents?" Bobby questioned.

"My birthday parties, my childhood. It's like I'm only just realising all the things I missed, because I was worrying about what I was missing."

"You're sixteen, not sixty." He smiled.

"I'm closer to being an adult than I am a child." Jade revealed how she felt. *'Mixed emotions.'*

"Responsibility is scary." Bobby agreed with a nod.

"Why does childhood have an expiry date, when adulthood could last for who knows how long?" Jade felt her being a teenager would be over before it began? "Two years and I'll be eighteen, four and I'll reach twenty." Her words were thought filled as she glanced around what was the place which would always keep her childhood contained.

"Sounds like you're wishing your life away." Bobby told her she should enjoy life one stage at a time.

"My life is running away from me." She smiled.

"I can't ask you to wait." Bobby repeated. "I love you." He told her. "But I don't know what my future will be." He admitted to being nervous about what he was facing.

"It'll be like you always imagined it, your dream is coming true." She said. "We will always be friends." She assured him.

"Friends?" He questioned.

"Always."Taking his hands into hers, she saw how he glanced at the ring still shinning on her finger. "I will wear it always." She promised. "Friends forever."She smiled.

"I love you." He said. The words which not so long ago had seemed none existence, now echoed inside her head like the loud ringing of church bells. Was it three? Four, or five times he'd revealed his inner most feelings. As Bobby bent forward to kiss her lips; Jade knew he meant what he was saying and saw what he said as making her sixteenth birthday complete. "I don't want to leave." He admitted.

"You're frightened about going so far from home." She said it was understandable to be wary of change.

"I found you and now I have to let you go." He said.

"I'll miss you too, but if you throw away this chance you'll end up hating me. You have to go." She urged him to look at the positives and remember his dream. "You worked hard for this."

"You'll miss me?" He asked. Jade assuring him she would. *'She'd only just found him too.'*

"Before you came into my life I didn't have one." She revealed.

"Roland?" Confused by what he was being told Bobby questioned what he was hearing. "Tamara said you and he."

"Weren't right." Jade shook her head.

"You still like him?" Bobby observed.

"Tamara must have found great pleasure in telling you everything about me." Her tone revealed her not liking the thought of being talked about. "Gretchen reckons she's jealous." The frustrated female interrupted, preventing her companion from saying something she didn't want to hear.

"Do you have feelings for him?" He asked.

"To be honest." She sighed. "I don't know, but I'm not lying when I say I'm going to miss you. I'm going to miss you like crazy." She insisted.

"Like crazy." He smiled. Allowing her to place her hands up around his neck

"Like crazy." She nodded. Kissing; the two embraced, tightly, holding one another longingly and lovingly. Allowing his hands to wander; Bobby ran his fingers down and over the back of her dress; his gentle touch causing a tingle which sent a shiver the length of her spine. Excited, each allowed the kissing to deepen. Happy, with Bobby, she felt her heart pounding and being aware of the fact they were out of sight she wondered how far they would go? Close, in such a situation, she should be declaring her feelings too. Fond of Bobby, he made her happy, he gave her confidence and helped her feel special. Bobby made Jade feel safe; so why didn't she love him? *'Perhaps she did?'* How would she know how it felt to be in love? To love somebody was something the text books couldn't teach.

'Maybe this was the beginning?' Perhaps she was learning how to love and experiencing how it felt to be loved? *'Sixteen?'* Aged sixteen; it would be legal to give into his advances. Together, surrendering to his intentions wouldn't be unlawful, but would it be right? *'Was she reading him right?'* Had Bobby told her he loved and said he would miss her, to get what he wanted? *'What every boy wanted?'* Was Bobby being like others and saying what he believed necessary in his quest for sex? *'What was she doing?'* What was she thinking? From having her breast touched on the outside of her bra, outside her blouse, her jumper and outside her fastened coat, to going all the way with a boy who said he loved her? She wouldn't, would she? Back when fifteen, her brief encounter with Rojay had left her knowing she wasn't ready for more than a kiss. Was she now considering a full sexual experience? *'Was taking her virginity what Bobby wanted?'*

"You're beautiful." He whispered. His kisses moving down onto and over her up-stretched neck. "Beautiful" He repeated, lifting Jade off the ground and wrapping her within his strong yet gentle arms, kissing and holding her beneath the stars, swept away by the romance, Jade felt lost in a mix of sensations. Surrounded by what she saw to be love. *'Was she in love?'* Certain, if she wanted; she could put a stop to what was happening; perhaps it was the trust she had in her partner which caused her to want to see how far things would go? *'How far would he go & how far did she want to go?'*

"I have your present." Placing her back onto the ground, he said he had something for her.

"You gave me flowers." She reminded him. *'Shocked.'* She thought she'd done something wrong, watching as he released his passionate hold to search the inside pocket of his jacket. *'Boy was he sexy?'* Broader, Bobby appeared larger when dressed in his padded designer baseball jacket and tight black jeans. *'Boy was she lucky.'*

Jimmy and Sawyer were right, there was nothing not to like, nothing not to admire and absolutely nothing not to want about Mr. Bobby Hallas. "Here you go." He announced. Handing over a box she again recognised as coming from a jewellery store. *'A top named jewellers used by the elite.'*

"Thank you." Pleased, she was relieved the box was too large to contain another ring. Lifting the hinged lid as the moon reached its highest, brightest peak, the golden colour to escape the dark red box; shone directly up into her eyes, illuminating her smiling face, a solid gold heart on a golden chain. "It's beautiful." She gasped. Draping the long, delicate chain over and between her fingers as Bobby pointed out the inscription

To Jade
Happy 16th
I will never not love you
Bobby

"It's beautiful." Kissing her cheek as he assisted with putting the sparkling, solid item around her neck.

"Something to remind you of me." He smiled.

"I won't ever forget you." She assured him.

"Nor me, you." He whispered.

"But I haven't given you anything to take with you." Jade realised if this was goodbye, she should give Bobby a token of their friendship

"I took the liberty of ordering copies of the photographs from the photographer, wallet size so I can carry you with me." He smiled.

"The way the camera's been clicking, you'll need a suitcase." She laughed.

"He knows a thing of beauty when he sees one." Clicking at what was both posed and informal, Jade believed there was more than one reason the photographer agreed to stay to the end of the night. Informing Bobby of how the one yet to find his feet in the media world could be on the hunt for his first big money shot, the soon to be well known footballer agreed there would always be vultures hungry to feed on scandal and asked she never believe should anything scandalous be printed about him.

"No one is a saint." She promised she would never forget the person she knew him to be and would always follow her own instinct when deciding what she did and didn't believe.

From greeting her guests to blowing out her candles; the young male whose personal business card introduced him to be Mr. Martin Greaves and advertised his services to include portraits, prints and everything in-between was young and ambitions. Dressed to impress; his designer suit was the type purchased to blend seamlessly whatever the occasion. Polite, Mr. Greaves knew all the right things to say; while listening to what was being said alongside his looking for the perfect picture.

"A picture of the happy couple." Pointed in the right direction by Mama and Suzann, Bobby and Jade agreed to posing together so long as Mr. Greaves agreed not to sell or publish the shot without permission.

"Papa is paying for every shot you take tonight, which means they're all confidential." Nodding, Martin said he was happy to hand over all and every image captured by his large professional camera. Together under the light of the moon, when out in the garden, together with their friends; Jade insisted group shots include Jimmy and Sawyer, sitting together on the couch swing and dancing together within twinkling fairy lights. With Mr. Barris's permission, Greaves agreed to printing an extra copy of whichever picture Bobby wanted.

"When do you leave?" The question had to be asked.

"A week, maybe two."Being the answer."I'm here tonight." From holding hands to dancing, from joining in the gossip filled conversations, to walking around the garden by themselves. Yes, Bobby was there now and his being there helped make her birthday special. Loving, loyal and kind, the two agreed to continue seeing one another till he left.

"A good sort." Jimmy agreed he would drive carefully when asked to take Bobby home. *'Permitted to join in with the party, but not allowed to drink alcohol incase his chauffeur services were required.'* Sawyer and Jimmy said they had the best time, especially the part when being photographed with Bobby, especially when upon realising the truth of their relationship; no one caused a scene, instead welcoming the couple with open arms. *'New friends?'* Jade assured Jimmy he'd always be in her gang and he agreed to always knowing she had his back in the same way he had hers. *'Sixteen & all grown up.'* Preparing to say goodbye, she giggled when the young chauffeur commented about expecting a big tip. *'Or at least an autograph?'* Having partaken in more than the odd glass of fizz; Bobby agreed to leaving his car. Having partaken in more than the odd glass of bourbon, Mrs. Hallas had called upon Jimmy's driving skills earlier when taking her staggering husband back home, Jimmy knew where Bobby lived.

"Goodnight."Jade smiled.

"Night."Parting from their goodnight kiss, both agreed to looking forward to their planned dates.

"Bye."Bobby would collect Jade after school on Monday. "Can't wait." A picnic and dinner, the two planned to visit their favourite places, she would watch him train and they agreed to one final cinema trip, things weren't going to be the same without him. Bobby promised he wouldn't let her down.

"Good birthday?" Her parents' inquired.

"The best."She smiled. Unlike others; Jade's sixteenth turned out to be a birthday she didn't want to forget, surrounded by people she never wanted to lose. Yes, she'd had a good time. "Thank you." She said when Papa agreed to Jimmy taking Sawyer home too. "Thank you." She said before rushing up to her room, wanting to watch the boys drive away. Excited, the birthday girl smiled a smile she never wanted to be without as sitting by her bedroom window she watched the last of her guests head for home. *'Wonderful.'* Watching as the large silver car made its way at a snails pace, she couldn't help but imagine the conversation taking place inside. *'Both Jimmy & Sawyer made no secret of the fact each adored Bobby.'* Alone with their hero, he would be a gentleman and they were bound to ask something they shouldn't. *'Did he love her?'* Proud of him, Bobby saying he loved her left Jade wondering if he would tell anyone else? *'Smiling?'* Looking out ahead of those who were leaving; her gaze fell upon the large electric gate as it opened. *'Should she blow him a kiss?'* She knew he wouldn't be able to see, but felt she should, leaning in toward the window, as she raised her hand to her lips her eyes fell upon a scene to cause her fluttering heart to stop.

♪70♪

One, two three, all large, noisy and powerful, one and two, as the third motorbike screeched to a sudden and stubborn halt, the wall it formed prevented Jimmy from driving any further. No! She wanted to shout but realised in the same way Bobby wouldn't see her blowing him a kiss; he wouldn't hear her call.

"No!" She shook her head. Watching as each removed his helmet, all enabling her to be sure they were who she believed them to be. "Don't." She hoped Bobby wouldn't get out of the car. *'What were they doing?'*

"Jade?" Entering to say goodnight, her aunt and uncle asked what was wrong, both looking out at what she could see, it didn't take long for the adults to realise what was happening could mean trouble.

"Friends?" Kevin's expression shown he knew they weren't. *'Friends?'* He asked because he needed to know how to react. *'What did they want?'* Shaking her head, Jade agreed he did; when asked if Bobby needed help? Bobby wouldn't hear her and she couldn't hear them. *'What were they doing?'* Jade wished she knew why Rojay had brought Spike and Denzel with him? Watching those who dismounted their static bikes; Kevin ran out of the room to try to do something and Jennifer picked up the bedside telephone to call the police.

"No!" Watching as first Jimmy and then Bobby got out of the jag. "No." Jade willed them to get back inside the car. "No!" Watching as the riders left their motorbikes and walked over to Bobby; she felt her eyes fill with tears. "No!" She couldn't hear, but she could see as those approaching closed in. "No." Jade knew without doubt what it was they were about to do. "No!" Removing her shoes, she raced downstairs, ran out of the house and headed up the drive as fast as her legs would carry her.

Silence; Bobby said nothing as two of the three approached one from either side. *'What?'* Watching the third rider dismount and remove his helmet, the one they were there to see believed he knew why. Silent and intimidating, Bobby felt he had no choice but to endure the punishment about to be inflicted by the male who believed actions spoke much louder than words.

"Let's not." Jimmy's attempt to intervene was met with a leather gloved hand being held up to his face and him being warned to stay out of things. Silence, leaving their bikes, the three leather clad riders walked around before approaching the one they were there to do who knew what to. Intimidating, before taking hold; Spike moved close and shouted Boo! Placing his face as close as it could get to Bobby's face; the elder male laughed.

"Boo!" He asked if the one standing his ground needed a change of underwear? Falling back into the side of the car behind him; Bobby looked to those whose actions intimidated.

"Get off him." Jimmy told those intent on causing harm, he would call the police. Shoved and pushed aside Jimmy lost his balance and fell as first Spike and then Denzel took a tight grip on Bobby's arms, one each, one on either side, they held him so tight, to struggle would only hurt more

"She's mine, she was always mine." Close enough to be heard Rojay flexed his fingers, interlocking and cracking them before forming a fist. "Mine." He repeated. With Spike holding one arm and Denzel the other; Bobby was powerless to resist the punch delivered direct into his unprotected stomach. One punch; as his head fell forward, the one being beaten felt sure his entire body would follow his glance to the ground should his captures release the hold each had on his outstretched arms. Deep and hard, he knew the punch was intended to cause harm and believed things would have been worse had he not had the parked jag behind for him to lean into. Having gotten out of the car on the other side, Sawyer was checking on Jimmy, the two at a loss as to what they could do to help.

"You big college windbag."Rojay continued, lifting and punching Bobby in the face.

"Not such a pretty boy now."Denzel laughed. Spike reminding his angry friend of the fact a footballer couldn't play football without his legs.

"A few broken toes would do the trick." The eldest biker amongst them pointed out how the posh boys designer pumps were no match for steel heeled and metal toe capped bike boots.

"No!" Back up on his feet; Jimmy attempted to step between Bobby and those intent on injuring him and his career. "No!" He told them and they told him not to get involved.

"You will have to get by both of us." Sawyer placed himself beside where Jimmy was attempting to keep his eye on those behind and Rojay standing in front of him at the same time. A wall of two, they knew it wouldn't take all three to overpower them, but they had to do something.

"That is enough!" Having used his golf buggy, Mr. Barris and his brother-in-law Kevin arrived just in time to prevent Rojay from doing what others saw as the unthinkable."What is the meaning of this?"

"Go back to bed grandads." Denzel warned the older males not to interfere as with Jimmy and Swayer stepping aside, he and Spike positioned Bobby so Rojay could jump on his legs.

"Stop." Never had Jade heard Papa sound so angry, as she continued to make her way; joined by her brother Jeremy and his friend Daniel; all were able to hear what was being said as they approached.

"Stop this now." Placing himself between Bobby and Rojay, Kevin was also loud and demanding. "Stop." He said and as she arrived Jade agreed.

"The police are on their way." Jeremy stated and Spike laughed. Releasing Bobby from their grip; both he and Denzel laughed at the weakened form slumped against the car to prevent his falling to the ground. Walking back towards the waiting bikes, Denzel and Spike brushed themselves down but said nothing.

"You cowards." Jade accused those to have ganged up on one of being weak.

"You best pull her into line Ro." Spike shook his head as back on his bike he replaced his helmet.

"The Princess should know her place." Denzel told Rojay to get things sorted as he and Spike prepared to leave.

"If you lay a finger on my daughter," Mr. Barris warned those making mischief to back off if they wanted to stay out of prison.

"Papa." Walking up to where Rojay stood, Jade demanded to know what he wanted? "Why?" She asked, looking to Bobby being assisted by Jimmy and Sawyer.

"You know these boys?" Kevin expressed his surprise.

"Better than you'll ever know, daddy dear." Spike winked as Jade replied by saying she thought she knew one of them. Continuing to laugh and smirk Spike and Denzel started up their bikes and left.

"Shouldn't you join them." She wondered why Rojay wasn't leaving? "Go." She wanted her words to show how upset and disappointed he made her. *'FLASH!'* A camera flash almost blinded the injured male whose blood stained lip and bruised face was the last thing he wanted photographing.*' A picture?'* Rojay had stepped back and his thugs were leaving. *'The money shot.'*

"Wait." Mr. Barris called out, but Greaves had gotten what he waited around to get and without delay or hesitation, he was in his car on route to develop and sell his prize.

"What the?" Trying to make sense of what was happening? Kevin shook his head.

"Let's get you back up to the house." Papa instructed Jeremy and his friend to help Bobby into the golf cart while instructing Jimmy to wait in the car to take him and everyone else back to the house. *'Sorry.'* Standing with Rojay, Jade's eyes told Bobby she wished she'd stopped what happened.

"Jade."Papa said she should get into the jag with him.

"I'll walk." She said. Kevin insisting he would wait and walk with her, agreeing to stand inside the gate while she remained outside with the only remaining biker. Unsure as to what she should do, Jade waited for Rojay to make the first move once all but her uncle were gone.

"You look nice." He announced. Approaching as Jade contemplated her next move. *'Nice?'* Didn't this head strong moron know any other polite words? That's nice: Did you have a nice time? Did you have a nice birthday? "I bought you a present." He revealed. Nice? *'Nice, bloody nice.'* How come he hoped and thought everything was, or should be so dam nice when nothing about him, or anything in his world was ever nice?

"No."Jade refused the small gift wrapped parcel.

"It is your birthday?" He requested confirmation. "Sweet sixteen?" He smiled. "You look good." He told her, his smile growing broader as he saw she was minus her shoes. "No need for you to worry about whether or not the photographer got your good side." He mocked.

"Did you plan that, is he paying you?" Rojay's silence proved his guilt."Why would you do that?" Unable to believe what she was learning, Jade shook her head when her companion blamed Spike. *'Older but far from wiser?'* The leader of the biker boys appeared to be all brawn and no brains.

"Spike." He told her.

"No."Jade refused to have him blame the one all bikers worshiped. "No, you're not who I thought you were." She told him. "I have to go." Turning to follow those already back in the house, Jade told Rojay to go home before the police arrived.

"I'm jealous." He called. Allowing his macho image to momentarily slip and stopping the leaving female in her tracks, eager to hear more and wanting to know what it was he was trying to say, she shrugged her shoulders as she stood and he approached. "I'm jealous." He repeated. "I know. I understand you had to go to the dance with him, with the college wimp, but."

"Bobby, his name is Bobby." Jade surprised herself by defending the injured party. "And the only wimps are the ones who have to gang up three to one. It's you who looks weak from where I'm standing."

"I told you. I'm jealous." He repeated.

"That's no excuse to have him held while you beat him." She scolded what was cowardly. "What you did could have ruined everything."

"I wouldn't have." He reminded her of how it was staged for the camera. "I barely touched him. Jade I want, I need to talk to you." He pleaded she listen.

"I have to go." She insisted. Aware her waiting uncle was listening.

"Tomorrow?" He asked.

"I'm not interested." She told him. Walking away and joining Kevin whose look told the following male to go.

"Meet me after your dance class." He called. His question followed closely by the roar of his bikes' engine and him disappearing into the night.

Fuss: fuss: fuss. Mrs .Jemima Barris was an expert when fussing was what was called for, fussing while Mavis and Jennifer were tending to Bobby's injuries. Having rushed him into the kitchen, the women quick to take on the role of nurse, set about doing what they saw needed to be done.

"Do you think we should take him to the hospital?" Fuss: fuss. "Telephone his parents' Jerald, let them know what's happened. Tell them he can spend the night with us." Fuss, fuss. Nag, nag, Jemima truly did have all the required qualifications for being a mother and wife, even if her words rarely matched her actions.

"Yes."Papa agreed. "Best they hear it from us before they read about it over breakfast." He signed. Leaving to make the necessary telephone call.

"Out of those clothes." Mavis said what was blood stained needed washing before it was ruined. Jemima informing her son and his friend to make themselves useful by bringing something for their guest to wear.

"Will we be in the papers?" Jeremy asked as he and Daniel left to do as they were asked, both discussing how they'd cope with the fame.

"I think we should take him to the hospital."Jemima said she didn't like the amount of blood, or the look of skin which was badly bruised as Bobby removed his clothes. *'I barely touched him?'* Jade may not have seen, but she would know when she saw what others could see how Rojay had lied.

"The young man is strong and he will be just fine." Mavis assured everyone, no missing teeth, no cuts to be stitched and no broken bone, with Bobby stripped to his boxer shorts the most experienced female in the room assured all that everything was under control. "He will have to endure more than a few bruises when he's a professional footballer, all those twists and sprains." With a wink; Mavis told her patient not to worry as she helped him clean what needed cleaning.

"What is going on here?" Jennifer questioned what her sister appeared to be allowing to get out of control? "Jemima?" She demanded. Watching as Bobby winced when dabbed with the ice cold, clear liquid from the medicine cabinet labelled witch hazel. "Who was he?" Jennifer referred to the one who had done the punching as having checked Mavis could manage, she followed her sister from the kitchen to the lounge.

"Jade's ex."Jeremy sniggered. Passing the concerned females when returning with a pair of sweat pants and a dressing gown, both him and Daniel being eager to rejoin the injured party.

"Her ex?" Jennifer questioned.

"Men behaving like children." Jemima instructed her husband to have Trevor make up a third guest room while Mavis was busy.

"Jade's boyfriend?" Jennifer continued to question what she heard.

♫71♫

"Your boyfriend?" Kevin questioned when escorting Jade back up to the house.

"He isn't as bad as he seems." Why she was defending Rojay she didn't know. Why she hadn't said no, when asked if he was her boyfriend, she couldn't say. *'He wasn't.'* Not anymore and not for a long time. *'Would he be again?'*

"No, I can see he's much misunderstood." Kevin attempted to sound like the voice of reason. "I can see we got him on a bad day." The older male shrugged, struggling to understand what he was being told. "He must really like you."

"Really?" Jade failed to see how Kevin worked that out. Rojay had spread rumours and been cruel to her before calling in the heavies to help beat Bobby. How did any of that equal him liking her?

"Brave of him to stay back and talk to you."

"Brave?" Jade continued to question what her elder was trying to say, the two finding themselves being followed up the long driveway by a police car, the driver of which asked them to stop.

"He risked being caught by these guys." Her uncle whispered before approaching the officer getting out of the car with the blue flashing lights. "Sorry officers, I fear there may have been a misunderstanding. Boys on motorbikes hanging out outside the gates, I'm afraid my sister-in-law panicked. When we spoke to them they moved on." Bending the truth to protect Bobby from more bad publicity, Kevin assured the officers of the law everything was under control and agreed to keep the security gates locked once they left. "Will they catch up with him?" Kevin asked. Jade telling him Rojay was a good rider who knew all the best hideouts. "Not your boyfriend?" His tone indicated how whatever she was saying, he and a big part of her was thinking different.

"Are you all right?" Pushing her way by two thirteen year olds happily re-enacting their interpretation of the unfortunate event, moving aside Jimmy and Sawyer stood ogling the sportsman stripped to his waist. Jade wouldn't blame Bobby if he never wanted to speak to her again, but she had to see him. "I'm so sorry." His new career had barely begun and his first news report wasn't going to include any mention of the sport he played.
"I'll be fine." He struggled to get down from off the worktop on which he was sat. Sawyer restraining the urge to wolf-whistle as the muscle bound sportsman stood to greet Jade.
"He'll live." Mavis agreed. Collecting the items of clothing she insisted she wash and telling both Jimmy and Sawyer to stop their star gazing and help her with the clearing and cleaning up.
"What? No, Out, out, out." Back to check on his progress, Mama hushed Jade out of the kitchen, unhappy to have her daughter see the undressed male. Jemima asked why Bobby wasn't wearing the dressing gown?
"Spoil sport, I'm guessing there'll be no dates round the pool for those two." Sawyer grinned. Making fun of the female's embarrassment and commenting on Bobby's struggle not to laugh despite his discomfort and pain. "I'll help." He rushed to assist the one pushing his

strong arms and broad shoulders into the heavy velvet housecoat."Burgundy, the colour suits you." Sawyer smiled. Jimmy reminding him they had work to do.

"He could have cracked a rib." Mr. Barris arrived to inform their unexpected houseguest his parents were aware of the situation. "Do you know those boys?" He asked.

"No Sir," Bobby denied all knowledge of his attackers identities. *'Another prepared to protect Rojay.'*

"And you have no idea what it was about?"His elder asked.

"No sir," Bobby shook his head.

"Thugs, what is the world coming to when the streets are full of such thugs." Mama commented. Passing the families first aid box to Mavis to put it away.

"Jade knows one of them." Papa said he needed names and addresses if he was going to press charges.

"I'll be fine." Bobby said he didn't want a fuss.

"Are you telling me Jade associates with boys who have motorcycles?"Jemima interrupted.

"Boys are bound to come calling when you have a beautiful daughter." Bobby smiled. His words preventing any row and disagreements.

"He's got it bad." Sawyer sniggered in a whisper as standing beside Jimmy; one washed and the other dried the crystal glasses unable to go in the dishwasher.

"Perhaps."Mama half heartedly agreed with what Bobby said. "Nevertheless such attentions should be discouraged." Hearing the words being exchanged from outside the closed door and not feeling in the mood for explanations, Jade made her way up to her room, where she wasted no time in getting washed and changed for bed. *'What a night? What a birthday?'*

"Goodnight."As all still inside the Barris house retired to their beds, Jade found herself listening for the closing of doors and clicking off of lights. Sitting on and not in her bed, she wondered if anyone would knock to ask to come in and see her before calling it a night. Poor

Bobby, how loyal and how typical of him not to tell all he knew, how like him to be able to smile and make light of the situation. *'What a brute?'* How dare Rojay interfere in her life? How dare he tell her he understood? *'How could he?'* Why should he? It had been six months; why admit to missing her and why say he was jealous? Concerned for Bobby, when it came to hating Rojay? Dislike seemed the strongest word she could, or would use against him."Goodnight." Listening as all retired to their beds, Jade felt sure she wouldn't, because she couldn't sleep. Three in the morning, glancing at the bedside clock, she wondered if Bobby had gotten any rest? Climbing out of bed and putting her peach, silk dressing gown over the matching knee length shirt style nightdress, the young female decided to find out? Tapping lightly on the guest room door, hoping Bobby could and would be the only one to hear, Jade couldn't help feeling like an intruder in her own home.

"Who is it?" He inquired. Her whispered reply gaining his invitation to enter. "Are you not able to sleep either?" He asked. Shaking her head, Jade was encouraged to sit alongside where he struggled to sit himself upright.

"Don't get up." She insisted. Making certain the door was shut firmly behind her before joining him, switching on and dimming the bedside lamp. "Is the pain getting worse?" She asked.

"It's a little tender." He winced.

"I wanted to tell you how sorry I am." She admitted.

"It wasn't your fault, you didn't tell him to do this."

"No."She agreed. She hadn't and she wouldn't.

"He likes you." Bobby commented.

"Rojay likes himself." Of that she was sure. Roland Jackson was obsessed with self imagine. Proud of his rough, tough, can have anything persona, Rojay only had time for those who shared his interest in motorbikes.

"I like you." Jade told Bobby. "And I'm going to miss having you around." She admitted. Sitting by his side and taking hold of his hand.

"Maybe I shouldn't go." He sighed.

"You have to. Your parents' are so proud and it's everything you've worked for." She reminded him of his love for his sport and the people relying on him to succeed.

"I could be a salesman instead." He suggested.

"And miserable."Jade shook her head.

"That photographer's probably ruined my prospects anyhow." Concerned about how the newspapers would interpret the photographed incident, the male tipped to make it to the top of his chosen career; knew his new team wouldn't be happy.

"I heard Papa calling people who know people."

"Meaning?" Bobby questioned what she was saying.

"It was the photographer got them to do what they did, he paid them and my guess is my uncle heard Rojay telling me. Papa's contacts will make sure Mr. Greaves never works with a camera again should any of those photographs get printed."

"Pays to have friends in high places." Bobby smiled.

"They don't come much higher than every judge in the land." Jade told Bobby she doubted there was a newspaper willing to risk the lawsuit attached to every photograph taken by Mr. Greaves."If you miss this chance to get into the career of your dreams; you will never forgive yourself. Football is what you want and this move is what you need. We're young, we're friends and as your friend; I want you to go." Jade hoped Bobby would agree. "You would make a dreadful salesman." She smiled.Delivering a kiss to his cheek.

"Ouch." Bobby winced.

"Sorry."She apologised.

"I'll survive." He smiled. "You're cold."He observed.

"A little."Jade admitted as he pulled back the large soft, warm quilt and suggested she climb in beside him.

"But."She hesitated. Unsure to the male's true and full intentions, she knew he would never do anything she didn't want him to do, but didn't know what she wanted him to do. Snuggling beside him, the only feeling Jade felt, was safe, safe and happy. When Bobby wrapped his arms gently over and around her, Jade felt she belonged.

Awoken by the giggles and adolescent remarks Jeremy and Daniel made having discovered the two huddled in one bed, entering the guest room curious to know how their local hero was doing after his traumatic night, to find more than they bargained for. Unsure who was more embarrassed? Jumping out from under the covers and hurrying out, Jade warned the two not to say anything. Despite nothing actually happening, she knew others would assume something had. *'A gentleman.'*

♪72♪

7: PERFECT
♪73♪

Despite nothing actually happening on the eve she shared a bed with Bobby Hallas, they seemed closer, happy to spend time with him. Proud to be seen together, Jade smiled when discovering he kept his promise and arrived to collect her from school.

"You look better." She said. Pleased to see a much healthier and more upright Bobby open the passenger door of his topless car. *'He wasn't sure the team physio bought his story about tripping while running downstairs, but the exercise given appeared to be working.'* "Where we going?" She asked. Both happy to make the most of their time together, she was told their destination was a surprise. *'Happy?'* As Bobby attempted to reverse out from the school carpark, both he and his passenger were shocked to have the exit obstructed by members of the biker boys alongside some from the elder, official bikers club fronted by Spike, Denzel, Baz and Rojay. *'What did they want?'* Where had they come from and how had they gotten where they were without being heard?

"I don't believe this." Having to slam down on the brakes to prevent a collision, Bobby was both shocked and angered by what he saw to be irresponsible.

"Let me handle it." More angry than she was shocked, Jade requested she be the one to challenge the intrusion.

"You don't have to face these thugs." Bobby said he wasn't going to allow bullies to intimidate him, insisting this was her fight, she said she didn't want him to sustain more injury by defending her honour. "I know what I'm doing." She assured her concerned companion who reluctantly agreed and remained seated.

Waiting, Bobby watched in his rear view mirror as those sat astride their bikes minus their helmets noticed Jade approaching the one dismounting his bike to greet her.

"You don't listen do you college boy." Arriving to prevent his getting out of his vehicle; Spike and Denzil positioned their bikes close enough to be heard.

"Enjoy getting a beating do you?" Denzel smirked. His words causing others to laugh as Jade reached Rojay.

"Jade?" He smiled.

"Call the dogs off Roland." She demanded.

"Dogs? You should look in the mirror more often missy." Baz stated. Rojay lifting his gloved hand to indicate he and those laughing should stop.

"Leave us, leave me alone." She instructed.

"I just want to talk." He sounded sincere, but whatever he had to say was all too little too late

"There's nothing to say." Despite pleading his case, Jade informed him, he was wasting his time. "Why are you doing this?" She asked.

"Because you're my girl. We never argued and we never split up." Unable to believe what she was hearing she shook her head. "You're only with him because it's what your parents' want."

"No."She disagreed. "That isn't true." She insisted when aware Bobby could hear and was listening.

"Are you saying you prefer him to me?" The leather clad male said she had to be kidding.

"Leave us alone." She advised he get over himself and stop wasting everyones time.

"Meet me after dance class?" He asked. Ready to return to the one waiting for her, Jade felt smothered when Rojay followed and stopped her. "Meet me and listen to what I need to say?" He asked.

"If you promise to leave Bobby alone." She attempted a deal, as without comment the insistent male returning to his motorbike, indicated Spike and Denzil back off , all riding away.

"Mum is expecting us." Bobby told his companion they were late. Aware he heard and saw everything, Jade hesitated before climbing back into her seat. "You're going to meet him?" She knew the question was coming.

I MAY PRETEND

She also knew she couldn't lie and said she didn't know. "Do you want to?" He asked. Watching as Jade shrugged her shoulders. *'Keeping the peace?'* Aware of and understanding Bobby's disappointment Jade couldn't help wondering what else she could do? Needing to stop whatever it was Rojay was doing, she saw her talking to him could be a good thing.

"Please be careful." Bobby said she shouldn't trust someone proving himself not to be trustworthy.

♪74♪

Two weeks, fourteen days, a fortnight, when enjoying one another's company, two weeks seemed like no time. Restaurants, the zoo and a picnic in the park, together the two went on nighttime drives which included moonlight walks. Two weeks, the time passed in a flash, repeating the fact he couldn't and wouldn't ask her to wait, Bobby assured Jade he would always be there for her and never not love her; while she assured him they would always be friends. *'Friends?'* He had to be free to dedicate his energy and emotions into becoming the sportsman he was born to be. *'A footballer?'* Jade agreed when his parents' told him he could and would make it to the top of his chosen sport. Two weeks, picking her up after school and spending every second they could together. Jade and Bobby agreed whatever was meant to be, would be. Friends agreeing to write and exchange telephone calls when possible. Bobby would work hard and take full advantage of the chance he'd been given while Jade would get on with the less exciting job of finishing school. When finally it was time for the two to say goodbye. Jade and Bobby agreed to them being friends forever. *'Just friends?'* When the two came to the end of their last night together, neither wanted to let the other go, but knew they had no choice. *'She would always wear his ring.'* He would carry her picture in the wallet he kept close to his heart, agreeing they'd look back and laugh at the sentimental sentiments, Jade wiped his and Bobby kissed away her tears.

♪75♪

As the after school dance class finished, despite it being two weeks on from when he asked, Jade waited to see if Rojay would turn up. Feeling guilty, deceitful and sly, like promised she would continue to wear the ring which shown she and Bobby were friends, but like he said she shouldn't, she wouldn't wait for him. *'Free & single.'* The only vow the two made, was to tell one another if either met someone else. *'Was this Jade wanting to meet someone else?'* Honest and open, it had been quite sometime since she needed to be deceitful.

"You're late." Pulling up by her feet, he handed over the spare helmet she put on and secured in place before climbing onto the purring machine behind him.

♪76♪

The railway embankment. *'Where else?'* Where had she expected him to take her? Rojay didn't do fine dinning, but he had done something. Surprised to find a prepared picnic with all the trimmings. *'How?'* Shocked to be invited to sit and join the biker on the checked picnic rug lay before them.

"Hope you're hungry." He said.

"Hope this hasn't sat here for a fortnight." She answered his enquiry with a question. Her reply causing her companion to smile as he led her towards the feast of food and drink.

"I bought fresh." He smiled, pouring champagne for her to drink.

"I can't." She refused.

"Too posh to use a plastic cup." He told her the bubble filled liquid wasn't the cheap stuff.

"I'm not permitted to drink." Jade said her parents' would sniff it out if she had even a sip.

"Lucky I have mints." He smiled. "I won't tell if you don't." He insisted his guest relax and enjoy. Tasting what was on offer Jade swallowed the sparkling, sweetness, almost choking on what fizzed up her nose; she assured the watching male, she was fine when what tickled caused her to sneeze.

"What is this in aid of?" She asked.

"A belated birthday surprise." Smug and pleased with his achievement. Acting like the cat that caught its' favourite mouse, his smile went from ear to ear.

"It was a nice thought." She thanked his generosity

"I guess I should thank Mr. Sport for leaving." The gloating male boasted and she reminded him her friends' name was Bobby.

"A professional footie player?" He mocked.

"I'm proud of him." She smiled.

"Are you in love with him?" Rojay inquired.

"I"

"If you were, you wouldn't be here." Confident and accurate. Jade wasn't in love with anybody. Her being where she was, was nothing more than curiosity. As Rojay refilled the plastic cup with champagne, Jade wondered what the rough and ready rebel was trying to prove? Wondering what it was he was thinking, she wanted to know what he was doing? *'What was she doing?'* "I see you kept his ring." Observant like always; Jade nodded as she glanced at the mentioned token shinning from off her finger. "Here you go." Handing her the wrapped gift refused on the eve of her sixteenth.

"Another belated birthday gift?" She questioned. Her curiosity getting the better of her as she opened the small square parcel. "A key?" She gasped. A key wasn't what she expected.

"The key to my heart." Rojay smiled. "You hold the key to me." He insisted. Moving closer and taking hold of her hand. "Actually, it's the key to a very special place." Kissing her hand, he moved his slightly separated, quite dry lips up onto her lips, his sudden and unexpected action sending a strange and sharp sensation throughout her nervous system. *'What was he doing?'*

"Stop." Pushing him and his advances aside. "Stop it." She insisted. "We can't do this." She stated. Reminding him of how any relationship between them wouldn't work. "Our friends' and families' won't allow it." What was she saying and why was she thinking about the two becoming a couple?

"Your friends' and your family."He revealed where he believed blame should lay. "Mine think you're quite feisty." He laughed. "You still like me." He said. "I saw you looking." He smiled. *'Facts she couldn't deny.'* How could she not still like him? How could she stop looking at the boy she spent years watching? Insisting she needed to go home, Jade said her being where she was, was a mistake.

"I should go." She told him. "I asked Jimmy to pick me up from the sports centre." Her chauffeur was waiting.

"We need to give us another try?" Ignoring her request to leave, Rojay suggested they put the past behind them and start over. "I thought you would like this." He said the picnic was all his doing.

"I appreciate it, but I have to go." She said.

"I'll take you." He agreed.

"Thank you."*'What had she been thinking?'* Panicked by the thought of losing control if she drank too much, and worried his failing to make Bobby pay; meant Rojay would hurt her? Jade agreed to them going to meet Jimmy.

Arriving at the sports centre carpark, Jimmy got out of the drivers seat followed by Sawyer stepping out of the passengers side.

"Looks like he brought backup." Rojay smiled as Jade climbed down from behind him to remove and return his helmet.

"Do you blame him?" She asked.

"Meet me tomorrow?" He asked as she walked towards the waiting jag. "Let me show you the special place." He said he wanted to see her again.

"Sorry."She couldn't."Exams and assignment."She apologised for being busy.

"Wait." Rojay dismounted his bike, removing his helmet as Jimmy and Sawyer stepped forward to get between him and the one he followed. "It's okay." Rojay held up his hands. "I'm not going to do anything." He assured those watching, calling to Jade, stopping and encouraging her to turn back. "What use is a key if you don't know what it unlocks?" Looking at him for his explanation, he said if she met him, he would show her. Grinning; Sawyer sniggered when whispering about how he heard it called worse. "I'm not playing games." Unimpressed by those there to take Jade home, Rojay said he understood her not trusting him.

"Okay." How could she refuse? If nothing else she was curious? At home and in school, whenever her head wasn't buried in a book and her mind not filled with assignment notes, her dreams were clouded by the image of Rojay. Roland Jackson was again accessing her every thought and working his way back into her life.

June:
Rides out in the countryside, being back on the bike feels like nothings changed.
♪77♪

June into July, with Jimmy and Sawyer happy to cover for the one sneaking out to join her biker boyfriend when she should be visiting the library, or attending after school classes. *'What was she doing?'* Jade enjoyed afternoons in the park and even managed to catch the early evening showing at the local cinema. *'Rojay didn't fall asleep like Bobby had.'* Mornings, afternoons and sometimes at night, Jimmy and Sawyer would collect her whenever from wherever she said, so long as she didn't tell anyone about what they called their cursing; in which ever of Papa's car was being used. July.Mixed up and confused. Jade struggled to keep up with what was happening as she moved from the seat of his motorbike into his strong, leather clad arms. *'In secret?'* Meeting whenever possible, Rojay arranged for Papa's cars to be valeted at his fathers' garage just so he got to see his girl. Confused, with Rojay, Jade was happy yet still she found the time to read and write the regular letters exchanged between herself and Bobby. *'She should to tell him.'* Friends, she couldn't help feeling there was more being said in-between the lines of the words he wrote. *'Bobby wrote a lot.'*

Dear Bobby,
I am so pleased to hear everything is going well for you. So happy you are making new friends.

How could she tell him she was with Rojay? Whenever a letter arrived or being prepared to send, Jade found herself feeling unfaithful, sneaky and sly. Reading his, her every attempt to put pen to paper and tell him what she knew she should; ended up in the bin.

Dearest Jade
Hope you are well? Everything is fine here, training is going swell. I haven't managed to score for the new team yet. My team members reckon my scoring is only a matter of time and once it starts I'll be escalated into the first team. You were right, I am loving my dream. Did you speak to Rojay? Hope he isn't giving you any grief. I hear Tarquin, Gretchen, Tamara and Greyson are still going strong. I wonder how long it will be before we hear wedding bells. Write soon.
Love Bobby xx

♫78♫

Dear Bobby,
About Rojay, he doesn't give me grief, not anymore because the two of us are back together. I know not everybody likes him and I understand they see him to be a bad influence, but he isn't. He isn't the rebel he makes himself out to be, he's a nice person, he's good to me and we have fun.

It didn't matter how many times she wrote it, or in how many different ways she phrased it, Jade could't tell Bobby the news she knew he had a right to be told, not in a letter. With the summer break upon them, when packing to visit her aunt; she felt it only fair she tell Bobby her news face to face. With his new team training less than a mile from the village, Jade felt sure her bumping into the hardworking footballer would only be a matter of time. "You'll tell him." Rojay needed to know.

"Yes."She assured him. After all it had been Bobby who insisted she didn't wait for him, it was agreed they were just friends, surely he would understand? Lay on Rojay's outstretched arm beneath the hot rays of the high afternoon sun. Lay, up on the flat tin roof of the place he called his special place, despite everything, Jade felt content and happy with the way their new found relationship was going. Friends' suspected, but this time the two were being careful, agreeing them being together should remain their secret. Exchanging secret smiles, what was frowned upon by others, again caused Jade's heart to flutter.

"Will you miss me?" She wanted to know.

"You going somewhere?" Rojay mocked. His smile revealing he would. "Maybe I'll follow you." He teased.

"So you will miss me." She nodded.

"Maybe."And maybe she would miss him? Or maybe there wouldn't be time to miss anyone? Feeling like she was the meat in a sandwich. *'The ball bounced between Bobby & Rojay.'* Jade Jennifer Barris found herself fighting with her feelings and wondering which boy she preferred? *'Who did she want?'* "Would I be welcome?" His question snapped her thoughts back to what was the reality of her situation. *'What was he implying?'* "If I followed you, would I be welcome?" He repeated. "I can see it now, me, you, the sun, the sea and all that sand." He laughed. Jade agreeing to it being a nice thought. *'A holiday?'* Rojay had once revealed the fact he'd never been on holiday; describing how the first time he visited a beach was when he got his motorbike and found himself there by mistake; having taken a wrong turn. "Would there be a bed for me?"

"There's a local campsite." Searching for a practical solution to them spending time together, she said he could pitch a tent, or rent a caravan.

"Think waiting here will be better." Their special place was a place Rojay said he felt safe. Hidden, the place for which Rojay had given Jade a key was a large abandoned rusting trailer, the type normally seen being pulled behind an articulated lorry. Positioned a few steps from a stream, sprawling plant life had attached itself in a way which camouflaged what shouldn't be where it was, unseen unless one really looked. With no road in and a steep hill to navigate, it was like the large metal box had fallen out of the sky. *'His den?'* Rojay's spacial place was a tin box sat in amongst a picturesque landscape lay between farmland and the local national park. *'Hidden?'* From the outside it looked like nothing unusual, from a distance it seemed like there was nothing out of the ordinary nestled within the tall grasses, cluttered bushes and surrounding trees. When standing, sitting and lying on top of the solid structure it felt like being on a platform suspended in the air. *'Different & unusual?'* What had become their second special place, started life as Roland Jackson's secret den? *'Every boy had one?'* Be it a branch filled bush, a sturdy tree branch, or a garden shed, every boy had to have his secret place and own space to be. *'His man cave?'* The abandoned trailer, concealed from view and converted for comfort; was a space most teenagers could only dream of escaping to. Accessed via a hidden door in the wood and metal floor, there was a magical, warm, homely feel to the tin box converted into a room. *'His den?'* Rojay told Jade he never shared what was his secret place with anyone. *'Only she & he had a key.'* From nothing, the boy who was good with his hands created something which was practical. Inside, the trailer was clean, illuminated by battery operated lamps and flickering candles, the grey metal walls were decorated with a mix of pictures and posters placed over oddments of carpet, providing colour, texture, insulation and sound proofing, that which he had taken from off the doorsteps of the local carpet shops and found in skips, covered the floor, walls and ceiling. Large beanbags and an old reclining armchair sat around an old teak chest used as both a table and storage. *'Rustic?'* It all added to the illusion which turned something unwanted into a place someone would want to be. Sleeping bags, pillows and blankets were available should the heat from the double ring gas burner not be enough. The structure of tin and wood turned cold in the winter, but Rojay had everything he needed to survive should his secret space need to be used as his temporary home. A pan and whistling kettle, bottled water was kept cool in a pot of sand and a suspended chrome bar with coat hangers kept coats and other clothes tidy. *'His home from home.'*

June.
I had no idea where I was going, from off the street we walked down a path leading us across a wood railway bridge before descending towards a river off which I could see streams of varying size. Steep, I honestly believed I would end up rolling from the top to the bottom, Rojay advised where I should step and helped me along the path he'd taken a thousand times. I couldn't see anything but plants, fields and the river. He laughed when I struggled over the protruding water pipe he balanced across with ease. Narrow, the stream below was shallow but it was a long way down. Sitting on my bottom, I shuffled and used my hands where he walked upright. The stream was much too far below to walk through. Thick and green; the leaf filled bushes, stubborn plants and tall sprawling trees didn't make the remainder of the trek easy and I have to admit I felt a little frightened and concerned about the distance from anywhere and the absence of anyone else.

A GEORGE

Trapped, as he led me through the vast greenery and pulled me up in-through a hidden door, I thought we'd entered a shed hidden in someones garden. Inside, it was larger than expected, resembling what I imagine to be a bachelors bedsit, no one would blame me for thinking he had an ulterior motive for wanting us to be on our own. Rojay's special place, he could live there if he wanted. Beanbags and battery operated lamps; there's a radio and it wasn't hard to see how when he was twelve, he found and made the abandoned trailer his go to place when wanting to escape his world. I needn't have worried, the more I see and the more time I spend with Rojay, the more I understand. His hideout, his secret place is the place he goes to when things get difficult for him to be at home. Rojay doesn't talk about his family and I fear things aren't easy for him. His dad is helping him become a mechanic and take over the Jackson and sons garage, but Rojay's dad doesn't live with him, his mum remarried and when at home Rojay appears to have responsibilities no one his age should have, not yet. When he works he works hard and he tells me his working hard allows him time to play even harder. Sometimes I struggle to understand and keep up with what he talks about, but when it is just him and me, he is kind. I like being at our special place. I enjoy being with the Rojay who is nothing like the biker boy others see, not when he is with me.

♪79♪

Waving to Mavis, Trevor, Jimmy and Swayer through the window of the train, Jade and Jeremy smiled. When visiting their aunt Jennifer and uncle Kevin the maturing teenagers knew everything would be fine, sure of a good time because Jade and Jeremy Barris enjoyed time away from fussing parents'. No homework and no one checking they were where they should be. *'Time spent in amongst others their own age.'* Visiting the popular holiday destination meant them getting to know people they would see time and time again, alongside the hundreds of strangers met in passing. *'Once in a lifetime encounters.'* Jeremy was better when it came to being social, but both siblings agreed to feeling more relaxed around those they knew didn't know anything about them and where they came from. Regular visitors, those who were neither holidaymakers or local, visited for a few weeks every summer. Participance in what each found to be a welcoming community, not a long way, the holiday destination in the same country felt a million miles from the type of life the brother and sister were being brought up to lead. *'Intelligent, wealthy & wise?'* When out of the classroom and let off their short leash, the Barris youngsters were given the opportunity to blend and be like everyone else. *'Being like everyone else didn't mean being themselves.'* Taking the seat assigned to them in the first VIP class carriage; as the train gradually gained speed, Jade found herself looking over at her younger brother reaching down to pull his comic style magazine from out of his rucksack. Whenever he ditched his briefcase Jeremy left his snuffy, snooty well-educated manner behind with it. *'Out of school.'* Unable to stop herself from smiling when thinking about the times they spent with their aunt and uncle, Jade felt pleased and was happy not to have to travel alone. Glad of the one another's company. *'Together'* Over the years on just such a journey, the siblings managed pleasant, polite conversation, shared problems and exchanged gossip, sometimes revealing secrets both promised would never be told.

Only the best, the first class VIP ticket included a private carriage with on call waiter service. Chaperoned when younger, the brother and sister had at times joked around, driving those assigned to cater to their every need almost to destruction with odd requests and impossible demands. *'Spoilt.'* During the frequent trips, both understood the comments and remarks made by others. *'Spoilt & privileged?'* None ever said the words, not wanted and abandoned, none that was except for

Jade and Jeremy; who long since stopped questioning why their parents chose to send them away instead of keeping them home, or holidaying with them whenever school took a break. *'Necessary inconveniences?'* Heirs expected to carry on the family name and look after the family estate. *'A lifetime of imprisonment?'* Both agreed to preferring what their aunt and uncle would leave upon passing. *'No children of their own?'* Jennifer and Kevin lived lives which were physically demanding; in a place which was lively and interesting. Peace filled and beautiful, Jade couldn't normally wait to go to the place visited since each could toddle, but this time meant leaving Rojay and having to face Bobby. *'This time would be different.'* Who could Jade talk to about her? Would her aunt Jennifer understand what her own mother would never talk about?

Shocked to see her brother swap his comic for a full colour football magazine and not his usual chess monthly, Jade didn't want to answer when he asked if she was going to meet up with Bobby.

"For sure.""Being the answer to pass her lips.*'If I must.'* Being what the coy female was thinking.

"I bet your heart is pounding." He teased.

"Why would it?" She blushed.

"Are you saying you're not excited by the thought of being back in the arms of your lover?" Jeremy's smile sent Jade into shock as she demanded an explanation for his statement? "You did sleep with him." He shrugged.

"I shared his bed." She corrected his sniggering. Aware of what he was thinking, she realised the conclusion he and Daniel had come to when finding her in Bobby's room; wasn't the right one.

"There's a difference?" Her obvious upset confirmed for Jeremy that the answer was, yes. "Are you telling me you didn't?" He laughed. "Are you telling me you're still a virgin?" He gasped.

"Aren't you?" Shocked as her younger brother advised she get real, Jade reminded him he was only fourteen.

"Almost fifteen." He winked and she asked him never to wink like that again. Aged fourteen and sixteen; it transpired the younger of the two was more worldly wise and far more experienced. *'Shocked.'* Jade refrained from asking, when, where, how many times and who with? Jeremy was her baby brother; why wasn't he waiting, and what type of girls had he been seeing? *'Unaware of his ever having a girlfriend.'* With many questions rushing around inside her head, all Jade really wanted to say was yuk!

♪80♪

Praise, hugs and kisses, reactions displayed only rarely when at home were plentiful once Jade and Jeremy disembarked at the familiar destination. Walking into the welcoming arms of those waiting, aunt Jennifer and uncle Kevin were kind, warm and welcoming. Arriving at the seaside village was for Jade and her brother like being home. The village where their aunt and uncle owned and ran the small post office, come general store was compact. Reliant on visitors to sustain and maintain a comfortable livelihood was said to be what encouraged local residents to be experts in being warm and friendly. In a place where everyone lived and worked side by side, those who felt restricted and isolated when inside their large detached house, felt privileged to be accepted as part of the close community where all were happy to work hard and play even harder. Having arrived late; it was a feast of freshly toasted bread accompanied by mugs of hot chocolate before going to bed. Drawing back the delicately patterned, light cotton curtains to allow the heat of the early morning sun to enter, Jade knew she was rising later than she intended, refreshed and raring to go. Ready and more then willing to embark upon the many things she enjoyed. Strolls along the country lanes, sunbathing on the soft, sandy beach and swimming through the clear, cooling ocean waves. Jade enjoyed assisting downstairs in the shop and past visits had seen her offering her services not only to her aunt, but also to their neighbours Mr. and Mrs. Burnley who ran the coffee shop/snack bar across the road. A counter assistant, shelf filler, delivery checker and occasional waitress. *'At aunt Jennifer's, Jade could read as many teen magazines as she wanted.'* Stood at her guest bedroom window; looking over to the cafe; the returning teen noticed Mr. Burnley and his only daughter Shannon busy putting out the many white tables and chairs before pulling and putting up the heavily starched lemon and white parasols, preparing what was needed in readiness for the busy hot afternoon ahead. Watching the close, happy community awake and come to life each morning felt like watching the petals of a flower gently unfold as everyone did what they knew needed to be done. *'A true community.'*

"Sleep well?" Jennifer inquired.
"Fine thanks." Jade smiled as she entered the shop.
"You know to get your own breakfast." Jade's aunt reminded her of what was the daily routine. Living by themselves; meant Kevin and Jennifer doing all work, domestic and other for themselves. *'No paid staff.'* Taking it in turns to rise early to collect the morning post and newspapers meant the day beginning around 05:00 and anybody wanting breakfast after 06:00 was to fend for themselves, or go without. *'Busy people.'* Lunch was a sandwich and piece of fruit prepared and placed to keep fresh in the fridge each evening before bed, that; or else Jade and Jeremy could dine out. Whether they stayed for one week, or six, Mr. Barris gave each of his children £1000.00 so they could enjoy their holiday. *'Generous?'* Jerald insisted in-laws Jennifer and Kevin take payment amounting to £1500.00 for taking in their niece and nephew over the summer. *'Guilt money?'* Both Jade and Jeremy had long since concluded how their high earning parents used money to ease their conscious,

especially when doing what others saw to be wrong. While their children spent time with their aunt and uncle Mr. and Mrs. Barris would be jet setting around the world. *'Jade & her brother learned not to care.'*

Dinner in the Perron household would consist of a large, three courses meal, eaten at the table each evening after the shop closed at seven, that which Kevin and Jennifer called the main meal of the day, was shared even when it was just the two of them. *'Family time?'* It was the same, but different, because there were no staff and everyone at the table was willing to engage in conversation.

"I've had some fruit. Is Jeremy about?" Jade asked. Watching as her aunt continued her daily chores and speaking between customers.

"Gone to the beach"

"Eyeing up the talent is my bet." Kevin announced. Kissing Jade on the forehead as he entered to deliver Jennifer's freshly prepared mug of coffee. *'Very probably her third or forth of the day?'* "He is growing up fast that brother of yours." The elder male smiled, his smile broadening as he aimed it at his wife. *'Another house rule was nothing which contain caffeine to be consumed after midday.'*

"Tell me about it." Jade sighed. Remembering the short in-depth conversation the two shared on the train.

"So too are you." Kevin complemented Jade's natural beauty as Jennifer spoke of remembering the day she was born.

"I can hardly believe you turned sixteen so soon. You were such a good baby." She swooned.

"I was?" Jade gasped. "You remember?" She asked.

"Of course I remember." Jennifer appeared somewhat distant as she reminisced inside her head.

"Were you at my birth?" Jade questioned. Kevin stepping in to change the subject. *'Why was Jennifer struggling to reply?'*

"Bobby rang for you earlier." Her uncle interrupted.

"Did you tell him I was here?" She asked.

"Shouldn't I have?" The elder male apologised for not keeping up with what was and wasn't cool?

"He's visited a few times. He and your uncle get along famously." Jennifer smiled. Kevin agreeing Mr. Hallas was a fine young man.

"Yes, he is." Jade nodded. Bobby was everything a girl could want.

"And very fond of you, though you should be warned, you have competition."

"Competition?" Jade felt shocked. All the time when thinking about herself and worrying about how she was going to tell him about Rojay, she never once contemplated the fact he could be seeing someone?

"Shannon." Her aunt informed her.

"Shannon?" Jade gasped in disbelief upon hearing her female relative confirm the name of the one playing for Bobby's affections. *'Miss Shannon Burnley.'* Friends for years. "And he like her?" Wanting more detail Jade hoped Bobby was moving on, but her hope was shattered when Kevin assured her the soon to be professional footballer was much too wrapped in her to notice other females.

"We're just friends." She made her position clear.

"That is exactly how your uncle and me started out." Jennifer winked. A family of holidaymakers distracting her as they entered and Jade excused herself.

Leaving through the shops front door, the visiting teen was going out to say hello to those she'd gotten to know. Shannon and her parents, the butcher, the baker, all small shop owners and the local vicar. The village was a place where everyone was a friend and all friends were treated like family. Waving to Shannon and her father; Jade realised she hadn't asked why Bobby telephoned? Was he coming to see her? *'Did she want to see him?'* When beckoned to speak to the nineteen year old whose family loyalty saw her assisting ageing parents' Marie and Stanley in the running of their thriving family business; Jade felt a sudden pang of jealousy. *'She didn't want*

Bobby to be interested in another.' It was selfish and if she was Rojay's girl, it was wrong, but Jade didn't want to imagine Bobby with another; especially not her more mature and very pretty friend Shannon. *'Shannon was lovely, but never loyal.'* A born flirt, the nineteen year old blamed the place she lived and the fact no one stayed long enough to form a relationship for the way she lived her love em and leave em lifestyle.

"Staying long?" She inquired. Encouraging Jade to join her as with her father's permission the girls sat and ordered refreshments.

"Three weeks."Jade replied. Shannon telling her how nothing had happened since her last visit. "I keep expecting to arrive and find you married." Jade admitted

"To who?" Shannon shook her head.

"You meet plenty of people." Over a thousand visitors passed through daily in the height of the holiday season and the one fast approaching her twentieth birthday was no stranger to the odd summertime romance. *'Love in the sun & tears in the rain.'*

"Plenty?" She laughed. "They pass, but none want to stay." The elder teen sighed.

"I wouldn't mind." Jade had often thought about living in the village.

"Its cold and lonely in winter." Shannon informed her as Mr. Burnley brought the requested drinks, his special cream and chocolate chip topped milkshakes. *'A treat he never normally had on the menu so early in the day.'*

"On the house."He smiled. Refusing the offered payment and informing Jade the special drink was to welcome her back.

"Thank you Mr. Burnley." She told Shannon her father was lovely.

"He can be." Shannon agreed. Both watching as he walked away to serve customers. "You are more likely to become a bride than me." Returning to what had been the topic of conversation; Shannon revealed the fact she'd met and approved of Jade's boyfriend.

"You can't have." She shook her head.

"We met at your aunts." Shannon insisted. "I joined your uncle to watch him play."

"You mean Bobby." Jade gasped.

"Of course I mean Bobby, who else would I mean?" Shannon questioned as Jade said no one. "Nineteen and a professional, you done well for yourself there kid, wish I had your connections."

"Bobby has a natural talent." She agreed.

"He's a real man, not like the wimps we normally get passing through."

"I seem to remember you having your fair share of hunks over the years." A serial romantic. *'Shannon made no secret of her enjoyment of the opposite sex.'*

"I did think him a little old for you." She stated. Jade reminding her friend she was now sixteen. "Big party?"

"Isn't it always? My last." She sighed as Shannon saw and inquired who purchased her necklace?

"Bobby." She smiled. Touching the token which like the friendship ring, remained where it had been placed.

"A man with taste." Shannon commented. Looking as the gold chain and heart caught the reflection of the brightening sun. "I would be after him myself if he wasn't so wrapped in you." She remarked. *'Wrapped in you?'* As Shannon finished her drink and returned to work, the words wrapped in you, echoed inside Jades head.

♪*81*♪

Aware she should be happy, Jade felt ill prepared.

"I've missed you." He said. Arriving that afternoon and taking her into his arms. Holding her close Bobby told Jade she looked great.

"Shall we take a walk?" Suggesting they get away from everyone; it was an automatic reaction to take his offered hand as they began the lengthy stroll down to the local beach. Walking to a beach which would be almost touchable was it not for the high rocks and vast greenery between it and the village; obstacles which redirected visitors out along a mix of country lanes before leading down through sand dunes. Together, they approached a beach filled with couples. *'Together?'* In amongst couples ready to enjoy the sea, sand and sun, Jade and Bobby saw many who were in love. *'Did she love him?'*

"You look great." He told her. *'A gentleman?'*

"You too." She smiled. "The tan suits you." Bobby's pale skin had caught the hot rays of the summer sun and his tan was deepening by the hour as it covered his soft, smoothness. *'Did she have feelings for him?'* Larger, stronger, broader, fitter and healthier than she remembered. "Everything okay?" She inquired. Referring to his football, which he said was good. "Good." Removing her hand from his as their pace slowed; the confused teen became immediately aware of how her action was something her companion hadn't expected. "Sounds like uncle Kevin is becoming a fan." She said in attempt to continue the conversation to have halted due to her releasing his hand.

"He's a good man." Bobby agreed. "Is everyone well?" He asked. Inquiring after Gretchen, Tamara, the boys as well as Jeremy and her parents?

"Fine." She nodded.

"Is something wrong?" He asked. Feeling knots slowly tightening inside her stomach; Jade feared she wouldn't be able to do the right thing. On one hand she was truly pleased to see him, on the other she knew it was wrong to put off the inevitable. *'She should tell him about Rojay.'* Jade knew it was wrong to lead him on, they were just friends, weren't they?

"It really is good to see you." She said. Avoiding his question as she placed her hands up around his neck and kissed him hello.

"Good to see you too." He agreed. It was only a peck and Jade knew he expected more, she hoped it helped. *'They were still friends.'*

"Still training hard?" She asked. Leading him down the narrow sandy entrance to the over crowded public beach.

"Training is my life." Bobby nodded

"Made many new friends?" She continued in her quest to discover how happy he was.

"Some." He admitted. *'Everyone needed somebody.'* Finding space to sit, the two sat themselves side by side, smiling as the sun shone down to warm bare arms and uncovered legs, relaxed. *'Friends spending the afternoon together?'*

"Lucky Mama isn't here." Jade pointed out how Bobby wearing shorts was enabling her to see his bare legs. Smiling, the two recalled the eve of her birthday when he'd removed his shirt, causing Mrs. Barris to shoo her daughter out of the room.

"I can see yours too." He observed. Placing his hand onto her raised knees; Bobby leant in to deliver a kiss which was more than a peck. Falling back, with the soft, warm golden sand around her ears and in her hair, with her eyes closed and Bobby's soft, damp lips pressed against hers; she failed to question her surrendering to his advances. Feeling his heavy, strong, solid, lean male form above hers, Jade found herself catapulted from the busy beach and onto an even warmer, much quieter tropical island. *'Why wasn't she stopping him?'* Why hadn't she told him? Why had she not yet mentioned her newly formed, reignited relationship with Rojay? "I love you." He whispered as to her surprise she found herself having to bite her lip and hold her tongue to prevent repeating his words. Was that why? Did she? *'Did Jade love Bobby?'*

Following a long, hot, enjoyable and relaxing afternoon spent in his arms, her question remained unanswered. *'Confused.'* Three weeks, there was three weeks before she returned home. Three whole, long luxurious weeks away from the restrictions of the house in-which she lived, three weeks for her to explain to Bobby about Rojay. *'Rojay?'* If seen with Bobby the dilemma would be sorted then and there. Roland Jackson, Rojay sorted everything his way. His fist on Bobby's face. Maybe his large male hands would make contact with her face too. *'Would she blame him?'* Wrong, where Rojay was uncontrollable and unpredictable, Bobby was gentle and kind, choosing to use words before physical, brute force; Bobby would never use his feet, because his feet were much too valuable to be used on anything other than a football.

♫82♫

Placing the white football into the back of the apposing teams' goal, Jade watched with her uncle from the crowded terraces. If she was to let him go; Bobby wouldn't be short of female companionship. Shannon was far from the only one eager to step into her shoes. When watching Mr. Bobby Hallas out on the pitch, Jade noticed how many a willing member of the opposite sex would willingly rush into his arms should he ask. *'Was she jealous?'* Aware of how some would gladly push her out of the way, Jade noticed those making a bid for the footballer's attention. *'How could they?'* Revealing their wishes and desires within the screams and shouts called in his direction; few left how they felt about him and his teammates to the imagination.

"I'll rub you down Ally!"Ally being Bobby's given nickname, it was clear his fan base was growing.

"He is gorgeous." They called.

"What I wouldn't give to be his bar of soap after the match." Some said.

"I'd give my right arm to be the mud on his legs." Jade smiled when realising not all such comments were being made by the females in the mixed sex crowds. Smiling, she hadn't noticed the photographers taking official snaps. Smiling; Jade wondered if she would ever be able to smile again when the morning newspapers reported her to be Ally's girlfriend soon to be fiancée. A surprise visit from his childhood sweetheart was said to have put a spring in his step and a number of goals into the back of the opposing teams net. How could they write what wasn't true?

'No!' According to the reported stories printed within the pages of the local newspaper, super striker Bobby Hallas was betrothed to his hometown darling. *'No!'* Under the headline.**The Love of Sport:** Jade and Bobby were pictured arm in arm. Photographed with the girl said to be his intended fiancée, the couples' loving and loyal relationship was documented as having started in primary school. *'Lies.'* **The Princess & the footballer Prince:** The nationals elaborated on what local newspapers saw to be able to attract younger readers along with a new generations of football followers. None of the photographs were posed, all showing the two standing together. Why would people who knew nothing, print what wasn't true? Local residents were ecstatic about having who they saw to be celebrities in their mist. Nodding, Shannon told Jade she said she would be a bride first. *'Everyone was happy.'* Kevin said he was proud. *'A handsome couple.'* While some saw the news article as putting the local area on the map, others questioned the young and tender age of the couple said to be in love.*'Too young?'* Having only recently discovered the joys and pitfalls of teenage life, Jade didn't want to be tied down. *'It wasn't true.'* Celebrities in their mist, the local estate agent had gotten a free advertisement by listing available properties for sale in the area fit for those wanting to live like a footballer and his soon to be wife.

"Jade?" Leaving her husband to take care of the shop Jennifer followed her niece out into the cosy cottage garden to the rear of the building. "Why are you upset?" She asked.

"Because it's not true." The distressed teen agreed to her aunt joining her on one of the wooden benches with the large wagon wheel sides.*'Compact & comfortable.'* That which was the private outdoor space belonging to the building in-which her aunt and uncle lived and worked was a space designed for relaxation. Neat and tidy, an array of seating was placed within and around a maze of raised and low flowerbeds. Walking through what was walled and led to a perfectly manicured lawn. Kevin was proud of his garden, both he and Jennifer having chosen a low maintenance option, using hardy plants, large stones and sand. When designing what was a space ideal for outdoor dining, sitting and relaxing, that which was lawned was space enough for a kick about, game of tennis, or to use the high basketball net. Fun in the sun, it seemed like forever since the niece and nephew spent their time where Jade sat. Both preferring the cottage garden to what was the vast amount of ground around their house. *'Too much of a good thing?'* Smaller, was more manageable and compact more sociable.

"We know you're not engaged." Jennifer assured her.

"We're not anything." Jade prevented her elder from correcting and connecting the truths."Just friends." The distressed teen told how the two said they would be just friends; when agreeing Bobby's chosen career and the distance between them gave reason for them not to ask one another to wait.

"They're only photographs." Her aunt said few people believed what they read in the news.

"We're not together." Overheard by Bobby entering the garden as he arrived.

"Aren't we?" He asked. Jennifer excusing herself to allow them to talk."Whats happened?" He didn't understand. *'Why should he?'* Jade had done nothing but act like his girl since she arrived.*'Sorry.'*

"This isn't right." She said. Bobby walking over to replace her aunt by her side.

"You've seen the newspapers." He said his parents' had telephoned to ask what was going on and assured her he understood if Mama and Papa were confused by the reports. "Are they angry?" He asked.

"They're on holiday. I doubt they've even read it." She dismissed what was incorrect."I don't they would recognise me." She sighed. "I'm not your girlfriend." She reminded Bobby how the two had left things.

"Just friends?" He questioned. "I love you." He told her as with her head lowered in shame; she realised her only choice was to do what she should have done earlier. There was no one else to blame, this was her fault. "I thought we meant something." Confused by her repeating the fact they were friends.

"I'm sorry." She began. "I like you." She said.

"But?" He questioned

"But I'm."

"Seeing Rojay."He completed her sentence. Telling her there was no need to explain, seeing Roland Jackson as the type of person who wouldn't have given her a choice. "I told you not to wait." He sighed. Agreeing to what she reminded him of. "I should go." He said. Standing to leave.

"Friends?" It seemed a reasonable request, but Bobby was hurt. Confused, he arrived expecting them to laugh about what the newspapers printed. Wrong, what was put on the pages which some nationals awarded a double spread was translated as being a true life fairytale, it not being accurate was no longer what mattered. Upset, Bobby hadn't seen what was printed to be a complete lie.

"I have to go." He insisted .Leaving Jade not knowing what to say? What she wanted to tell him was that she loved him. *'Why?'* She wasn't sure, probably because it was the truth. Never, not once had she felt the urge to say any such thing to Rojay. Being back with Bobby, Jade found herself biting her lip and holding her tongue. When with Bobby, Jade found herself preventing those three little words from escaping uncontrollably. *'Jade was in love with Bobby.'* How could she put right her mistake?

"I'm sorry." She blurted. Having never felt more sorry about anything. *'Confused.'* It wasn't his fault she was struggling with her emotions. *'Fighting with her hormones?'* When watching him leave; she wondered why? Why wasn't she saying how she felt and telling Rojay they were over?

♪83♪

Inside the shop Jade felt shocked to find Bobby talking to her uncle, both males leaving as her aunt approached to ask if she was okay?

"If things aren't working dear it's best to be honest." Her elder attempt to avert Jade's gaze from the males who continued their conversation outside.

"He hates me." She sighed.

"I doubt he could." Jennifer said disagreements were all part of growing up. *'All part of the getting to know one another.'* "But if he isn't right." Apologising for how everything; Jade said she was to blame.

"I never meant to hurt him." He sighed.

"Are you hurting?" Jade didn't know. She didn't like how she was feeling. Struggling to contemplate never seeing Bobby again. Yes, everything including her heart was stinging. No, Jade wasn't tearful, disappointed and confused, sad and heartbroken. How could she know what it was she was feeling when she had never felt what she was feeling before?

"Kevin will see Bobby is all right." Jennifer things had a habit of sorting themselves out. What would be, would be? Retuning to serve those entering to purchase postcards. "I could do with a hand." Nodding Jade agreed to assist those wanting ice creams.

♪84♪

Rojay and Bobby, Bobby or Rojay? How could two who were so different cause her to feel the same? Unable to put her feeling into words, assuring her aunt and uncle she didn't need to talk. *'Shaking his head.'* Jeremy asked why? She didn't know. *'Which did she want?'* Her younger brother told her it wasn't right to want the one she was with depending on which one that was. *'What had she done?'* Rojay was bound to see the newspapers, if not him, someone was bound to show him what would be the top of the gossip list everywhere including back home. *'What would he say?'* Was it Bobby she loved.

'Not heartbroken?' Sixteen, Miss Jade Jennifer Barris knew without doubt she loved Mr. Bartholomew Robert Hallas, but didn't know if her love for him would or could last? With four years of her teens and her whole life yet to be mapped out, Jade was too young to think about settling down. *'Life had only just begun.'* Jade being Bobby's intended bride scared her because she didn't know what she wanted. *'College & university?'* If she failed her education, Mama said she would need a wealthy husband. *'A wife?'* Falling asleep that night, the lone female told herself what she needed was to experience life. Did she love Rojay? When asking herself about the one waiting for her to return, Jade found herself saying he was fun.

♪85♪

8: D.I.S.C.O
♪86♪

Keeping herself to herself, Jade chose to assist her aunt in the shop, serving customers, stacking shelves and doing the stocktake. Avoiding what she saw to be awkward conversations, when not working, the one visiting the village spent time up in her guest room. *'Another bedroom?'* Standing by the window while listening to the radio, stood observing the many goings on within the village. Watching those enjoying and those helping others to enjoy their holiday, Jade felt for her, the holiday was over. *'Did she want to go home?'* Jeremy was out with pals, boys of a similar age who spent the summer working in which ever role they could; at the nearby campsite. *'Friends & acquaintances?'* Boys and girls, teenagers happy to spend the school and college breaks manning the teen bars, ice cream vans and deckchair hut. *'Good people.'* If Jade said she wanted to go home, Jeremy would have to go too. *'Okay?'* She couldn't and wouldn't be the reason for having to leave early. Emotional, a female could blame her hormones when wanting the males around her not to fuss. *'Her hero's?'* Not that she would ever let them know, she knew her uncle and her brother were two men who would never let her down, not when it mattered.

"No." She repeated as for the fourth, could be fifth time he asked if she wanted to join him? Insisting those the two had known for years would really like to see her. Jeremy attempted to help his sister feel wanted.

"Come to the disco tonight? Uncle Kevin said he'll drive us." He continued to pester until; if only to shut him up, she agreed.

"Okay. Okay." She sighed

"Promise." Jeremy requested assurance.

"I promise." She said. Pushing her annoying sibling out of her room and telling him she needed to get ready.

A GEORGE

'Why was being a teenager so difficult?' Why was everything so complicated? Opening up her wardrobe, she decided the long cotton dress with lace up bodice would be appropriate. *'In vogue.'* For a summer night disco the loose breathable fabric with lace shawl would be understated and comfy, her agreeing to go didn't mean she had to dance. *'Who would she dance with?'* The perfect place to sit back and watch how those on holiday let their hair down. *'Sun, sea, sand & shandy?'* While those earning extra cash between lessons were well educated and ambitions, the type of people who chose to holiday under canvas and inside a caravan were in the main of a certain class. *'Working class?'* When attending the camp disco, Jade found herself enthralled by those who enjoyed themselves without planning. *'Making the most of their free time.'* She agreed when Jeremy reminded her of the fantastic times they'd had.

The disco held twice weekly during the summer months at the largest of the two nearby campsites was somewhere many youngsters went, a place where all were welcome. A gathering place for locals and meeting place for strangers who would always be remembered, strangers becoming friends. With summer jobs taking up their days, many who lived in and around the village looked forward to kicking off their shoes from aching feet. *'Catch their breath, meet up & relax.'* The local church dances held annually, at Christmas and on midsummers night. *'A true community.'* There was weekly bingo and film nights whenever the vicar got his hands on the latest video. *'Fun & friendly.'* It was little wonder Jade and Jeremy looked forward to and took full advantage of the many events and leisure facilities the village, beach and campsites provided. *'Fun in the sun?'* The brother and sister were more local than the visiting holidaymakers, but not so familiar, or confident either would go anywhere on their own.

Yes, it's off the shoulder neckline and long shin length skirt was perfect. Bright blue swirls intermingled on a black background with a glittering silver thread, the dress looked perfect when worn with low strapped shoes and her hair swept back with silver and crystal combs. *'Stunning.'* Gypsy, some said the style was hippie or boho, perfect, her aunt and uncle commented on how fast Jade was growing up.

"I wish you were my date instead of my sister." Jeremy gasped as she walked out to meet him and her uncle by his waiting 4X4.

"Sometimes having you as a brother is kind of nice" She smiled. Flattered by his remark as Kevin agreed whole heartedly. Admitting to wishing he was ten years younger.

"Only ten."Jeremy commented and Jade blushed.

"Cheeky, come on or you'll be late." Opening the rear door to allow his passengers inside, Kevin told his niece and nephew they didn't want to be last to arrive at the event which was popular with all ages. *'A night with her brother?'* It amazed them how different they were when spending time together away from over protective parents. *'Nervous?'* Jade knew Jeremy would keep his promise to take care of her, even if he was younger.

♪87♪

"Here she is." Leading his sister into the large area set up for youngsters to meet, dance and have fun. *'Here she was.'* Jade had been there before, glad the place in-which holidaymakers and others gathered hadn't changed, she liked when her surroundings were familiar. Taking his sister over to the all male table where friends Mike, Johnny, Kieran and Loui sat waiting, she could barely believe twelve months had gone since last they'd met. Older and more mature. *'Older & wiser?'* As each stood to greet her, she couldn't help but wonder why it was boys got taller quicker. *'Friends?'* The teens who lived in and around the village and local town, were those who spent the long school and college breaks helping others to make the most of their time by the sea.

"Hello Jade." Kieran smiled. Pulling out a chair and inviting her to sit before joining Jeremy to fetch drinks.

"So, you are Jay's big sister this year." Loui smiled.

"This year and every year?" Jade nodded.

"You look different to the girl who was here last year, you lost the pigtails." He continued. Jade admitting to that being the price paid for getting older. Smiling, the lone female felt comfortable as those she knew,' welcomed her back into their company.*'Good people.'* She'd forgotten how friendly and fun loving others could be. Anxious Jade made her brother swear he wasn't setting her up on a blind date and as the night continued, she was glad he knew what would cheer her up *'Relaxed?'* When joined by girls to include her brother's chosen holiday romance Gemma; Jade agreed she was having a good time.

♪*88*♪

Loud music, flashing lights, dancing and light hearted conversation enveloped within a carefree atmosphere, each in attendance found themselves caught up in the enjoyment of being with and making new friends. The night couldn't be doing her more good had it been bottled and prescribed by the doctor. This was what others her age did and what she should be doing. *'Stunning?'* Her brother wasn't the only one heard commenting and complimenting on how she looked. *'Easy going & easy to get along with.'* Included. Like those around her, Jade was having a good time.

♪*89*♪

"You have a sweet smile, you should smile more." Left to sit together when others invaded the dance floor, Johnny informed Jade he was glad to see her, watching as the music slowed and those dancing took one another into their arms. "Should we?" He asked.

"Lets." Agreeing, Jade was aware it had taken courage for the shy young male to ask what he had. *'Who was she to let him down?'* He, Johnny Hamilton was the eldest yet most timid of the group who teased him for his quiet, gentle nature. A good sort, another gentleman in the making, intelligent, perhaps he was a little geeky? Teased for wearing gold rimmed spectacles and being skinny, his beanpole like physique was something he attempted to disguise beneath his designer clothing. *'A swot?'* Mr. Hamilton was studying to be a doctor and one of the ones working at the camp to help pay his way. *'Why not dance with him?'* Moving onto the dance floor, she smiled at what she saw to be his gentle clumsiness, his actions reminding her of herself. *'Shy?'*

"Don't look so worried, you should smile more too." She said. Assuring her dance partner; he was doing fine as the beat of the music changed

♪*90*♪
♪*91*♪
♪*92*♪

"Hi Jade," Hearing someone call her name she smiled when seeing Shannon, her pleasant surprise changing to shock when noticing her friends' slim frame being held within Bobby's strong arms.

"Hello." Her shaky reply revealed how surprise turned to shock, her smile fading when the male asked if she was breaking someone else's heart? Stern but slurred, he didn't normally drink anything stronger than water when training, his speech and sluggish body language indicating his being drunk. *'What was he doing?'* Guilt ridden and awkward, shocked and taken aback. Jade didn't know what to do as she broke away from his stare.

"An old boyfriend?" Johnny assumed. "I expected him to have better taste." *'Over her already?'* At least he could be sure Shannon liked him, her reputation for having had a lot of male attention was public knowledge, but she did only date one boy at a time.

"Shannon is okay." Jade forced a smile. Shannon was a friend. *'Older & more streetwise?'* Shannon Burnley had been amongst the first to welcome and befriend the shy, timid girl seen sitting on her own when visiting her aunt and uncle. *'Good friend.'* The two having become close when aunt Jennifer and Mrs. Burnley encouraged them to picnic together on the beach while sunbathing. *'Sharing many memories & all the gossip.'*

"A bit full on."Johnny being a regular visitor and more local than most, meant he knew the rumours and had seen enough to know Miss Burnley wasn't his type. *'Too easy?'* While some saw a fast maturing Shannon to be someone behaving irresponsibly, Jade saw her being with Bobby as him being someone out to gain experience.

"None of us are perfect." She defended her friend.

"She should come with a health warning." Believing Johnny wouldn't say such without good reason, Jade listened. "She takes." He said. Admitting to having taken her out on a date. *'A broken heart?'*

"You don't seem her type." She didn't mean to sound rude but knew Shannon preferred brawn over brains.

"It was my turn." Smiling, the look each shared said no one should judge a book by its' cover, both realising, neither were what they seemed. With his confidence building Johnny whirled Jade away from prying eyes, disappearing into the centre of the crowded dance floor like a pair of mischievous school children avoiding the teacher, each continued to enjoy one another's company. *'Friends being friends?'* When dancing and chatting, Jade and Johnny had fun, laughing and joking, together the two continued to enjoy the night. *'No strings.'*

♪93♪

"Glad you came Sis?" Jeremy inquired. Him and his girlfriend rejoining the table where all admitted to it being an enjoyable evening. Back at the table where those to have rekindled their holiday friendships laughed, drank and caught up with campsite gossip, Jeremy and Jade were treated like family. *'Enjoyable?'* A good time had by all, all agreed to meet up again soon.

"Goodnight."All said.

"Take care." Johnny smiled when leaving Jade to wait for her uncle by the entrance to campsites carpark.

"You too."Thanking him for his company she said would be fine. When watching Johnny walk away, Jade's eyes fell upon her brother kissing his girl goodnight. *'Or goodbye?'* Sweet, sitting beside her on the wall which edged the roadside of the camps carpark; Jeremy looked like the cat to have eaten all the cream.

"Gemma goes home in the morning." He sighed.

"So come sunrise it's down to the beach to checkout the new talent?" Teasing the one showing himself to be more experienced at being a teenager, Jade fell silent when he admitted to loving the girl he didn't want to see leave. *'Love?'* How come everyone found the four letter word so simple to use and easy to say? How could her younger brother understand something she struggled with? *'Maybe love wasn't for her?'*

"We're going to write and her parents have said I can visit. Do you think Mama and Papa will allow her to come stay with us?"*'Probably not?'* Jade laughed at the thought of Jeremy asking permission for his girlfriend to spend the night. "You could say she is your friend. Jade? Jade?" Her brother begged her to help.

"Okay." She agreed. Her attention momentarily drifting back into the carpark where Shannon and Bobby were stumbling around looking for his car. A car she realised was directly behind the wall on which she and Jeremy were sat. *'No?'*

"Fantastic car Bobby, pity you were late, daddy would have been well impressed." Shannon said upon finding what they were looking for. *'How could this be happening?'* Listening because they were too close not to be able to hear; Jade kept her back to the giggling twosome fast approaching their intended destination. *'Late?'* Shannon would have to get use to Bobby being late. *'Lucky her?'* Jade struggled to prevent her thoughts as upon hearing the commotion, Jeremy turned to say hello.

"J my boy, where's the cutie I saw you with?" Bobby stuttered.

"Safely tucked up in her caravan." Jeremy smiled.

"You know Shannon." The intoxicated male introduced his companion.

"Sure do, Shaz." Jeremy nodded.

"Hi Jezza, is Jade all right?" She questioned his sister's quietness as he assured her, Jade was fine.

"Her bloke tucked up for the night too?" Bobby slurred, causing Jeremy to shrug his shoulders and ask who he was talking about?

"Still heartbroken over you." Shannon commented. The sound of glee in her words."Her loss is my gain." She smiled. Jade struggling to retain her composure as she continued to glance down at her feet, listening to the conversation as it continued around her.

"Jade prefers motorbikes." Bobby snarled. "Rough and not smooth." He grinned. Shannon telling him she took after her father when it came to appreciating fine vehicles.

"Evening all, had a good night?" Kevin asked as Jade walked directly over and climbed into the front seat of his 4X4. "Problems?" He turned to Jeremy who in turn indicated the presence of Bobby with Shannon.

"He shouldn't drive." Jeremy gave his uncle a look which said he didn't know what to do.

"Bobby?" Kevin told his nephew to join his sister as getting out of the drivers seat, he approached the two he realised had, had much too much to drink to be responsible. "You weren't going to drive were you?" The elder questioned Bobby holding his car keys. "Why don't I take you back to Shannon's and you can call a cab, or I can run you back to the club once I drop my two home?" He offered.

"I'm fine thank you sir." Bobby insisted he could take care of himself as he attempted to unlock his car door.

"No."Jumping over the low wall and stepping in-between the drunken male and his car, Kevin took from Bobby his keys and insisted he and Shannon get into the

I MAY PRETEND

4X4. "I can bring you to collect this when your soba." He insisted.

"We can walk." Bobby reluctantly agreed he shouldn't drive, but said he couldn't accept the offer of a ride.

"In these shoes."Shannon said she wasn't walking anywhere except over to what Jeremy helped her into. Climbing up and into the rear seat of Mr. Perron's high vehicle; the female calling her companion stubborn, thanked those willing to help.

"Coming?" Kevin asked. Watching and waiting as a reluctant Bobby agreed.

"Rojay? Roland Jackson?" Jeremy gasped. Watching their uncle drive away having dropped him, his sister and Shannon in the village. Waving Bobby goodbye, Shannon told the brother and sister goodnight when removing her shoes to cross the road to her home. "Roland Jackson? You and the biker boy, a grease monkey over a professional footballer." Jeremy accused his sister of being mad. "Tears? Really?" He questioned. Passing his handkerchief; he heard her say she and Bobby had parted as friends when. "Cry over all your friends'?" Her worldly wise sibling observed. How could she blame him for being disappointed when she was disappointed in herself?

♪94♪

Packed, ready to go. From her guest room window Jade took one final glance at the village. There they were; there, where the two could be seen daily since the eve of the disco. *'Shannon & Bobby?'* Placing his drink before him and running her fingers through his hair as he smiled. Three weeks and they resembled a couple preparing to become man and wife. *'What she wanted?'* Unlike Jade, Shannon wouldn't be letting her footballer go. *'Old enough?'* Had the two fallen in love?

"Man and wife before I return." She said out loud as her aunt entered to assist with her luggage.

"I doubt it." Jennifer replied. Looking down through the netted window."He is still in love with you and if you're honest with yourself, you will admit to loving him." More like sisters, the two often sounded like gossiping friends. *'Together?'* Jade and Jennifer spent as much time as they could together whenever they were in the same place, heard discussing everything from the weather to the tangled love triangle in-which Jade was caught up, there was nothing they couldn't say. "Take care." Jennifer told her nephew and niece to be good. Hugging and kissing them goodbye."Be yourself."She told Jade. Holding her slightly longer than felt necessary, Jennifer always seemed to have something more she wanted to say.

"Jade?" Turning, the leaving female felt shocked and wanted to run away. Bobby? "Jade.I want to say sorry." He said. Stopping by her side."I shouldn't have." He apologised and she admitted to being sorry too. Her eyes catching sight of Jennifer whose body language and eyes said she told her so. Jade also saw Shannon watching on from the garden where her father insisted she hurry with waiting the busy tables.

"Goodbye."Continuing to climb up into her uncles' waiting transportation.

"Jade you were right. I think we should stay friends, can we?" Bobby asked as with a nod and forced smile she agreed they could. Resisting the temptation to look back as her journey got underway, Jade couldn't help wondering what their friendship would be? Looking to Jeremy sat shaking his head. Jade agreed she didn't deserve anyones loyalty. *'What would be, would be?'*

♪*95*♪

9: WILD WORLD
♪96♪

September meant being back home and back to school. *'Older?'* Sixteen meant sixth form, no uniform, free periods for extra study and a much less military style atmosphere, more relaxed. For Jade Jennifer Barris; school was still school and like the house she lived in her school was a place where her parents' and the authorities kept her trapped. Back, before returning to her place of education she was able to avoid the inevitable. No one called at the big house unless invited.

"You okay princess?" Stepping back into his role of chauffeur. Jimmy revealed how he was enjoying the job. *'Right place, right time?'* James Kingston said he never saw himself wearing a suit and waiting around to transport those who paid his wage as a long term role, but did see his being given such a fantastic opportunity to be his fate. *'Staff?'* The young, handsome male agreed to being happy to continue for as long as needed. *'Experience.'* The secret world of a chauffeur, he wink whenever Jade asked how his day was? *'What happens in the backseat, stays in the backseat.'* "Why so glum?" If no one else, Jimmy was bound to notice how low and lost Jade looked since returning from her aunts house.

"Have you ever made a mistake?" She asked the one taking his lunch in the garden; Jimmy apologising for not realising there was anyone home, Jade insisted he remain where he looked comfortable.

"We all make mistakes." He pointed out his thinking he could do whatever he wanted without his employers knowledge. "I saw the newspapers." He also revealed his knowing what she was talking about? Knowing it all, he knew about Rojay because he was her alibi and the one who brought her home safe. Shrugging his shoulders meant he knew her dilemma and wouldn't know who to choose either. "Both handsome." He winked. "I wouldn't say no." He teased, quickly becoming aware she wasn't in the mood for his jokes."Sorry." He assured her, he was living proof of it being okay to be different.

James Kingston was happy to dress up and enjoyed looking macho, something he was anything but. *'Jade knew him & his secrets too.'*

"You looked great." He assured her. "Sawyer approved and you know how fussy he can be when it comes to the perfect pose." He smiled and she said she was glad they were still together. At least there was one relationship going from strength to strength. "Do you think you're with the wrong man?" He asked. Jade laughing at the thought of Rojay and Bobby being referred to as men.

"Have you seen him?" She asked.

"Rojay?" Jimmy required clarification. "He rode by." He nodded. "But he'd need a telescope to see in. I told him you were still away." He said the burly biker had also approached him while filling up at the local petrol station. "Why?" She didn't need to answer. It was clear she was avoiding what she believed would be a difficult reunion. "It will be okay." Placing his arm around her shoulder, Jimmy reminded her people like Rojay didn't read newspapers.

"No."She forced a smile. "But they look at the pictures." Jimmy agreed that the pictures had told their own story. *'Should she laugh, or cry?'*

"It will be fine." He said if she needed him, he would be there.

♫97♫

"How did it go?" Planting a kiss on her cheek as she stepped out of the jag on the first morning back at school. Rojay asked Jade about her trip to the sea?

"Good."She nodded.

"You stayed." He looked to her hesitate chauffeur as he sought clarification.

"Is that a problem?" She asked. Her nod indicating Jimmy could go

I MAY PRETEND

"Meet me at the trailer." Before she had chance to tell him no, Rojay rode away. No longer a full time student, the biker boy had places to be. Not expecting to see him.

"Not again."Tamara gasped, as she and Gretchen made no secret of the fact they's seen her with the one they called the wrong one.

"We thought you were with Bobby. The newspapers said." Gretchen began.

"You shouldn't believe everything you read." Jade interrupted before insisting they go to class.

♫98♫

Requesting directions, Jimmy was told by Rojay that their destination wasn't somewhere he would be welcome, promising to come looking if she was late. Jade's driver made no secret of his mistrusting the one collecting her from the community centre carpark. Arriving at what was their new special place.*'The trailer.'* There was no disguising her struggle to regain any enthusiasms for her everyday.*'Hating home.'* Jimmy agreed to wait where she left him.

"How is the job?" Rojay's apprenticeship alongside his father and elder brother had been made official, within two years he would be a fully qualified motor mechanic. The few lessons he continue to attend in school would now be tailored to compliment what would be his adult career and Jade wanted him to know she was proud.

"Well."He nodded. "What happened with Bobby?" Unlike Jade, Rojay didn't want to change the subject started when going out of his way to meet her. "Did you tell him about us?" He asked.

"Of course." Following him up into the trailer; she questioned his stern attitude and unhappy expression as using his handheld torch, he found and switched on the lamps."Is work tiring?" She attempted to make excuses for his sharpness when he demanded she inform him about what happened? "I told him." Pointing out the fact she was still wearing another mans ring, it was clear Rojay didn't believe what he was hearing. "Because we're friends, it's a friendship ring." She gave her reason. Moving towards her, Rojay lifted her hand to look more closely at the trinket shinning from the finger on which it was placed. "It means Bobby is my friend." She said.

"You told him you're my girl?" He asked.

"Yes."She nodded.

"My friends' think different." Thrusting a copy of the newspaper to have reported her being engaged; into her hands, Rojay demanded she explain. "Friends," Shaking his head. It was clear he wouldn't because he didn't want to understand.

"Uncle Kevin and me went to watch him play. We didn't know they were going to print the pictures and make up a story." Jade told how it was.

"You posed?" He accused her of enjoying her time with the up and coming sports celebrity.

"No."She shook her head. "The photographers were everywhere." She reminded him of the time he played dirty so a photographer could get a picture to go with his story. "Journalists lie." Telling him she would go if he wanted her to, she said she was sorry for how it looked continuing to insist she and Bobby were just friends. "He's with Shannon." She sighed.

"Shannon?" Rojay questioned.

"She lives in the village." Jade shrugged.

"He left you?" Her companion smirked.

"He wasn't with me." She repeated. "The two are very happy."As a couple, the footballer and the waitress had become inseparable. Placing his lips onto her lips, Rojay told Jade he missed her. *'Had she missed him?'* Lifting and holding her in his strong arms, Rojay lay Jade down across the three beanbags positioned side by side.

"I missed you." He repeated. His kisses becoming more urgent as first he lay on top and then beside her.

"You're not angry with me?" She asked. Watching as he shook his head. "And you're not tired." She said.

"Definitely not."He assured her. His hands moving her hair from her neck as his kisses began to explore. *'What was he doing?'* Aware his tongue was tickling her skin; Jade didn't know if the goose bumps and tingling was excitement or anxiety? "Relax." He whispered. His lips and hands wandering over the top half of her body; she suddenly felt threatened.

"No."She shook her head. "No," She told him. Sitting herself upright and preventing his attempt to unfasten the buttons on her blouse.

"What? What's wrong?" He questioned

"I"

"You're shy." He assumed. "No one can see." He assured her.

"I don't want to." The unsure female stuttered. Pulling away like a frightened child from the holds which her companion had on her; Jade repeated the fact she didn't want what he wanted.

"I thought you were ready. I thought you were my girl." He questioned her reaction in a way which made her feel she was wrong to be where she was.

"I am." She agreed.

"A girl I'm not allowed to touch." He shook his head.

"Not if I don't want you to, no." She told him and he assured her, he would never hurt her, repeating how he thought she was ready and reminding her, she was sixteen.

"What's age got to do with it?" Listening as he attempted to persuade her to come round to his way of thinking, stunned, she struggled to believe what she was hearing? "If I'm not ready, I'm not ready." She told him to backoff and asked why the rush? Being legal didn't make something compulsory.

"If you're worried about getting pregnant you can go to the clinic." Shocked by his flippant attitude, Jade told him there were more things to worry about than an unwanted baby."No." She repeated the fact she didn't want to. *'Did she?'* Rojay advised she visit the local family planning centre so she would be safe when she was. *'Shocked.'* He said if the two were going to continue being a couple; their relationship would move on one day. "You know how much you mean to me. You're the only girl I've ever brought here. The only one I've given or wanted to give a key to." Was that supposed to make his intentions acceptable? "You know how special you are." Absence was said to make the heart grow fonder, Jade hadn't heard of it causing lust to become uncontrollable.

"No." She shook her head. "It's not right." Not yet at the stage she imaged she would be when ready for her first time, Jade didn't want her first sexual experience to be something she wanted to forget. *'Ones first time should be with someone they love & feel loved by.'* Uncontrollable passion and experimentation, the belief young love will last forever. Jade was aware of all the reasons and the many circumstances, peer pressure or a want to be like everyone else. Whatever it was to have happened to others, Jade believed any and everything to happen to her should happen when she saw and felt it to be right.

"Would you still respect me?" Why was she asking? What a stupid question, any and everyone being asked what she was asking was bound to say yes and he did. Whether she believed him or not didn't matter, looking deep into his bright blue eyes and feeling his body close to hers; with his breath hitting her face, Jade found herself considering what he wanted. *'Not heard.'* Maybe she was afraid of saying yes and maybe she was ready for what he called the next level in their relationship.

"At least say you will think about it?" He asked.

"Are we over if I say no?" She questioned and he assured her them being a couple wasn't based on what they did and didn't do?

"I care for you. I thought you knew." He sighed. "I missed you." He asked if Jimmy mentioned his asking about when she would be home? "I don't want us to fall fowl of a mistake, we're a couple and it could happen." His concerns seemed genuine. *'Confused.'* He made it sound like what he wanted was for her sake, not his need.

"Will we have to make an appointment?" What was she saying? *'What was she thinking?'* What was Jade doing? While he heard none of what she said, she listened to his every word. *'Could he be right?'*

"Don't worry, I'll arrange it." Would he? Why was she not surprised by the fact Rojay was acting like he had done what he proposed doing before?

♪99♪

"Dr. Butler will see you now." A polite young nurse by the name of Susan Goods announced before showing both Jade and Rojay into the small consulting room and closing the highly polished, solid door behind them. *'Nervous?'* Like being called in to see the head, they sat before the doctor sitting at his desk.

"Hello." Dr. Jonathan Butler opened what turned out to be a somewhat lengthy conversation of questions and answers. Inside, the consulting room felt cold and quiet, but its' quietness was the only similarity between it and the local library where Jade was meant to be. *'Jimmy was waiting one street away.'* Jimmy asked Jade if she was sure. *'Contraception or abortion?'* Jimmy advised she think carefully. *'Eliminate risk.'* Offering to come in and hold her hand, Jimmy assured her he was there if she needed him and she thanked him for caring. *'Her hero?'* Her young chauffeur joined her uncle and brother as being someone on who she could, would and often did depend. *'Contraception equalled precaution.'* Like the legality of age, that which Jade was agreeing to do didn't mean she had to do anything else. *'Safe not sorry.'* The intelligent female managed to turn what was happening in to what was logical. *'Disregarding fact.'*

"You are Miss Jade Jennifer Barris and Mr. Roland Jackson." Feeling like the two were entering into marriage, being married was what two people were meant to be before doing what was being contemplating?

"Yes."Both confirmed their identities. *'Would her parents find out?'* Jimmy promised not to tell. *'What happens in the backseat, stays in the backseat.'*

"Ages?" Questions varied from how long the two had known one another, to how many previous partners they'd had?

"None?" The doctor continued to probe, having requested Roland wait outside, the one there to assist those in Jade's position wanted to clarify she was sure.

"None."Aware she should feel proud, what she felt was fear. *'What if the doctor said no?'*

"Are you sure about this?" Nodding, she knew it was her looking to the ground which prompted his next inquiry. "Is Mr. Jackson putting pressure on you?" The unsure female felt sure the doctor had seen and heard it all before. *'Why was she shaking?'* The professional in his chosen line of expertise was only doing what he was paid to do.

"He's my boyfriend." She found herself using the same reasoning Rojay used when suggesting they take their relationship to the next level. *'Expected.'*

"You're certain?" The Doctor continued his search for confirmation and reassurance. Reminding her again of how she didn't have to do anything she didn't want to.

"Yes, I mean no, I mean." She stuttered.

"I've met lots of girls like you, you can say no." The elder professional continued to tell her of her choices, informing her, her body belonged to her and no one else.

"Yes."She agreed. "I know." She assured him.

"Then I take it you have read through the available leaflets and fully understand the dangers, as well as the pleasures of having a sexual relationship?"

"Yes."Jade nodded

"You know saying yes is the hardest part and after your first time; saying yes gets easier." It was clear the medical professional was sensing reluctance and uncertainty. *'Right.'* Jade wasn't sure of anything. Both knew the law prevented him refusing her request even when it was clear she wasn't sure if, or when she would need it. Having come this far, both Jade and the person she came to see were aware her leaving with nothing, wouldn't be wise.

"Which contraception?" His words sounded as reluctant as she was feeling, embarrassed, yet confident in her reply, she recited what she researched in hope the time spent considering her choice would convince the doctor she wasn't some scatter brained lovesick teenager or desperate fool, not that any female should be seen as foolish or wrong when it comes to preventing unwanted pregnancy and the spread of STD's. *'A stereotypical slapper?'* Aware of the looks she and others her age had gotten from those who were older; when sitting in the waiting room, Jade wanted to tell them she wasn't what they thought, the truth being she felt exactly that. *'Like everyone else?'* Jade didn't want to be like those her friends saw as being easy and desperate. Having experienced being a girlfriend, Jade didn't want to run head first into what boys expected and many accepted as being the next stage of a relationship. *'What was she doing?'* Dr. Butler was right when he said she didn't have to do anything.

"I believe condoms are safer when it comes to preventing diseases." She began. Having taken a much needed deep breath. "And it would seem the pill is much more reliable when it comes to preventing pregnancy, especially in the case of inexperienced teenagers."

"I couldn't have put it better myself. You're a very intelligent young lady. Have you also researched the risks?"

"Everything from headaches to blood clots and death, I could die in childbirth just as easily." Jade attempted to assure him she knew what she was doing.

"The sensible thing would be to continue to say no." He said. "At least until you're sure." Was he reading her mind?

A GEORGE

"What happens now?" Aware the consultation was becoming somewhat lengthy and Rojay was waiting outside, Jade attempted to move things along.

"We will put you on the pill." The doctor said. Signing for her the requested prescription and informing her she would be given the condoms on her way out. "We will need to keep a check on you." He said.

"Weight, blood pressure and smear tests." Jade again revealed the full extend of her awareness, before arranging her follow up appointment for three months time. September, she agreed, but wasn't looking forward to what would be her next clinic visit in early December.

♪100♪

September into November, Jade felt uneasy, but didn't know why, close, most of the time she and Rojay were happy, unlike expected, he wasn't pushy, respectful he kept his promise not to do anything she didn't want him to do. *'Not pressured.'* Understanding and patient, his being understanding wasn't like Bobby understanding her. With Rojay there was a tension which signified his waiting for opportunity. *'Biding his time?'* He said he wouldn't force her and promised never to hurt her, none of which stopped him protesting whenever she insisted it was time for her to go.

"Again?" He complained when she said Jimmy was waiting. *'Her alibi & friend.'* Jimmy said should she ever be more than five minutes late, he would be rushing in. *'Followed by police.'* September through October, into November, due to planned building works taking place over the Christmas festivities; the annual school Ball was moved to coincide with extended bonfire night celebrations. *'More fire sparkle than glimmering glitz.'* Many preparing to attend what should be a grand affair said they still intended to dress to impress. Ignoring the fact what normally took place indoors was being advertised as a mix of fire pit huddles, sky high displays and barbecues. Most insisted the larger event include the traditional DJ and live band, so not to miss out on the glamour of the occasion which was the annual Ball. Many wanted the opportunity to dress up and dance and for Jade and her friends' this would be their last ever school Ball.

♪101♪

The school Ball was the reason she gave for breaking dates with the one whose own commitments and responsibilities were beginning to encroach on his free time. *'Growing apart?'* Full of apologies, she said Jimmy would be waiting to take her to Mama and Papa in time for dinner. *'How she lived.'*

"You'll be seventeen next birthday."Rojay complained about her not being able to meet up with him later.

"Yes."She agreed. "Age means nothing to my parents." She signed. *'No more parties?'* Mama and Papa had made it clear any future birthday celebrations would take place around a table in a restaurant and Rojay guessed right, when guessing he wouldn't be invited. *'Family only.'*

"Is he worth it?" Having watched the two approaching and witnessed a less than amicable goodbye, Jimmy questioned why Jade was still doing what she was doing? Right; when saying the excitement and adventure had subsided. "Do you even like him?" Not so long ago she was asking herself if she loved Roland Jackson, when Jimmy said like? She wasn't sure.

"I'm fine." She said she knew what she was doing and nodded when he asked if she was happy? When not disagreeing, the two had fun, when not tired, they continued to go out for rides, walked hand in hand and snuggled up to keep warm inside the den. Smiling when remembering the good times, Jade continued to repeat the fact she was fine.

♪102♪

Having signed up to their chosen college; Tamara and Gretchen shown concern about their friend being unable to decide. *'A gap year?'* Accusing her of spending way too much time with her chauffeur and having her expectations lowered by her rebel boyfriend. *'A gap year?'* Mama and Papa agreed to allowing her more time; while both aunt Jennifer and grannie invited her to spend time with them. *'Could, should she leave?'*

"Will he be there?" As the girls got themselves ready, all knew Tamara's reference to he, meant Rojay. Standing before her dress mirror; she could hardly believe it had been so long since the last time the three used her bedroom as their personal changing room and her house their beauty parlour. *'What was once regular, now happened when necessary.'* Approaching the year when she would turn seventeen, Jade was no longer the frightened child she perceived herself to be, that didn't mean she knew what she wanted? *'The last Ball?'* Bobby had taken her when last she entered the school hall to find it decorated with fairy lights and filled with the sound of music. Yes, she would be meeting Rojay.

"Any plans for Christmas?" Gretchen attempted to change the subject, Jade telling them Mama and Papa planned to visit grannie in Canada. "Without you?" She asked.

"They're leaving you?" Tamara gasped.

"I'm almost seventeen." She reminded and informed them her aunt would be coming to supervise Jeremy.

"I really must get some new clothes." She spoke her thought out loud. Gretchen assuring her, she looked fine.

"Daddy is taking us skying for Christmas." Tamara bragged. "He asked Tarquin to join us."

"Really?" Gretchen gasped. Revealing the fact she and her parents had been invited to join Greyson and his family on boxing day. "I love Christmas." She smiled and Jade admitted to never being able to plan so far ahead for fear of everything going wrong. *'Remembering the Christmas grannie brought forward so her terminally ill gramps wouldn't miss out on the time of year he loved.'* Taking a deep breath, Jade said she hated when things went wrong.

♪*103*♪

I MAY PRETEND

Inspecting appearances, the friends' took it in turn to comment on one another's chosen outfit. Gretchen wore green, a trouser suit, the jacket was fitted and the full length trousers flared. Teamed with a sparkling navy blue blouse. *'A school teacher.'* Was how both Jade and Tamara described the created look. *'Strict & organised with clean lines & a hidden hint of glam.'* All agreed Gretchen's look was smart and sophisticated, while she pointed out how the trousers resembling a long skirt made them easy to hide beneath her long overcoat when outdoors while being stylish and easy to dance in when enjoying the main aspects of what each saw to be the unusual Ball. Tamara wore rose red, a dress with full skirt and black belted waistline. *'A true party girl.'* Tamara had a flare for design and a natural knowing of what looked right. When told she would feel the cold, Tamra revealed her full wool tights and laced ankle boots, her coat was a black dress coat with red belt and her hat a red beret. Smart and stylish, up to date because mummy could never allow the one to represent her be seen in something last season.

Unlike her friends' Jade's chosen outfit of deep black crushed velvet trousers and long length off the shoulder smooth silk knit sweater embroidered with diamanté around the shoulder and cuff wasn't multi functional, especially when teamed with low black studded ankle boots. *'Outdoor only.'* Jade said she wasn't planning on spending much of the night inside.

"Are we going to the same event?" Tamara questioned the casual attire. "Are you going ice skating?" She asked. "Where did you even get that?" Her snootiest friend checked the labels in disbelief when being told it was all designer?

"You'll be too hot?" Gretchen worried.

"I'll be fine." Jade's attempt to silence the fussing twosome failed.

Leaving together, approaching the waiting vehicle, the one to have stopped playing gooseberry by only joining her friends' for all girl events, said she had her own plans for the night and could get Jimmy to drive her if Greyson wasn't happy.

"He doesn't mind." Gretchen smiled. Kissing Greyson as he held open the doors to his father's seven seat land rover.

"More the merrier."He smiled. Encouraging Tamara into the rear and assisting Jade to climb up into the back, where she felt shocked to find Bobby sitting on the opposite pull done seat.

"Bobby, what a nice surprise. How are you?" Tamara stated. Her expression showing her pleasure. *'Grinning like a cat.'* Jade never felt more uncomfortable.

"Fine thanks." He replied. Wriggling as with the only place to look being at one another; both he and Jade struggled to avoid eye contact. *'Had they fallen out?'* Less than three months ago they'd parted as friends. *'He agreed to be friends.'* "Sorry," He apologised as their short journey got underway. Jade telling him it was fine, it was clear neither knew what to say.

"How long you home for?" She inquired as Bobby made an attempt to speak at the exact same time.

"Are you?" He began. "Sorry," He blushed. Informing her, he was home for a short break. "How is everything with you?" He inquired.

"Good."She smiled. Bursting to ask about him and Shannon; she didn't want to give the wrong impression and held her tongue. *'Tamara would tell all later.'*

"Don't you worry Bobby mate, we'll not leave you out." The biggest goodie amongst them interrupted. "We have a hot little number lined up." Tarquin smiled when reaching their destination where Bobby asked what they were talking about? Watching Jade rush away into Rojay's open arms. "Friends wouldn't invite you to play gooseberry." Patting him on the back, Tarquin told Bobby he should forget those all were watching.

I MAY PRETEND

♪104♪

Passing Bobby and the others as they sped away, Jade hadn't meant to smile. It felt good ridding on the open roads as part of a group and it was exciting to watch each speedy rider take a turn to lead the large convoy within which each felt warm and protected from the cooling night air. November, there was no avoiding the ice like wind pockets each passed through as they rode on two wheels. *'What was she doing?'* What? Her actions didn't matter. Jade felt free. More free than she ever felt before, holding on tight to Rojay, confidant and happy to put her trust in his skill and judgment. *'Did she love him?'* She enjoyed being with him. Pulling back and opening up his powerful engines. When Rojay sped forward to take the lead, his passenger felt incredible. Out ridding with the group, she felt feelings she never felt before. *'Belonging?'* Speeding down road after road and swerving around lane after lane, the bikes came to a halt within what could only be described as a camp in the trees.

♪105♪

Removing her helmet and shaking free hair she chose to wear lightly curled but loose, feeling bemused by what met her eyes? Hundreds of motorcycles, as day light faded into night, like someone placed a dark, star spangled blanket over the sun, the one unsure where she was, struggled to make out the many heavy shadows surrounding her. Conversations and the sound of laughter echoed alongside the snap, crackling and spitting flames of many a campfire. *'A gathering?'*

"Where are we?" Unable to hold back any longer, she asked her question in a whisper, too afraid to allow her words to be heard. When dismounting the bike and stepping onto what was damp, dark and cold, Jade wanted to know where they were? Encouraging her to join him, her partner smiled, taking her gloved hand into his; Rojay led Jade to one of the many warming, roaring, yellow, orange flamed fires.

"Rojay." A large, leather shrouded female called. "Long time no see." She continued. Not standing, but raising her hand for him to kiss, their contact caused both to smile. "Join us darling." She invited and finding a space on the other side of the dancing flames he agreed. Pulling Jade down to sit between his outstretched, parted legs, both sat on laid waterproof sheeting. "Introduce." The woman Jade saw to be in her mid thirties, insisted and Rojay obliged.

"Ratbag, this is Jade, Jade meet Ratbag." Surely Rojay wasn't being rude? *'Her nickname?'* Jade would learn how all females associated with bikers were called their old ladies and each old lady earned a nickname. *'What would hers be?'* Peering through the flames to see who she was being introduced to, Jade failed to see how the name given, related to the one who was large, loud, proud and demanding. Straight, jet black hair down to her waist, a large rounded face and big, dark brown black eyes. If it hadn't been for the blue, black lipstick, the brown leather Indian style headband and the studded neck collar with matching wrist bands, Ratbag would look gentle. *'Agony aunt?'* To many, membership of a bikers club was a way of life and as she was introduced to others, Jade couldn't help the thought stereotypical; entering her head as everything she imagined sat, stood and moved before her eyes.

"Hello sweetie." When not shouting, Ratbags' voice was gentle.

"Hello." Jade stuttered.

"The name is Ratbag dear."

"Hello Ratbag." She said with more confidence.

"And these other's here are Angel, Kenny, Rosebud, Mez, Petal, Blue, Peaches, Carter and this hunk of a man is my Stork." Stork was nothing like the type of partner anyone would put with such a fierce creature. Younger, next to the larger than average female, Stork looked small. Nineteen or younger? His hair was short, shaven and dyed blonde, Stork looked more her pet than her partner as he sat by her side. Nodding hello like an obedient puppy would raise its' paw, Jade felt sorry for him. *'Happy?'* When seeing Storks smile she questioned how she looked to others when with Rojay?

"Take them a beer." The dominating female instructed and he did her bidding. Was Jade doing everything Rojay asked of her own free will?

"Not for me thanks." When she refused, Rojay insisted she take it.

"Warm enough?"Kind, considerate and thoughtful. She was fine, but felt her first taste of ale would be her last?*'Wine with dinner & toasts made with the finest of champagne. Beer could stay in its' barrel.'* "They are a good crowd." Wrapping his arms around her, safe in the arms of her boy, the one who had never been anywhere like where she was, attempted to assess her surroundings and weigh-up the company. *'Warm in a place which was cold.'* Was she safe?

♪*106*♪

Dancing and chatting, drinking and laughing, Bobby was a gentleman not enjoying his time with the female others had set him up with.

"Do you have a girlfriend?" Tamara asked when sensing his discomfort around the one happy to flirt and see herself as lucky to be out with the local footballer.

"I didn't come home for this." His reply didn't answer the question, but it did let those at his table know he was far from happy. Never rude, Bobby told his date he was sorry he wouldn't be joining her on the dance floor, or escorting her home."Sorry."He shook his head when she asked if she could see him again? Wondering if they would be waiting to take Jade home? All noticed how the one struggling to be in amongst them; continued to check his watch.*'Where was she?'*

♪*107*♪

Dancing, drinking, eating, kissing, talking and walking, everywhere Jade looked she saw people doing whatever they wanted to do. Food, drink and drugs, few hid what was happening out in the open beneath star spangled skies. *'Having fun?'* Laughter filled the air and spit roasts gently turned over open flames creating an atmosphere the like of which she had never experienced. Free spirited and masters of their own destiny. Some of what she saw caused her to question her being where she was?

"Don't worry, everyone will meet at midnight." Jade was informed when inquiring as to the whereabouts of Spike and the others.

"Midnight?" She repeated. Concerned as to what time Rojay planned on taking her home?

"Yeah, midnight, the witching hour."Ratbag laughed out loud in a shriek like fashion. "Have you not told her Rojay. Does your filly not know what happens when the clock strikes twelve?" She asked.

"Its when we all meet up and make out like crazy?" Stork lent in to whisper, his eyes turning to Ratbag. "Sometimes we share." He smirked. All around smiling while Jade didn't know what to do? *'What should she say?'* She was taking the pill as instructed by Dr. Butler, she knew Rojay carried a packet of three in his wallet, but a full scale orgy? *'An anything goes sex party?'* That wasn't how she imagined her first time? Not that she had imagined her first time. This wasn't what she wanted. *'Not casual sex.'* Glancing into Rojay's eyes; she searched for reassurance

"We're leaving before midnight." He smiled.

"Not willing to share." Carter smirked as all continued to laugh, talk and joke, Rojay excusing himself and Jade when aware of her escalating uneasiness.

"New friends?" Jade realised they were in amongst those who made up the official club Rojay would soon be a fully fledged member of. Stopping beneath a dark, shadowing oak tree having walked away from the others. Rojay assured her, Ratbag was teasing.

"They wanted to meet you." He revealed as she realised she was being tested.

"How often will you come here?" She asked. Lowering his shaking head, Rojay told her, not often.

I MAY PRETEND

"I really like you." He said. Stepping before her as she stepped back to lean into the tree and they kissed. *'Strange, different & scary.'* Jade had to agree she was; when asked if she was enjoying her night.

♪108♪

Eleven thirty, Mama and Papa said she was early when inquiring if she enjoyed her night? Having thought to take a spare key for the electronic gate, Jade allowed herself in, entering the house and telling those greeting her, her night was fine; before retiring to her room and denying them the chance to question her further. *'What a night?'* She saw Bobby for the first time since August and gone out of her way to make him jealous. *'Was he jealous?'* Why did she want him to be green with envy, when she was the one feeling envious? *'Wasn't Rojay enough?'* When remembering what she use to write inside the pages of her diary, Jade realised she had gotten everything she wanted. *'Rojay's girl?'* She now sat astride the leather seat of his motorbike whenever she wanted. Why, whenever she had her feelings under control did something happened to bring back the confusion? Why when with Rojay was she thinking about Bobby? *'You can't keep both.'* Recalling her brothers' words, she asked if she was with the right one?

♪109♪

November 1st

Almost twelve months ago I went to the school Ball with Bobby Hallas. What a difference a year makes? My intention then was to meet up with Rojay who promised to save me a dance, he didn't. Rojay was with Stacey. I stayed and returned home with Bobby, a nice guy, a true gentleman, Bobby was one of my kind. We got together and had fun. Tonight I was meant to attend what would have been my final school Ball, instead I met up with Rojay and we danced under the stars. Tonight when I was kissing Rojay; I couldn't get Bobby out of my head. Was he there for me? Why did he come back? Bobby or Rojay? Who do I love? Am I capable of loving either and why do they make me feel like this? Could I be in love with them both?

<u>*November 2nd*</u>
Jeremy ran into my room this morning to tell me Bobby telephoned last night to check I got home safe. Why would he do that?

<u>*November 7th*</u>
I'm only permitted out on the fields; but Rojay says everyone should know how to handle a motorbike. He is doing well at the garage, his dad says he'll make a top mechanic ahead of his elder brother. Bobby returned to his team, I never got to ask about Shannon. I haven't seen or spoken to any of the others. When I watch Rojay at work, he makes me smile, does my being proud of him mean I love him? Jimmy calls me one confused teen, while saying what he wouldn't give to have my problem. He calls Bobby and Rojay my cake and desert. I struggle to share his enthusiasm about one being covered in grease and oil, while the other gets sweaty out on the pitch and wet in the showers.

♪*110*♪

10: LIVE & DIE

♪*111*♪

With Jeremy and his friend Daniel climbing into the jag so Jimmy could drive them alongside Mama and Papa to the bonfire night celebrations being held at Gretchen's house, Jade was feeling rotten, a cold. Waving from her window, wrapped in her dressing gown and snuggling her hot water bottle, with tissues to hand, she said to give her apologies. *'Sorry.'* Having woken with a head cold, all knew she would be there if she could.

"Too many nights sleeping with your bum out of bed." Jimmy told her to get well soon and Mavis brought a tray of hot lemon, honey and warm buttered crumpets, telling her to eat the large orange if nothing else, the hard working housekeeper never failed to show how much she cared. Bonfire night, the celebrations always went on for much longer than they should when the official date failed to fall at the weekend. Coloured lights lighting up the dark night sky and bangs as loud as thunder. *'Stay safe.'* Papa insisted his little girl stay tucked up and keep warm. Moving her bedding over to the deep window seat, Jade snuggled herself down to watch what when younger she called the magical stars and exploding rockets decorating the black sky. *'Ill?'* Why hadn't she suffered such ailments when there was nowhere to go and no one to be with? Jimmy told Rojay she was sorry she wouldn't be out. *'Ten days rest was Dr. Tombrink advised.'* Sat watching as Jimmy drove away and pulled out onto the main road, Jade sat bolt upright when noticing the motorbike speed in through the closing gates. *'What?'* She worried he would be hurt upon hearing his vehicle screech to a halt by the front door. *'What was he doing?'* Why was Rojay off his bike? Had he crashed? Banging on the front door like a mad man? Rushing down to tell Mavis she would sort things,

A GEORGE

Jade found Trevor asking Rojay what he thought he was doing?

"Jade is ill." Mavis advised the demanding male to telephone whilst telling Trevor to come inside.

"You need to leave." Trevor insisted. Rojay telling his elder to get out of his way when seeing Jade exit the front opened door.

"What's happened?" Walking out onto the doorstep, Jade questioned why the biker was behaving like he was. "Rojay?" As the one who was always strong and in control collapsed into her arms, through his tears he told her it was Spike and she told Trevor and Mavis they could leave them. "We'll be fine." She moved her body down with Rojay's onto the steps as she struggled to hold his weight, sitting beside him, she held him and he held onto her. As the night skies above them exploded into a thousand colours, as Trevor and Mavis watched from inside, Rojay told Jade, Spike was dead.

♪112♪
♪113♪

Ashes to Ashes: Dust to Dust: Rubber to Rubber: Metal to Rust: Amen: Dressed in black, she stood beside the one she was there to support, her family disagreed, but she insisted she needed to be where she was. Those she stood in amongst said losing someone to speed was inevitable, crashing and falling from ones motorbike was much more a question of when? Not if? *'Unfortunate?'* Standing by Rojay's side, Jade heard how those who spent their days putting their lives on the line for the love of two wheels normalised death. A life lost to the road was a life well lived. Ratbag said being a biker meant understanding the road was king, with everyone and everything on the road seen as the enemy. Stork led the prayers as all heads bowed to remember a life taken by the only murderer to receive regular maintenance and never a sentence. Shock, for some it was their first funeral while others would stroll the graveyard to pay respects to those they'd stood to see buried over the years. *'Not slaughtered by a rival gang.'* Spike wasn't on

I MAY PRETEND

anyones hit list.*'Not taken by a life threatening illness.'* Spike had been young and healthy. *'Lost to his love of the open road.'* Spike lost control in the wrong place at the wrong time. All knew the driver of the lorry he and his cycle slid beneath would never forget his not being able to get out of the way of the young man whose motorbike had taken back control. *'It could happen to any of them.'* Every time it happened to one; others counted their blessings, fingers, toes and all vital limbs. Most had, had accidents and many carried injuries and scares inside and out, but few would contemplate giving up what each loved and valued more than life. If each was to prove themselves to be a true biker, none could quit.

♪114♪

A church service and burial, those wearing leather stood back as a sign of respect to the family of the one they called Spike, real name Terence Simon Sharp. Waiting for family and family friends to do what they needed to. *'Blood red roses.'* Each allowed the long stemmed floral tribute to fall from their hand into the open grave. *'Silent tears.'* His mother couldn't look at those she blamed for her son dying before he lived; while the look on the face of Mr. Sharp was one of respect. *'An ex biker.'* Spike made no secret of being proud of the fact his father had once rode with the largest biker gang around. Tattoos and long hair, many a suit wearing male didn't hid the fact they once did what others around were doing. Standing and paying their respects from one side or the other. *'None wearing leather was invited to where those wearing suits were heading.'* Silent respect, stood watching; Jade never realised there were so very many unwritten rules. When the funeral cars began leaving, Ratbag led all to have ridden with Spike to his graveside. Aware of what was tradition; the vicar nodded and stepped aside. Happy to stand back, those employed to fill in what had been opened to accept what was lost, gravediggers kept their distance. Unsure what to do, Jade was told to stand with Ratbag when all leather clad males gathered around the hole in the ground. Watching other females walk away, many shedding tears, some sobbed uncontrollably. Unsure what she should say. *'Devastating?'* Her own relationship with Spike had been short lived and somewhat frosty but nothing made his sudden death any less sad.

Trinkets, scarfs, badges and letters, each had something to give as each placed what was to be buried with the deceased, inside the grave.
'Gone, he would never be forgotten.'
"It never gets easier." Ratbag asked Jade if she was prepared for what she was getting herself into? "It could be any one of them next time." Her elder advised she leave if she couldn't handle the thought of her man going out one day and never coming home. "Bikes come first." Those Ratbag and Stork watched over, were nothing more than fledglings awaiting their introduction from biker boy to biker club member. "If he stays," The elder female told how a loss like this sometimes caused a biker to go solo. "If Rojay doesn't leave us, I believe he will go all the way and his going all the way means he won't appreciate being held back by a princess." Feeling like she was being warned off, Jade wanted to hold onto Rojay when he returned having filled in what would now allow Spike to rest. "Sweet." Ratbag told everyone they were invited back to hers. *'The burial complete.'* Jade reminded Rojay, Jimmy was waiting. He told her it was okay, he would be okay, when Rojay rode away with the others. Jade wondered if he would stay? He had his apprenticeship and the garage, but when he was with those who rode motorbikes; she saw how Roland Jackson became the real Rojay. Within the world of the biker, Rojay had the family support Roland Jackson lacked when at home.

Hit and used as a punchbag to prevent his alcoholic step father beating his drug addict mother. It had been his older brother Jake and his father Jack who revealed the truth of what was happening, when Rojay told her his numerous bruises, cuts and bust nose were the result of him coming off his bike. His brother and biological father were there to help, but he refused to leave his mum. When he arrived at her door she feared it was his mother who was dead. When he collapsed in her arms; she hoped he hadn't done something he would regret. Walking over to join Jimmy waiting by her fathers' car, the confused female said she knew; when he said he was sorry. Her chauffeur had only known the worst side of Spike, but like all, Jimmy was sorry about what happened.

♪115♪

November 23rd
I never saw it before; the murderer beneath our feet, it never moves yet it goes everywhere. All it takes is a drop of water, an oil spill or drop in temperature, a lapse in concentration, a raised manhole cover, a stray stone or like in Spike's case, a motorbike taking back control. Rojay said skidding on ice is like flying and all described how if a bike stops working, there is no coming back. All said Spike would've felt no fear, because an accident like his allowed no time for feeling, thinking or reacting. Gone in an instant, it is hoped his life was extinguished before hitting what sliced through him like he was paper. Spike's death seems to have mellowed Rojay, instead of talking about bikes and cars, he talks about getting his own place and starting his own business. I never realised someone like him could be vulnerable. Perhaps Ratbag was wrong about him being a born biker. When on my own I wish I could bring my boyfriend home to meet and spend time with my family, when with him, I'm beginning to feel glad its' just the us two.

♪116♪

Three months on, sat waiting inside the starchy white cubical, despite a light blanket being placed over the lower half of her body, she felt completely exposed. Having kept the appointment because she felt too afraid

not to, she hadn't had sex. Jade made every excuse not to be more intimate than she felt comfortable. With a little help from Jimmy and his ability to sound a car horn; Jade was still a virgin, but saw her missing the arranged appointment leading to a letter being sent to her home which could result in her parents finding out something where there was nothing to know. To miss the appointment would mean her repeat prescriptions being cancelled, something else the teen believed to be too big a risk to take. Jade was still with Rojay and when he wasn't working, when she stopped studying, the two had fun. *'Sweet & caring?'* They went for rides, strolled hand in hand and assisted one another with assignments and practical learning. Jade helped Rojay service and fix his bike and he shown her how to ride. Together whenever they could be, together the two visited Spikes' grave.
'Tears?' When laying the posey of deep red roses tied with a black ribbon, Jade saw tears in Rojay's eyes.

"Don't look so worried." Nurse Goods assured Jade all would be fine. "I'm just going to take a little blood first, standard practice, to check for sugar."

"Okay." Not able to watch, when asked if she disliked needles? "I don't mind." Was her reply, feeling the tightness of the elastic strap being placed around her upper left arm, followed by the nurse tapping and then the sting of the incision as the sharp, narrow, metal point of the needled made its' way through her skin.

"Are we all done?" Dr. Butler asked upon entering.

"All done."The nurse smiled. Cleaning and placing a plaster over the tiny hole in her arm.

"Hello again Miss Barris. How are we today?"

"Fine." She forced a smile as nurse Goods excused herself to send the blood sample to the lab.

"We'll wait for nurse to come back before we begin." She was told. "She won't be a moment." Funny how a moment when waiting; feels like a lifetime yet a moment when rushing takes no time at all.

"Raise your legs, knees together, then relax them and allow them to fall apart, keeping your ankles together." The doctor instructed upon the nurse's return. Following the instructions which sounded more appropriate for a yoga class; Jade complied as the male in the white coat positioned the long armed spot light to enable him to see more clearly what he was looking at? *'What was he doing?'* The metal contraption shown earlier; suddenly seemed fierce and threatening. *'Why was she putting herself through this?'*

"Deep breath."Nurse Goods advised. Stroking her arm and attempting to put her at ease. "Relax, nearly done." Jade felt wet and sticky, the sharp coldness of the alien object had seemed unexpectedly refreshing as the doctor carefully inserted it into position; but as he moved it around and took the required tissue sample, she would describe the feeling as that which one felt when listening to fingernails being scraped across a school chalkboard. For a split second she was sure she stopped breathing.

"All done," When re-straightening her legs, the teen was sure she was bleeding, alarmed by the way her legs shook and quivered uncontrollably, she felt she was losing control.

"Just tension." Nurse Goods assured her as the doctor requested she sit up before writing and giving her the prescription needed for the pill, along with a large box of condoms. *'All done?'* Jade was told to return in twelve months. *'All done?'* She had done it. *'Why?'* It was over, her first smear test was done. Aware she was not yet sexually active. *'Why?'* Why had she put herself through what she had?

"Continue taking the tablets as instructed." Dr. Butler wished her all the best before he and his nurse left her alone to dress.

Do *Take the tablet at the same time each day.*
Don't *Take two if you miss one.*
Do *If you miss one; repeat the course from the beginning.*

Jade had read the instructions over and over; taking the tiny pill regularly, religiously, but with no intention of having sexual encounters. *'Why?'* Maybe it was so she could experience what others girls her age did. Maybe Jade was doing what she was doing purely because she could. *'Did she want to?'* Jade was unsure what it was she wanted.

December 12th
Rojay is throwing himself into his work. I attended my follow up appointment on my own. What is it I'm thinking? He greets me with a kiss and tells me he misses me, but we've stopped planning dates because of his work. His dad assures me its all part of the grieving process and him working hard isn't a bad thing. Is my being proud of him the same as my being in love with him? I'm there for him and I try to understand. Is it wrong of me to want to see him smile again?

♪117♪

"Wish I was going grannies." Jeremy sulked when alongside aunt Jennifer, he and Jade waved their parents goodbye. Feeling what her brother was expressing, she said she missed grannie too. *'Maybe Jade loved those she missed so much there was no love left for anyone else?'* "Why aren't we going?" If Jeremy hadn't asked she would. "Is grannie ill?" Both wanted to know. Jennifer assuring them her mother was fine. Christmas without Mama and Papa? Unlike many would, Jade and Jeremy didn't mind being home alone, especially when Jennifer promised to do the best she could to ensure a good time.

"How are you?" With her brother rushing away to telephone Gemma; their aunt turned her attention to Jade the two entering the spacious family lounge together, the younger aware Mama had kept her sister up to speed.

"Fine." Jade admitted.

"It can't have been easy." Her elder said she was there if she needed to talk.

I MAY PRETEND

"Spike was Rojay's friend." Shrugging her shoulders she intended her tone to convince her aunt she didn't care about what happened, but she did and the wall she was putting up was as transparent as glass.

"Your boyfriend?" Jennifer requested clarification and she nodded. "Mr. Motorbike?" Jade wasn't surprised to hear Jennifer use one of the many names used by Jemima. *'A kinder name than some.'*

"Roland, his friends' call him Rojay." Aware Jennifer would use what was correct once she knew, Jade nodded when her elder repeated.

"Rojay: Bikers never use real names, it's the code."

"You know about biker code?" Jade was shocked.

"No, but I got you to smile." Smiling; Jade wasn't surprised when her aunt pointed and said there it is. Smiling; Jade said she was pleased Jennifer agreed to join them for Christmas.

♪*118*♪

Switching on the battery lamps as they climbed up into the trailer, both shivered.

"Cold?" Rojay asked and Jade nodded as sitting herself in the chair, he threw her a blanket. "Soon be Christmas." He commented as with a nod she agreed. She was already up to December 21 in her diary and the local area was glowing with a dazzling assortment of tree decorations and fairy lights. *'Almost Christmas?'* Having assisted Jimmy and Trevor in searching out a blown bulb and found herself laughing at the younger males poor attempt to hook lights over and around the trees he said would look pretty if dressed for the festivities. *'This one not that one.'* Jade was glad Sawyer had been on hand with his design expertise and critical eye when preparing the Barris's house and vast garden for the arrival of Santa. *'A house full of fun without Mama and Papa?'* Christmas, snow continued to refuse to fall from the low, white fluffy clouds, but that didn't stop it feeling cold. The absence of snow didn't prevent the ground from freezing and the route to the trailer becoming slippery. Sat wondering if she would make it back up what she had slipped and slid down, Jade said maybe they should stop visiting their special place until the winter weather got better.

"Do you know what you'll get?" Rojay inquired. Disinterested in his companions' concern.

"For what?" Jade hadn't been listening either. Having had her words ignored she was thinking back to previous Christmas's when as a shy, quiet, timid and unsure school girl she spent it alone. When passing a mirror; she barely recognised her reflection. *'Jeans?'* Time had changed many things.

"For Christmas?" Rojay asked what she was expecting to find under her tree on Christmas Day?

"Aunt Jennifer asked if you would like to come to dinner." Avoiding the actual question, the thought filled female said yes, when asked if she and her aunt had been talking about him?

"Me, in your house?"His shock was clear.

"Invited by my aunt." She reminded him Mama and Papa were out of the country. "Will you come?" The closest he gotten to the Barris's grand house had been the front steps on the night Spike died, not even in a state of distress was he permitted entry. *'Staff couldn't authorise visitors.'* "I think she is interested to see why I like you?" Jade blushed. "And why Mama and Papa dislike us being friends." She continued because she felt she knew how the mind of her favourite aunt worked. *'Friends close & invite your enemy in.'*

"When do I arrive for inspection?" He asked.

"Christmas Eve," Previously on the eve of Christmas Day Jade and her brother would be encouraged to accompany their elders in going to the home of whoever's turn it was to host the no expense spared ceremony which was the cutting of the Christmas cake and drinking of port or sherry.

"Do you want me to come?" Rojay looked to Jade for approval, as with a smile she nodded.

"I will." He agreed. Should they ever find out, Mama and Papa would hit the roof and everything else in sight, but then they would also go crazy should they learn their daughter had spent over £300 on a Christmas gift she hoped Rojay would like. *'Only money?'*

♪*119*♪

A couple, with Mama and Papa away Jade experienced a freedom never before permitted, able to go out and be with Rojay. Aunt Jennifer saw it safer to know where her niece was, who she was with and when she would be back. *'A couple?'* Allowing others to see them together, Jade was instigator when suggesting they go Christmas shopping. *'His dream jacket.'* When wandering from shop to store and checking out the Christmas market, Jade listened, looked and learned.

"You like that one?" She asked. Watching when Rojay looked through the rail of thick heavy, brown, black, blue and red leather jackets at one of the outdoor stalls.

"Not really." He shook his head. Replacing the chosen items, he said he wasn't looking to renew his wardrobe or revamp his image. *'Boots, jeans, plain t'shirt & black leather jacket.'* Jade was aware his look hadn't changed in years. *'New overalls?'* Out for hours, still she was struggling to know what Christmas gift would be right.

♪*120*♪

Christmas shopping, both had individual lists and their own money, but as Jade purchased items for her family members, household staff and friends, she noticed Rojay's reluctance to buy for others. Out together, laughing and joking as they shopped till they dropped. *'Carefree?'* In amongst the Christmas decorations, twinkling lights and jingling tunes, both felt warm. Shaking his head when Jade suggested they lunch in a top restaurant, she smiled when joining him and others to taste what was on offer from the many street venders cooking and selling their produce at the Christmas Street Market. Huddled together to protect themselves from the sharpness of the cold fresh crisp winter air, they checked out what was on offer in and outside the area dedicated to all things retail. Perfume for Jemima and something more expensive wrapped in a silk scarf for her aunt. Aftershave for Papa, uncle Kevin liked books. For Mavis her craving for Belgium chocolates and must have face cream made buying easy. Commenting on how those working for the Barris family got better gifts than he and his family exchanged, Jade said what she was doing was traditional. Explaining how staff felt more like family. Driving gloves for Jimmy and a new tool belt for Trevor, making light of what was her long list, she saw how her shopping companion struggled to know what to buy. Purchasing a silly themed sweater for Jeremy, another family tradition. *'Silliest boxing day jumper?'* The winner got to choose the afternoon movie. *'Fun?'* Whilst Jade spent money, Rojay shook his head at the numbers printed on the numerous price tags of the items he picked up, only to put back down. His mother, his father, his elder brother and his stepdad, maybe? Not a long list, but for him it seemed what he should buy for his family wasn't an easy decision. For Sawyer Jade purchased a set to include a water carrier and bicycle pump before stating how the hard work was yet to come, she still hadn't started the hunt for the ideal gifts to buy Gretchen and Tamara, the instruction being glamours, the rule was expensive.

♫ *121* ♫

21st December.
Spent the day with Rojay at the trailer, we decorated our own tree and he agreed to join us for dinner on Christmas Eve. I will be crossing my fingers and all of my toes, because I want aunt Jennifer to like him.
♫ *122* ♫
Late getting later meant keeping everyone waiting?

"Unreliable," Jeremy's words echoed inside her head as she waited for her guest to arrive, despite reassurances from her aunt that nothing would spoil; Jade felt embarrassed to see ten minutes turned to twenty and twenty become thirty before her eyes. When the clock struck o'clock for a second time, the waiting female convinced herself, her brother was right. Sure Rojay had backed out and gone to party with the bikers, she apologised to those waiting and said they should have dinner without him. Jennifer informing Mavis to give it another fifteen minutes before preparing starters. *'Where was he?'* Maybe his meeting her aunt was too much, she knew he didn't do family. *'Why agree to come?'*

"Roland Jackson?"Jeremy grinned. "Instead of Bobby Hallas, I never said this before, but I think you need help sis." Perhaps he was right, maybe she was and always would be too naive to understand the actions and reactions of others, but others were allowed to be late. *'One hour & five minute late.'* There were a million reasons why, but when waiting for Rojay, Jade failed to think of one which would make sense.

Pressing the buzzer on the gate, it was clear the one attempting to gain entry was out of breath

"Barris residence, can I help you?" Jimmy requested he identify himself.

"Rojay, Roland Jackson."Not wanting anyone to see him wearing a shirt with black instead of his usual blue jeans, he was keeping one eye on the road when stating his reason for being where he was.

"Come in." Watching on the security camera, Jimmy smiled when his father asked if he should fetch the golf buggy to go collect him. Out of breath, the approaching males body language revealed his dismay when faced with the extensive driveway to stretch from the main gate to the house. "I think he will manage." Jimmy said the expected visitor was a resourceful type.

"He's already late." Trevor told his son to inform Mavis, as shaking his head, he kept one eye on the security screen and the male who was out of his depth. "No flowers and no sign of a bottle of anything." Trevor sighed. "Good thing the Master and his Barbie aren't hosting this one." Years of employment with the Barris family meant the full time gardener anytime jack of all trades becoming an expert on what the family expected and found acceptable, their daughter dating a boy with a motorbike didn't even make the maybe list. Not suited and booted, wearing a ruby red shirt with black jeans, his leather jacket and boots weren't the type worn when ridding, but neither were they quite right. *'Dressy?'* Roland Jackson wore his brothers' three quarter length overcoat to keep out the cold, but wished he thought to wear gloves, a scarf and a hat as he arrived at the front door able to see the breath he decided to catch before making his presence known. Mr. Roland Jackson wasn't use to travelling on foot.

"Roland."Trevor greeted the one those inside awaited. "This way." The older male took from him, his coat before leading him through to the lounge.

"Apologies."Rojay said when accompanying the one leading the way.

"I didn't do the cooking son." Trevors' eyes indicated the door to the room where others were waiting.

"I was rude to you the last time I was here." The one inside what he had only imagined repeated the word sorry.

"Forgotten."Trevor smiled with a nod.

"Cricky, this place is like a hotel." Mesmerised by the height of the ceilings and amount of doors, Rojay relaxed and asked the staff member if he ever got lost?

"Roland!" Jade struggled to contain her excitement. "You know Jeremy."She got the introductions underway.

"Jeremy." Rojay greeted.

"Good evening Roland."The right and proper younger male attempted to use where he was and what he had, to gain the upper hand over the one he would fear if they met on the streets.

"And this is aunt Jennifer." Jade continued. Sending her brother a look which told him to behave.

"Pleased to meet you." Jennifer smiled. Offering her hand for Rojay to shake.

"You too.Wow! That television is like a cinema screen." Sounding like an excited child, he observed and took in his surroundings, stopping and apologising when becoming aware of the attention and concern his reactions attracted. *'Was he drunk?'* While Jade saw his behaviour being due to nerves, Jeremy commented on their guest having partaken in the consumption of a little Christmas spirit.

"Dinner is ready." Leading everyone through to the dinning room; Jennifer assured her niece everything would be fine as in a whisper, Jeremy said dinner had been ready for hours.

A grand oak table with twelve chairs set for four, white crockery sat within silver cutlery beside crystal glassware on a deep green tablecloth. Rojay was invited to sit beside Jade, who told him not to look so worried. To start there was melon followed by asparagus soup and an assortment of fresh bread rolls. Mavis smiled when the visiting male asked if the meal was over prior to receiving the main course. *'A tin of soup & a butty?'* He admitted to never having eaten more than two courses at one mealtime. Roast lamb with rosemary and mint jelly, the guest at the table gasped when noticing the amount of serving dishes being placed before him, each and everyone filled to overflowing with food. Mashed and roasted potatoes, roast parsnips and mashed carrots mixed with swede, cauliflower cheese and grilled courgettes, Jade said he didn't have to try it all.

"We can save desert to have with coffee." Jennifer also noticed their dinner guest struggling with more than the amount of cutlery laid before him. *'Christmas cake.'* There was black forest gateau, strawberry and chocolate cheesecake and a raspberry meringue if he preferred, but tradition was; the first slice of the homemade Christmas cake be eaten on Christmas Eve.

"Jade tells me you are a mechanic." Having allowed those around the dinner table to enter into whatever conversation they wanted, back in the families lounge, Jennifer began her inquires.

"Yeah."Rojay nodded. "It's a family tradition and I've always liked messing around with engines. I like fixing things." Proud of his achievements, his smile broadened when those with him agreed his career choice was challenging and worthwhile.

"You have your own motorbike." Jennifer continued and received a second nod. Complementing and thanking his hostess on the meal, Rojay said it would have been fish and chips to share if he stayed home.

"You must be Jade's aunt with the shop by the sea." With his confidence growing, he revealed the knowledge gained. "This place must feel big to you too." He said. Commenting on the house being overwhelming

"Big and cold."Jade admitted.

"I'm not cold." He disagreed, but she wasn't referring to a lack heat.

"Coffee?" Jennifer inquired as they took their seats.

"Do you have beer?" Rojay's inquiry caused Jeremy to smirk while Jennifer asked if he was planning on ridding home? "I'm on foot, that's why I was late, sorry." He explained his leaving the dream machine at home. "Black ice warnings." He told those listening it was what a biker couldn't see they needed to be wary of. "I don't take unnecessary risks." He apologised again for not having realised how difficult or expensive it was to get a taxi on Christmas Eve. "I walked." He told them. "And on slippery pavements in these boots, that wasn't easy." His words caused those with him to smile.

"Whisky, vodka, port or a sherry." Jennifer recited the contents of Mr. Barris's over flowing drinks cabinet before Jeremy informed her the beer was kept in the back fridge.

"Whisky."Rojay assured all; he could handle a proper drink.

"Wine Jade." Sending the tray of coffee and cake back to the kitchen, Jennifer told her niece she was opening a bottle of white and instructed Jeremy to have Mavis make him a shady.*'Everything in moderation?'* It was agreed a second glass of their chosen tipple would be plenty and Christmas cake would taste just as good accompanied by hot chocolate before bed.

Carrying his second tumbler of ice and whiskey, Rojay followed Jade on a tour of the building he found to be more like a hotel than a house. *'Not a home?'* She agreed when he said more than one family should be living under the huge roof. Hand in hand, she led him out into the hallway, leaving Jennifer and Jeremy to watch television, Jade led her boyfriend into and through one room and then another and another. Struggling to believe his eyes; when inside the fully fitted kitchen, both admitted to being stuffed; when asked if they wanted to join Mavis, Trevor and Jimmy making a meal from some of what was left over. *'Aunt Jennifer hated waste & told those working, to help themselves & make themselves at home whenever she was in charge.'*

"We're good thank you." Jade apologised for having interrupted the staff's down time.

"I can drive you home when ready if you like." Jimmy offered his chauffeuring service and with a warming smile which said thank you, Jade said they would let him know. *'Good people'* Rojay asked if the staff ever got any time off, in the same breath as enquiring how she and her family kept an eye on everything, when they had so much?

"We respect those we employ and in return they have never taken advantage, or given us reason not to trust them." Shaking his head. Rojay said he couldn't see himself living either life, not the lord of the manor. Mr. Jackson said he wasn't the type to give, or take orders.

"A mechanic."Jade reminded him he served those whose vehicles he fixed and he said what he did was a completely different kind of service. On through to the morning room and into the wrap around conservatory; where when looking out of the window, Rojay told Jade she lived in a hotel surrounded by a park. Having made their way around and back to the dinning room, her observant companion commented on the staff being good at their job, everything having again tidied and cleared, the room looked perfect. The Drawing room, not the same as the lounge, no television in the high ceiling multi windowed space where matching leather sofa's stood either side of a long, low coffee table before a large fireplace. *'A second reception room.'* Jade explained how the drawing room was for those whose visits were short, a room used for meetings. The large door beside the fireplace took the two into the library with his and her office areas

"Wow!" Once he got started, Rojay didn't want to leave any stone unturned or door unopened. In the basement the one living in what her companion called a maze; revealed the well stocked wine cellar and Papa's cigar lounge beside the family den ready and awaiting their next film night. *'Papa's man cave.'* Back up on the ground floor, the attached double garage was a place. *'The first & only place.'* Rojay said he would like to have should he ever own a house he could call his own. Space to keep his motorcycles and cars which was warm, clean and organised. Next was the indoor swimming pool and small private gym, showers and a changing room. *'More rooms found in a hotel.'* Rojay said if he was allowed back, he would bring his swimming shorts. Remembering back to when they first met, Rojay commented on how he could see why she never went anywhere. *'No need to leave.'* There was nowhere and nothing outside her house Jade could possibly need. *'Except for people.'* Sneaking up to her room, Jade shown Rojay the space in-which she spent most of her time.

"This place is a palace." He gasped. "If I lived here, I'd need a map to find my way around. Hope I don't get desperate for the bathroom."

"Second left down the hall, or through that door." Jade pointed to her personal ensuite.

"You got your own bathroom." Curious to see exactly what lay on the other side of the white wood door, Rojay walked over and entered. "With your own shower." He gasped.

"Spoilt bitch." Saying it before he did. Placing one of her long playing albums onto the turntable as he returned to be with her.

"You have everything." Nodding in agreement, Jade's companion told her, he would never use the word bitch. "Not inside a palace." He smiled.

"Expensive gifts to make up for the lack of love, attention and parental guidance." Telling him how things weren't always how they seemed, Jade said having things, didn't make someone happy.

"You're unhappy?" Mesmerised and overwhelmed, Rojay walked over to the padded window seat to look outside. "You can see the world from here."

"Yeah, the great big, wide, wild world." She sighed. "It's all out there going by while my world remains in here." She said as he apologised for letting her down by being late, loud and arrogant.

"I drank whisky and I'm sure I used all the wrong cutlery." He admitted.

"You were yourself and I'm pretty certain aunt Jennifer was impressed."

"Jennifer is great, like a proper parent." It seemed unfair how two people who knew instinctively how to parent; had never had children. It was their first meeting and Rojay saw how mothering came natural to Jennifer.

♪*123*♪

Listening to the low playing music, Jade felt shocked when Rojay asked her to dance?

"Here?" She questioned.

"Why not?" Why not; standing as he took her into his arms, together the two moved to the slow, low tune being played. Holding onto one another, they danced in one another arms. The mood, the scene, everything was perfect, ideal. *'A bed?'* As his lips met her lips, as his arms held her tight, as the two lost themselves in the music, in the heat of the moment, Jade wasn't surprised, but she was disappointed to be interrupted by Jeremy rushing in to say it was time for Rojay to leave.

"Jimmy is waiting." He said. "And aunt Jennifer knows the two of you are up here." He whispered his words. Informing his sister, his being there was so he could warn, not annoy her.

Rushing downstairs, those who didn't want to disappoint the woman allowing them time together; found Trevor waiting with Rojay's overcoat.

"Hope you enjoyed the day." Jennifer smiled when exiting the lounge to say goodnight. "Cake and bits." She said when having assisted him with his coat; Trevor handed Rojay a bag and box.

"The whole cake?" He questioned the size of what he would have to be blind not to realise contained much more than a slice.

"Left overs, biscuits and cake." Jennifer disagreed when what she asked Mavis to put together was seen as charity. "You were invited to share a slice of cake and everything else is what you left. An extra Christmas present. The biscuits can go to the boys down the garage." When Jennifer finished Jade heard her brother whisper the word ungrateful.

"Sorry."Rojay said. "Thank you." He smiled.

"Visit tomorrow." Jade suggested. Jennifer and Jeremy leaving the two to say goodbye as Trevor offered to take the box and bag out to the waiting car.

"Christmas Day."Reminding his partner of the time of year, Rojay admitted to it being the only day his family made an effort. *'She understood.'* Being with his family was important. "I will try." Climbing into the car, he promised to get away for an hour or two if he could.

<u>24th December.</u>
I'm glad Mama and Papa left us behind, being able to walk freely hand in hand and arm in arm with Rojay is exactly what we needed, it's what I need, what I want,

it's what's been missing from our relationship. I can't wait to surprise him with what he referred to as the ultimate dream jacket. He's no idea what I bought him.
♪*124*♪

Christmas trees, snowmen and tinsel, bells and sledges, decorations inside and out. *'Would there be snow on Christmas Day?'* This was a Christmas like no other, if home; Mama and Papa would be going out. If at aunt Jennifers' or grannies' there would be a traditional lunch to be shared sitting around the appropriately dressed table. Jennifer had given the staff the day off, inviting them and their families to lunch. Different, Jade saw what was planned to be something long over due.

"Merry Christmas."Jeremy announced. Sitting around the branch filled, ceiling high Christmas tree the youngest passed to his sister her first gift. *'Perfume & Chocolates.'* Not surprised. Thankful her brother bought something which wasn't embarrassing to go alongside the tradition sweater, a deep red knit with glitter filled baubles and bells hanging from a garland set over a fireplace with flames which waved as she walked.

"Wonderful."She admired his bad taste. *'His from her had a reindeer with snow globe nose.'*

"Fantastic."Jeremy declared himself the boxing day bad taste sweater winner, unwrapping the latest in magic tricks and a book said to uncover the mystery and myth surrounding the magic circle. It wasn't the money each spent on the other, it was each appreciating the fact the other listened, because listening resulted in each getting from the other, what he and she wanted. On Christmas morning, breakfast was whatever one wanted, which when the Barris children had been smaller included chocolate snatched from the selection box aunt Jennifer and uncle Kevin always included in what they requested from Santa.

Christmas morning, Jennifer said she had breakfast and four mugs of coffee while waiting for those too old to get up at the break of dawn to see if the man in red had emptied his sack under the tree.

"I miss this." Their elder sighed. "Families should be together at Christmas." She smiled. Jade asking what time Kevin would arrive? "Upstairs changing."When informing her niece and nephew, her husband had drove through the night to be with them; Jeremy apologised for not waiting before beginning to give out and open the gifts, many of which still sat beneath the tree. "He won't mind." Kevin's niece and nephew nevertheless said them having breakfast before present opening would give their uncle time to join in with what was traditional.

♪*125*♪

Joining in with what was happening inside her house; from welcoming Mavis, her husband Tim and their girls alongside Trevor his wife Carol, Jimmy and Sawyer all looked forward to the role reversal afternoon. Sitting at the same table. *'Big enough.'* Good food, fun conversation and the playing of parlour games. A traditional Christmas Day, The Queens speech and a movie. Kevin insisted Trevor be left to sleep; when seen catching z's while watching a Christmas Carol. *'A Christmas like few others.'* Aware of the hours ticking by, Jade hoped Rojay would arrive so she could present him with what he called his dream jacket.

"Want me to go collect him?" Jimmy offered when noticing her watching the clock. Shaking her head, she knew he would be there if he could.

♪*126*♪

The ultimate leather jacket, the equivalent of a top named designer dress, if asked Jade would have to admit to seeing all leather jackets as looking the same.

"That is the ultimate." Walking in and out of shops and stores, wandering around the Christmas Street market, sharing food and enjoying one another's company, while Jade ticked off the items on her list, Rojay continued to window-shop. "The ultimate jacket." Should he graduate to a fully fledged biker there would be patches for him to earn and his chapters waistcoat to wear, gaining his colours didn't mean he wouldn't need a real leather jacket? *'Standing out whilst blending in with his crew.'* Glancing in and up at the showroom dummy stood in the large window of the motorcycle outfitters, Rojay told Jade the jacket on display was amongst the best money could buy. "Not that I will ever have that kind of money." His sigh was deep and loud, his eyes telling how his heart felt. *'Wanting the dark gunmetal grey/black waist length coat.'* "Timeless, a masterpiece." He swooned and Jade agreed it looked fine, smart, tough and just the right mingle of colour to form a black which would stand out in a sea of pure ebony. *'A Worn look which meant it always looked new.'*

"Smart." She nodded. With a price tag of three hundred and thirty-three pounds, Rojay explained the history of what he said was hand stitched and especially made to the exact design first worn to protect more than a statement of fashion. "Nice." He said the price tag containing three threes was due to suspicion, meaning it would never change. Smiling, Jade wanted to say he was lucky it wasn't three sixes, but the fact he said he could never justify spending so much of his monthly salary on his dream when there were bills to pay; caused her to feel bad. *'Pocket money?'* Her family spent more on a night out and half the amount on a bottle of fine wine. Rojay's hard earned cash went towards essential amenities and filling the kitchen cupboards so he and his mother didn't starve.

"Let's go inside. I need new gloves." She thought quick when coming up with a plausible excuse for entering the store to have attracted and kept his attention.

"I think the gloves are over there, I'm just going to check out the jackets." Once inside Rojay was quick to take the opportunity to get closer to the jacket he dreamt of owning. Alerted to their interest, those who would have stopped his trying on what he described as being like a second skin, backed off when Jade flashed her platinum bank card.

"And this one?" As those there whose wage was dependant on commission assisted Rojay to try jackets and waistcoats for size, giving thumbs up or thumbs down, Jade smiled, laughing as her boyfriend modelled what the sales staff suggested he wear. Everything from individual items to leather all-in-one designer pieces, from the latest more streamline helmets to bandanas, like a male model, Rojay looked great in everything, but said only the jacket of his dreams felt right. New gloves for herself, a black scarf featuring studded skulls which she liked, his and hers designer sunglasses and a fragrance gift set advertised to be every bikers' must have. Jade said she could gift what she purchased to Ratbag if she changed her mind. Buying, while Rojay assisted with the returning to the hangers and shelves what he tried, Jade approached the nearest available assistant, made her purchases and arranged for her shopping, including a jacket in Rojay's size, to be delivered direct to her address later that day. *'Did she love him?'* Was it love which urged her to buy the most expensive Christmas gift she ever bought. *'He looked good.'* Jade liked when Rojay looked good.

♫*127*♫

"Roland is here." Jennifer said. Showing their expected visitor into the lounge. *'He made it?'* Kissing Jade on her cheek as she stood to greet him; he said his not turning up would be rude.

"Merry Christmas." She smiled.

"Merry Christmas, cold out is it?" Jeremy asked and Rojay nodded. "Dad dropped me at the end of the road." He revealed. "He reckoned he could get lost if he brought me up the driveway, either that or arrested?" He smiled, Telling those there; it looked like it was going to snow.

"I love a white Christmas." Jennifer said. Inviting their guest to remove his out door clothes and sit close to the fire. "My husband Kevin." Meeting under different circumstances than when first the two saw one another, both males said they were willing to move on. Aware

Rojay probably hadn't shared what was a traditional Christmas lunch with his own family, Jennifer sorted the turkey sandwiches and other nibbles so she could serve them early.

"Drink and nibbles." Jade informed her guest it was the staff's day off as he sat in amongst her brother and uncle alongside Trevor, Jimmy, Sawyer and Mr. Tim Martin. All males together, Rojay took a deep breath followed by a sigh of relief when welcomed without question.

Good food, free flowing drink and interesting conversation filled with talk of motorcars and motorbikes, as the men happily discussed all things mechanical, their intrigue and enthusiastic topics covered everything from models, performance, speed and engine size, to wheel trims, with both Mr. Martin and Trevor agreeing to give Rojay and his family garage a call if needed.

"For you."Jeremy announced. Handing Rojay a box when the time for gift giving resumed. Mavis had made everyone a hand knitted scarf and from Trevor each received seeds and a pot to grow them in.

"For indoor or out." The male who was proud of his agricultural skills said what he chose would thrive in a garden or window box, telling Rojay how placing some plants out and inside the customer areas of the garage would improve the atmosphere as well as the air.

"I'll get it sorted." The young visiting male promised. "Thank you." From Jeremy, he revealed a designer scarf and personalised pocket road map. Stunned, he was told his reciprocating wasn't necessary when apologising for not bringing anything. All continuing to watch as first Kevin and then Jennifer unwrapped perfumes, gift cards, chocolates and jewellery. From their absent parents; Jade and Jeremy received notes telling them money had been deposited into their accounts for each to go out and purchase for themselves whatever they wanted. From their aunt and uncle the two received gold bracelets,

Jeremys' being a thick link chain with identity plate inscribed with his name, Jade received a delicate charm bracelet from which her initial J hung alongside a delicate gold Christmas tree. *'Meaningful & thoughtful'* Their aunt and uncle always managed to choose gifts which were stylish and worth keeping.

A true family Christmas, with the staff and their families heading home and their elders' saying they needed to walk off the vast amount of food consumed, Jade excused herself to fetch what she presented to Rojay.

"Thanks again for the gift." Jeremy told their visitor he was welcome, before asking why he was with his sister?

"She's a great girl." Rojay nodded.

"Why Jade? You can have anyone. You've had almost everyone." He revealed what he knew.

"You don't think I'm good enough." The biker assumed his being a young rich kid meant Jeremy not knowing any better than to judge a book by its' cover and never by its' content. Rojay didn't blame him, he would protect his sister too, if he had one.

"I don't believe she's your type." Jeremy corrected his companion's assumption.

"Why the present?" Rojay struggled to understand.

"Jade likes you." The younger male shrugged.

"Yes, I do." Jade admitted upon her return. Passing to Rojay a large gift wrapped box and informing him it was his Christmas present.

"You gave me something already." He reminded her of the sunglasses and gift set presented earlier. Asking as to whether or not there was a law stating one person; one gift, Jade insisted he open the box. Watching as he fell speechless and the jacket of his dreams met his wide and surprised eyes, Jade saw the excited little boy she suspected to be hid inside. "It's perfect." He gasped. Kissing her as she sat beside him, handing to her a small, unwrapped black box from out of his pocket. Earrings and a matching pendant, colour black and gold, the

I MAY PRETEND

design was a motorbike inside a heart, unusual, it was the thought that counts. Cheap, Jade managed a smile and thanked him with a kiss, as they kissed and they kissed and they kissed.

♪*128*♪

They kissed and they kissed, together, they kissed and they walked the grounds, they kissed and they swam in the pool, exploring the house as what began on Christmas Eve continued with Rojay becoming a regular inside the Barris household. Happy to help when Jimmy asked he teach him about cars and Trevor needed assistance with the sit-on lawnmower and its' add on bucket used to remove ice and snow. Spending time together, Rojay and Jade kissed and they kissed, chasing one another from out of the swimming pool, neither heard Mr. and Mrs. Barris return, each running into the home comers to enter the house with grannie. *'Cold?'* This was what Jade meant by her home being cold, things turning from warm and fun filled to frosty in an instant, this was the reason her house would never be a home.

"What the?" Mr. Barris gasped. Each acknowledging the other's presence, all were shocked by what they saw.

"Jade."Jemima snapped. Watching Rojay as he looked around for something to cover the fact he was wearing nothing but his swimming shorts. "What is going on here? What is he doing in my house?" She demanded.

"Who is he?" Grannie asked. *'The glint in her eye revealing how she liked what she saw.'* What should have been a happy home coming; was in a matter of seconds turned into a family feud?

"Jemima?" Jennifer gasped. Entering the reception from out of the main lounge alongside Kevin. "Mum?" She questioned why no one said they were returning?

"Was it you who allowed this thug into my home?" Her elder sister insisted she answer as Jade said Rojay was her boyfriend.

"No."Papa disagreed.

"Mama, Papa, grannie, this is Roland." She continued in attempt to have her point heard and Rojay's reason for being where he was understood.

"I thought I told you to stay away from my daughter." Jerald said. "Kindly explain why I've returned home to find you here?" He requested an explanation. His eyes and expression showing his dislike of the fact the male was in a state of undress.

"He was invited." Jade interrupted.

"Roland is Jade's friend, I invited him over." Jennifer gave her support.

"You had no right." Jerald informed his sister-in-law she had no authority in his home.

"Papa." Jade was told to be quiet.

"I want that boy out of my house." He demanded. Kevin stepping in and suggesting the two be permitted to dress before anyone went anywhere. About to follow Rojay back to the changing room by the pool, Jade was told she had clothes up in her room. With a nod, Rojay assured her he would be fine as entering ladened with bags, Jimmy entered to be told to keep an eye on the one needing to dress and leave.

Insisting he was able to dress himself, Rojay told Jimmy to keep his distance.

"Just doing my job." Jimmy said he was sorry. "If they'd telephoned for me to collect them, I could have warned you." Dressed and ready, Rojay said he knew it was no ones fault. Meeting and kissing Jade on her cheek as she came down from upstairs, before the adults could speak; Rojay held his hands up and headed for the door.

"No." Jade disagreed. "Why?" She demanded. "Why not give him a chance?" She asked.

"He is a nobody." Jerald told his daughter the one leaving was no good for her, but she failed to understand how he could judge someone he barely knew. "I know his kind." Putting on his professional hat, Mr. Barris told his only daughter to go back to her room and calm down.

Attempting to get to the front door to follow Rojay, she was intercepted by Kevin; telling her it would be for the best if she did as she was told. *'Cold & dark outside.'* Not late, winter days turned into night by late afternoon in the absence of the sun. What had he expected? Rojay knew he would never be accepted by those who looked down at others because they had more. *'Annoyed?'* He wished he knew how not to be angry, humiliated because he hadn't known how to react. Walking out, he realised he'd forgotten his coat. *'What a difference a few days made?'* Walking, Rojay realised he had nothing, what little money he had and his house keys were in his coat pocket. Wearing another shirt borrowed from the wardrobe belonging to his elder brother Jake, black jeans and boots, in his hast he forgot the three quarter overcoat others told him was smart and as his anger subsided, the cold began to take hold. Watching as the electronic gates in the distance opened, Rojay was tempted to turn around and tell those wanting him gone, he wasn't ready to leave. Snow. *'There had to be snow?'* Folding his arms across his front, he knew he could walk the vast distance from where he was to his house and felt sure someone would be home to let him in, as the flickering flakes fell heavier and heavier, he didn't think he could be outside minus his coat.

"Get in." He didn't hear the car approaching. "Hurry." Jimmy hadn't turned on the headlights of the jeep, because he didn't want to be seen. Jeremy had helped with putting the needed coat and other items to include more leftovers from Mavis into the boot before instructing the chauffeur to find and take his sister's friend home. "Will you stop being so stubborn. I'm risking my job here." Putting on the brakes; Jimmy waited for the male growing colder with every step to stop, turn back and get into the passengers seat.

"Hope daddy dear scrubs the security footage." Jimmy assured his reluctant passenger the one he called geek boy was already on it. Jeremy was also the one keeping the security gates open as they continued along the driveway, turning out onto the main road before switching on the needed headlights and speeding up the windscreen wipers to clear the falling snow. Pleased he hadn't chosen the jag as the weather worsened, Jimmy said Jeremy was the one who ask he take Rojay home.

"They're not as bad as they seem. Mr. Barris is just looking out for his daughter." The one who knew the family best, attempted to have his passenger see things from the other side.

"I'm not good enough." Rojay said he wasn't stupid.

"Jade likes you." Having known Miss Barris since she was a toddler, Jimmy said she was someone who always got what she wanted. "Be patient." For someone like Rojay; his being patient was easier said than done. Rojay was someone use to getting what he wanted, when he wanted it. Roland Jackson didn't do waiting.

♪*129*♪

Within minutes a knock on the door she slammed caused Jade to avert her gaze.*'Watching the snow.'* She saw Jimmy stop for Rojay and felt more at ease knowing he was safely on his way home.

"Grannie?" She gasped. Having expected her follower to be Papa. "I'm sorry." She apologised. Assuring her eldest relative the tears she wiped from her eyes were being shed in anger; not pain or upset. "Come in." Inside the bedroom the females reunited after so long waisted no time in making themselves comfortable. Snuggling together beneath the throws in amongst the cushions on the deep window seat, the two to have been separated by miles and would always be separated by generations; agreed to liking to watch the snow falling from the darkening sky. At last, finally she had someone she could talk to. Back where Jade wanted and believed she belonged, close enough to hold and to be held by. In the excitement of getting what she wanted, Jade forgot to question why?*'Why was Loti back & where was Sam?'* "Welcome home." She smiled. A warming hug and welcoming kiss, when her elder inquired about what was going on, she agreed to having seen something she didn't understand.

"Who is the young man?" Like she always did, grannie asked Jade to tell her side of the story. Seeking confirmation to what she surmised. "A boyfriend your parents' disapprove of." Loti called her eldest daughter the most disapproving person she knew. Accusing Mama and Papa of not being fair, Jade told her listening grandparent her parents hadn't given her friend a chance. "How well do you know him?" At least grannie asked questions before making judgment.

"My boyfriend." Hoping her reply covered everything, the upset teenager revealed her having met his father and brother. "A mechanic." She attempted to paint what was a true picture of the boy she enjoyed spending time with.

"Do you love him?" There it was, the question she saw as being the most difficult to answer. "Enough to cause all this trouble?" Loti asked.

"I don't want to stop seeing him." Snuggling down with her grannie, Jade wished she could feel the same respect and acceptance, love and understanding from Mama and Papa. Inside her head, Jade told herself if Mama and Papa didn't want her, she wasn't going to stay.

'Drowning in a black sea of nothingness; tensions closed in like a volcano preparing to erupt & the egg shells on which I am walking have all cracked.'

♪*130*♪

Sweaters, blankets, underwear, toiletries and every penny she saved, collecting together everything she saw necessary to enable her escape. Jade was prevented from going anywhere without a chaperone, her every move was watched and her every word monitored to the extent where Dr. Judd was brought in to complete an unofficial assessment of her mental health. *'Brain washed?'* Mama saw her daughter as a victim, blaming her change in behaviour on others having blinded her to what was real. Jade having stopped listening to those whose rules she was told to follow, left her parents no option but to keep her under constant surveillance. Tired of the arguments and physically drained, for no other reason than her acting like a teenager. Mama and Papa raised concerns about her mental health and having overheard the plan to send her away for treatment; Jade felt her need to leave becoming more urgent. *'Some will want to go away & no longer be there.'* Teenage hormones mixed within a tangled web of messed up emotions, the being suspended between a life void of responsibility and the unknown phenomenon of becoming an adult. *'Veering from the path supported by parents & carers down the road of self discovery, uncertainty & independence.'* What would running away do to solve the life puzzle which was adolescences? Running away seemed easier than staying in a place where she no longer belonged. *'Changing when others wouldn't.'* When grannie left with uncle Kevin and aunt Jennifer, Jade had no one to turn to. Dr. Judd reporting her behaviour as risky, caused her parents to look into sending her away. A private hospital, an institution for troubled teens. Dr. Judd agreed to make enquires; leaving Jade little time to carry out what she planned. *'What she saw as being the only thing she could do.'* Having seen her house as her prison Jade felt sure that should her parents have her locked away, they would never let her out.

♪*131*♪

Party food and drink to include a bottle of whisky, champagne and red wine, taking food from the buffet table and overstocked cupboards. New Year's Eve gave the ideal opportunity for someone to slip away unnoticed. *'Her head hurt & her mind was unclear.'* When found floating in the swimming pool; Papa thought his daughter had tried to drowned herself and whenever she failed to answer the regular knocks on her bedroom door due to listening to her music, whoever was there rushed in, in dread of what they would find. *'Telling Dr. Judd she no longer wanted to be here.'* She meant here inside the house, not here in the world. Jade didn't want to die, did she? *'Her being dead wouldn't be something she thought about if others didn't keep mentioning it.'* Did they want her dead? If yes, none would be disappointed when she was gone. *'Suicidal?'* It didn't matter that she never actually said the words and never mentioned wanting to die, the fact Jade said she didn't want to be here, along with her displaying a dislike for her teenage life was immediately interpreted as her being capable of taking her own life. Ticking all the wrong boxes and being incapable of hearing the words not being said. It was the paid professionals' failure to incorporate the simple things, which blew everything out of all proportion. *'Suicidal?'* Not being asked the right questions, led to Dr. Judd filing a report which said Miss Jade Jennifer Barris was at risk. *'Unofficial, papa paid private.'* When confronted, what teenager would be brave enough to tell the pen pushing box ticker; his or her paper led judgement was wrong? *'Down.'* Dr. Judd told Mr. and Mrs. Barris their daughter was in need of counselling and shouldn't be left to spend time alone. *'A private institution?'* Jade believed she had to run, leave before she was sent away and escape before she was truly trapped. Teenage emotions misinterpreted and manipulated so the professional with certificates in all maters of the mind was able to reach a conclusion to tally with what years of research equaled a null hypothesis. *'Sense equalling, nonsense because it eradicates logic & made no common sense.'* Jade was nothing more than a teenager struggling to cope with what everyone was fighting against and quarrelling about. A teen left out, because no one was able or willing to explain them being against what she believed she wanted. *'Learning to think for oneself.'* Know your own mind. Grannie told Jade her knowing her own mind wasn't an instruction, it was needed. Told no one else can help you become you, Loti told Jade there will be life stages when others will be there to help see you through, protect and redirect you from what you find scary. *'Suicidal?'* There isn't anyone who hasn't said they don't want to be where they are. Sixteen, Miss Jade Jennifer Barris no longer wanted to be in the house she saw as being her cage, with parents acting like prison wardens. *'Time to go.'* Mama and Papa were planning to send her away, driving their frightened and confused daughter away. *'Talking often leads to walking, but no communication should equal misdirection.'*

♪*132*♪

Being the turn of Mr. and Mrs. Barris to host the New Year's Eve celebrations, the arguments to arise from Rojay being permitted into the Barris house meant visiting family members leaving early. Not wanting Jimmy to risk the job he saw as his ideal start out career, Jade left alone. Under the shadow of darkness, with everyone distracted by the welcoming in of another new year, the one certain she could no longer stay where she was, took what she saw as needed and left. *'A rucksack & suitcase.'* Behind her she left a house bursting with people, abandoning all the expensive gifts and valuable belongings. *'Possession rich, people poor.'* Behind her, she left a beautifully furnished, cosy, comfortable bedroom and the only security she had ever known. *'No time to sit around waiting to be locked up.'* Away from the familiar, nothing mattered, Jade no longer cared for the uncaring, unloving people not trying to understand. Those calling themselves family; didn't deserved a second thought and not even from the gate; did she award them a second glance. *'Struggling?'* Nothing but the barest of essentials, what she carried quickly grew heavy. *'Not strong enough.'* Jade's only thought was to where she was going to go. *'Where?'* Her aunts? There wouldn't be a bus or train for two days. Struggling to escape the long driveway, once out on the dark streets, she didn't know where she was heading, but knew anywhere was better than where she was. Jackson and son's garage would be locked up. Jade didn't know where Rojay lived. *'Where to go?'*

Cold, dark and unwelcoming, there wasn't anywhere else? Walking and stopping, resting in the bus shelter and watching those out on the streets celebrating another new year. *'Would they notice she'd gone?'* Sure it would be Jeremy to be first to check on her, she left a note telling him she would keep herself safe. *'Cold & alone.'* She hadn't expected what was wet and muddy to be so slippery and hard to move over. Underestimating the difficulty encountered when moving what normally slid with ease on its' wheels; over the rough and uneven ground. Up and down, down and up, over, slipping and sliding, descending and climbing, dragging, pulling, pushing, pulling and carrying her suitcase along with the rucksack. Awkward and heavy, dark, in the absence of artificial light she couldn't allow what she needed to get away from her. How would she cross the pipe? *'Dark?'* Night had never felt so empty and black, her hand held torch only shone on what was directly before her. *'What was that & who was there?'* How was she to get herself and everything she had over to what was her intended destination? *'Too heavy to throw.'* If it slid down the embankment she would never retrieve it. *'Clothes & toiletries?'* Carrying what she saw to be a weeks worth of food rations in the rucksack, what she lacked was the extra hands and physical strength needed to get where she was heading, the only place she could go because there was nowhere else. *'Return?'* Could she divide what she had into more manageable bags and take them one at a time? She could empty her rucksack to use for what she saw taking numerous trips. Not confident when crossing what required balance and nerve. *'Defeated?'* Rain, what she left to the elements would be ruined if it got wet. *'No washing machine or clothes dryer.'* The distance wasn't vast, but the terrain was proving difficult to navigate in the absence of light. *'Defeated?'* What was she thinking? *'Could she return?'* Rain? What was cold would soon be wet? If she fell there wasn't anyone who knew where she was and it could be days before she was found. *'Death by hypothermia?'* If found dead, her death would prove a wrong Dr. Judd to be right.

Wet, cold and tired, she couldn't remain outside if the weather got worse. Taking her rucksack first and telling herself not to look down, when reaching the other side she took out the picnic rug packed to give extra warmed and used it to place her bags contents onto before returning across the pipe to lighten what was much too heavy. Once, twice, unpacking and transporting smaller amounts, it took what felt like days and was most defiantly hours, with each crossing more treacherous than the last due to the weather worsening and the dark getting darker. Three times, four, five, six, Jade lost count of the amount of unsteady crossings she made before the suitcase was light enough for her to lift and balance across what was narrow and becoming more slippery. Fast moving, deeper than it looked and icy cold, when concentrating on the job in hand, her transporting, rearranging and repacking what she couldn't be without saw times she felt sure either herself or her belongings would end up in the water. *'If she fell, who would find her?'* If injured, how would she get help? *'Why hadn't she thought things through?'* Cold, wet and more physically tired than ever before. What was she thinking and what had she done? Leaving the heavy bottles wherever they rolled, she didn't care who found them, reaching unlocking and climbing up into the trailer, she hoped no one else was inside. What would she do if the shelter was inhabited, it wasn't warm, but it was dry and anyone or anything could be hiding in the dark? *'Rojay with someone else?'* Unlocking the door and throwing her collected belongings inside, night was making way for daylight when she eventually crawled up and into her chosen to hideout. *'Hiding because she didn't want to be sent away.'* Using what was her fading torchlight to find and switch on the lamps, she could barely believe she made it. *'Cold, wet & tired.'* Much too tired to worry about others being where she was, she snuggled down beneath a mix of coats and blankets. *'Alone?'* Not once had she thought about how it would feel to be on her own. *'Would she sleep?'* Wishing herself a Happy New Year. Her hope was that things would be better in the year she would turn seventeen.

♪*133*♪

One day, two? Opening her eyes because she needed the bathroom, the realisation of what she'd done began to hit. Waking inside what was minus any artificial warmth and attempting to focus where there was no natural light. *'No toilet?'* Having thought to bring tissue paper; there was nowhere to flush, nowhere to store rubbish waiting to be collected for appropriate disposal and nowhere to wash ones' hands. Suddenly realising all the things she and others took for granted, the one believing she would manage, feared giving up and having to return to her family home. One day, her getting wet while crouching in the long grass; made her feel like she was an animal and shivering alone beneath cold, damp covers had her questioning her choice. When one of the lamps flickered out, Jade realised she should have thought to bring batteries. Sat reading one of the three books intended to be read while traveling, the lone female worried she hadn't brought anything which was right. One day, two, two nights, three, did people know she was missing? *'If found, what would she do?'* Her returning to find the lost bottles gave her something to do, when outside she saw no one. *'Rojay?'* Experiencing a cold which penetrated her bones, if nothing else; she chose the wrong time of year to be without what a person needed to feel warm and comfortable. One day, two, three? Being the only other to know about Rojay's den, Jimmy searched, searching for a place he had never been, when what turned from mild to wintery and fierce Jimmy's searching resulted in his finding nothing, looking in the wrong places, he got close when checking beneath the railway bridge and standing at the top of the steep hill, having his sight obstructed by a thick blizzard meant Jimmy missing the figure whose footprints were immediately erased by heavy snow. Helpless and out of ideas, when in amongst those asking for information; Jimmy said he didn't know. *'When had Mama & Papa realised their daughter was missing?'* Out at a party. Her parents believed she was with those she shouldn't be with, believing she would be back when the party was over. Almost seventeen, Jerald said the police wouldn't want to know what they would call a domestic misunderstanding. *'She wouldn't?'* Why did Jerald and Jemima suddenly change their made up minds and see Dr. Judd as getting Jade wrong? Jade being missing would reflect badly on the couple whose career's required each to be cleaner than clean.

♪134♪

Having fallen into a deep sleep. *'Eight thirty?'* Looking down at her as her eyes flickered open; her morning visitor asked what she was doing?

"What are you doing here?" Rojay questioned?

"What?" Allowing her body to take a much needed stretch, she struggled to wake from what had amounted to nothing more than a catnap.

"The big guy with attitude came to see me." Rojay's words echoed as they rebounded off the cold, damp walls and Jade realised she could be found before she was lost.

"Is he here?" She realised people had started looking?

"No, but he was knocking my bedroom door down at the crack of dawn. How did he know where I lived?" *'Jade didn't know where he lived.'* When meeting, the two never visited his family home. "Jimmy." The inquirer realised. "Saint chauffeur." He sighed. Informing the one attempting to take in what was happening, his stepdad hadn't taken kindly to having his drunken slumber disturbed.

"What?" Hoping he hadn't said anything to anyone, she said she was sorry for having caused trouble.

"I told dear papa to sling his hook." Upset and annoyed. Rojay said he couldn't have police sniffing around, he had to put his bike club first. "I told him his sort weren't welcome in my bedroom." Smiling at the thought of papa being sent away, Jade's eyes sought the reassurance which was given when her companion said he hadn't told anyone anything. How could he, he didn't know."What are you doing here?" He repeated. "Have you ran away." He asked.

"I guess." Pulling the thick wool blanket around herself when moving to sit in the chair; Jade told Rojay she hadn't thought things through.

"You plan on staying?" He questioned how? Unsure, Jade knew she wasn't going home. "Why here?" The truth was, there was nowhere else. Having had time to think and considered going to her aunts, Jade realised Jennifer would have no choice but to send her home and her next home could be a mental health institution. "Do you need anything?" Rojay asked. Bottled water, cereal and a little milk, biscuits, bread, butter and jam. Asking if he would replenish what was dwindling and turned, he agreed when she said it was risky for her to go shopping.

"Batteries."She revealed her fear of losing what supplied her with light, sure she would be fine so long as she kept herself from starving. Rojay agreed to sorting something to help her stay. Agreeing to help; he shook his head and told her she was being foolish, calling her mad for walking away from everything she had, she couldn't tell him her family were thinking the exact same, for different reasons. *'Was it worth it?'* Told she left because she didn't want to be where he wasn't accepted, Rojay smiled and assured her, he would do anything for his girl.

"This makes you my girl." He said.

"You know I'm your girl." She agreed. His accidentally kicking the bag into which she placed the rescued bottles of wine and whiskey resulting in her telling him she took things from the New Years party. "I thought we could have our own celebration." She smiled and he agreed they would, when he finished work.

"My girl."He kissed and told her, he would be back.

His girl, her being with Rojay wasn't the only reason she was where she was? Leaving the only place she'd ever known was because she hadn't wanted to be sent away. Arguments and disagreements, Rojay being in her life had created a storm in amongst the calm, if she hadn't left, she would be forced to go. Did Rojay see her leaving her family to be a declaration of her commitment? From being trapped within the safe and comfortable security of her family home, Miss Barris hadn't wanted to be locked away for her own wellbeing, but now feared her attempting to escape, resulted in putting herself in a position where she would become more and more vulnerable by the hour. Looking to see if she had everything, Jade realised how in her haste she failed to pack what she took daily. Her pill? *'Taken just incase.'* What would protect her, wasn't where she needed it to be?

♫*135*♫

"I don't know." First, Mr. Barris hassled him in his own home and later that day Jimmy was asking if he knew where Jade was? "I haven't seen her. Maybe she went to that aunt she loves so much." Not the type to invite scandal, the Barris family were keeping their growing concerns in-house. Aware authorities wouldn't put his sixteen year old daughter to the top of their priority list, neither Jemima or Jerald was willing to believe Jade had run away. *'Gone?'* Mavis confirmed there were things missing and Jeremy had seen his sister with her rucksack and suitcase on the cctv. *'Gone?'* Searching? In truth Mr. and Mrs. Barris were refusing to admit there was anything wrong. Not contacting Kevin or Jennifer, believing if she went to them they would let everyone know. *'No news is good news.'* Jimmy told Rojay he was worried his friend had, had an accident, or gotten herself into trouble and Rojay assured him if he heard anything, he would let him know.

♫*136*♫

Their own party? *'What had she said?'* Whiskey, wine and party nibbles.

♫*On my Radio*♫ As the radio played they sang along.
♫*137*♫
♫*A new royal family, a wild nobility, we are family.*♫ When the song changed, they danced before singing again.
♫*138*♫
♫*I was born in a wagon of a travelling show.*♫ They sang, they danced and they listened. Alone, together, it was nice not to worry about being seen by others, nice for Jade not to be on her own, but there being no one to disapprove; meant there being no one to hear and nothing to use as an excuse should he want to get closer than she wanted him to be.
♫*139*♫
♫*140*♫
"The door is locked." His assurance sounded more like a warning as he held her close, wrapping her in his arms he allowed his hands to wander. *'An expert in seduction?'* She was aware of his experience because she knew the type of girl he liked. *'Did he like her?'* A skill, as he released what held her bra tight, Jade stepped back. *'What was he doing?'* Her attempt to laugh off what had been intentional by calling it a wardrobe malfunction sounded silly. *'What was she doing?'* Having exposed her awkwardness, the lone female said she was cold, too cold, she wanted him to back off. "My girl." He said what would be his most repeated words. Being his girl didn't make her his property. "You said you wanted to be with me?" He questioned her actions.

"I left my pill behind." Why she said what she did, she wasn't sure. "We can't." What she wanted to say was she didn't want to. *'Could she go back?'* Having left three days and four nights ago, Jade wanted Rojay to say he understood and tell her he was sorry.

Drinking, eating and dancing, had Rojay gotten carried away and found himself lost in the moment.

"Okay," He nodded. "It will be fine." He said he would fetch whatever she'd forgotten.

"No," How could he not see she wasn't ready and didn't want what he wanted? *'Not yet, maybe never?'* Sixteen, in this new year Jade would turn seventeen, not ready. Old enough, no longer a child, maturing but not yet ready to become an adult. *'What had she done?'*

"Don't worry." Approaching and continuing to touch, embracing and continuing to kiss her. *'Was this what she left for?'* Was this what she wanted? Continuously reassuring her as she sat back in the armchair, he placed his legs astride her lap. Kissing and touching from her face to her neck, over her shoulders and down over her breasts. *'No!'* Jade wanted to cry. *'No,'* She wanted him to stop, powerless to do anything when being held beneath what was his stronger, more dominating form. Afraid and nervous, the tension caused her to struggle to breath and her lack of breath meant she couldn't speak. *'How was she meant to feel?'* Was this how it felt for other girls? *'No!'* Feeling the urge to callout and shout, she wanted to tell him no, she couldn't. As his kisses ventured further down her body, the female whose every instinct told her to cover up, felt helpless to resist. Naked, within seconds flesh was being pressed against naked flesh. *'What was she doing?'* What was he doing to cause the strangest of feelings and most unusual of sensations to sweep over her? What was causing her body to tingle with an intensity leaving her incapable of preventing what felt like nothing felt before? *'Say no?'* At times she felt herself wanting to tell him not to stop and heard the word inside her head change from no, to yes: Shaking, he kissed and touched every part of her from her head to her toes, she hadn't said no and as he wrapped her in his arms and covered them with a blanket she realised he hadn't done anything she didn't want him to do. Unsure, Jade found herself describing her first sexual experience as nice. *'Not full intercourse.'* Unsure if he would stop if she asked? Jade was pleased he

I MAY PRETEND

hadn't tried more than heavy petting. Feeling safe and warm when lay in the arms of the one asking if she was okay? Jade found herself believing she and everything would be fine. Having taken her body to places it had never been, the boy who called her, his girl, assured her, he was there for her. *'Always?'* How long would always continue?

♪*141*♪

A GEORGE

11: RUNAWAY

♪*142*♪

Arriving in the early hours; having travelled through the night via train, bus and foot, Jennifer apologised for waking her nephew, too early for staff to have taken up their posts, the unexpected family member insisted Jeremy go back to his bed while she made herself at home. *'Black coffee.'* The one well acquainted with the Barris household said she would wait for her sister and brother-in-law to wake. *'Thoughtful & kind?'* Setting a fourth place for breakfast, Jennifer apologised for a second time when her presence caused Mavis to jump and Trevor to look for his trusted baseball bat.

"Did you think I was Jade?" Like all loyal employees would, neither made comment about what was being kept hidden. *'The family secret?'* Jennifer told them, they didn't have a clue.

"Black coffee?" Mavis offered more of what she noticed their unexpected houseguest drinking.

"If I have another I may drowned." Jennifer knew she wouldn't be welcome. "Do you know where she is?" She attempted to gain the information she was seeking.

"Sorry," Mavis shook her head. "I'm sure people will be down for breakfast soon." The one to have always treated the Barris offspring like they were family, said she would be sure to prepare enough food to go round.

Sitting at the table, when asked what she was doing? Jennifer told her sister; she was there to see Jade. Two months, over eight weeks, unable to believe what she was hearing, Jennifer wanted to know why she was being lied to when told Jade was with friends.

"I know she's missing." There was no disguising the fact Jemima would be looking to blame a staff member for what her younger sister discovered.

"You shouldn't be here." Having waited until Jeremy left to join friends at the local library, Jemima told her sister she had no right to turn up uninvited. "Jade is none of your concern."

"Do you know where she is?" Assuming the laid back attitude meant there was news, Jennifer reminded all of the fact she was family.

"Jade is sixteen, she can be wherever she wants to be." Jerald continuing to quote the law only caused their visitor more concern. *'Unfit to be parents?'*

"Jade is your teenage daughter and you don't know where she is." Jennifer asked Jerald which part of what she said sounded right?

"She left." Jemima defended their reluctance to take action or responsibility.

"She could be dead." Asking if either read the newspapers, the only one showing any concern accused both adults of living in a bubble wrapped dome.

"We would have heard." Jerald believed his work meant he would be the first to know if there was a murder or accident.

"Is every body, found?" Jennifer accused her brother-in-law of burying his head in the sand and filling his ears with tissue paper. "Don't you want to find her?"

"A gap year." No, they didn't know where Jade was, but believed they knew why she left. Both Jerald and Jemima felt sure the teen had known where she was going. "She took a suitcase." Jemima reminded her sister Jade was intelligent and resourceful.

"You take a gap year from education, not from your family." Shaking her head, Jennifer's inner fear turned to frustration and anger as she was told they didn't know if Jade had any money, the look they passed between one another proof they knew she couldn't get any more. Shrugging, Jemima shook her head when asked what had been taken? *'What was in the suitcase?'* "Did she take food?" Searching for hard facts; Jennifer couldn't believe nothing had been done to try to find the missing teen.

"I contacted her boyfriend." Jerald grunted before

shaking his head and admitting to have found nothing.

"She's no longer our daughter." Jemima's interruption and harsh words caused her sister to send a look which warned she should rethink what she was about to say. *'Not thinking.'* Requesting permission to check her room; Jennifer said she was looking for any and everything? *'The only one looking to find Jade.'*

♪143♪

The stables, Jennifer spoke to Tamara and Gretchen, neither of who had any idea, because neither knew their friend was gone

"Jimmy drives out every chance he gets." Not wanting to appear completely heartless, a concerned Trevor and upset Mavis said they were doing all they could. The Jackson Garage, Rojay was ready to give Jimmy a mouth full and tell him to get lost before noticing Jade's aunt. Telling his father he could manage, Rojay calmed himself before saying he hadn't seen Jade since the day he was thrown out of the big house. Nodding, he said maybe, when asked if he believed she may have taken herself off on a gap year. Returning to the car, neither Jimmy or Jennifer believed what they heard, both agreeing they hoped Rojay was keeping her safe.

Her friend, her companion, her boyfriend, days and early evenings spent listening to the radio, playing cards by candlelight, walking arm in arm and strolling hand in hand through what surrounded them, winter wasn't the time to be outdoors, when the wind joined the snow and rain, the trailer proved to be a poor shelters. A proper sleeping bag and small oil filled radiator, Jade hid when Mr. Jackson helped his son transport what she needed to where she needed it. Draughty, damp and cold, as one month moved into another; Rojay promised things would be better when the weather improved. A gas ring, Jade worried about causing a fire; but when sat shivering, she also worried about what she would do if the gas and oil ran out. Blankets and hot water bottles, Rojay stayed over occasionally, but he couldn't lose his job and wouldn't risk his failing to gain entry into the bikers club now showing interest in offering Jackson's garage the type of contract they couldn't refuse. Arguments, blame and accusations, while Jade was left counting her money and dividing her rations into equal daily amounts. Telephone calls between family members were filled with anger, upset, blame and growing concern. Papa, her aunt, grannie, her brother, Jimmy and Sawyer, all looked but none could find what they were looking for. Afraid the scandal would lose him the position and career he worked hard to gain. It was with a heavy hearts Jennifer and Loti agreed the authorities shouldn't be involved. *'A family secret?'*

♫144♫

No disagreements, no misunderstandings and no one getting between them, bathing in a tin bath Rojay created from an old oil drum, it took two large pans and a kettle of boiling water collected when it rained to make the temperature of the water tolerable and its' depth enough to cleanse. *'Strip washes with soap & a flannel, cold showers standing under tipping buckets wearing her swimming costume.'* Jade wasn't looking forward to fetching water from the river in the absence of enough rain. Wet, muddy and cold, she hated when her needing the bathroom meant having to go out in bad weather or the dark. *'A bucket for wet emergencies only, never to be emptied close by.'* Sometimes she surprised herself with her housekeeping. Evenings spent listening to the radio, sometimes singing and dancing along, Rojay always said she smelt good on a bath day.

"I love you." Did he? From holding one another; he stood. "You love me." He said. *'Did she?'* Watching as he began to remove his clothes, she felt she should close her eyes, removing his jeans to reveal bright red and white Y'Fronts, she doubted he noticed the fact she hadn't answered. What was he doing and why had he said loved? *'Lovers?'* They hadn't, but they could, would they? From holding, kissing and caressing; things had moved on a little. Picking up the packet of condoms to have fallen from his pocket, she knew she should be glad he remembered the small matter of precaution. *'Were they ready?'* Closing her eyes tightly shut; she wasn't sure how they got to this point, but knew there was no going back. Not wanting to look, Jade didn't want to watch, but couldn't prevent herself from hearing, unable to close her ears; she lay blinded by nothing but her own eyelids, her inability to see not stopping what she was imagining. Unable to stop the images inside her head, she knew what was happening and her knowing made her want to sneak a peak. *'Had they agreed?'* Like when you get into the seat of a rollercoaster and the safety bar locks; there was no turning back and no way of stopping what was about to happen. From talking to kissing, that to have advanced quickly was now out of their control. *'Was this how it always happened?'* From kissing and caressing, that which had become passion filled, created an urgency carrying each of them away in the moment. Yes, she said yes and now neither wanted to say no. *'Unable to stop.'* They were of legal age to consent, in a trusting relationship, they knew one another well. He asked if she was sure and she told him yes. *'What had they done?'* As he lay heavy upon her, it was over. He was the one who knew what he was doing and what he was doing, he did quickly.

♫145♫

Where were the sparks and the fireworks? Was he hiding the big brass band, because from where she lay beneath him; it felt like the earth was holding firm and rock steady, nothing had moved. *'What had they done?'*

"That was fantastic." Rolling off and laying on his back beside her, all Jade felt was confused. A tingle, some fumbling around, a strange cramp and a little discomfort, why was he breathless? His breath, his lips and his hands, his flesh against her flesh, having experienced the mechanics, what occurred lacked emotion. *'Her first?'* When he said fantastic, she wanted to ask if that was it? Physically, she knew what had happened, emotionally she was left feeling nothing. Not sad, not happy, when he said he needed to leave, she was left disappointed. *'What happened?'* Wondering if what had happened had been wrong? *'Your first time should be special.'* Everyone said so, Jade couldn't laugh and she didn't want to cry, neither had done anything wrong; leaving her to conclude what had happened; had happened with the wrong one. *'Sex.'* Not happy and not feeling sad, all she felt was sure that with Rojay; she wouldn't be having sex again. *'Did she love him?'* Neither had done anything wrong, yet nothing felt right. Bringing chocolates, a card and roses, she apologised for not being able to go out to get what on Valentine Day was exchanged by those said to be in love. A night invented for lovers, what happened, happened on a date which wouldn't be easy to erase.

"Fine." She assured him everything was okay, but realised nothing was how it should be. Noticing how he watched whenever she took money from her bag, she waited for him to leave before splitting and placing what was her everything, into places she hoped he wouldn't look. *'Would he steel from her?'* He said he loved her, was it because she knew she could and would never be in love with him. Wary? Her first? Jade promised herself their first full sexual encounter would be their last. *'He had done nothing wrong.'* He was just the wrong one.

'Fish & chips eaten by candlelight.' Romantic, if she loved him, Rojay was doing everything right. *'What had she done?'* What should and could she do when what seemed the right thing was creating all kinds of wrong? February brought so much rain there were times the trailer became inaccessible. *'Never seeing herself as being someone who would be thankful for a pair of wellington boots & a bigger bucket with a lid.'* March through into April. The beginning of another month brought showers which sometimes caused floods high enough to submerge the pipe needed to cross, to get to where she was. *'Nobodies fault.'* Minutes, hours and days, with time losing all meaning, her being alone was

proving to be nothing like she thought it would be. April was a month known to change dramatically from its beginning to end.

"You look ill." Passing the flask of hot soup meant for his lunch, Rojay made no apology for the amount of time allowed to pass since his last visit.
"A chill."Attempting to convince both him and herself that the constant headaches and shivering was nothing more than a common cold. Jade pushed his advances away when he attempted to get close. "Can you fetch me something to help? From the chemist."She said she didn't want him becoming ill.
"Sure."Snatching the money she took from her pocket, the male preparing to leave said he would be sure to fetch body spray and mouthwash too."Anything else?" Sniffing and wrapping her shaking form in the blanket she allowed to slip, Jade told him no.
"Can you bring what I need tomorrow?" Finding and placing the sleeping bag over her shivering and sneezing form. Rojay kissed her forehead and bid her goodnight. *'Looking a state.'* If feeling well, she wouldn't blame him for wanting to get away from her. If feeling well, Jade felt sure she would be doing all she could to get away from herself. *'Homeless?'* Having done all she could to prevent what was inevitable when fitter and more able bodied. *'Washing when able.'* Jade was ill and Rojay failed to visit for days. *'He took her clothes to put in with his washing when he could.'* Items found by his mother, were items she would never see again because he told her they came from charity shop. *'Gifting her clothes to cheer his mum up.'* Rojay's helpfulness was leading to Jade running out of things to wear. *'Ill?'* For the first time in her life Jade didn't have anyone to look after her. *'Alone?'* All she wanted to do, was sleep. Cold and tired, run down and running out of everything she needed to keep her physical self together. Dark, cold and lonely, having lived in the trailer for months, she felt weaker than weak. Lay alone, Jade felt frightened. *'The*

illness?' Startled by every strange sound. *'Alone?'* Nervous and unsure, she knew the sounds supplied by nature to indicate the difference between night and day. *'Unwell?'* Drifting in and out of uneasy sleep, she felt worse each time she woke. *'What was she doing?'* Where was she? Her nose seemed three times its natural size, her head felt like it had been hit by a hammer and her aching body shook uncontrollably, pain filled, sore and tender to the touch. Paper tissues filled the wicker wastepaper basket and sweat poured from every pore. *'Her punishment?'* Was this Jade receiving her reward for running away? *'Why had she ran?'* If it had been so she could be with Rojay, it was time to admit her mistake and go home. *'Would Mama & Papa send her away?'* Would her being institutionalised or incarcerated feel anything like she was feeling? *'Forgetful & confused?'* Pill boxes and a glass of water, her vision was blurred while her life felt how she'd imagined it.

♪146♪

"Again! More! Again!" Everything was white, a buffet laden table with a three teared wedding cake. "Yes." Rojay's smile turned to a smirk as he walked forward, encouraging the one he was holding to step back. *'What was he doing?'* Moving from the dance floor to up against the table, he lifted the layers of net, silk and lace which skirted his brides' long, soft, flowing gown. "Yes." He repeated. "Yes, yes, ye," Why was he saying yes when she was telling him no? Lay back and shutting her eyes, her mind was clear, thinking of nothing, she held her breath, clenched her fists and prayed. *'Mrs. Jackson, Mrs. Jackson?'* Had he really done what she didn't want him to do? Opening eyes she would rather keep shut; the faces of friends' and family circled what was her upright stature. *'Had they seen?'*

"Mrs. Jackson?" All encouraged the bride and her groom to retake the floor.

"We told you." Seeing smiles beside looks of disapproval when twirling into the arms of her new husband, Jade had no clue where she was? Mama, Papa,

Tamara, Gretchen, Tarquin, Greyson, Swayer, Jimmy, Trevor, Mavis, Ratbag, Stork, Stacey and Spike? *'Spike shouldn't be there. Spike couldn't be anywhere.'* Grannie, aunt Jennifer and uncle Kevin, Bobby stood with his parents. *'Why?'* Where were they? Where was, there? Everything was white, was she in heaven? Her wedding? Jade didn't want to be married. *'Married before doing what they did.'*

"We told you so."
"You wanted him."
"You asked for it."
"You got him now."
"Mrs. Jackson."
"His girl for keeps."
"Yes, yes; yes!"
"Mrs. Jackson."
"Yes, yes, yes!"

"No! No!" Screaming out; she released the word to have gotten stuck deep inside her throat when taken by her husband on the buffet table. "No." She cried. Her eyes opening as she awoke to discover herself alone. A dream, another nightmare? Unaware of the time, her not knowing what day or date it was, didn't matter as her fever broke and she drifted into a much more restful and peace filled sleep.

♪*147*♪

Another day, April would soon make way for May?

"What's the time?" She asked when Rojay found her sitting by the river. Having lost count of the amount of days and nights spent drifting in and out of her fever filled nightmares. Feeling better, she spent the day outside, having bathed, she was wearing clean clothes when her infrequent visitor commented on her looking more like herself. *'Her hair needed cutting & a manicure was well over due.'* Cleaner, she remembered how he said the word cleaner when comparing her to his other girls. *'Was he seeing another girl? Stacey?'* The truth was, he could do whatever he wanted while she was keeping herself out of sight. Feeling better, Jade felt it was time to go.

"Seven," Having waited all day for him to bring essentials, it was clear he was also growing tired of the ongoing situation. "Do you want to go for a ride." He asked. Declining, she said it was late, he was late. Complaining about how they never did anything, Jade heard herself apologising for being ill. "Your loving Mama and Papa are out of town." He assured her, she wouldn't be seen if she joined him.

"Where?" She asked?

"I forgot to ask." He mocked her stupid question.

"I should leave." Admitting to things having gone on for longer than they should, Jade told Rojay there was no need for him to stay.

"You're going home?" He asked.

"No," She shook her head.

"Then you can't leave." He said if she had nowhere to go, she would have to stay.

"I can't stay here like this for the rest of my life. It's time to start over." She sighed. "I doubt I'll survive if I fall ill again." Her feeling better and her parents being away, meant it was time to make a move.

"You can't leave." Rojay protested.

"Why?" She asked

"Because you are my girl." He told her.

"You'll find another." Remembering how he was rarely alone for long, she assured Rojay he would find someone else. "It's been fun." She forced a smile. "I will always appreciate all the things you did for me." She said. "I will leave the key when I go." She promised.

"I won't let you go." Taking a grip of her arm."I can't let you go." He told her. "I love you." He said, but she disagreed. "I need you." He insisted as she pulled away, shaking her head and telling him no. "Jade I love you. You know I love you." He insisted. *'What was that look in his eyes?'* Why were her words causing him to look scared and angry? Why was him looking scared, frightening her?

"I have to go." Her mind was made up, their relationship was over. A good person, Rojay wasn't the right person. *'Young & foolish?'* Having allowed herself to be blinded by the excitement of something different and fallen under the spell which was the enjoyment of everything new. Realising her feelings for Rojay had been infatuation. *'She was sorry.'* Assuring him, he would be all right, she promised to clear his name should she hear him being blamed. "I will leave in the morning." Bidding him goodnight and making her way back to the trailer, she expected him to go, she thought he would be relieved. *'No more looking out for her.'* No more keeping her secret and having to sneak around. He could have his den and his life back. *'Jade needed to move on.'*

"No!" Turning and lunging himself forward. His sudden action caused his stunned companion to run. Noticing what was in his eyes turn to hate as he took chase, Jade felt the need to get away. Running she realised she was still weak, reaching and attempting to climb up into the trailer, her intention was to lock herself inside. "No, you don't." Catching hold of her leg, he pulled her down onto the hard, cold, damp ground. *'She wasn't dreaming.'* "You're mine." He told her. "Mine, mine, mine." He insisted as she struggled to regain her freedom.

"No, this is wrong."Attempting to reason with her capture; she quickly became aware her escaping his grasp was impossible. "No!" She yelled. "No, I don't want this." She screamed, continuing to scream and tell him no. Large, heavy and strong, his male hand struck her across her face with a force almost rendering her unconscious. "No," She wept. *'Not a dream a nightmare.'* When it was over, Rojay had taken from her, her pride. Taken against her will, when taking her for his own sexual gratification he had taken her everything. *'Why had he done that?'* "Let me go." Having screamed and

311

sobbed, her shouts, protests and tears had been in vein. Lay across the bean bags inside the trailer, her entire body trembled, shaking uncontrollably, she continued to cry silent tears. Having begged him to let her go. *'What had he done?'* Who was this beast? How could he love her and do what he did? From a place which felt like a prison, Jade found herself imprisoned.

Bruised, scratched and sore, unable to move for fear of further punishment, in the scuffle, her companion referred to as being a bit of fun, she was beaten, injured and abused. *'What people in love did?'* Was he really so blind he failed to see the fear in her eyes, why was he ignoring the fact she was hurt? *'He hurt her.'* She told him no, but he did. The sexual assault following the physical attack was brief. *'How could he?'* She told him no, crying and begging he stop. Too fast, too heavy and much too strong, her body had given up and surrendered the moment he and his took what he wanted. *'His girlfriend?'* He said it was what boyfriends and girlfriends did. Why hadn't he listened when she said No? *'Unprepared?'* His forcefulness resulted in her sustaining injuries, leaving her pain filled inside and out. *'Not what she wanted.'* His strength and continuing dominance left her feeling vulnerable and weak. *'No meant No.'* Jade found herself wanting to be left alone.

"When I don't go to work tomorrow, Jake will think I've run away to be with you." Insisting he keep a twenty-four hour visual on the one wanting to leave, Rojay said he was staying because the two had already spent too much time apart, there because he loved her. *'There for her?'* If this was him caring, she wished he would stop. "We should go to the cinema." When he talked she listened. "A good gangster pic, I see myself playing one of the bad guys." *'How & why would she disagree?'* Apologising for having caused her skin to bruise, he refused to see what happened as wrong. *'Playing rough.'* Telling her, he told her he loved her.

'Just a bit of fun?' It was four days before he returned to work and for four days he took care of and looked after Jade. Holding her to keep her warm at night, their conversations strayed from what had happened to talk about what would be. Rojay said he wanted to make the trailer into their forever home, while Jade avoided saying what was on her mind. *'Jade wanted to leave him.'*

April, May would bring another birthday. *'Flinching when he came close.'* No longer sure what he would and wouldn't do, she wasn't fast enough to out run him and no way strong enough to fight him off should he attack again. April, if she had her diary to write in, she wouldn't know where to start. If Rojay wanted to become an actor, she could write a plot where he played the bad guy. *'A big bad baddy?'* Keeping up the pretence, happy when fooling everyone including himself. Naive and vulnerable. *'Educated in the classroom created a novice in life.'* April, the installing of extra locks meant her companion come capture being able to make sure she stayed inside whenever he was out. *'Why?'* He said he was looking after what he loved, loving her didn't mean he owned her. *'Her bad guy?'*

"No," She shook her head when offered a biscuit.

"It's no wonder you get sick, you hardly eat." He said. Entering the fourth week in the month of May meant Jade would soon turn seventeen, eating little because she was feeling sick. *'Cold & tired?'* Rojay saw what was genuine as being pretend, her way of getting to go outside. *'Being physically sick.'* Her companion come prison warden said it couldn't be anything she ate, not when she was eating next to nothing.

"I need to see a doctor." May, she didn't want to turn seventeen while imprisoned and wondered if her parents would celebrated her birthday in her absence? Like when she said no, her pleas for help went unheard.

"I wouldn't run. I couldn't. I'm ill." She sighed when saying she needed air.

"Again?" Rojay complained. "You are always ill."

"This place is damp." The ailing female searched for an explanation to what she saw as being another cold. *'The flu?'* She would feel the true heat of summer soon. *'Not soon enough.'* Finding his hostility difficult, Jade refused to accept his actions' as being his way of showing how much he loved her. *'Afraid of losing her?'* Couldn't he see he already had? May ninth. *'How had May come around again so fast?'* Insistent on how spending time outside helped her feel better. *'In need of vitamin D from the sun?'* Her hope was the more times they climbed in and out of the trailer, the more likely it would be he would forget to engage the locks?

Another mistake, Jade was becoming expert in doing the wrong thing. *'Had he gone?'* Searching for her money, she discovered what had put the fear in his eyes. Robbed. Why? If he asked she would have given him her money. Had he taken it so she couldn't leave? What she had in her jeans pocket plus fifty pound hidden in her makeup bag and another fifty placed within the lining of her handbag. *'He had taken everything?'* Having arrived with savings of almost two thousand pound, what was left totalled £153.27. Despite promising she wouldn't, when the opportunity arose; Jade left. Thankful for a dry day, never in her life had she felt so wobbly and unsure. *'Which way?'* She couldn't go home. Struggling up what was steep and in places bumpy, moving across what was slippery, she almost gave up. *'Not strong enough?'* Blaming the way she felt on her lack of nourishment, aware this could be her one and only chance, she knew there was no time to waste. The bright daylight dazzled causing her to feel dizzy. *'Low blood sugar?'* She needed to get away. *'Where would she go?'* There was no going back. Unsure how long she had, she knew she was taking too long. *'What else could she do?'* Leaving her suitcase, the rucksack packed with next to nothing felt heavy and her balance created a stagger which would cause others to steer out of her way.

Why had he turned from friend to foe, going from her boyfriend to captor? Was he mad, crazed or insane? Whichever? Whatever? She had to leave, she had to get away. Having crossed the pipe and climbed the hill, she questioned whether she should go over the railway bridge, or follow the track to the next exit which would lead her onto a road. Needing to remain out of sight; the latter was what she decided, making her way down to the buzzing train track, her eyes struggled to focus when it was time to cross. *'Would she hear a train?'* Wobbly and uncoordinated, when looking down at the two sets of tracks she stood on the wrong side of; she saw many more than the four solid rails. *'Unable to get up if she fell.'* Jade didn't want to trip and couldn't risk taking a fall. One foot in front of the other, she looked left and then right and then left again. *'Much quieter than crossing a road?'* Lifting her feet high to avoid the hazardous obstructions. *'More catastrophic if an accident should happen.'* Being blinded by daylight made it difficult to see. Jade wished she could rush, but knew the best her body would manage was to hobble her way along.

♫148♫

A bus to take her to the train station. *'Where else would she go?'* Like many an escapee; she felt the urge to rush and wanted to run, she couldn't. *'How far?'* Not far, not much further, repeatedly telling herself she could and would make it, with every step her eyes scanned her changing surroundings and with every flicker glimpse of something; her heart skipped a beat. With Rojay out and about on his motorbike, her standing at a bus stop was a risk and her walking meant she should keep listening if she was to remain out of his sight. *'She could do this.'* Weak and tired, making herself as presentable as was possible, it hadn't been her intention to allowed her hygiene and health to suffer, but knew she didn't look or smell her best. *'Aunt Jennifers?'* There was nowhere else, it was where she should have gone. *'A bus?'* Her ears worked so hard they hurt, the sound of the approaching transport being joined by the sound of an accelerating motorcycle left her questioning what she should do? *'Which would get to her first?'* Others in the bus shelter moved in readiness to embark what was approaching, visible to all who passed, she couldn't not get on what was on time, she didn't know when the next would come. *'Please don't be him.'* Aware of the fact not all motorbikes sound the same, what Rojay rode was popular and what was about to go by could be him.

"One please." All buses went into the city centre and the centre would be more crowded, a safer place for someone not wanting to be found. All buses went into the city, but no bus was quicker than a motorbike, if not him, it wouldn't be long before others would be on her trail. A rebel, he wasn't the brightest light on the Christmas tree, but unlike many believed; Roland Jackson was far from stupid. Her house, the bus and the railway station, it wouldn't take him long to workout her options. The bus, if not a widow seat, she wouldn't see him coming, if taking a window seat, she risked him seeing her first. *'Upstairs or down?'* Too weak to waste energy. *'Front or back?'* Other passengers made it clear they didn't want her sitting beside them as she sat alone.

♪149♪

"One way, thank you." She told the enquiring female in the ticket booth she was fine.

"I'm fine." She repeated. When while on the platform a young baggage attendant asked if she needed help? "Fine." She lied. Sitting on one of the wooden benches away from where others using the busy station could see. *'Needing a ticket to get where she was.'* Jade knew Rojay would jump the turnstile in the blink of an eye should he spot her.

"Why not get yourself a cuppa, this train isn't due for ages yet." She understood he was only being helpful, aware he was going beyond what was his job description, she didn't want a fuss.

"I'm fine, honestly." Relieved the friendly male wasn't someone who knew her, she hoped he wasn't a friend of Rojay's. *'Aware not all bikers wore leathers & patches twenty-four seven.'* Jade knew her not knowing the friendly male, didn't mean he didn't know her. Rojay's old lady? Not yet of an age to have made any of his pledges. Ratbag warned her how being with Rojay would mean her life no longer being her own. *'Jade hadn't realised her body & mind wouldn't remain hers either.'*

"Going somewhere nice?" Sitting by her side, his concern was clear as he engaged in conversation.

"A friends."Jade couldn't trust who she didn't know.

"A short stay is it?" He noted her lack of luggage.

"Not sure, maybe I'll stay forever." Going and staying away was what she wanted. Introducing himself, Simon asked if she was ill? Jade looked ill.

"Flu, I can't seem to shake it." Wasn't that the truth, at least she would be warm and properly fed at her aunts, Coughing and shivering, looking forward to being comfortable and warm after so long of feeling nothing but cold. *'Lucky to survive?'* How could she be so foolish? What was she thinking? What she was thinking now was how her parents' wouldn't understand and her friends' would never forgive her. A lack of nourishment caused by her reluctance to eat, her not wanting food was because she didn't want to be sick, she couldn't stop feeling sick. *'A chill, the flu?'* Over the passing weeks there was plenty of time to think and ponder, time to wonder and worry about her presenting ailments. *'Sick?'* She reached a number of conclusive could be's, she could have caught anything, a virus, or a fever? *'An allergy?'* Suspecting all and everything from an allergic reaction to a sexually transmitted disease, everyone had heard the horror stories which surrounded unprotected sex. Having read the facts and explored the myths; Jade still knew next to nothing about the symptoms of the many things all sexually active people were told to fear most. Maybe that which felt like it was eating away at her, was the big C? Feeling constantly sick, weak and tired, drained of all energy and much too frail to muster any emotion. Had what took Gramps returned to take her? Maybe Gramps saw her as being better off with him? *'Her wish was to talk to gramps?'*

"Here," Having left momentarily, Simon returned with a cup of hot chocolate, sweet and creamy.

"Thank you." Gratefully accepting his kind offer, if nothing else, the warmth from the cup heated her hands. "Have you no work to do?" Her inquiry wasn't her being rude or ungrateful, it was merely a question.

"My break, my next job is your train." Sat awaiting her transport, she was pleased when the platform got busier, while not being able to prevent her everything from urging the train to arrive on time. "Are you running away?" Unable to answer truthfully, she shook her head. Telling Simon not to worry, she drank the chocolate and repeated the line about being fine."I see em all the time." He nevertheless began."Runaways." He continued."Few ever return once they board." His tone lowered as his words told of what he knew. "I see the parents too." Listening; Jade knew he was only trying to help."They sit here for days in hope of being reunited with someone they've lost. I've seen them get down on their knees and pray, asking the trains to return what they take." He sighed.

"You'll not see my parents." She assured him.

"You are on the run?" He continued to pry.

"No."Jade shook her head.

"At least your getting onboard and not planning to go under."A purchased ticket. "And you look old enough to be on your own." He commented.

"Seventeen."She nodded. *'Almost?'*

"I've seen them as young as seven."

"Seven."Jade gasped.

"Like I said, it's the parents I feel sorry for." The parents? In all honesty Jade had stopped thinking about Mama and Papa a long time ago. Better off without her. *'Confused?'* Assisting her to board, Simon insisted he escort her to her seat, passing a bottle of water, an apple and a small chocolate bar he called the best she would ever taste. *'Kind & thoughtful.'* She thanked him and said she hoped he wouldn't get into trouble. "Perks of the job." He smiled. Refusing her offered payment. "You take care." He said. "Hope to see you back soon." He nodded before leaving.

"Thank you."All she once felt sure of now left her feeling afraid. A place to sit and plenty of time to rest, the train was warm, so why was she struggling to get comfortable. Seven? Seventeen? Was there a difference? Age? Years? Time? Jade wanted to cry, she wanted to scream, to shout and call out for help. Instead she took her seat and sat in silence, quickly becoming mesmerised, hypnotised by the passing scenery she drifted to sleep, relaxing, sitting alone on the train Jade drifted away to somewhere else? *'Was she dying?'*

♪150♪

Wherever she was, leaving.

"Can I help you?" Coming across the one running onto the platform as the train pulled away, Simon was just doing his job? "Can I see your ticket please?" Running and rushing; the one to have left his motorbike in the carpark didn't have a ticket. "Sorry you missed it, the next to that destination is tomorrow." Helpful, Simon directed the angry looking male to the ticket booth.

"Did you see who got on that train?" Rojay asked.

"A lot of people got on that train." Simon struggled not to smile. "Were you looking for someone?" He asked because he wanted to delay whatever could be the biker boys next move.

"My girlfriend," Later than late, Rojay's eyes saw nothing but the rear of the train as it disappeared down the track.

"I noticed a lot of couples and families." Simon said he was sorry he couldn't help before insisting the searching male leave the platform, or purchase a ticket. "The next train is going into the city." He said.

A GEORGE

"Where was that one going?" Having failed to check the departure board, as Simon looked up to see the trains destination disappear from what was constantly changing, he said Scotland. "Glasgow," Watching as his information caused the one carrying his motorcycle helmet to back up and go look elsewhere, Simon believed his white lie hadn't done anyone any real harm. Watching as the leather clad male checked the list of trains ready to leave; Simon saw what looked to be the look of angry being replaced by disappointment. *'Glasgow?'* Rojay saw it as possible his wealthy girlfriend would run to a place she wouldn't be found while seeing her not being at the station as a sign she had very probably returned to her rich, comfortable home. *'If home? He had all the time in the world to find her?'*

♪*151*♪

Wherever Jade was going, she was leaving everything to have happened and all she had known behind.

"Hello, Hello can you hear me?" Opening her heavy, tired eyes, the white brightness of light almost blinded as it took from her, her vision, sinking directly down into the back of her eyes, hurting her head. Lay flat on her back, she felt shocked to find a young, uniformed female standing over her. "Hello, I'm nurse Thompson." What was happening? Had the train crashed? "You are safe, you're in hospital. Do you remember what happened?" Shaking her head, Jade had no idea where she was? Simon and sitting on the platform, she remembered taking her seat on the train. "You collapsed." Collapsed? Jade remembered closing her eyes. *'Was she dreaming?'* "Do you feel any pain?"

"Fine, I'm fine." More lies. She felt weak, dizzy, tired, sick, frightened, lonely and confused. "I need to use the bathroom." The feeling she felt was urgent.

"Of course." Assisting Jade into a sitting position nurse Thompson said she regained consciousness only a few moments before being admitted onto the ward. "Slowly." The nurse held her arm so to lead Jade over to what was an ensuite inside the private sideward.

"I can't stay." Thanking the smiling female for her help, Jade said she was sorry. Having used the bathroom, the confused teen found herself put into a wheelchair and wheeled into a private consulting room. "I can't stay." She repeated. Feeling afraid of what she was going to be told, she wasn't sure she wanted to know what the nurse and doctor had to tell her? *'What kind of hospital was she in?'*

"The doctor would like a word."

"Dr. Burlington," Young, the attentive female entering the room introduced herself as she sat opposite where Jade waited on the other side of the large oak desk. "How are you feeling?" Telling nurse Thompson she could leave. Dr. Burlington looked to her patient.

"Fine." Jade continued the lie.

"Do you remember what happened?"

"I collapsed." Believing someone had struggled to wake her from her sleep, Jade repeated what she was told, not what she actually remembered. *'Remembering nothing.'*

"And why would a young girl like you do that?"

"I'm tired."Exhaustion.

"I need to ask a few questions?" The concerned doctor began."How old are you? Sixteen?"

"Almost," Jade corrected the assumption. *'Almost?'* The calendar beneath the wall clock said May eleven, Jade would be seventeen in ten days.

"Are you anorexic? Do you know what that means?"

"Yes, and no, I'm not anything but tired." Jade insisted she just needed to rest. *'A good meal & a warm bed.'* Grannie said either was good for you and both could help anything feel better. *'Aunt Jennifer would help put everything right.'*

"Nevertheless you seem malnourished. You haven't been eating properly." Jade guessed the female wouldn't be a doctor if she didn't know what she was talking about and there was no disguising what the medical professional was looking at.

"I guess not, no." She shook her head.
"Can I ask why not?"
"I haven't felt hungry." It was as good a reason as any.
"Have you felt sick?"
"A little," She nodded.
"Have you actually been sick?"
"Yes," Nodding, Jade realised the doctor and some expert advise was what she needed, seeing no sense in holding back the facts, she wouldn't openly reveal what were her true suspicious.
"Where are you going?" The health professional said she needed an address?
"To visit my aunt and uncle." Jade said she didn't remember the postcode or house number.
"Have you been living rough?"
"Not exactly."Yes, it had been rough, but she hadn't been out on the streets.
"No?" Dr. Burlington questioned what was negative.
"I've not been living in a house, it was a trailer." Unhappy about having to talk about what she wanted to put behind her, Jade kept what she was willing to disclose to a minimum.
"Are you a traveler?" It would make sense if she was.
"I left home for a while to live with." She hesitated.
"Your boyfriend? Could you be pregnant?" Pregnant? Pregnancy was the only thing not to have crossed her mind. Pregnant?
"Yeah," Yes, unfortunately it was possible and yes, she and her boyfriend had been in a relationship."Yes." Without intention or hesitation, without a second thought the word escaped her lips and her thoughts flashed back to when she said no. *'Why hadn't he stopped?'* Terrifying, painful and not what she wanted, his urgency left no time for precautions. *'What had he done?'*
"I'll need to do some tests." Jade felt her everything cringe. "I need blood and a water sample."
"Okay,Yes, Right." Pregnant? Her head was spinning, she didn't want to be pregnant, almost seventeen, she

didn't want to carry Rojay's child. *'No!'* Jade wasn't willing to be the one to reincarnate a monster. Shaking her head, she didn't want to think about what could be? "Then can I go?" She said she would be fine if the doctor allowed her to leave. "Please." She begged and was told to wait for the results.

♪152♪

Sat waiting, Jade didn't want to be pregnant but realised the choice may no longer be hers to make. No, unfair, it couldn't be, it was crewel. *'Why her?'* This didn't happen to girls like her. Sat in the chair by the hospital bed appointed to her, she used the ensuite to shower and put on the clothes she carried inside her rucksack. Waiting, when Dr. Burlington entered with her recorded results, Jade felt sure she stopped breathing.

"Did you know?" The doctor asked.

"You won't tell anyone." She didn't want anyone knowing. She didn't want to know, but it was there, the result was written in black on white.<u>Positive.</u>

"Who is and isn't told is up to you." Informing her shocked patient of the reason she collapsed. Dr. Burlington said she was there to help.

"I don't want anyone to know." Jade repeated.

"The father?" People were bound to ask.

"It's over." The truth was, it had never began. Told she couldn't keep her secret indefinitely, Jade felt the build up of tears behind her eyes and wanted them to stop. "I don't want it." She blurted. In her eyes this wasn't a pregnancy, not a baby, what was growing inside her was a monster. Touching her stomach she felt invaded and unclean. *'Over reacting?'* Jade was scared.

"This is clearly a shock." Sitting on the edge of the bed beside where Jade sat in the chair, the doctor said she should think things over before deciding anything.

"I never wanted this." Shaking with shock, her distress was obvious. "I don't want this." She said.

"Are you asking for an abortion?"

"I don't want this." Jade cried. "I want to go. Can I go?" Shocked, confused and distressed. Despite the doctor's objections, having discharged herself, Jade climbed into a waiting taxi and continued to her intended destination. *'Pregnant?'* How could she? How stupid, what a fool, a tart, a slag, despite her dislike of the words loose and easy, loose and easy was how she felt. Disgusting, dirty and disappointed in herself, what would she do now? *'Why hadn't he heard her telling him no?'*

Pregnant? They must have gotten the tests mixed up and labelled her samples with the wrong name. *'Mistakes happen?'* They were busy, the doctors were taking forever and the nurses barely had time to catch their breath. *'Pregnant?'* She wasn't old enough, not ready to be anyone's mother, recent events proved Jade to be incapable of looking after and being responsible for herself. *'Expecting?'* When the taxi driver asked where to, she gave her aunt and uncles' address. Twenty minutes from the local train station, she hoped the large hospital on the outskirts of town wouldn't put too many miles on the clock. Rojay having taken her money, meant her having little cash to spare. *'Penniless & destitute?'* She knew her aunt and uncle wouldn't be expecting her and hoped they wouldn't turn her away. *'Where else could she go?'* Pregnant? How had she allowed such a thing to happen, falling pregnant didn't happen to girls like Miss Jade Jennifer Barris, she was one of the smart ones, wealthy and well to do, should mistakes be made wealthy parents like Mama and Papa paid to cover-up and remove what could cause a scandal? Mama wouldn't and Papa couldn't help. *'Disowned & disgraced?'* Jemima and Jerald had made it clear that should she leave, she would be on her own. Would Jennifer and Kevin feel the same? *'Why hadn't she come to them sooner?'* Pregnant? Why had this happened? Recalling the facts of what she hadn't wanted, the distressed teen reminded herself of how she said no, she told him no. *'Hadn't she?'* Inside her head Jade told Rojay to get off and go away, in her silent tears she begged her attacker to leave her alone and inside her mind she fought hard against what she didn't want. Bringing the hectic horror to the foremost of her memory, she found herself struggling to say with complete clarity that the two letter word had escaped her lips. *'If she heard, he must've heard.'* Shaking her head, she had run from his unwanted advances and attempted to push him away. Struggling with him in a physically fight, she remembered her choice being taken. *'No!'* She felt certain she told him no, when running from his unwanted advances. *'No!'* She didn't want to be pregnant. *'No!'* She hadn't wanted him to do what he did. *'His girlfriend?'* Him calling her, his girl didn't make it right. *'No!'* Surely that which rushed through her head at full volume had escaped her lips more than one time. *'No!'* If at no other time, when Rojay started what he was determined to finish, she had told him No!

No! No, no, she hadn't wanted him to do what he did and she didn't want to be pregnant with his baby. Young, inexperience and not trust worthy enough, neither was ready to become mum and dad. No longer together, Jade wasn't sad about them being apart, they were over. *'No.'* Maybe if she stopped thinking about it, it wouldn't be. Maybe she could wish it away. Aware the sadness she felt was born of a bitterness created through anger, the one at a loss about what to do refused to believe what she was told. *'A mistake?'* Hoping it wasn't what it was. In the absence of funds to solve what would become her growing problem, her asking her aunt and uncle for help and advice would result in them being disappointed. If what test results confirmed was real, Jade didn't want others judging her for something no one would or could understand. *'An abortion?'* Given leaflets, Dr. Burlington said she had time. How much? Pregnant? Jade had nothing against babies, if happening to someone else or under different circumstances, at any other time; she would be pleased and struggling to contain the news. What happened made her being pregnant all kinds of wrong. Unable to see what was inside her as a child, not welcome, not invited and not right. Frightened and alone, with no one to turn to; she was left with no other option but to put right what had gone horribly wrong. *'On her own.'* On holiday, or just visiting? She told the hospital she would continue her care with her family doctor when home. *'Would she ever go home?'* Maybe she should run away to somewhere no one would find her and begin a new life on her own. Knowing what she knew meant there was a chance Jade would never be on her own ever again.

♫153♫

I MAY PRETEND

12: ONCE BITTEN
♪154♪

Hugs and kisses, welcoming embraces and smiles of relief, standing outside the postoffice he watched the arriving cab, rushing to help when recognising his missing niece. Mr. Kevin Perron insisted he pay the fare and fetch her bag. Having called to his wife, Jennifer exited the front of their retail establishment to see what the fuss was about?

"Jade!" Her aunt gasped. Rushing to greet her as she stood on the pavement. "Jade!" Jennifer failed to prevent the tears of relief shinning in her eyes. Happy, neither heard when the inquisitive male ask the waiting cab driver where he'd come from? Watching his wife, the concerned male questioned why the teen had, had reason to visit the local hospital? *'Glad to see her safe.'* Kevin knew it wasn't the time to ask what he wanted to hear answered. Apologising for not warning them she was coming, Jade failed to mention the fact she was where she was because she had nowhere else to go. *'Disowned.'* Shocked but happy to discover grannie hadn't returned to Canada.

"Good to see you princess." Her uncle had to squeeze between the females caught in a tight embrace to get the hug he said he needed. Welcoming her with open arms, Kevin said he was happy to man the counter while his wife settled their guest. Treated like she had never been away, all agreed the only thing to matter was the fact she was safe. *'A visit?'* Relieved when told she could stay for as long as she wanted. *'Forever?'* Back with people who cared for and loved her. How could such loyal, loving, caring people understand? *'Would they accept her back if they knew?'* After a second much needed shower, Jade changed into clothes borrowed from her aunts' wardrobe before rejoining those waiting to hear everything? *'Not wanting to say anything.'* Telling would lose respect, and saying the words out loud would make it real. *'Sorry,'*

♪155♪

House-hunting, ageing gracefully, when sat at the dinner table, grannie made the conversation all about her. Aware her granddaughter would talk when ready. Mrs. Loti Louise Denton-Stableford eased Jade's concerns when revealing she was where she was without her younger husband because they needed a base, a cottage or apartment? *'Not ill, no marriage on the rocks?'* The property being sought would be unoccupied for much of the time and in need of a caretaker. Kevin told how he would help if he could, all agreeing the second home could generate income for all, by doubling as a seasonal holiday let. Big plans, Loti said she needed to sort things for what would be her twilight years, a place to be closer to family and enough in the bank to lay her to rest beside her first husband. *'Forever in love with gramps.'* Understanding, Mr. Samuel Fernando Stableford agreed that should he out live his elder wife, he would inherit everything they owned together in his homeland of Canada. Happy? *'Loti & Sam were fine.'* Upon noticing the panic on her granddaughters tired face, Loti assured all, she wasn't planning on joining her first husband any time soon. *'Not ill.'* Her getting older meant it was time for making in need of making. A home to be kept in the family and used to keep a roof over whosoever head needed it. Income as a holiday let would be split between her two grandchildren when she was gone, with Kevin taking what he needed for the upkeep and his time.

"Sorting my legacy."Loti assured Jade everything would be fine. "It's good to have you back safe." She also said she hadn't been looking forward to living the rest of her life with the hole in her heart where her only granddaughter should be.

"Where have you been?" Concern shone almost as bright as her smile. "I was worried." Jennifer being next to speak; the look Loti sent her youngest daughter warned now wasn't the time. Kisses, cuddles, tea and sympathy, all agreed there was plenty of time for questions. Loti staying in what was usually occupied by her brother; meant Jade being placed in what had always been her room. Safe, no one asked, but she knew they wanted to know why she ran away. *'With friends?'* Kevin wondered if it had been her or a friend in need of the visit made to the local hospital? Her visiting friends was a plausible explanation, her wanting to be with her boyfriend was another? *'Where had she been?'*

Safe and sound, back with her family.
"I'm okay." It was like she forgot how to tell the truth. Informing her aunt it was fine to enter, Jade pulled herself up from beneath bedcovers she wanted to hide under forever.
"You look terrible." Awarded time to collect her thoughts and settle. Ten in the morning was late for breakfast in the Perron house. "I made toast." Jennifer revealed what was on the tray
"With eggs, you need meat putting back on your bones." Trust a grandmother to notice, trust grannie to fuss as she entered behind Jennifer. If fussing was what shown how much someone cared, Loti would have a cabinet overflowing with trophies. Back with the family, Jade wished she'd never left. "You look shocking." Not one to hold back, grannie told it like it was.
"So everyone keeps telling me." The teenager sighed. Another day, more hugs, more kisses and tears were followed by the questions which had to be faced sooner or later. *'An emotional reunion?'* Confused, but glad to be with people who cared. *'Would they still love her when they found out?'*
"Not feeding yourself properly will help no one." The eldest family member shook her head at Jade insisting she was all right. "Get the breakfast down you."
"Thank you." Hoping she would manage a nibble without being sick, what granddaughter wouldn't do her grandmothers' bidding. Grannie knew best, but Grannie didn't know everything.

"I telephoned your parents." Jade guessed someone would have to and it was just like grannie to do what she saw as needing to be done.

"What? Why?" She nevertheless gasped

"Yeah, why?" Jennifer asked.

"To let them know where you are."

"Like they care." Jade's aunt shook her head.

"I'm not going home." Jade didn't want to have to face Papa and his jury. Not yet, not ever if she could help it. "I want to stay here, you said I could stay." She panicked.

"You can, for as long as you like." Jennifer agreed. Informing her niece, she would never go back on her word and sending a look to her mother which shown disappointment.

"They're pleased you're safe." Shouldn't parents be relieved, happy and wanting to see the daughter missing for more than four months? Relieved, what else had Jade expected from people who no longer wanted the person she was.

♪156♪

A cake with candles, sandwiches and a balloon, not even on her birthday did her parents make an appearance, not so much as a card. Jeremy telephoned and Jimmy thanked her for allowing him and Sawyer to breath again. A full page of words showing how much her friend cared, words written within a card reminding her of his home telephone number if she needed it. There if she needed him. Jade found herself nodding when reading how Jimmy believed she should have gone to him. Caught up in the excitement and romance of it all, Jade hated herself for forgetting how dreams are only dreams until they become reality and reality is rarely what is perceived.

♪157♪

Watching May drift into June in a small seaside village meant the true beginning of the next holiday season arriving with a vengeance.

"Josie can't join us this year, expecting." What was exciting and thrilling for some, made Jade feel sick, what others looked forward to, Jade couldn't face, not yet and maybe never?

"It's fine." She agreed to what would be part time and keep her busy. "I'm here when needed." She smiled, but her concerned relatives said she didn't have to take the job for which she intercepted the advertisement before it was put in the window.

"Are you sure you're well enough to work?" Both Jennifer and grannie asked. *'Too soon?'* Jade pointed out the fact she was only across the road. *'Not going to get better anytime soon.'* Her physical condition may appear to be improving, but no amount of healthy food, warmth, love or medicine could cure what she was suffering.

"£50 per week?" Some called it slave labour. £50 per week was Jade's first step in building her new life. *'A fresh start?'* £50 plus a share of tips, not enough, but better than nothing. A new book, asking if she could take the rainbow coloured notebook, Kevin told her to go write her masterpiece. It had been a while since she sat to put pen to paper, having left her diaries in her bedroom back home, Jade wondered if anyone had read them. *'Where had all her hopes & dreams gone?'* Was she strong enough to start again?

June 1st:
I began work today, finally I'm doing something for myself, by myself. I need the money, I've no option but to save for an abortion, the only way. There's nothing else I can do.

"You're keen." Shannon said when opening the door to Jade arriving before six on the first morning of her first day of work. *'Any excuse to miss breakfast.'* Her first day of work, her first day of her first paid job. A fresh white, clean page, a fresh new start, a brand new book, a brand new beginning. Keen? Yes, she was keen, keen to work, keen to get on with her life, keen to prove to both herself and others she could cope; while all the time wondering how she was going to manage. The white metal tables and chairs were heavier than they looked, too heavy for someone in her condition. *'Shannon helped.'* On her feet as much as she needed to be. Aware none of what she was doing was good for her. *'Not illness?'* Jade knew the demanding work could harm someone as delicate as she was feeling. *'What was she hoping to achieve?'*

"Study the menu, it only changes Sunday." Shannon shown her old friend and new work colleague all she needed to know and everything she was expected to do. Put out the chairs, tables and parasols, having helped before; Jade was aware of some of the daily routine.

♪158♪
WIPE EVERYTHING DOWN.
FILL THE WATER BOILER.
EMPTY THE DISHWASHER.
FILL THE CUTLERY TRAYS.
FILL THE MILK JUGS,
FILL THE SUGAR BOWLS & SAUCES.
SERVE THE CUSTOMERS.
FILL THE CAKE DISPLAY
FILL THE CRISP & SNACK COUNTER.
SERVE THE CUSTOMER. At the end of each day everything out had to be put away. Not easy, not ideal and not always pleasant, there were some smells she struggled to stomach and others which assisted in her getting her appetite back. *'Sickness & cravings?'*

"Tea and cream scones for four."

"One of your finest cheese and ham toasties."

"Two teas and two milkshakes,"

"Two burgers, two bread rolls with chips, four cola's."

"Tea and cake choice for one." Old, young, couples, families, single people, locals and visitors. Jade enjoyed meeting and talking to the many characters who called into the small, busy family cafe/coffee shop. Two hours four, sometimes eight, she wouldn't let down those to have given her the seasonal contract of employment.

"Tired princess?" Shannon asked as they sat treating themselves to a well earned and welcomed refreshing milkshake at the end of what turned out to be one hell of a first week. "You don't look so good."

"I'm fine." Jade seemed to be forever telling people she was fine; when what she really should do was tell them she was scared. *'Terrified.'*

"Profits are looking good." Mr. Burnley announced as he finished bagging the takings. "Must be the new pretty face on the team, keep up the good work." He smiled when presenting his new employee with her first ever pay packet.

"Thank you." Her forced smile wasn't because she wasn't grateful, it was because she knew he wouldn't be quite so pleased once her bump began to show.

"Its good to have you onboard, you feel like one of the family already." Family? If Jade didn't sort herself soon, a family would be exactly what she would be, a one parent family. *'How many weeks?'* Her having stopped being sick didn't mean her secret wouldn't reveal itself.

"Fancy the camp disco tonight?" It was good of Shannon to ask, but she couldn't.

"Bath and bed for me." Saying goodbye before having to answer more questioned, Jade agreed to join her friend on a night out soon.

Two hundred pounds, counting the money paid along with her share of tips at the end of her first month. Pushing all notes back inside the handmade pyjama case to have sat at the foot of her bed for as many years as she could remember; Jade shook her head.

"Not enough."She scolded herself. Inquiries having led her to discover the cost of a private termination was around three to six hundred pounds. *'A private abortion was the only way to keep her secret.'* Want would soon turn to need, did she still want to rid herself of what she couldn't keep secret? Private, her not being registered with a local GP left no choice but to go private if she didn't want her business becoming public knowledge. *'£200.00 per month wasn't enough.'* It taking at least another three months to save anything near what she needed would be too long. Since her arrival, both her aunt and grannie had done their utmost to feed her up, not wanting to pile on the extra pounds, over her six week stay Jade found reason to avoid and hide food whilst taking up jogging. Afraid of anyone noticing what she felt sure she could see, she worked hard, volunteering her services on her days off, her wanting to keep busy helped, but it wasn't the kind of help she was in need of.

1st July:
I no longer know what to do? If I ask Mama and Papa for the money they'll want to know what its for. Trapped, I tried to access my savings account but the bank tell me its frozen. Desperate, perhaps I should swim out to sea and hope I never return. I don't want this. I want this gone. I can't go back to the hospital because I told them my name was Jade Hallas. Why did I do that?

Closing her diary, she continued to think about her final entry and last sentence, words she said accidentally when asked her name. Miss Jade Hallas, giving her school address when asked where she lived, she shook her head when asked if she knew the details of her family doctor. Could, should she swim out to sea? Her ink had flown so freely from the nib of her pen it felt like someone else was writing. With the fresh breeze blowing through her hair, she sat with her knees pulled up almost under her chin and her hands stroking her lower leg as the soft, gentle ripple of the cool ocean waves hit the tips of her curling toes. Despite the large beach towel hung around and over her shoulders, she shivered. It was dark, the high, full set moon casting its' shadow far out to sea as her eyes followed its' silver glow. No-one would know, everyone would believe she'd run away again. It would be weeks, months and maybe even years before anyone discovered the truth. Some bodies are never washed ashore. *'Suicide?'* What other option did she have? Dr. Judd had gotten everything right by accessing her and everything about her wrong. *'Psychologist or psychic?'* Having had dealings with both; grannie said there was no difference because each predicted what a person would see for him or herself if they took the time to stop and look. *'Directional misguidance?'* Loti called psychologists psychics with more money, less control and next to no common sense, because the books they read and the boxes they ticked dictated their prediction. *'Witches without the craft.'* Dr. Judd would be the first to tell Mama and Papa how their daughter was depressed, while Loti would insist her granddaughter wouldn't have ever considered taking her own life if the dotty professional hadn't put the idea in her head. Dr. Judd was forever referring to suicide as being the ultimate and only way out, calling it wrong, no one listened to the positives within the negatives when pulling out the words they saw to be most important to them and their needs? Standing and allowing the towel to fall to the cooling sand covered ground, she glanced around herself to check there was no one else there. *'Alone?'* Never before had she felt so by herself, even with her aunt, uncle and grannie so close, Jade felt alone. Shivers ran the length of her spine and the whole of her body felt icy as she entered the cool blueness, the sharp coldness and the constant movement of what was the oceans' waves. Cold, what swirled around her ankles slapped at her knees before rolling into and around her thighs. Plunging herself forward, she began to swim. *'What was she doing?'* Her head was meant to be clear, yet she found her thoughts filling with her wants. Jade wanted grannie to be happy, Loti would be sad. Jade wanted Jennifer and Kevin to have their own family. A baby for her aunt and uncle was too late. Jade wanted her brother to be whatever he wanted to be and she knew he would. Mama and Papa would still have Jeremy and he would never let them down. Smiling as she swam into what got deeper, her holding herself above the water became more difficult with every stroke. Realising how far from the shore she was, what should cause panic caused her to smile as she felt her worries drift away. *'She could do this.'* Did she want to? There was no one to stop her, no one knew where she was. Swimming further and further, within seconds she was out of her depth and within minutes she was out of sight of the mainland. Surrounded by nothing but water and engulfed in a blackness which was never ending. Enveloped by nothing but the gentle ripple of the deep, blue/black ocean. What looked refreshing and welcoming in daylight, appeared mystery filled and murky in the dark. Gracefully gliding through what contained hidden pockets of sharp coldness to bite into the softness of her exposed skin, it was what hurt; which caused Jade to panic. *'Was something else there?'* Unable to see, out in the ocean on her own, it was the turn of her imagination to enter the space created when her worrying thoughts moved out.

"No!" She screamed. "No!" She shouted as like a toddler losing her balance, she lost all control. Splashing, screaming and shouting! "No!" As her line of vision slipped from above to below the waterline. "No! No!" Jade yelled. "No!" She screamed. "I don't want to. I changed my mind." Whether she said or simply thought the words; she couldn't be sure, as breathing became more and more difficult, her vision blurred and calm turned to a helplessness she wasn't able to fight. Breathless, like a rag doll weighed down by led weights, from sheer and utter panic her body succumb to its' fate as it began to sink. Sinking deeper and deeper; her ability to fight, like her body began to float away in what was a breathtakingly and wondrous nothingness. *'Gone?'* It was over. She had released her last breath,

I MAY PRETEND

walked her last step and swam her last swim. *'Gone?'* How and why had she ignored her doubts? Why hadn't all the things she wanted and the feelings of others mattered? *'Selfish?'* If she could, she would tell people she did what she had done because she had to, the truth is no one has to do anything they don't want to do. *'Why did she?'* If she could return and tell them, Jade would say she had gotten lost, become frightened and panicked. Before entering the water she hadn't thought of anyone or anything not even herself. If she could explain, she would tell others the point at which a person realises their thoughts, worries, inner demons and concerns are no longer as terrifying as they seem, is the point where clarity kicks in. If she could, she would do what she could to let others know how one reaching what feels like being released from ones everything; is the point from which there really is no return. The point of no return is the point which causes the realisation of how very precious every life is.

"No!" Opening her eyes, Jade realised it had all been a dream. A disturbing and frightening eye opening dream. Looking around her room, sitting herself up and switching on the bedside light, she wished what was growing inside her was nothing more than a nightmare.

"A dreams?" Having rushed in to find her niece looking like she'd seen a ghost, Jennifer insisted she take the next day off work.

Pushed out, grannie told Jade to go spend the day on the beach and get herself some much needed colour. *'Time off to relax.'* Time to herself. Mr. Burnley agreed to Loti covering her granddaughters shift, leaving Jade with no choice but to do as she was told.

"Putting weight on at last."Jennifer announced as Jade squeezed herself into the swimsuit kept in the draw alongside other summer outfits stored at her aunts because they weren't needed when home. Standing before the long dress mirror in her room, the teenager jumped when her aunt entered to place fresh towels on her bed. "Sorry, I didn't mean to startle you." She apologised. Stood checking the stomach which despite all effort was beginning to change in shape and size, upon noticing her aunts' presence she covered herself with her large t'shirt.

"Off to the beach?" Jennifer asked. "Or is it the pool?"

"Beach, grannie's orders." She continued to gather what was needed.

"Do you good, you should start looking like a local if you intend being one." Jennifer's smile couldn't be brighter.

"I am a little pale." Jade agreed.

"Will you be back for lunch?" Saying she would eat while out, Jennifer asked Jade if everything was all right?

"Fine." Hoping her elder would believe her, she was told she hadn't seemed herself. "I'm fine." She repeated. "A little tired." She wasn't lying, her feeling exhausted was just one of the many symptoms being experienced, probably due to poor sleep. *'How does one sleep when ones mind refuses to rest?'*

"You began work too soon." Jennifer agreed a day or two spent resting would be good for her. "Mum will manage." She smiled at the thought of Loti being a waitress. "Not sure Mr. Burnley will survive the day though." Both laughed when looking out across the road and noticing the elder male taking Loti a breakfast of tea, boiled egg and toasted soldiers. "I hope it's not too runny." Loti didn't hide her true feelings about how she liked things to be and her boiled egg had to be just right.

"Maybe I." Jade began.

"You go hit the beach and grab yourself some sunshine." Her aunt said she should enjoy her day.

"On my way." Having placed the long baggy shirt over her one piece costume, she slipped her feet into a pair of comfortable sandals and placed the bag carrying everything she needed over her shoulder before setting off to join devoted sun worshipers, holidaymakers and those who worked on the hot, golden sands of the local beach.

♪159♪

Lay beneath the hot, bright, burning rays of the sun, she wished she could be like everyone else. *'Why try to escape her fate?'* Having protected her skin with a high factor sun lotion, the lone female wished there was a way of protecting her everything from what others would think when they knew the truth? *'Holidays?'* Time to relax and have fun, no cross words and no worries for a week, maybe two? As children built sandcastles and teenagers swam and surfed within the cooling ocean waves, parents and elders relaxed. Soaking up the bright and cheer filled atmosphere whilst relaxing beneath the sun's soothing rays. *'Parents?'* Sitting herself upright, Jade glanced from behind her sunglasses to observe those around her, watching those there with children. *'Parents?'* Jade didn't want to be a parent, not ready for the responsibility which came with being answerable for someone else. *'Not ready?'* Jade Jennifer Barris was too young and no way mature enough to deal with what was happening. How could someone who wasn't ready to have children contemplate having a child she didn't want? Not the fault of the child?

"There you go, put some cream on darling." Two years if a day? The sweetest smile on the rounded cheeky, angelic face, blonde hair falling in uneven curls. *'Girl or boy? Would her baby look like Rojay?'*

"David," His proud mother sounded relieved that on such a soft surface her tiny jewel could not be injured as he toddled and stumbled around, giggling when she told him whoops a daisy. "Silly Billy," His mother smiled, picking him up and dusted him down, cradling and preventing the tears the arrival of which was indicated by his fallen bottom lip. Proud and happy, loving and kind. *'Jade couldn't do that.'* Surrounded by scenes of idyllic family life, she couldn't be a mother to what should never have been conceived. *'Rojay knew nothing.'* Should she tell him? What would be the point if she was never going back to where he was?

Feeling uncomfortable being low down on the sand, Jade decided to hire a sun bed, gathering her things and walking over to the beach hut, she smiled when being recognised and recognising the one greeting her.

"Hello Princess, what can I do for you?" Johnny? Usually found behind the bar inside the holiday camps teens only area, Master Johnny Hamilton. *'A friendly face.'* When admitting to being by herself, she accepted the invitation to join him sat in amongst the sun beds, surf boards and deckchairs for hire. Fun in the sun, having Johnny to chat with in-between his assisting, sometimes flirting with the many holidaymakers; led to Jade experiencing a rollercoaster of emotions. *'Not carefree?'* No one knew and she hoped no one was able to see, Johnny said she looked well and why wouldn't she? Jade wasn't ill, even if she couldn't remember feeling worse. *'Wanting to feel like herself.'* Told to cheer up and smile when caught drifting off into deep unwanted thoughts. *'No reason to be unhappy.'* Sun, sea and sand, Jade was safe, standing on her own two feet, she was earning her own money surrounded by people she liked in a place she loved. Embraced by warmth, Miss Jade Jennifer Barris was in a place where she felt she should be. Not unhappy, not sad, Jade was frightened and confused. *'No one else to blame.'* With no one to turn to, Jade was upset because she was on her own. In amongst so many, Jade felt alone.

♪160♪

Fun in the sun, sun hats and ice cream, sitting side by side in reclined deckchairs, Jade and Johnny discussed those they observed. The children alone and in groups, busy building castles in the sand, first timers daring to paddle in the fluffy white breaks while those with experience rode the rolling ocean waves, bathers and sun worshipers, Johnny pointed out the girls silently competing in the; I look better than you in a bikini contest, Jade telling him she related more to those she saw attempting to hide beneath parasols, wearing oversize tops and wrapped in beach towels. Singles, couples, groups and families, all around people were playing, eating, drinking, sunbathing, swimming, walking and relaxing. Sitting with Johnny, Jade said she didn't mind when he assisted a group of girls with putting up their deckchairs and she took payment from a family in need of four sun beds and two parasols. *'A family?'* Her own was okay in their own unique and dysfunctional way. *'A one parent family?'* Jade didn't want what was growing inside her, neither could she give her baby away.

♪161♪

The time wasn't right and what had happened added up to a million kinds of wrong. *'Unwanted?'* Too young, what was happening was unfair.

"A drink sleepy head." Apologising for having drifted off, Jade accepted the cooled can of lemonade. Waking to find things on the beach changed, Jade felt shocked to discover the game of football taking place close by. Back away from the sea, with the waves heading out, those who hadn't left, had followed the shoreline, creating space enough for beach games. Kite flying, badminton, volley and what looked to be a somewhat professional game of football. "He blends in well doesn't he." Johnny nodded to the one Jade felt shocked to recognise. *'What was he doing there?'* "He's down here at least once a week."

"Why?" The question escaped without her meaning it to, he was a professional with a training ground and official teammates to kick a ball around with. *'Jade Hallas?'* Why had she said Hallas and not Jackson? Why hadn't she given her actual name? Had grannie and aunt Jennifer known he would be there? Jade told Johnny she should go, standing at the exact time the ball was kicked in her direction, hitting and knocking her from her feet to her knees. *'Was it instinct caused her to cover her stomach.'* Jumping up from his seat, Johnny asked if she was all right. Picking up and throwing the ball back to those awaiting its return, the deckchair attendant told them to be more careful.

"Are you all right?" Insisting she take a seat inside the beach hut, Johnny helped Jade into the comfy armchair stood in amongst what was stored for hire. *'The bad weather chair.'* She told him she felt stupid, avoiding all eye contact with those looking to see. "If you wait I can drive you back to the village." Johnny offered.

"I'll wait." Her feeling dizzy left her no choice but to regain her composure and balance. "But I'll be fine. I can walk back when I'm ready." It being almost time for him to pack up, Johnny told his companion she was welcome to stay and sit for as long as she wanted, excusing himself to collect what needed collecting, Jade assured him she could, when asked if she would manage accepting what needed to be handed back in his absence.

"Fine." She repeated when asked if she was okay.

"Jade?" Having recognised him, she now recognised his voice. *'Why him & not one of the others?'* "Jade how are you?" Did she really have to repeat her most repeated reply? "Wow, how have you been?" Did he really want to know? Not able to tell him the truth. "Who are you here with?" His questions continued as she struggled to find the words needed to reply.

"Johnny, myself," She said watching as Bobby entered the hut to sit in the deckchair beside her.

"The two of you?" He asked and she shook her head. "Are you visiting your aunt?" A nod. Despite the awkwardness it was nice to see another friendly face.

"Okay." Why she agreed to wait for him to finish his game; she wasn't sure. *'Did she want to?'* Having agreed to wait, she waited. *'Aware she shouldn't.'* Could she turn to Bobby for the help she needed?

♪162♪

Looking and feeling better, there were times she believed the hospital must have gotten things wrong, times when she felt normal, there were also times when smells sent her running to the bathroom and nights she sat up eating the items purchased and kept hidden in the bags up inside her room. Bobby said he enjoyed their time together and Jennifer noticed what she called the return of her nieces brighter smile. *'Happier?'* Jade hadn't made arrangements, but agreed to seeing Bobby if he was around. *'Would he come around?'* Not if he knew the truth about what had happened. No one would want Jade if they knew what she had and was planning to do.

♫*163*♫

Pawing through the back pages of the magazines, Jade checked newspaper adverts in search of a solution to what she knew would become more and more difficult to hide *'Feeling fine.'* Purchasing what she needed to check for herself and taking the test in the public toilets down by the beach. *'Pregnant?'* Not wrong, nothing she'd suffered had erased what she saw to be a mistake. *'Pregnant?'* Weeks were running into months and time was running out. *'Happy?'* Why was happiness forever overshadowed by a threatening cloud of upset and despair? *'Pregnant?'* Struggling to find the service needed at a price she could afford within the area she was able to travel, her working and saving hard seemed pointless. *'Unable to ask Papa.'* All access to her saving accounts had been frozen because Mama saw Rojay as the type who would take every penny if there were pennies there to take. *'He had.'* Rojay had taken everything, leaving Jade with a problem she couldn't solve. *'Maybe her parents' were right.'* Too proud and much too stubborn to ever see things from Mama and Papas point of view. *'Sending her away?'* How had she gotten everything so wrong? Jeremy would struggle to keep it to himself if she went to her brother and no one else had the type of money she needed. Jimmy would help if he could. When she spoke to her dear friend, she was pleased to hear he and Swayer were happy. Grannie was much too busy house hunting and neither her aunt Jennifer or uncle Kevin had funds enough to spare. *'A mess?'* Looking through the yellow pages and local telephone directory while standing inside the local telephone box, the only place Jade found able to answer her questions was the family planning clinic situated in the neighbouring town. *'What did she have to lose?'* What she wouldn't give to lose what she had.

♫*164*♫

Not planning a family, neither was Jade in need of help or advise about contraception. *'Too late for prevention?'* In search of a cure, Jade needed the name, location and price list for a place registered to do what she needed doing, an address she could get to and price she could pay. *'Private?'* Needing to keep what was her business to herself. Weeks, she didn't have months, Jade had days to sort what needed sorting. When heard being sick by Shannon, she said she had a chill on her stomach, checking what she was expecting to see growing; daily, her cutting down her food intake wouldn't prevent what was getting bigger and her drinking water to keep hunger pangs at bay couldn't drowned what was living inside. *'Lucky she never had a flat stomach.'* When grannie took her shopping, Jade picked a size larger than what was normal, baggy and heavily patterned but not too bright, comfortable, not stylish, the teen said what she wore were clothes she could relax in when Loti questioned her style being a little hippie. *'Pale?'* When her uncle commented on her sickly complexion, Jade admitted to feeling a little stressed. Wanting to turn back time, the one feeling lost and alone wanted what was happening inside her to stop. *'Did she deserve to live?'* If able to take a life, what gave her the right to live one?

Weeks, while enjoying her time with her family, Jade didn't want them to be disappointed. Loving and loyal, it would hurt much more than she was hurting if those she loved pretended what had happened was okay, when it wasn't. Yes, they would cope, aunt Jennifer and uncle Kevin would be there for her, maybe they'd have a solution she hadn't thought of, but Jade didn't want what had been created without consent. Jade didn't want to live how she was living and feel the way she was feeling anymore. Taking the bus, she hoped no one would follow or workout where she was going. Having prevented her uncle from being her chauffeur by telling him she needed to shop for personal items.

"Underwear," She thought fast when Kevin pointed out the postoffice/general store sold most things. Embarrassed, her uncle apologised for being insistent, but she knew he was only being kind. *'Restoring her faith in men?'* Mr. Kevin Perron was the exception to the rule. *'Frightened & on her own?'* Keeping her fingers and toes crossed, she hoped her visit to the local clinic wouldn't be in vein.

Unsure, entering the establishment providing all things related to sexual heath, her not making an appointment was because she planned to look around. *'Relationship advice?'* Jade hoped she wouldn't have to talk to anyone. Posters, information leaflets, cards and pamphlets. Hoping not to be noticed, her mission was to leave no printed advertisement unread. *'Mother & baby classes?'* There was baby yoga, baby milk and breast is best information. *'Fathers have rights too.'* In her search for something to rid her of what she never wanted, Jade's eyes fell upon much she would rather not see. Happy smiling images, she didn't need family planning, in amongst those there for all kinds of reasons; Jade hoped she was blending into the background as she scrutinised the noticeboards and examined the display stands.

"Just looking," The truth was she was just passing through on her quest to discover what she desperately needed to find. *'Mums, bums & tums?'* Coming across groups and classes for before and following birth; her eyes moved from information about vitamins and nutrition to descriptive diagrams displaying any and everything from conception to pregnancy and on through birth and sexually transmitted diseases. Not seeing anything she hadn't seen before, she wished she was seeing what was, with different eyes. *'No,'* Subconsciously shaking her head, she couldn't, not even if she wanted to, how could Miss Jade Jennifer Barris do what was needed to carry a baby and give birth?

'*No,*' She had said it then and inside her head she was repeating it now, Jade didn't want to be a mother.

"Is this your first time?" Was he old enough to wear the white uniform and name badge stating him to be a nurse? Glancing from his face to what officially displayed his name; she felt sure Mr. Jack Sellers was younger than she was. "Are you okay?" He was only doing his job, there to help. Jade had no idea how to ask for the help she needed.

"I'm new in the area." She replied. "Which means I don't have a doctor." She stuttered as Jack encouraged her to sit with him so he could get her registered. "No," She snapped. "No, I was only looking." She panicked. "Just learning my way around."Placing his hand on her hand as they sat; Jack said she should relax.

"No pressure."He assured her. "Which contraception do you use?" He asked. Jade informing him she was on the pill. *'If only she hadn't forgotten to take it?'* Blaming herself and her own absentmindedness for the situation she was in, the teen struggled to recall how she could have been so stupid. *'Every morning after cleaning her teeth?'* Two things no self respecting person should neglect, her teeth and her sexual health. *'When had she gotten so grown up?'* If Jade had been a grown up, she wouldn't have forgotten and if she was a woman, she wouldn't have allowed what had happened.

"Sorry, I should go." She apologised. Telling Jack she would make an appointment on her next visit.

"Wait." Following her to the door, the young male nurse asked Jade to at least let him fetch the registration form and list of local GP's taking on new patients. Reluctant but not wanting to appear ruder than she had already; she waited in the covered area outside reception by the main door. A parking bay for prams and pushchairs, the lone female saw no harm in checking the larger noticeboards filled with cards and advertisements for things being sold and people for hire. Interesting, bikes and dollhouses placed beside designers, counsellors and undertakers. Old Mrs. LK would knit anything you wanted if you bought the wool and she had the pattern. *'Personalised baby blankets & teddybears made from babies first clothes.'* While some things stood out, there were also many items Jade wished she hadn't seen. *'Incontinence pads?'* The one with the searching eyes stopped when coming across someone who would take a plaster caste of your babies hands and feet. *'Dead or alive?'* A keepsake to remember what should be happy, something to keep should things turned sad. *'Thoughtful or cruel?'* Shaking her head without realising. *'Adoption?'* Stunned, stopped by Jack's return, she took the offered papers and thanked him for his time.

Where was it? *'Adoption?'* Returning her glance to the cluster of cards beneath the sign which said please take one; she couldn't believe she was telling herself to check all options? *'Jade had no option?'* Not a solution, it wouldn't be easy to hide what would develop and multiply over one hundred percent in size before handing it over, but maybe? And maybe someone on the other end of the telephone line waiting to help would know more? Maybe she would have to go through one avenue to reach another? *'Or maybe she'd found what she was looking for?'*

BERRY WELL HOTEL
&
NOOK CLINIC

Could what she was searching for be disguised behind what was advertised as well-being and good health? Taking what was printed with pictures, an address and contact number; the voice informing her what she'd taken wasn't a spa; told Jade she'd forgotten to check if anyone was watching.

"Those hotels aren't the type where you go for a holiday." Shannon apologised when realising she'd startled her friend. "You should have said where you were coming, we could've shared a cab. I hate that bus, full of old pissy-pants and pregnant housewives. I had to stand most of the way." Asking Jade if she was all right? Shannon said she would be in and out. "Wait for me."

"Sure."Jade agreed. Placing the cards and papers she'd collected into her bag before stepping back to allow a young mother with her newborn to park her pram. Dressed in blue, he was tiny, like a doll. Perfect, he was sleeping soundly as like she'd read her mind; his mother told Jade looks can be deceiving.

In and out, Shannon shown no shame or embarrassment when announcing she was where she was for her repeat prescription. *'The pill & a large box of condoms.'* The happy go lucky female laughed when telling Jade they always supplied her with enough to share.
"Did you get what you needed?" Nodding the truth was that she hoped so.
"A list of local doctors." She said she was out and about seeing what was on offer. *'There to stay.'* Jade didn't want to have to leave where she felt safe.
"I can show you around." Shannon said she loved a bit of window shopping and agreeing they should indulge, Jade said she would love to when asked if she wanted to taste the best coffee and cake in town. "Then we can share a cab home." How could she say no to seeing the window display Shannon called her fantasy shoe collection? *'A small town?'* From the cinema to the bingo hall and into the glass roof market hall where her eager guide pointed out the best place to purchase designer copies and the best run-resistant tights. *'Every girls must haves.'* The local showing the new arrival where she should, could and shouldn't go when in town. If she didn't think it strange, Jade would thank Shannon for turning a dull day bright. If she didn't think he would turn her away, she would have run up to and stopped Bobby when catching sight of him getting into his car. They were friends, not back together.

♪*165*♪

Markets stalls, designer and charity shops, beauty salons and hire stores. *'Friends having fun?'* For a time Jade thought about nothing but what she was looking at. *'No longer able to buy what she wanted.'* The one use to never having to worry about money or her needs being met, listened when Shannon gave tips on how to save on everything.

"What next?" Having placed an order for two Frappuccino and cake selection, the one more use to being the waitress joined Jade at her chosen table by the window and asked if there was anything else she needed help with? Having seen much, Jade said they should arrange for more sightseeing when next the two had the same day off. "Don't you forget what I said about Berry Well, it is defo not your type of spa." Her companions look told Jade she'd seen her keep the card she'd taken. "Locals call the Nook Clinic the hook clinic if you know what I mean."

"I'll checkout what the travel agents have on offer." Jade told her listening friend she was looking for something which would be a treat for her aunt. *'A relaxing weekend away while grannie was around to help.'* Becoming accustomed to telling white lies, Jade realised the Nook Clinic was exactly the place she needed.

♪*166*♪

'One thousand & five hundred pound?' By the time she saved what was needed, it would be too late. *'Seven hundred pound for a daytime slot?'* The one day only procedure omitted aftercare, painkillers and rest. £700.00 Thanking the person to have answered the telephone, Jade said she would call back to make the needed appointment, but even if she went for the day, she was £400.00 short. No one to turn to, no one who wouldn't ask questions, no one who wouldn't be disappointed and no one to understand. How could she tell anyone about what she struggled to tell herself? Late, she wasn't normally late, but having had her hopes raised before being buried, Jade needed to be on her own. Having accompanied Shannon in the taxi cab home she told her uncle she was going for a walk and headed to the telephone box which stood at the gates to the camp, not wanting to be seen or overheard. Kevin asked that she be back in time for super at seven, it was after eight. Late, she telephoned her aunt to say she'd met up with friends, but

since leaving the telephone box Jade had spent her time wandering and sitting on her own. *'Alone?'* Sand normally heated by the sun felt firm and cold underfoot as she shivered. *'Why had she walked onto the beach?'*

"Jade?" When Johnny said he was all done for the day and heading through the village if she wanted a ride, she sighed and agreed she was going his way.

♪*167*♪

One step at a time, one foot in front of the other, one day, one hour, one minute, one solitary second at a time, that was what she decided to take. What else could she do? Go with the flow and do what was expected. *'Expect nothing & everything is a bonus.'*

"No Bobby?" Shannon wasn't the only one wondering why the local football hero was only making intermittent visits since they'd met on the beach. "Are the two of you back on?"

"No."Jades' interruption was her convincing herself; as much as it was her informing the one inquiring of how she and Bobby were just friends. *'They promised they always would be.'* Just friends? "Just friends,"

"What's your letter?" Having received what looked to be a card in the morning post, Jade waited till her break to sit and see what it was? Arriving with their usual break time refreshment, Shannon said she could sit somewhere else if she'd rather open the envelope alone.

"Stay." Jade agreed.

"Maybe it's fan mail?" The more experienced waitress said she received her fare share of compliments from those too shy to approach in person. "Though they usually leave em on the table under the salt. Mum and dad have had more than the odd shock when opening what gets left for my eyes only." She watched as Jade read her note.

"An invitation."

"To somewhere nice?" Shannon asked.

"A wedding?" Was anyone she knew old enough to marry? Jade knew she should be pleased.

"Is it Bobby?" Shannon sounded as shocked as Jade felt sure she would be had the invite been to witness Mr. Hallas pledge his troth to another.

"No." She shook her head.

"Then who's the fool getting hitched?"

"A friend, someone I went to school with." Jade said she would understand if Mr. Burnley couldn't spare her, it was short notice and she would be away for almost a week. Shannon assured her friend she would manage and insisted her dad give her the time. One week? Another week in-which she would be unable to do anything about what needed to be done, a week of no pay. Jade would say good luck and send her best wishes, but she didn't want to return to where she would run the risk of bumping into people she didn't want to see.

"Tamara? Little Tamara?" Grannie repeated as like she'd promised, she informed both Loti and Jennifer of the envelopes contents. "Are you going to go?"

"She wants me to be her bridesmaid."

♪168♪

A bridesmaid, dressed in a full length, sky blue, silk dress overlaid with silver lace and wearing a ring of blue and silver sprayed flowers in her neatly arranged hair, Jade could barely believe she'd agreed. *'Glad the style wasn't fitted.'*

"You ready?" Gretchen asked. Looking almost identical as she entered to say the cars had arrived.

"Is Tamara ready?" Friends' Tamara and Gretchen now seemed more like strangers. *'A wedding?'* Dressed like fairytale princesses, never had Jade felt more plan.

"She'll follow." Gretchen said Tamara and her father had a bridal car. *'One bride & two bridesmaids?'*

"Is she all right?" Since being back, Jade felt there was something she wasn't being told, believing she was there more out of duty than want, she was told everything and everyone was fine. *'Not in-touch?'*

"She looked pale." Jade worried her friend was ill.

"Nothing your Mamas' makeup artists won't be able to put right." Jemima remaining friends with the mother's of Jade's friends meant her offering what all agreed to be a brides must have, on her big day. *'Able to solve the problems of all, but her daughter?'* Jade wasn't looking forward to seeing her parents. Having met those she knew to be Jemima's most loyal employees, she quickly realised the reason no one had mentioned her being away was because none had been told, or rather they believed she was spending time with relatives. *'The family secret?' The family* embarrassment?

Bridesmaids wearing identical dresses, Gretchen made comment on how Jade's developing tan caused her to look much better in the chosen colours. *'Gretchen looked fantastic.'*

"It feels a bit rushed." Jade was only showing concern as she continued her enquiries inside the car on the way to the church.

"It is." Gretchen nodded. "She's pregnant."

"Tamara is expecting." Miss prim and proper? Miss goody, goody two shoes? Tamara? The one with all the high principles? Tamara was having to wed because she was expecting? Having a baby? Aware of the look crossing her face, Jade also knew she had no room to say anything. Would anyone notice what the two in the main wedding party were attempting to hide? *'Was Tamara Happy?'* Gretchen said both Tamara and Tarquin were over the moon, but their parents' didn't want the news getting out before the wedding. A perfect, beautiful, hot summers day, a church, of course it had to be a church, a proper white wedding with all the trimming, a bride hiding her growing condition behind the glamour of doing everything right. Bridesmaids and a long white flowing gown, inside Jade envied Tamara. Envy, because she knew she couldn't condemn. Jade had no room to make comment or criticise. Not like Tamara would criticise should the situation be reversed. *'Pregnant?'* She appeared so happy as on her fathers' arm she climbed out of the cream and silver, ribbon fronted Rolls Royce. Her smile was so bright the fussing cameraman said it was blocking the sun. *'Beautiful?'* Standing calmly while her friends' straightened out her long trail and placed her veil over her face prior to taking their place's behind. Tamara managed a few words of thanks. *'Nervous?'* Inside Jade still hurt, she ached though she was unsure why? Throughout everything she couldn't erase the thought Tamara and Tarquin were happy and proud despite their troubles. Proud to be and to stand by one another. Happy to commit to one another.

"I do."

"I do." Following the newly weds around to witness and sigh the marital register, as chief bridesmaid Jade felt uneasy, a fraud to have to return arm in arm with bestman Bobby. Covered in coloured confetti and posing for photographs, Tamara kept her four month secret hidden throughout, allowing what was happening to be overshadowed by the excitement of the day, both bride and groom played their part to perfection. *'A perfect wedding day?'*

♫*169*♫

"How are you?" It was Papa who approached and spoke first, making his inquiry and speaking to her like she was one of his clients. No longer his daughter, she knew she would be disowned

"I'm fine." Jade lied. They may not need her, but for three maybe four months their only daughter had needed them. Jade needed their understanding, strength, support and parental guidance. When running away she could never have foreseen how she would become so very lost. Jade needed Mama and Papa to find her, physically there, their little girl was emotionally missing.

"Lovely dress," Mama commented as Jeremy rushed up to greet his sister with a warm and welcoming hug. Unable to go home, Jade's hotel room was all part of the gift awarded from the bride and groom for her standing as their bridesmaid. Grannie had paid for the train and her working was the excuse she needed not staying longer than she needed.

"You look great." She said and he beamed. All grown up, taller and broader, her six month absence seemed more like six years when seeing how her younger sibling had developed and matured. *'Wow!'* The little brother she left appeared more a man as he towered over and held her in his strong arms. Jeremy was the only one to admit to missing her. *'Him & the staff.'*

"How's, grannie, aunt Jennifer and uncle Kev?" He was also the one to ask about other family members.

"They send their love." Jade nodded.

"Are you happy living with them?" Papa interrupted.

"Yes," She agreed.

"Jennifer always did want you to herself." Mama commented as with a look which could kill, her husband stopped her from saying anything more. *'What?'* Where were the happy tears of reunion? Why weren't they telling her they were there if she needed them? How could Mama be such a bitch by calling her only sister for showing more consideration, caring and loving than she ever had? Jade hadn't seen nor spoken to her parents' in over six months, she knew she'd done wrong, but why were they talking to her like she was a stranger and why was Jemima acting like her sister had taken her favourite doll? Why? Why was Mama treating her more like she was an object than a person? In worrying about what would be her future, Jade found her head filling with the unanswered questions surrounding what had been her childhood and her past.

"Jade quick, Tamara is about to throw her bouquet." Excited, Gretchen pulled her away from her family to be in amongst the gathering crowd of single females. Tradition? Everything was being done in the very best of taste. Glancing around, paying little to no attention to the bouquet, her shock shown clear as the blue, silver and white floral arrangement placed itself into her hands.

"It was guided." Gretchen told her as Bobby kindly inquired as to whether or not she had a ride to the reception? Two bridesmaids and two best men. Tamara wouldn't miss the chance to have her wedding certificate sighed by the male on the verge of becoming world famous for the sport he'd been gifted.

"Me, us,"Jimmy announced as he and Sawyer stepped forward. "We can take Jade, we can take you both if you like." He smiled. Aware his interruption had saved embarrassment.

"I've others to take." Bobby said he'd see them there.

"Did I do wrong?" Her much missed chauffeur and life long bestfriend asked as all watched Bobby leaving.

"Probably not."Jade sighed. Not wanting to bump into anyone, there were few she hadn't seen, almost everyone had been invited to the wedding.

"You look great." Sawyer kissed her cheek. "And you caught the bouquet." He swooned as she presented him with the floral arrangement and assured her bestfriends' boyfriend he should keep it.

"What car are we in?" She asked. Linking her arms into theirs and allowing both Jimmy and Sawyer to escort her to the car her father said they should use, him having asked Trevor to be his chauffeur for the day. All the men Jade had once lived amongst looked smart. A wedding, the first to become man and wife, Jade smiled when Gretchen reminded her of how they'd fantasied about being married to those who escorted them to the Christmas dance. Married, one of them had done it. *'All grown up?'* Would Jade ever be grown up enough to stand up to her responsibilities?

♪*170*♪

Sitting, chatting and dancing with Jimmy and Sawyer, Jade danced with her brother when he asked and though it was awkward, she joined Papa for the father daughter waltz. A very traditional wedding with all the trimmings, when asked, Jade said she wasn't the marrying kind.

"Nor me, not till they make it legal." Having followed his friend out onto the patio surrounding what was the second floor hotel function room, Jimmy didn't have to speak for her to know he knew there was something not right. "He hasn't taken his eyes off you." His reference was to Bobby who's eyes would have burned through her if sight created laser beams. "I was worried." She'd written to Jimmy when settled at her aunts and she knew he was hurt by her not confining in him before she left.

"Sorry," She apologised for much more than he would ever realise. "I wasn't thinking." If only she'd reengaged her brain and stopped listening to her heart. She could have prevented Mama and Papa sending her away if she really didn't want to go. *'Would an asylum have been the better of two bad places?'* If asked, Jade would admit she'd been more than a little mad and her actions' crazy.

"He came looking, Rojay, after you left him."

"Escaped him." Jade sighed and Jimmy asked what she was saying? "It doesn't matter." She didn't want to cry.

"Will you be coming home?"

"I doubt it, pretty sure Mama and Papa have disowned me." She took a deep breath before asking what was happening for him? Still with Sawyer, they were looking to start their own business. Cycle and mini bus tours, Jade saw the two being the best at what made perfect sense.

"Mr. Barris is happy for me to work part time while we're setting everything up, he even helped us get backing from the bank .Mum wants us to go all out and include a B&B, dad is loyal and I doubt he'll agree to moving far."

"I think your parents would move to the moon to be with you." Jade told Jimmy he shouldn't underestimate those she saw as having always put him first by providing their strength and unconditional love. Funny how she saw in others what was absence in her own life. "You and Sawyer are so lucky." She said she was happy for them, Jimmy telling her he could see how very unhappy she was.

"You and Bobby?" He questioned.

"Probably not, no."Jade believed that boat had not only sailed, but sunk. *'A shipwreck not to be resurrected.'*

I MAY PRETEND

"He still likes you." Jimmy called her blind not to see.

"I don't like me." Jade shook her head. "It's been a nice day, a lovely wedding." She smiled. Sawyer rushing out to find his partner as a song both enjoyed dancing to, began to play, him telling her their conversation was to be continued as he was dragged inside and onto the dance floor.

♪171♪

A beautiful wedding, Jade continued to stand outside, looking out across the gardens belonging to the hotel.

"This is where you got to." Shocked, when turning, Jade found Bobby closing the door behind him. *'Why was he looking for her?'* Her entire body tingled as he approached. "You look nice." Jade agreed the choice of bridesmaids outfit was a good one. "I wanted to say I'm sorry."Bobby continued. Walking forward to stand by her side. *'What was he sorry for?'* The two hadn't seen much of one another following their meeting on the beach, he drop her back at her aunts, invited her and her uncle to watch him play and they'd agreed to be friends. His apology was because he hadn't thought to invite her to travel to the wedding with him. "We can travel back together if you like." He offered and she told him she was booked on the morning train.

"Please." He said he'd like the company. "Someone to talk to." He said conversation helped the journey pass more quickly and promised he would make the car as comfortable as the train. Agreeing to think about it and suggesting they rejoin the party before they were missed, Jade was reluctant, but joined in with the popular floor filling party dances when encouraged by Sawyer and Jimmy.

♪172♪

From being in amongst Jimmy and swayer to dancing with Gretchen and Tamara

♪173♪

Jade also agreed to dance with her brother as the two shown others what they learned during the hours a week both spent in ballroom dance classes.

♪174♪

♪175♪
When things got slower, Jade felt surprised to feel comfortable back within Bobby's strong arms.
♪176♪

The wedding:
Everything went well. I still can't believe Tamara is going to be a wife and mother. They seemed so happy, inseparable, standing side by side, walking hand in hand, holding one another, dancing with one another, hugging, touching and embracing. A beautiful bride and her handsome groom. Tarquin looked so proud, he also looked very smart in his dark grey top hat and tails. Gretchen said Tamara looked gorgeous and she did, stunning, in her white full length, lace sleeved gown. Barely showing, I saw Tarquin make a point of resting his hand on what in a matter of weeks will become a much larger bump. They're creating new life and making a family. Happy for them, I wish the three of them a long life and send them much love, peace and happiness. 'Jennifer always did want you to herself.' Mama's words continue to echo inside my head whenever I attempt to sleep. Why? What did she mean? Why did Papa silence her? "Jennifer always did want you to herself." Like I don't want my child, my parents' no longer want me, clearly not missing me, Bobby and me rode home together.

♪177♪

13: TOMORROW

♪178♪

Maybe it was gone? Taking the pregnancy testing kit to the public toilets by the beach, maybe this time it would be negative and she could restart her life? Telling those looking out for her, she would have dinner out, she didn't want anyone to worry.

"Johnny," When asked, she said she was meeting up with the one in sole charge of the deckchairs and surf boards. "Just friends, someone to talk to." She assured her uncle there was nothing going on and nothing for him to worry about. *'Wanting Jade with Bobby?'* Jade wished she'd never been with anyone else. The drive back from the wedding was filled with polite, engaging conversation, but neither mentioned them being more than friends. Bobby had his exciting career and Jade may still have her problem to solve. *'Pregnant?'* She didn't want to be pregnant. Placing what gave her the opposite reading to the one she wanted into the tall bin and pushing it down amongst the discarded hand towels, she washed her hands and wiped her tear stained face. *'Pregnant?'*

Johnny's day off, she didn't know the female telling her she would let him know she called in. Walking, sitting, paddling and sunbathing, how come time goes so slow on the days you want it to go fast? *'What should she do?'* What could she do? Dreams, daydreams and nightmares, when kept busy she didn't have to think. No one else knowing meant she didn't have to talk about what she wished wasn't there. Dreams and nightmares? Each and every time she closed her eyes, she saw something different whilst experiencing every emotions encountered in the same way, hurt, pain and fear? *'Where else was there for Jade to go?'* Where can one go when wanting to run away from them self?

♪179♪

Ridding with Rojay, the gentle breeze running like a thousand tiny fingers through her hair. *'Why had he pulled her hair?'* When with Roland Jackson, Jade felt free. *'Why imprison her?'* Them meeting in secret and the hundreds of unseen glances exchanged from the school corridor lockers to the playground and beyond, when it started it was exciting. Able to recall the flutters and skipped beats of her heart, what she felt had turned from excitement to fear. A sinking and not a fluttering, a thud as his fist made contact with what was her core, hurting, she felt the numbness she'd encountered when he said she couldn't go. *'Why hurt her?'* He use to make her blush long before they spoke. How she wished she'd continued worshipping the leather clad biker from afar. Jade never wanted to be anywhere near Rojay and his motorbike ever again, she didn't want to hurt anymore. Daydreams, every time she saw a motorbike she looked for him and every time she heard the roar of a bikes' engine, her instinct was to run. There to rescue her, Rojay searching to find Jade would be because he wanted to take her back to somewhere she didn't want to go. Daydreaming and hearing an engine, that which once caused her heart to fly, now caused her whole body to freeze. *'Would Rojay stay away?'* Dreams turning to nightmares, from a bright sun filled day to a darkening night sky. Shivering and shaking. *'Why stay so long?'* Trapped? Her staying hadn't always meant her being under lock and key. *'Why not leave sooner?'* Why had she left her own house? *'She could have talked her way out of being sent away.'* Jade knew Papas' money spoke much louder than any words. *'Was she mentally ill?'* The only thing she proved, was something she'd always known, the fact Mama and Papa didn't care. *'Why not leave earlier?'* In the beginning she stayed because she didn't want to be sent to an institution and then she stayed because she was his girl, because her staying made him happy. *'Was he happy now?'* Her being his girl didn't give him the right to do what he did. A nightmare? She ran and he chased, she told him. No! It wasn't an excuse to say he hadn't heard, he should have been listening. *'She was screaming.'* Turning from hero to monster. *'Why did he do what he did?'* In her nightmares she saw Rojay back with Stacey stood laughing, spending her money and mocking her innocence. *'Jade wasn't innocent anymore.'* Dreams turning to nightmares, the most repeated nightmare took Jade to the beach, sat on the cold, damp sand beneath the light of a full moon, sometimes someone called her name, but on more than one occasion nothing and no one prevented her from entering the rolling waves.

♪180♪

Late, she said she was meeting friends, but there was no one she knew. Why had she telephoned the Nook Clinic again? The one on the other end of the line repeated what she was told before. Another week, seven more days? Jade didn't have the luxury of time, something had to be done. Day turning to night, from being in amongst many; she found herself alone. Late, light turning dark. *'Was the moon full?'* She felt too afraid to look. *'Alone?'* There was much she didn't want to be able to see. Late, alone on the beach, having pictured herself where she was more than a thousand times; the lone female questioned her ability to do what she imagined and dreamt of doing. Surrounded by silence, with no one in sight she stood. Asking if she could put one foot in front of the other, Jade checked and double checked that there was no one watching. *'Alone?'* Allowing her bare feet to take her beyond the bright white break of rolling waves. Knowing the icy water would take from her, her breath as the deep darkening ocean washed over her, she hoped what would engulf her entirety was capable of cleansing her soul and washing her troubles away. Could she? Should she? Jade had to do something. She said she was out with friends from the camp, she'd warned those she lived with she could be late. *'People would worry if she didn't return.'* The note placed inside her pillowcase explained everything and would be found when next aunt Jennifer changed the bedding. *'If anyone, Jennifer would understand.'* Avoidance and white lies, Jade would do anything and try everything to buy herself more time and delay what would cause those who loved her, heartache and pain. *'Having gone missing before, could she put her family through her going missing again?'* Jade going missing this time, could mean her being missing forever. Not all bodies get found. *'Lost at sea?'* Aware of the fact the tide was going out; she intended to swim as far as she could. *'An accident?'* Many a holidaying teenager took a midnight swim. A dare gone wrong or one breaking away from a group and becoming lost? *'An excellent swimmer.'* If she didn't panic she could go miles, if she allowed the sea to take her, it could keep her secret for all eternity. What was tragic sounded romantic as she played the thoughts of others inside her head, once gone Miss Jade Jennifer Barris would soon be forgotten. *'Back with Stacey?'* Rojay had forgotten her already. Could, should she go? Prepared to sacrifice the life of the unborn child inside her; Jade saw it as only right she be prepared to take her own life too. *'An eye for an eye?'* Grannie said if everyone took an eye for an eye there would come a time when no one would be able to see.

A life for a life, she didn't feel pregnant, not broody or maternal, what Jade felt was violated. Inhabited by a trespasser, she hadn't felt any flutterings or strange movements. *'A baby?'* Tiny, the tadpole would be growing ten tiny fingers, ten stubby toes, blue eyes and a button nose. Agreeing; all babies born were beautiful bundles of joy, some saw their babies to be miracles, but everything beautiful and good has its' ugly, bad opposite. Violated, what happened to Jade was punishing and violent. Jade had said no and no meant she didn't want anything to do with anything resulting from what she wished she could forget. *'Not the babies fault?'* Jade would be to blame if she brought a child destined to live a terrible life into the world. *'No life would be the same.'* Jade couldn't mother what she saw as being a monster. *'Give the baby to daddy?'* Once born she could leave the baby for Rojay to bring up. Rightly or wrongly, Jade saw his not knowing as being for the best and felt certain he would deny it all. Sure he would see things to have been different, unable to take responsibility, like Jade, Roland Jackson was too young, left to erase the mistake, Miss Barris was fast understanding how it felt to be cruel to be kind.

Walking to the waters edge and stepping into the breaking waves, Jade allowed what felt sharp to slap into and wash over the parts of her body being submerged. What else could she do? *'If meant to live, she would survive.'* Maybe the cold would be enough to remove what was continuing to grip on to its' lifeline. From her ankles to her knees and up to her thighs before wrapping itself around her waist, it was when hitting her chest what appeared black took from her, her breath, inhibiting her ability to begin her swim. *'She had to swim.'* Late was getting later, if unable to leave the beach behind; she would have to return. *'An accident?'* Her aunt and uncle would understand her being wet if she said she'd been swimming with friends in the sea. 10:30pm. Lunging forward she refused to quit. *'Now or never?'* Lunging forward, diving and traveling under the fast moving water so to put more distance between herself and the land. Moving further and further away from what was solid, when out of her depth; what seemed rough lay calm. Swimming above, moving through and diving below, Black, like its' blue did during the day, the oceans' darkness joined seamlessly with what indicated day dissolving into night. Black, in the absence of any artificial illumination as she swam further and further from the shore the lone female lost all perception of depth and space. *'Her only option?'* How else can one escape their fate if not by destroying what fate holds? Swimming, sure she was heading in the right direction, leaving what needed to be left, when surrounded by what was black, Jade saw nothing. Stopping to tread water and catch her breath, the seamless line between water and sky felt like seeing nothing. *'Eyes open or closed?'* Where was she and which way was land? Swimming, that which now encased her entirely became heavy as its calm turned rough. Swimming, the one out at sea alone began to struggle when hit by one wave and then another. Hit by water which when turning and moving turned and moved her along with it. From still and calm to wild and rough, hit by one wave from this direction and the next from another she floated above before becoming covered, struggling to regain and keep her breath, each gasp was becoming shorter and shorter. *'Out of her depth?'* Doing all she could to prevent the panic she felt building; Jade struggled not to splash because she didn't want to make a noise. *'Not wanting to be found.'* Slipping from above to below, she wondered when it would be over? When sleeping deeply she woke gasping for air, when dreaming, she encountered all the things which when awake she would rather not have to face. *'Was it over?'* Opening her eyes and gasping for air, opening her mouth and gurgling on the vast amount of water raising from within as it poured out. *'Dream or nightmare? Imagination or real?'* A cough, a sputter and a shiver which caused her to feel like everything within was encased in ice. Where was she? What had happened? Was this heaven or was she in hell?

"What the hell do you think you were doing?" What was he doing? What had he done? A cough, a sputter and a shivering she couldn't stop, an iciness penetrating her bones. What had happened? *'Was she dead?'* "What the hell do you think you were doing?" She guessed he wouldn't believe her if she said she was enjoying a moonlight swim. *'What had he done?'* Why was he shouting? "I should call an ambulance, get you to a hospital."

"No!" Regaining her breath and finding her voice; having emptied everything including the content of her stomach, Jade insisted he help her up onto her feet.

"You almost died." *'Shocked?'* The fact he was wet was a clear indication of what he'd done. *'He could have died too.'* Bobby had recused Jade. How? Why? What was he doing on the beach so late? "Were you on your own?" While the honest truth was not exactly, she nodded. "What happened?" Could, should she tell him the truth? Assisting her up and walking with her off the sand, he led her over to his car helping her inside before climbing in and switching on the engine so he could start up the heater, passing her a towel, he climbed back out to open the boot and change into a tracksuit, finding for Jade his team jumper and telling her to remove as much of what was wet as she could. Having come across the abandoned bag, towel and shoes on the beach while out jogging, Bobby hadn't realised who it was he was looking for? Believing the items had been dropped or forgotten, it had been the sudden stillness of the ocean which caused him to look out to sea. Seeing her body slip beneath the water for who knew how many times? A female, only when he had her in his arms did he realise who she was. Aware there was much she wasn't telling, Bobby said if she refused to allow him to take her to the hospital, he was taking her back with him to his hotel room.

Agreeing to take a shower, while she warmed what felt frozen, he telephoned her uncle to let him know she was safe. Informing Kevin the two were at his following a late super, he said he would get Jade a hotel room and bring her home in the morning. A warm shower and soft fluffy bathrobe. *'Was she dreaming?'* Assuring Bobby she felt fine, he told her, her aunt and uncle said she should enjoy her night. *'Gone midnight, she'd have to apologise for Bobby getting her aunt & uncle out of bed.'*

"Kevin offered to come collect you." Aware everyone was doing what they were because they cared. "He said to have fun." Thanking him for everything, she felt shocked when room service delivered hot drinking chocolate and freshly buttered toast. "You can stay." Three bedrooms, two bathrooms and a lounge, Bobby's suite was large enough for her to be his guest. "Hot chocolate, toast or whatever you want from the mini bar." His having showered and changed meant Bobby insisting they relax and get their strength back.

"Nice room." The penthouse suite of the most expensive hotel in town, his career and growing popularity meant his being able to command the best of the best, not that he would. Bobby being where he was, was more to do with his dad not wanting him getting mixed up with the rough. "Posh," She made reference to the relaxing multi seat sofa and giant television.

"You can take your pick of beds." Bobby offered to give and get her whatever she needed as both sat on the half moon sofa.

"The guest bed will be fine." Jade couldn't smile when Bobby was telling her he was worried.

"What happened?" He wanted to know. Having saved her life, he deserved an explanation. Sitting so they faced one another, dressed in matching dressing gowns and drinking hot chocolate from large mugs embossed with the hotel logo, Jade knew she should say something. Sat within what under different circumstances would be fantastic, she wished he hadn't asked, because she didn't want to answer.

"I'm pregnant." Finally admitting to another what she was denying to herself. "I can't keep it." She shook her head. "It isn't right."

"Is it?" Bobby interrupted.

"Rojay?" She said. "Half his and all," Stopping what was her next thought, she told Bobby she hadn't wanted to. "I said I didn't want to."

"He's forcing you to keep it." The listening male misinterpreted what he heard.

"I said no. I told him no." Jade felt herself begin to shake.

"He forced you?" Bobby gasped.

"I told him no."As her eyes filled with tears; she wiped them away and told Bobby she didn't want to talk about it, his hearing the gruesome details wouldn't be fair and she needed to stop reliving what she wanted to forget.

"Does he know?" Apologising, Bobby said he shouldn't ask. Shaking her head, Jade told Bobby she didn't want anyone knowing.

"I." Bobby stuttered. "You weren't out swimming were you." He realised. "Did I stop you?" He asked. "Were you going to kill yourself." He gasped in disbelief. "We need to get you checked out."

"No."To everything said, Jade told him no,

"Why?" He wanted to hear why she couldn't go on? "It's a baby." His attempt to have her see there were worse things didn't help. "You won't." Shaking her head, Jade said she couldn't promise, because she didn't remember entering the water. Shaking her head, Jade couldn't deny her intentions because she didn't know what her intentions were.

"Sorry."Seeing her cry, Bobby asked if he could hold her. *'Was she dreaming?'* Being held within his strong arms helped her to feel safe. *'Was this real?'* Bobby told her his running on sand helped build his leg muscles, three times a week and always after dark so he wasn't interrupted. He went out late so he didn't trip over anything and because it was when the beach was cooler. "Are you hurt?" She sniffed. Shaking his head, he told her, his using the beach gave him an excuse to call in and say hello to her aunt and uncle. "Did you call in tonight?" Was he out looking for her?

"I was running late." He said the postoffice was closed when he passed, with his own parents' hundreds of miles away, he revealed the fact he now called Jennifer and Kevin his aunt and uncle too. "Sorry."He apologised. Jade telling him she saw both relatives having more than enough love to share.

"I didn't want what happened." When it was her turn to talk, Jade warned Bobby he may not like what she had to say. "No one knows and I don't want them knowing. I don't want this." She said she was running out of time and her options were minimal. In truth, her options were none. "Hideout and have it adopted." She shook her head when told her family would understand. "I don't want them to."

"Running on the beach helps me think and sometimes I think about you. I never thought I would find you in the sea." Taking a deep breath, Bobby told Jade he would do whatever he could to help. Continuing to talk, he realised the one he was holding had fallen asleep. Lifting and carrying her into the guest room, he covered her sleeping form before kissing her forehead and wishing her sweet dreams. *'Was she dreaming?'* Jade had fallen asleep believing she was dead and wondering why Bobby was with her in heaven? When he took her home the next morning, she hoped he would keep his promise never to reveal her secret.

♪181♪

Two hours of sitting in the same position, travelling alone, Jade found herself in amongst families, couples and groups of friends. Agreeing to change seat so an elderly couple could sit together, the male beside her was only interested in the whiskey he drank from the thermos he held onto for dear life. Irritable, his being a smoker meant he couldn't wait to get off what continued moving. *'A well deserved holiday.'* The words of those who told her to have a good time; echoed inside her head as she watched what was outside the window going by. What would they say if they knew? Whenever she closed her eyes, she found her mind reflecting on her lies, why couldn't she be honest and true with those she loved? *'Who was she to say others wouldn't understand?'* Able to see their smiling faces, Jade had accepted the money grannie gave her so she didn't have to be reliant on Bobby. Dear sweet Bobby, whatever money she earned or was given was his. He promised he would help and helping was what he'd done.

Arriving when arranged to collect her from the village Mr. Bobby Hallas agreed when Kevin asked he take good care of his niece. Helping her into his car and taking from her, her suitcase. *'Kind?'* Everyone was pleased for them, a holiday, two weeks in the sun on a private island away from it all. Bobby was taking Jade to meet his teammates and their families, his chance to unwind and her opportunity to see if she could fit in. *'Jade wished their story was true.'* Bobby was going to a training camp and she was on her way to somewhere she didn't want to go, leaving to do something needing to be done. Waving and telling the two to have the best of times, those there to say goodbye had no idea of the truth. *'A happy couple.'* Shannon was shocked to hear they were back together, but even she wished them well. *'Together?'* Having avoided being photographed, the two blamed what was their shared history when saying they wanted to give their relationship a chance before going public. Respecting what they called their privacy, those pleased to see Jade with Bobby, understood it could be more complicated second time around. *'Older & wiser?'* Bobby's public profile was huge and his fan base vast, allowing them time, none witnessing what was pretence saw through what was nothing more than a show. *'Two weeks?'* Both would be away. *'Not together.'* The training camp where Bobby assisted those he saw as benefiting from his expertise was top secret, something he did yearly. Bobby was keeping the promise he made when telling those he helped, his fame wouldn't change him. *'A gift?'* Paying for Jade, Shannon told her she was lucky, but no one would see her as being fortunate if they knew the truth. Waving them on their way, grannie gave her blessing while Jennifer and Kevin called what they saw happening, a true fairytale. Good being underpinned by what was bad, Jade needed her nightmare to be over.

♪182♪

Friends, the short car journey to the bus station was silent. With those waving fading into the distance neither driver or passenger knew what to say, both believing everything had been said. *'Generous?'* Jade promised and promised again to pay him back. Before getting out of the car Jade thanked Bobby for everything.

"I'll be fine." His not being seen meant his taking her to her destination impossible, out of the question, while she would be forever grateful, Jade wouldn't allow her friend to risk his good name and professional career. *'Not his problem?'* Bobby had done much more than he needed to do. Pulling into the large bus station, he asked if she was sure? *'Stand C.'* Nodding she agreed she had everything she needed. Offering more money so she could take the train and book herself into a first class carriage, she said she owed enough already. Pulling into the bus station carpark, Mr. Bobby Hallas couldn't risk being seen anywhere near where Jade was going. *'The Nook Clinic?'* Bobby preferred to use the Berry Well Hotel when referring to the establishment into which she was booked for the next ten days.

"Don't go." Preventing her from leaving the car, he asked she reconsider. "Don't go." Jade didn't want to hear what she knew he was going to say, because she couldn't do what he was asking.

"No."She told him she was sorry. "We can't." She shook her head. Her mind was made up and as she left the car to get her suitcase from the rear seat, she told him she would be forever grateful. "Thanks for the ride." While working out how to repay him his money, Jade knew she would be forever in his debt for everything he'd done. Loyal, loving, caring and kind, she hated the two of them having to pretend and keep up the white lies, but she couldn't risk anyone else finding out. When Bobby attempted to get out of his car, Jade closed the door on him and wished him all the best. "Enjoy the camp." Her returning without him would be because the two had fallen out and their brief pretend relationship would be officially over. When Jade retuned to the village, that would be that. *'Just friends?'* Directing her eyes to a man with a camera hanging around his neck. Bobby said he should go and drove away. *'A sightseer waiting for his girlfriend to buy tickets?'* Jade smiled when realising the camera carrying male wasn't press. *'Cute couple.'* She hoped she would be as happy as the two looked one day.

♪183♪

Two hours sitting in the same upright position, how she wished she and Bobby were doing what others believed they were. *'Friends having fun.'* Friends spending time together and taking time out to relax, two hours gave a lone traveller a long time to think. Two hours, stiff and tired, when arriving in a place she'd never been; Jade didn't want to do what she was about to do.

"Not a problem miss, let me get the bag for you." Aware digression was in his job description, she knew he had very probably made the journey a hundred times before when realising there was no disguising the question in his eyes. *'What was a young girl like her doing, going to a place like that?'* Having done her research, she discovered much about what took place within the walls of the establishment into which she was heading. A private clinic hidden within a hotel? Cosmetic surgery, figure enhancements and slimming pills, that which she sought wasn't mentioned in the advertisement flyers, but everyone knew what went on. A place for the rich, it was rumoured to be the place to go if you were a celebrity with a mistake in need of correcting. Jade didn't blame anyone for wondering, but was thankful to her driver for holding his tongue and pleased he knew where he was going. Arriving at the large electric gate, he said he would need the name she was booked in under.

"Jade," Those running the establishment told her surnames weren't needed.

"Not heard that one before." Her driver said the usual names used were a mix of cartoon characters and comic strip heroes. Jade should have realised real names were optional in a place where money did the talking.

"Will you be okay?" Having taken her bags up the steps and into the reception area before she could stop him, she followed and gave the requested fare with five pound tip. "Take care." Looking at her like she was his daughter, she felt shocked by the fact a stranger sounded more sincere and compassionate than her own Papa. Jerald Barris said those providing a service for which they received a cash payment would always have a ploy or hook to earn them a larger tip.

"Thank you." Jade wondered if Papa had ever been sincere?

A long gated driveway leading to a large manor house, the landscaped grounds were manicured to perfection. Elitist, the deep green sign with gold lettering advertised a five star hotel specialising in rest and relaxation.

Shannon hadn't been right when saying there wasn't a spa, stretching from floor to ceiling, the hand painted list of amenities included much, some of which Jade had never heard of. *'Not inclusive?'* The list headed with the word Spa treatments incurred extra costs. Rehab, continuing on to a second list the one standing alone read words to include therapy, counselling and addiction. *'Everything under one roof?'* The one visiting; wished she was there purely to get away from it all. A mix of lists and full colour photographs, the reception area advertised a Jacuzzi, sauna and full size swimming pool alongside fine dinning and fully stocked bars to include a traditional public drinking area, fruit and energy hydration bar. Offering everything anyone could ever want, outdoor and inside, together and separate, the numerous places designed for relaxation, treatment and recreation offered whatever was ones individual preference. *'Wow!'* Aware she wasn't, the teen and other visitors could be fooled into thinking they were on holiday. Top to toe experiences for all, rooms were a choice of one king or two queen size beds with ensuite and optional butler service. *'Luxoury beyond belief?'* With no one around, the one waiting to book in, began to feel lost within what was mesmerising and vast. *'Nervous?'* What would she do if she was in the wrong place? What if she'd got the wrong date? Walking over and up to the half moon desk Jade noticed a plate with the word reception alongside a bell, could, should she ring it?

"Can I help you?"A receptionist, a more mature lady who knew what she was doing because she'd been doing what she did for a long time, well dressed, the female introducing herself as Ms Ford wasn't a stranger to the surgeons knife and Jade couldn't help wondering if her bright white, perfect teeth were her own? "And you are?" She encouraged the stunned teen to give the information needed?

"I'm Jade, I'm here."

"I know why you are here." Interrupting her stuttered words, Ms Ford lifted the desk top telephone receiver to her ear and spoke to someone called Louise, informing her to come over and collect her guest.

"Sorry."Jade apologised. Believing she was in the wrong reception, she offered to wait outside but was told to stay where she was.

"Louise will be over directly and I will see you in the next day or two." While her ability to smile appeared hindered by the tightness of her skin; Ms Fords' sternness wavered when assuring Jade everything would be fine.

"Hello, my name is Louise, sorry I wasn't here to meet you." Young and attractive, some women were made to wear white. Clinical, Louise looked the type born to be a nurse. Young, attractive and confident, having appeared from a back room, she asked Jade to join her, ticking off the clipboard checklist as they went; Louise stated Jade's registered name, allotted patient number and bed. Hurrying her along, Louise said she was there to help and asked if she was sure? *'Jade had no choice.'* Walking out from a side door and over to a long single storey building which started life as the stable block, Jade apologised again for having gone to the wrong reception.

"You didn't." Louise said it was she who should say sorry for the one she called old frosty knickers. "She hates when she sees the before, but Joan is second to none when it comes to being able to co-ordinate the care you will need after." Rustic, that which from the outside appeared to blend seamlessly, on the inside was starch white and sterile. Distracted by the rows of black and white photographs telling the story of how the Nook Clinic began life as a travellers inn, before becoming a manor house and stud farm, bought by a famous acting couple who transformed it into the private hotel and specialist clinic, having themselves discovered a need for somewhere to escape to.

"There is a book in the gift shop if you're really interested in the history of this old place." The female leading the way and conversation told Jade she could buy the book for three pounds. "I can get one sent to you if you like." Unsure if her interest was genuine or purely a deterrent, Jade had to admit to not bringing anything substantial to read when Louise said reading could help pass the time. Unable to remember the exact contents of the suitcase beginning to feel heavy as she pulled it along. "In here," Asking her to wait in a side room, Louise introduced the male who joined them. "Joe will take your bag. Bed three please Joe." His noticing the luggage wasn't designer caused his eyes to reveal the fact he knew there wouldn't be a big tip. *'Should she tip a porter?'* Was Joe Holt a hospital porter? Like Louise, the male smiled and was friendly. Like Louise, Joe wore what was a nurses uniform.

"Doctor Sutton." Old enough to be her grandfather, Jade felt she was about to be judged.
"Doctor Jones." The female professional appeared a little more approachable, but that didn't stop the one there seeking their help from feeling trapped between the angel and devil everyone carries on their shoulders. "We need to ask a few questions." Telling the medical professionals she'd filled in all forms, Jade was assured everything was routine, a few questions, most of which could be answered with a yes, or no, all of which she should know the answer to. *'Nothing too personal.'* Jade was assured any and everything was confidential.
"When was your last period?" If her dates were accurate, that which was growing inside her was between eight and ten weeks. "Why do you want a termination?" Looking to her for her reply, Jade felt dumbstruck, unable to speak, she didn't want to say. Not wanting to be judged, the lone teen didn't see how anyone else would understand without she revealed every detail? Disbelieved, she and Rojay being girlfriend and boyfriend would no doubt have elders shaking their

heads and saying the two should have known better. Rojay being her boyfriend could mean some would say he hadn't done anything wrong and she worried some would insist he have a say. *'His baby too?'* Jade struggled to see what was inside her as being a developing child. *'Not ready to be a mum.'* Why was it so wrong for her not to want what she believed not to be right? As both doctors looked to her, she didn't want to say.

"You do want an abortion?" Suddenly and for the first time Jade felt her certainty waver, both doctors telling their reluctant patients she needed to go for a scan. *'Why?'* A scan? Why did those about to take what was inside her, want a photograph? Jade didn't want to see. Told she could turn away. Dr. Jones explained what she called safe practice, a necessary procedure, both medical professionals insisted they be sure of everything, before doing what she wanted done. *'Did she want it gone?'*

"How will seeing help me?" Interrupting what was proving to be a long and descriptive explanation, Jade asked what would happen if she refused?

"We couldn't continue without the information the scan will give us, we'd need your medical records." She knew it made sense, but she wasn't sure she could cope with doing what other expectant mothers do. *'She would look away.'* Her not looking wouldn't mean she wouldn't see, Jade would imagine. *'A baby?'* Bobby had called what was inside her innocent. A baby? Would, could they pretend the baby was his and bring he or she up together? Why had she listened to him? *'Too young to be a mother.'* The two would always know the truth and Jade didn't want to mother Rojay's child. *'Did she?'*

"Here at the Nook we have everything you will need to aid recovery, you being with us for a few days means you have access to counsellors and therapists." Dr. Sutton advised she take advantage of what was there to help, while Dr. Jones assured her, she was in safe hands.

"We're here to help." Told there were rules, guidelines and policies which couldn't be overlooked no matter what the circumstances or who the patient. Aware privacy sometimes cost and realising she was in no position to argue or make demands, Jade agreed to listen.

The latest in medical equipment and a list of those at the top of their professional careers, looking and listening, Jade saw justification for the high price.
"Would you like to talk to someone before the scan?" Shrugging her shoulders caused the doctors to send for Joe, instructing him to take her to her bed. *'What was she doing?'* Feeling like a naughty school girl made aware she'd been stupid, she believed she deserved being treated like a silly child. *'Too young to be a mum?'* Jade still felt like she was a child. Not mature enough, not independent enough, seeing herself as having much to learn and things to see before settling down. *'A mistake which needed erasing.'* Wasn't everyone allowed at least one mistake. *'The baby isn't to blame.'* Adoption? Bobby mentioned it and she read about it. *'Yes,'* Seeing adoption as being the morally right thing to do, adoption would mean others knowing what had happened and her having to explain what she'd done? *'Not a baby?'* Knowing what was growing inside her was a new life, Jade told Bobby babies were created by those who love, respect and were committed to one another. What was inside her had been put there by force, greed and because Rojay hadn't listened when she said, No!

What was she doing? Why was she hesitating and why had she left her questioning what was her choice until now? Bed three, a single bed in a private room situated amongst five other private rooms at the end of a ward containing four beds, space for nine patients in total. Jade never realised there were so many others to have made mistakes in need of erasing. Bed three, Joe told her she would spend the time before her procedure and the first day following on her own. Then she would be moved out onto the ward before moving over to the hotel. How long would be dependant on recovery and need. The money Bobby insisted she take was enough for what would add up to a ten day, nine night stay. *'Booked & paid for.'* Why was Jade questioning what she was doing?

"I'll be back to take you for your scan." Was she meant to thank him? There wasn't anything to look forward to and nothing she wanted to do less than what needed to be done. "You have time to shower and get into your nightdress. Some ladies feel more comfortable in sleepwear. You have brought your nightdress, dressing gown and slippers." It was clear Joe was use to saying what he said.

"Yes," Having read and read again the list of essential items, her case was filled with what was vital. Toiletries, sleepwear and comfy clothes, Jade hadn't brought a book because at aunt Jennifers she didn't have any books, a few magazines, a pen and her newest diary. Maybe she should buy the book about the history of the Nook? *'A keepsake?'* Maybe she should go home?

Bobby had been the first to call what was inside her a baby. *'Too young?'* She couldn't bring up a child on her own. Bobby said he would help and believed she should tell others the baby was his, calling every child a blessing. *'Her baby?'* When thinking about being pregnant, all she felt was fear. *'Confused?'* Afraid of what others would say, afraid of letting people down, she didn't want Rojay in her life. Why was she changing her mind? Why was she no longer sure of what was the right thing? *'Would telling everyone Bobby was the father, keep Rojay away?'* Could she and did she want to? Jade agreed when he said it wasn't the babies fault. Would he forever blame her if she did what she was where she was to do? If Bobby wanted to be a father; he could go about it his way, the right way. Should Bobby want a mother for his child, there were many who would happily become his wife. If he was to be father to her baby, Bobby should be at the scan? Did she want him by her side? *'Had she changed her mind?'* Unable to make contact because no one knew where he was. Mr. Bobby Hallas had gone to ground, training those he promised he would never forget. Bobby wasn't with Jade. *'What should she do?'* What Bobby and others were saying, turned what was an unwanted pregnancy into a baby for the very first time?

"Do you want to terminate the pregnancy?" Her pregnancy? The baby? That which Jade attempted to deny couldn't be more real. Assured the scan and other tests were routine, there were more questions to which the answer was yes or no. *'Murder?'* She hadn't thought about anyones life but her own. "Jade?" The female asking the questions prompted her to answer what she said would be the last question.
"I'm not sure." Shaking her head, she apologised for being confused. "How long do I have to decide?" Told the electronic scanning device would be used to provide measurements and everything needed for her question to be answered more accurately, the confused teen was asked if she thought it could be too late to abort? "No." Shaking her head for what felt like the hundredth time, no, she may be out by a day or two with her dates, but felt certain she knew the day it happened. The only time they hadn't used protection, the time she said No.

Lay on the narrow bed covered with thick white tissue paper, she was told the gel needed to allow the scanner to glide more easily would be cold. Unsure if she wanted to see, experience taught her how her imagination didn't always conjure up the actual fact of the situation. *'Look or don't look?'* Louise turned the screen away and promised to be quick. Gentle and caring, the young nurse explained what she was doing as she pushed the hard plastic device down onto and across Jade's lower stomach. Pictures and measurements, probing and pushing. *'Quick?'* That which Jade was told would take minutes, seemed to be taking an age.

"Is there something wrong?" The way Louise was checking and checking again caused the one feeling like she was on public display to question what she was seeing? "What is it?" She questioned what she saw to be the nurses concerned expression; her first thought being the machine had discovered a monster. *'Two heads?'* It was clear there was something which shouldn't be. When Dr. Jones arrived, it became clear that whatever was wrong wasn't something which could be put right. Asked to dress and join the doctor in her office, Jade was told they needed to talk.

"Sorry," Too busy worrying about herself and what others would say. *'When?'* The word never escaped her lips, but the thought crossed her mind again and again as she listened to what she was being told. "Your baby has died." Why wasn't she feeling relieved? Gone? Everyone was sorry and Jade couldn't stop thinking this was the result she wanted. *'Gone?'* Taken before others could take it. It wasn't a baby, not yet and now not ever, she no longer needed to answer the question about what it was she wanted? *'Gone?'* Jade began to see that which had been growing inside her as being much smarter than she was. *'Gone because it wasn't wanted?'* Jade should be seeing what she was being told as being for the best. Gone, someone would talk to her and someone would be with her when it was time, instead of deciding whether or not she should terminate her pregnancy, become a mother, or have the baby adopted, instead of asking herself if she could tell everyone Bobby was the father. Jade was being asked how she wanted what had died to be remembered and lay to rest. It shouldn't have changed anything, everything had changed. Having prepared herself for being the one to allow what was growing inside her to be taken, Jade struggled to understand why she was feeling sad about the life inside her having gone.

A GEORGE

A baby, ten tiny fingers and ten toes with a cute button nose, what could have been, was no more, Jade's baby had stopped growing and ceased living. Everyone apologised for doing what needed to be done. *'Gone?'* When wheeled back to her room and bed three. Jade was told it was over. Drifting in and out of sleep, she wondered if Bobby would believe she wanted him with her at the scan. Considering his offer of help, Jade was thinking about changing her mind, only to discover the decision she had to make, taken away.

♪184♪

14: DREAMS

♪185♪

Walking towards his waiting car, Bobby commented on how good she was looking. Clothes borrowed from her aunt Jennifer and the few essentials she kept in what they called her room. Jade didn't feel good, but her regular showers, recent hair cut, manicure and a pedicure went a long way to her feeling more human. Choosing a mid-length dress in a floating A-line style, even her uncle agreed the deep pink and black colour combination was perfect for dinner with her parents. Feminine and respectable, its' rounded neck and elbow length sleeves were classy enough to be appropriate, her elders agreed she looked perfect as she and Bobby joined those to have arranged and booked the high class restaurant in the nearby town.

"Good evening" The stylish middleaged waiter greeted upon handing out the large leather bound menus and asking whether or not he could provide refreshments while they browsed. Glancing around, once orders were placed and taken, Jade felt relieved the dimly lite environment was neither over crowded nor empty. Dark, heavy wood furnishings and deep red velvet drapes braided with gold trim, what was warming would be romantic under different circumstances, an ambience magnified by the gentle flickering of strategically placed candlelight. The calm and soothing atmosphere didn't deterred the males at the table from embarking upon their favourite topic of conversation, from how Bobby was doing to what was being printed on the back pages of the local and national newspapers. While the content of the on going discussion felt natural, to Jade, Mama and Papa felt like strangers.

"You're looking well." Jemima commented.

"You too."Jade said."You and Papa both." She smiled, a smile which faded when Mama asked whether or not she wanted to come home? All knew sooner or later the question would be asked. Jade and Jemima also knew the question was being asked more out of courtesy, duty and commitment than it was out of love, loyalty or want. As all at the table awaited her reply, how she wished she could reply with a pass.

"Jade?" Papa urged.

"Sorry."Lowering her glance and shaking her head, she said she couldn't.

"What?" Mr. Barris was confused.

"I'm working." His daughter attempted to explain her decision to remain where she was.

"A few hours waiting tables in a tea shop." Jemima shook her head in utter dismay of what she was hearing.

"I enjoy it." Aware neither parent would be listening; she told them she was happy and enjoyed working at the cafe and alongside her aunt. Jade liked village life.

"I've arranged for you to attend college." Jerald assured his daughter there were favours he could call in, to get her education back on track.

"I don't want to go to college." Looking to each of her parents in turn, she saw nothing but disappointment, hearing only disapproval, she didn't want what they wanted. Why couldn't they see she wasn't the person they wanted her to be? *'Not who they saw?'* Jade didn't want to be the person others expected her to be, Jade had found herself and she was happy.

"You want to be a scrubber for the rest of your life." Mama's question was much more a statement.

"I'm a waitress." She defended her career choice.

"Is there a difference?" Jemima questioned upon releasing a deep sigh. "I can send you on courses to learn the beauty business."

"No."Jade shook her head. "No," She said. "No!"She shouted."No!" Why did no one ever listen to her? "No!" She called.

"No!" Woken gently by those there to look after her, her first thought was that Mama and Papa had succeeded in their quest to have her incarcerated within a place for those with mental health difficulties. *'A fever?'* Following what she'd been through; her sleep had been deeper and for much longer than anyone expected. *'The baby was gone.'* Waking, Jade was reminded of the fact she was a guest at The Nook Clinic and told of what had occurred in the same breath as being assured her being with Bobby and her parents had been a dream.

"Do you remember?" How would she ever forget? They said it only weighed around an eighth of an ounce but it felt heavier. 1inch in length, in amongst what left her body with the final push, she saw something much larger than expected. Blood? Had the baby drowned? A intra-uterine foetal death: Told what occurred was rare, it was confirmed the pregnancy had lasted eight to nine weeks. *'Unlucky?'* When looking at what lay between her open legs, Jade believed she was looking at the unluckiest baby of all. *'The baby?'* Had what would be forever unborn avoided the complicated life lay out before it? *'Unwanted?'* Why was she not feeling relief, the physical pain had subsided, but as her eyes fell upon what was the extinguished life lay out before her, she knew the phycological pain may never die. *'What had she done?'* The truth was, she'd done nothing, not an abortion. Some said the length of the pregnancy didn't warrant it being a stillbirth. What had formed life within, had also found death inside her, no heartbeat, arms, legs, fingers and toes? Had she imagined what she felt sure she'd seen? A baby, the baby lay sleeping in the position said to be the position all babies begin life, sleeping a never ending sleep. *'Was she sorry?'* Those around her said she had nothing to be sorry for, assured there was nothing she could or should have done, she was asked what it was she wanted to do? *'What was there to do?'*

An indued labour, what was gone had departed quickly; eliminating the use of what she had been told was on stand-by to remove what could prove stubborn. *'Toddlers & teens were stubborn.'* The baby would never have the chance to be anything but a foetus encased within a never-ending sleep of nothingness. *'Gone?'* Without experience there could be no dreams. *'Gone?'* What else was there for her to do? Asked if she needed some time? She'd looked when asked if she wanted to see, but shook her head when it was requested if she needed time? *'Gone?'* A plaster caste? A photograph? The ashes? Had she been dreaming when hearing the questions to sound horrific when associated with what had been, but was barely there?

"A name?" Everyone and everything has a name. No one could be certain of the sex and so she chose what could be either? It would have been easy and it was tempting to say Angel or Baby, but when asked, Jade told those needing to register what had happened; to print Spirit in the box requiring a name. Spirit. Nothing more nothing less, Spirit would mean what she'd lost being forever with her. *'Her second Spirit?'* The more she thought about it, the more the name seemed fitting. Spirit, it no longer mattered if the baby was to be a boy or a girl? Not of age to be an angel, old enough to be recognised as what it would develop into. When she asked if Spirit's heart had beaten, she was told yes, her emotions becoming mixed, she questioned what she'd done? What could she do about something she'd never been in control of. *'Is anyone ever in control of their own spirit?'* Spirit was a good name for what would now and forever fly free.

"You passed out." Jade remembered little about what was being referred to as her having fainted. Dr. Sutton said the next procedure was a D&C *(Dilation & curettage)* When Louise said what would happen was a clean out, Jade closed her eyes and woke shouting No! Had her seeing Bobby with a large bouquet of white roses been a dream? Rushing in to be told he was too late and asked to turn around, Jade felt sure she saw Joe escorting Bobby out of the room where she lay resting, recovering from something she never wanted to go through again. *'She would've agreed to whatever he wanted.'* Coming around to there being another way, why had what was wrong to begin with gone horrifically awry? Louise asked if she wanted a copy of the scan when questioning what she wanted to do? What did Jade want to do with the ashes? *'The baby was gone.'* Unsure, Joe advising she take what was on offer incase she regretted her decision later; only caused her to realise her mind had changed long before being denied its choice?

"Nothing."Jade said she didn't want any reminders or anything which if found could lead to others discovering what she wanted to forget, something she knew she would forever remember.

Nothing, no: "No!" Screaming, shouting and crying out like someone in pain, her pain wasn't physical. Walking to the cot in the middle of the night ready to feed the child she heard crying, the young mother discovered her baby was gone.

"No!" Waking in the middle of the afternoon to find Joe waiting for her eyes to focus and find him, Jade apologised for making a fuss, hoping she hadn't disturbed or upset anyone else. Joe told her the strange dreams and odd feelings were understandable reactions to what had happened.

"You need to come with me." Insisting she use the wheelchair, Joe said that as her nurse he needed to follow what was health and safety policy when taking her outside.*'Where were they going?'* Pushing and chatting to her as they moved from her room inside The Nook Clinic out into the garden and through a gate hidden within a stone wall. *'Troy's playground?'* Jade asked where she was? *'A grave yard?'* Joe explained the dreams and thoughts being experienced were because she was looking for what was no longer there. A small courtyard, a secret garden in the centre of which Jade noticed the tiniest of raised tombs.

"I don't understand." Looking around at what was being beautifully preserved and tended by someone who truly cared. Joe advised she see and take it all in, informing her how not everything was as it may seem. Dry stone walls enclosing raised flowerbeds, Jade saw trinkets, ornaments and planting in the shape of nursery toys. Windmills and teddybears, rattles, balls and spinning tops.

"He was two."

"Who?" Continuing in her struggle to understand why she was where she was, Jade requested more detail. Made of stone, marble, wood and the plants growing naturally, she saw a tall multi room dolls house built up against the main wall, ceramic balloons and twinkling metal stars, that which she was beginning to recognise as being a tomb, Joe called a playground. "Why bring me here?" Joe said it was to say goodbye and to see where the one she would be forever looking for would be. On top of the wall beside the raised tomb she saw a mix of silver and gold star shaped plagues, each inscribed with names and dates. Not many, Joe told her Spirit would be the sixth, the youngest and only the second to have died inside.

A playground for deceased babies, bodies and ashes lay together in the same safe place. Troys playground, Joe told how the high walled structure was a duplicate of what had been the two year olds nursery when he and his parents occupied what was now the Berry Well Hotel as their home. *'They never wanted their beautiful boy to be lonely.'* Star, Silver, Ruby, Lilly and Prince. Joe shown Jade where the plague for Spirit would go and said she could have more words inscribed if she wanted. *'What would she say?'* Star's plague said goodbye, Silvers' stated no more than the date and name, Ruby was told she would be missed, Lillys' said she would always be remembered and for Prince there was a poem.

"No," Joe answered the question before she asked, not all expectant mothers came into the clinic for the same reasons, some were there to hide and some were willing to pay for the care they lacked at home. *'A space for them to leave the secrets each needed to keep.'* Joe said it was sad how the passing of others brought hope to Troy's ageing parents because it stopped their little boy being on his own. *'Sad?'* It made sense, able to see why Joe had done what he did, agreeing she was ready to leave, Jade said she would think about what she wanted inscribed on what would show where she'd left her secret to hide.

Spirit
Within my confusion
I hope you found your peace

No regrets, two days in a room on her own and another on the ward where four beds stood side by side. Clean cotton sheets, hotel standards in a medical setting, why did she keep saying she was fine when she was anything but? On the mend and progressing well, Jade knew others were saying what they were to help her feel better. *'She couldn't feel worse.'* Chatty and sociable, the other females she lay beside each had their own story to tell. Mary was a mother of five, not able to justify another mouth to feed, her reason for paying private was because her family doctor said she was too young for the operation which would prevent future mishaps. Shelly said her fiancée didn't want her looking fat on her wedding day and Jill barely spoke, younger than Jade, all noticed how the one who said she wouldn't be moving over to the hotel cringed in the presence of the older, more dominant, demanding and commanding male arriving to take her home. His home, all assumed, but were told by staff how them getting involved and jumping to conclusions never helped anyone in the long run. *'People were allowed to keep his or her own secret.'*

"Will your man be coming to collect you?" Joe asked when helping Jade gather her belongings for the move to her hotel room?

"Tell him he can come join me if he's stuck for somewhere to stay."Arriving with her painkilling medication, Louise said Jade was a lucky girl.

"My man?"She didn't understand.

"We should keep confidence." Both apologised for talking out of turn.

"Who are you talking about?"

"Me" Turning, Jade felt shocked to see Bobby standing in the doorway of the ward she was about to leave. Her seeing him with flowers in hand hadn't been a dream. Bobby had come to change her mind and left when told what happened. "I'm so sorry." He told her he'd booked an adjoining room at the hotel, smiling when both Joe and Louise assured him he didn't need any work doing, he said he could do with the rest.

"Your man," Joe winked.

♪186♪
♪187♪
♪188♪
♪189♪

Adjoining rooms, Bobby told Jade to stop worrying about him being recognised. Smirking when Ms. Ford gave her disapproving look, together the two found amusement in those they saw to be at different stages in their treatments. *'The wired & the wonderful?'* The two knew they shouldn't, but couldn't help smiling when coming face to face with those bandaged like mummies. Uncomfortable, some had swollen lips, pumped up breasts and inflated biceps which looked ready to pop. Sore, there were noses of all shapes and sizes alongside tight eyes and entire faces disguised by scarfs, sunglasses and surgical masks. *'Strange & remarkable?'* Both agreed none would be bothered or worry about who was and wasn't there when priority was his or her own picture perfect self. Together the two had joined one another for meals and walked the vast grounds with many a hidden garden, exploring and being there with one another, Jade and Bobby spoke, during the daytime Bobby kept Jade company while at night she entered her room to be and to cry alone, when leaving, the friends realised them having avoided what both knew each needed to talk about caused their needing time apart.

Forever thankful, a debt to repay, Jade agreed they should return to the plan to have veered off track.
♪190♪
Returning earlier than expected; Bobby and Jade assured her aunt and uncle that all was fine, blaming his schedule, the two said them being back together might happen one day but not now. *'Yes,'* They liked one another and yes the two would remain the best of friends. *'Deep in their own thoughts,'* Having been through something both were struggling to come to terms with, Jade and Bobby told others they needed time to decide what they wanted for themselves before making a decision about being together. *'What would be would be?'* Loving one another to allow one another the space and time to go, neither had actually spoken about them wanting to be back together.

When returning to the village, Jade was told grannie had made her property purchase and returned to Canada to be with Sam. *'Sorry she hadn't said goodbye.'* Jennifer said there was an open invitation for Jade to spend time with Loti and Sam whenever she wanted to board a flight. *'Should, could she?'* July was busy and for a small seaside village August chaotic, if she was to go Jade said that maybe she would visit grannie at Christmas. Busy sun drenched days, Shannon helped Jade replace the smile on her face, her aunt and uncle made her feel safe, but no one and nothing could prevent the tears whenever Jade was given time to think about what happened. Never having accepted what was growing inside her Jade struggled to understand why what was gone left a gaping hole causing her to feel that there was something or someone missing. *'Gone?'* Would she be feeling what she was if the decision hadn't been taken from her? Could, would Jade Jennifer Barris have become a mother?
♪191♪
A busy and hectic summer, handwork and exhaustion helped when it came to being able to sleep, time assisted

and when boarding the plane to take her to spend Christmas with grannie Jade felt hopeful. Nights snuggled under thick blankets, sitting around dancing flames and roasting marshmallows. Never when home would Jade sit outside at night in the snow. Being cold while feeling warm, when in Canada there was plenty of time for Jade to talk to and with grannie. A grandmother knew when there was something troubling her only granddaughter. Aware of her upset Loti told Jade there was no rush to talk, what would be would be she assured her granddaughter she and other family members would always be there for her. When she asked why her mother would say her aunt Jennifer had always wanted her to herself, Loti said she would be best to ask Jennifer, reminding her of the fact Jemima rarely thought before releasing her words. A quiet, cosy Christmas, having posted all cards and presents before she left to be with Loti and Sam, Jade returned to find two small gifts and a card waiting under her aunt and uncle's Christmas tree.

♫192♫

January, welcomed back, having welcomed what Jennifer requested Loti sort Jade loved the winter coat from her aunt and uncle. Perfume from Jimmy and Sawyer presented in a keepsake treasure chest box containing gift cards and letters from Trevor and Mavis, her second gift was a wristwatch from her brother inscribed with the words *My Sister for All Time*. The note from Papa which said her bank account was unfrozen caused Jade to question whether or not Mama knew. Informed what was in her account was hers' the brief letter to contain nothing but words of explanation, informed Jade all future investments in her name were safe but there would be no regular allowance. Papa hadn't handwritten what came printed on officially headed paper, for Christmas; Papa was telling his daughter she was on her own. *'She knew.'* Almost an adult, taking a deep breath, happy to show her aunt and uncle what caused her smile to turn to a frown; Jennifer shook her head and Kevin assured their niece there would always be a place for her with them. The card wasn't to wish her a happy Christmas or prosperous new year, when opening what was addressed to her and her only Jade was unsure how to feel about receiving an invitation. Nothing from Bobby, from Canada she had sent him a postcard, playing away, winter was busy in the world of a footballer, he probably hadn't received it. Noticing how she looked to see if there was anything else Kevin shown the Christmas card sent to the village address, a card opened and put on display because it included the names of her aunt and uncle too.

♪*193*♪

Returning to the seaside village in the winter meant it being cold and quiet, returning to her aunt and uncle meant there being a warm welcome. More time to spend together, there was still the post and papers to sort, no holidaymakers saw most businesses reduce opening hours and lower productivity. Mr. and Mrs. Burnley left Shannon to cover coffee mornings, Sunday roasts and whatever functions people were willing to hire the village cafe to hold. Children's parties being her least favourite, she could relay on the local WI to assist with more than the cleaning up once their weekly meeting was finished. Helping when needed, there for Shannon when wanted, in-between contracts Jade agreed to work for cash in hand. Mulling over Mama's words about her sister wanting Jade for herself and grannie advising she speak to Jennifer, Worrying about the invitation to an event she wasn't sure she could go to, Jade knew all the things she should be talking about but didn't know how to say it? What questions should she ask? How mush of what was wandering around inside her mind should she reveal?

♪*194*♪

A christening, Jennifer said they were all growing up so fast and Shannon envied her work colleagues' event filled diary. A christening meant her having to return to where she didn't want to be and ran the risk of her seeing people she didn't want to see.

A GEORGE

"A Christening? A bit quick isn't it?" If Shannon had worked it out, anyone could and Jade believed everyone would. Yes, February 14, having a christening six months following a wedding was quick. Jade assured the one sat smirking, her friends' were happy about how things had turned out. "A girl? Does she have a name?" The answer was no, knowing Tarquin and Tamara they probably hadn't agreed? "And you're going with Bobby?" Shannon was as shocked as Jade had been about what arrangements had been made. It made sense for the two to travel together and his offering her a bed at his family home was thoughtful. "Are the two of you together?" Shannon assured Jade she wasn't bitter about what she called her fly by fairytale without an ending. Shannon could never be Bobby's girl, not his type, she laughed when saying he would never keep up with her. Unable to admit to missing absent parents' the strong and independent female assured Jade she would be fine when told the Christening would mean Jade being out of the village for three, maybe four days.

♪195♪

A christening, Jade had known when attending her friends' wedding that this day would come.

"You just got here." Bobby's fussing mother was reluctant to agree to him going out, reminded her sons' home visits meant his struggling to find time to fit in all the things he missed doing when so far away Suzanne said she hated what was their lack of family time.

"Leave the boy be." His father said there were people Bobby needed to see. Proud, Bobby would never forget his roots or neglect those to have helped him along the way. The Christening was Sunday, there was a charity match Saturday and them having arrived on Friday to leave Monday, meant little time to sit and chill. Happy to see Jade, Suzanne insisted they didn't leave until Monday evening so to give her time to host what she called a leavers lunch.

"Don't fuss." Bobby knew he was wasting his breath. There to be godparents, while his mother fussed and

I MAY PRETEND

organised, Bobby whisked Jade away to join Tamara and Tarquin at their house, invited to meet the baby.

Married with a home and family of their own, were any of them old enough to be what was seen to be adult?

"Great house," Bobby commented. "Are you settled?" He asked how things were going and Tarquin replied with a. *'fine.'* Stepping in from the kitchen Tamara brought the tray of requested refreshment as the four sat themselves around the coffee table in the lounge.

"Being married isn't as bad as the oldies make out." Tarquin told their guests they should try it. *'No longer a couple?'* Bobby became aware of where Jade's attention drifted. A converted barn close enough so her parents' could keep an eye and help out, far enough from the main house and stables to be independent. Tamara and Tarquin were man and wife, married with a home and occupied carrycot indicating a family

"You look great." Bobby commented. Whilst flattered Tamara complained about not yet getting her figure back. Like metal to a magnet; Jade was powerless to prevent her eyes falling upon and watching the basket containing their sleeping child.

"Come see her." Jade said they shouldn't disturb the sleeping baby. *'A love child?'* Aware of her discomfort, Bobby agreed with letting the little one rest.

"When was the big day?" He apologised for not recalling the birth date mentioned on the invitation?

"Three months today."Tarquin bragged with pride, stating how he and Tamara couldn't be happier. "Can't wait for you to meet her." He smiled. Tamara reminding her over excited husband how the child she'd carried, wasn't always the angel she seemed.

"We just finished the nursery, would you like to see." Not wanting to offend, Jade followed her hostess. Tarquin telling Bobby such things were girlie and insisting they remain in the lounge.

Peach and mint candy stripe walls, solid wood picture frames displaying an assortment of cute teddybears, puppy dogs, kittens and ponies. A swinging crib draped in brilliant white lace. There was a changing station, a wardrobe, draws and a bookcase. Toys, books and all the equipment a baby could ever need, everything their beautiful princess could want, to include a tall, wall mounted dolls house.

"Lovely isn't it." Tamara smiled. Happy to display the fact the candy stripe blind was the type to blockout all light and show how when switched on, the musical mobile over the cot would light up into a colour filled glow. *'A tall stone multi room dolls house?'* The one in the room was wooden and brightly painted, what Jade saw was the dolls house seen within Tory's playroom. *'Wanting to stop the lump forming in her throat.'* Glancing over to the changing mat; Jade noticed the tinniest pairs of knitted booties, laying side by side there was a pair in pink and another in blue.

"What's it like?" She found herself asking out loud what was running silently through her mind. Keeping her back to her friend, Jade didn't want the other female in the room to see her pain, heartache and sorrow?

"Being married?" Tamara assumed her friend was enquiring about what the four had been talking about. Sitting herself in the high back rocking chair. The wife and mother told Jade it was different. "No one telling us what we can and can't do." She began. "No one here to do things for us." She sighed. *'Jade saw Tamara sitting in the stone & wood throne standing inside the dead babies garden.'*

"Having a baby?" Jade shook her head to remove the wrong image and rephrased her words.

"Oh that."Tamara smiled with love filled pride. "It's taking some getting use to." She said. "But they say it will be worth it." Looking to her friend Tamara realised something wasn't right. "What?" She asked. Getting back onto her feet and walking over to where she saw

I MAY PRETEND

her invited guest and good friend in distress. Despite her not having wanted Tamara to see, Jade hadn't managed to disguise what was revealed by her inability to hold back her tears. "Jade?" Tamara shown concern.

"I'm fine." She insisted. "I'm being silly." She said. Asking if Tamara and Tarquin were happy?

"Of course." Tamara nodded. Settling herself back into the seat. "It isn't exactly how I planned my life to be, but Tarquin and me love one another. We're solid." She said. "Everything is happening earlier than we thought it would, but yes, we're happy." She nodded. Married with a home, a couple in love, a couple with a baby. How it was meant to be. Love, marriage and a family. Listening to Tamara as she described her life, the past, her present and all her many hopes for the future, Jade realised her friend had much to be happy about.

"Jade?" Again questioning her companions emotion, Tamara insisted Jade reveal what was wrong.

"Ignore me." Jade wiped her eyes. "I'm so happy for you both." She lied; all be it only a partial lie. Jade was genuinely pleased and very happy about how things for some had turned out. Sad because when she saw what Tamara had, it reminded her of what she lost.

"Good to see Bobby and you together." Switching the line of conversation, Tamara felt alarmed to see her words cause Jade to cry more. "Jade?" Getting to her feet again, she agreed when asked to fetch Bobby.

Attempting to clear the tears she couldn't stop, when left alone in the room fit for any little princess, Jade looked at what Tarquin and Tamara had created.

"Jade?" Bobby entered. His eyes darting from one thing to another, quickly covering and taking in all to have been perfectly designed and exquisitely decorated.

"Have you seen these?" She lifted and shown him the hand knitted booties.

"Jade?" He questioned her tear stained face. Stepping forward and taking her into his arms as she almost collapsed. "Come sit yourself down." He insisted she allow him to help her as both sat on the cushion topped bedding box.

"What have I done?" She asked?

"Nothing," Bobby reminded her how in the end, nothing had been her decision.

"You never approved." The upset female recalled how his words had assisted her change of mind.

"What is, was meant to be?" Not truly believing what he was saying. Both knew they needed to say the words neither wanted to say.

"I never realised." She sobbed. "Murder." She stuttered. Her chest tightening and her breathing becoming more shallow as she became more and more aware of what she'd almost done.

"No." Bobby attempted to give support. "No, you said you were confused." He told her.

"Tamara said her baby was created through love." Jade sniffed and Bobby agreed to that being the way things should be. *'Could he understand her distress?'*

"You said you changed your mind." Taking her into his strong, gentle arms. *'Young & naive.'* Would she ever be mature enough to understand all to have happened?

"I left everything behind." Jade told Bobby it hurt.

"Talk to Tamara." He suggested. Leaving the friends' alone, Bobby closed the door and encouraged Tarquin to join him downstairs.

"Jade?" Tamara questioned what she thought she overheard. "Are you pregnant?" She asked.

"I'm sorry." Jade sniffed. Not knowing where to begin and insisting Tamara make herself comfortable. "You have a lovely home." She commented. Allowing her friend time to settle back into the high back rocking chair before opening the conversation.

"Thank you, we like it." Tamara forced a smile, concern shinning from out of her eyes as she waited for Jade to speak. "Jade?" She urged.

"I'm pleased things are working out." She remained on track as she continued the conversation.

I MAY PRETEND

"For Bobby and you too?" Tamara nodded.

"We will have to wait see about that one." Folding and stroking her arms; Jade's body language revealed her discomfort and reluctance to speak openly about what she kept deep within her mind.

"Jade, I know we weren't always the best of friends." Tamara began.

"Are you kidding. You and Gretchen were my best friends, my only friends." She interrupted.

"Bobby seemed to indicate you may need my help, I'm happy to try if you'll let me." Tamara again asked Jade if she was expecting.

"No."Jade shook her head.

"It's nothing to be ashamed or afraid of. I was scared half to death and Tarquin said he felt like his world had come crashing in, but once the shock wore off."

"I'm not pregnant." Jade stated. Interrupting the well meaning words of wisdom. "I'm not pregnant." The distressed female repeated. "Not anymore," She sighed.

"You miscarried?" Tamara was clearly alarmed and saddened by what she believed her friend to have disclosed. Aware if she wanted; she could allow what was being misinterpreted to continue. Yes, Tamara was right, sort of. Shaking her head and falling silent, Tamara listened for a second or two, to the silence before unable to hold her tongue she urged Jade to tell her.

"I was going to kill it." She revealed.

"What?" The new mother questioned.

"I was so confused. I wanted rid." She knew those who knew her would disapprove, having realised her true feelings; Jade herself disapproved. Then something happened which she couldn't change, Jade's unborn child died. *'She changed her mind.'* But her baby was already gone. She paid for what was unwanted to be destroyed and her seeing Tamara caused her to realise she couldn't have been more wrong when saying what was inside her was monstrous. What had died inside her had been her first child? Her baby, her flesh and blood.

A GEORGE

When thinking about what could have been, Jade realised it wasn't about biology, it was about caring, love and life.

"You must have thought what you were doing was right." Her friend assumed everything had been discussed and agreed. "Bobby seems supportive."

"He was, he is." Jade agreed.

"A joint decision?" Tamara asked. Taking a deep breath Jade admitted to changing her mind and the baby having died, before informing Tamara the baby hadn't been his. *'Not Bobby's baby.'*

"Bobby wasn't the dad." She said and Tamara gasped.

"No." Her friend shook her head in disbelief, realising who had fathered Jade's child. "No," She couldn't believe what she was hearing. "Rojay?" She released the name inside her head out loud via her drying lips and Jade told her. *'Yes.'*

"I don't expect understanding." Aware of her friends' strong disapproval and the great temptations she must have to say. *'I told you.'* Jade nevertheless felt the weight she'd been carrying lifted.

"Some things aren't meant to be." Tamara chose to comment with logic rather than pity, saying she didn't have to explain. Jade told Tamara her baby lived and died inside her.

♪196♪

"Beautiful," Told she didn't have to if she didn't want, Jade told Tamara and Tarquin they had a beautiful daughter. *'Perfect.'* Tarquin was told to hush when stating it as strange for a female not to want to coo over a new born.

"Jenna Rose," Jade held the one dressed in white and looking like an angel. Small, precious and innocent Jenna Rose was priceless. *'A happy family?'* Tarquin's smile was one filled with mischief as he stated how he planned to extend his family soon. *'A house in need of filling?'* A girl? A tiny, beautiful baby girl, when holding her god daughter; Jade was able to smell baby, baby powder, baby creams and baby wipes. *'A baby girl?'* Jade knew Bobby was watching over her shoulder, but found herself wondering if she and Rojay could have worked things out? A baby girl, looking at Jenna Rose, Jade felt certain her baby had been a boy. Spirit? When leaving the church and walking into the surrounding grave yard, Jade felt she should have a place she could go to pay her respects. *'Brushed under the carpet?'* Bobby gave his silent support like always.

♪197♪

Watching from the terraces and standing by ones self in amongst the cheering, jeering excited crowd, she didn't feel like being alone. The charity match had been planned for over a year and it was by pure chance the dates coincided with Bobby being asked to be a god father. Having found the friendly kick-about impossible to decline, the local football hero made his guest appearance alongside the college team he'd belonged to before leaving. Bobby couldn't have looked prouder when celebrating his triumphant goal, but Jade had been distracted. *'What were they doing there?'* Not ready to spend the day with Tamara, Gretchen and baby Jenna Rose out shopping for last minute christening attire, Jade saw her watching Bobby as being a good idea. *'Why shouldn't they be there?'* Jade was in their hometown.

♪198♪

Had she thought about Rojay during the christening because she'd seen him at the football game? Unable to redirect her stare, she'd watched as the one sitting in the corner stall leant forward, burying his face into the nap of his companions up-stretched neck as she giggled. *'Why weren't they watching the game?'* Shocked, she'd felt physically sick and frozen to the spot as her eyes met the deep blue eyes of one Mr. Roland Jackson. Having noticed her first; his sly smile indicated how much he liked the gained reaction his presence caused. Arm in arm, flirting and kissing, Rojay and Stacey appeared happy. *'What had she expected?'* Following the match when rejoining Bobby, Jade wondered if he'd seen who she'd seen?

♪199♪

A lunch, Mrs. Hallas thought she was doing the right thing when bringing two families together to say hello and goodbye in the same afternoon. Pleased to see Jeremy, Jade saw how her little brother appeared all grown up, older, taller and much more mature, it didn't shock her to discover Jeremy was wiser than when she left. Awkward and uncomfortable, Jemima and Jerald made no secret of the fact they saw seeing their daughter as being a complete waste of their time. Wanting the time to pass quickly, when leaving the house; it felt like everyone had turned out to wave their local football hero goodbye. Pushed into the background, as family, neighbours, friends and fans, new and old arrived to wish Bobby all the best. Jade quite liked watching, because Jade Jennifer Barris didn't enjoy being in the one in the limelight. Smiling when fans requested his autographed and laughing when many a swooning female requested a photograph. Happy, Jade would do whatever she needed, to find new happiness wherever she could.

"Bye sis."Jeremy smiled. Her brother really had grown up. Assisting her with her luggage, the sibling she'd fought with more times than she could remember; kissed and hugged her before saying goodbye. How? When had that happened? Jade had blinked and missed his dramatic transformation from boy to man. Being hugged by the male she would always call her baby brother, Jade realised he was the one she missed most. "Are you sure you want to go back?" He asked and she nodded. "He is only going to become more popular. Are you sure you know what you're doing?" Her brother asked having noticed the longing look in her eyes. *'No hiding her feelings.'* Watching as the popular footballer signed more and more autographs Jade told Jeremy she and Bobby weren't together. *'Just friends?'*

I MAY PRETEND

"Visit soon." She told him not to be a stranger before climbing into the car.

"Take care." Jeremy smiled and as Bobby got into the drivers seat he asked if she was ready. Putting on their seatbelts, both agreed it was time to go.

Upset and happiness, them becoming godparents turned out to be quite the experience. Up one minute and down the next, both saw what it would be like should they decide to return home. *'Not together?'* Mrs. Hallas hinted about her not being prepared to give up on the two becoming man and wife, while Mr. Hallas told her to stop fussing and advised his son not to rush. Jeremy spoke about still being in contact with Jemma; while neither Mr. or Mrs. Barris said anything much. Interesting, if nothing else, the lunch organised for those who were leaving convinced Jade she was doing the right thing. Returning to the village and people who wanted and respected her. *'Would her aunt & uncle respect her if they learned the truth?'* When with Bobby, Jade wished she knew what he was thinking? In church the two had stood side by side. *'No rush?'* Mrs. Hallas wanted a reason to wear a large hat. The charity football match had put Bobby where he was most confident and looked more comfortable while the leaving lunch, left all feeling disappointed. Mrs. Hallas told her son she was sorry when Mr. and Mrs.Barris left before it was time to go. Different, Jade couldn't prevent the sigh of relief from exiting as they hit the open roads. *'Yes,'* She nodded when asked if she was happy to be leaving. *'Yes.'* Leaving felt like going home. How she wanted to ask if she and Bobby would ever be more than friends? *'Unworthy?'* She knew she didn't deserve more than what her friend was giving, his time, his company and his kind words. *'He was a footballer & she worked in a cafe.'* His life had remained on track while the life she was living felt derailed and unrecognisable.

♪200♪

A GEORGE

Sat side by side, as Bobby concentrated on the road, Jade wondered what would be? *'Friends?'* Smiling to herself, the young female was aware others her age would rather be out having their hair done and spending time with friends. *'Smiling?'* Jade was happy to watch Bobby fulfil his dream. *'Good friends?'* Her having seen Rojay with Stacey was how it should be.

"I saw you." Hearing his stern tone, his passenger questioned what it was Bobby was about to say. "I saw you watching them." He revelled his having seen Rojay with Stacey. *'A romantic date?'* What was it he wanted her to say? "How did his being there make you feel?" Wanting to say sick, the truth was; Jade didn't want to answer because she wasn't sure?

"Shocked." When speaking she kept her eyes facing forward. "I wanted to run, but I was there with you. He looked happy." She said.

"He doesn't deserve to be happy." While agreeing, Jade failed to feel the anger she heard in Bobby's voice.

"Sorry." She also disagreed when he attempted to say it wasn't her fault.

♫201♫

In need of refreshment, Bobby pulled off the fast road into a lay-by designed for rest. Getting out of the car to stretch his legs and fetch them each a drink. Jade had never felt more sorry, forever grateful for his help, she didn't want to lose his friendship. Sorry he'd gotten involved in what she realised would never be over. *'Not something to brush under the carpet?'* Bobby believed Rojay should know what he did and be told about what happened. Bobby didn't understand and Jade couldn't tell him how no matter how it had come to be, she was the one to have lost her baby, even when rephrased and described differently. *'Her baby had left her.'* Jade's baby leaving her didn't prevent her feeling like a killer, Jade had wanted what was inside her gone; for longer than she'd considered and recognised it as belonging to her. Upset, feeling the need for some air, Jade stepped outside the car as Bobby began his return. Having queued for refreshment. *'A motorbike?'* The roar of an engine and the screeching of brakes? Were they pulling into the lay-by because they'd seen her? Maybe they needed rest and refreshment too? *'No!'* Jade felt her heart sink and her skin sting in anticipation of the contact and connection which was about to take place. *'A meeting she didn't want.'*

Rojay and Stacey, removing their motorcycle helmets, both dismounted the bike parked close, but only he approached where Jade was standing. Nervous, anxious and a little frightened, aware Bobby would be by her side within seconds, there was no stopping Rojay reaching her first.

"You should have told me you were back." Jade wanted to run, she'd run away once already and knew there was nowhere to go. *'What did he want?'* Placing his strong stature to obstruct her direct vision of Bobby, Rojay demanded to know where Jade had been?

"It doesn't matter." She reluctantly replied. Standing upright and wanting to appear strong while feeling like a frightened child in need of rescuing, with his giant leather clad form shadowing over her, she didn't want to engage. Aware of her uneasiness, Rojay stepped aside while remaining close and lowering his tone when asking how she was?

"You're looking good." He commented. He said he missed her. "You were my girl." Both aware of the fact Stacey and Bobby stood close enough to hear what each was saying, they spoke.

"No." Jade disagreed.

"You knew I loved you." Keeping one eye on those stood listening, the uneasy female couldn't believe what was happening and didn't want to believe what she was hearing. "Why did you leave me?" He wanted answers to his numerous questions. "What are you doing back with Mr. Super Sport?"

"None of your concern." Her attempt to show strength was feeble as Rojay insisted she listen if she didn't want to talk.

"I looked for you. I went to your house. I thought we were happy." He said.

"And now your back with Stacey." She pointed out what was clear.

"Stacey is a friend. She isn't a patch on you. You broke my heart." Had she? Was Rojay being sincere? The only thing she knew for sure, was the fact she would never trust him. "What went wrong?" Unable to believe he didn't know, Jade asked if he was serious?

"Sorry."She said. Not because she was, because she didn't know what else to say.

"No, You're not sorry." He accused her of lying. Again attempting to assert his strength and misguided authority.

"You need to go." She told him he wasn't welcome.

"You heard what she said." Bobby shown his support. Walking around and placing the drinks and snacks he carried inside the car before walking back to place himself between Jade and the male neither wanted to be where he was.

"We should go." Jade told Bobby they should get back on the road.

"We're not running away." Bobby disagreed with them being the ones to have to move on.

"A footballer isn't much use to his team with two broken legs. Turns him into a real bummer." Rojay smirked as he continued his smug attack.

"What do you want?" Bobby asked.

"I want to talk to my girl." Rojay stated with a smile directed at an uncomfortable Jade who immediately shook her head.

"Jade doesn't want you." Bobby told him.

"I want to go." Jade continued in her attempted to persuade Bobby to leave.

"I love you." Rojay told her.

I MAY PRETEND

"You love her?" Bobby questioned. "If you treat people you love the way you treated Jade, I'm glad we're enemies." Oblivious to the fact Stacey was upset, Bobby continued to vent. "People treat rats better than you treated Jade."

"I love her and I want her back." Rojay spoke while revealing his usual smirk, Bobby informing him, he would never allow him to harm Jade.

"Not again."Instructing the dumb biker boy to go get back on his bike Bobby told him , he made him feel sick.

"I never harmed her. I wouldn't. What you talking about?" Rojay questioned.

"You really don't know." Sizing up to the male wanting to oppose him. Bobby sounded like he was about to reveal everything in front of everyone.

"Bobby?" Jade interrupted.

"He needs telling." Defending what was his intention, Jade begged her friend to leave it, her request allowing Rojay the opportunity to insist he be told what they were talking about.

"No," She shook her head. "Don't." She said. Informing Rojay there was nothing more to say.

"Its over."Bobby sighed. "Go."

"But-out sports freak." Dismissing Bobby's brave words, Rojay took a step towards Jade who told him no.

"No!" She yelled but it was too late. As Rojay stepped forward, Bobby hit out, his anger fuelled punch causing its recipient to lose his balance and fall to the ground. "No," Jade gasped. Asking Bobby what he'd done as she approached Rojay to check he was all right? She knew she shouldn't have, but she hadn't known what else to do. With Rojay getting to his feet and walking back to Stacey, Bobby got into his car.*'Would Bobby have told?'* He may know her secret and be able to forgive her, but she was continuing to struggle to forgive herself. Jade didn't deserve Bobby and found herself watching as having checked and kissed her man Stacey rode away with Rojay.

♫202♫

"Christ!" Within seconds of joining him inside his car, Bobby released his frustration by hitting the steering wheel with the clenched fists of both hands. "I shouldn't have hit out."

"No."Jade agreed. Rojay wasn't worth his energy.

"I can't believe he was here."

"No."His confused companion agreed.

"And back with his ex." Bobby commented. Turning and asking Jade if she was in the car with him because Rojay had gone to Stacey? Having seen her rush to join him as he picked himself up from the floor, he had to ask. "Why did you go to him?" She said he could've been injured. "Are you jealous?" Bobby needed to know.

"Jealous?" She repeated. Having felt nothing but fear, she was confused by what her companion was implying.

"You were his girl and having his." Stopping, Bobby prevented his words.

"His baby." Jade completed his incomplete sentence.

"Sorry."He apologised.

"No."She agreed he was right. Her being pregnant with Rojay's baby was fact, but she wasn't jealous, Rojay and Stacey deserved one another. "I felt fear." She admitted to having felt cold, frightened and alone, but never jealous. "They deserve one another." She repeated.

"Do we deserve one another?" Bobby asked?

"No one deserves me." Jade said he deserved much more as they continued their journey.

♪203♪

Continuing on to their destination, neither knew what to say. Instinct and not intention, Jade was the type who would always tend to the victim before listening to the attacker. Knowing how it looked, her going to Rojay when punched by Bobby didn't mean she cared. *'She should have left him to Stacey.'* Bobby shaking his head was because he saw what she'd done as wrong. Watching the changing landscape as they moved from one part of the country to another, neither was surprised by the changing weather conditions and both expected the rain. Being protected by the car didn't stop Jade feeling cold. From sunshine to dark heavy clouds releasing their contents. *'Just her luck & what she deserved.'* Like the raincloud, the build up of salt filled tears forming behind her sad and confused eyes also soared forward. In the same way raindrops penetrated their floating vessel, Jade's tears burst through what struggled to hold them back, making their escape and blurring her vision in the same way the thick and fast raindrops filled and blocked the windscreen before them.

♪204♪
♪205♪

Upset, her tears came from the heart, her aching, breaking heart which she felt crumbling under the strain of secrets and continuing lies. *'No.'* Rojay didn't know, he had no idea about what he did and she didn't want him to be told. Glancing around herself, attempting to see through tears which fell much more freely in amongst the falling rain, she felt lost. Years of being chauffeured to and from wherever she needed to be, meant Jade feeling safe when inside a car. *'Bobby had done what he had, to keep her safe.'* What could, what should Jade do? What more could she say, sat crying, she sat wondering what Bobby was thinking?

"Sorry." Apologising for what had happened and her tears, she dabbed her eyes with a tissue she found in her pocket.

"I'm sorry." He told her before asking if there was anything he could do? *'Why did he care?'* It was clear his anger had calmed as like he was reading her mind, Bobby said he'd done what he did because he loved her and in response she told him she loved him too.

"I love you." She repeated. The words finally escaping her lips as she looked across into eyes she saw questioning her everything?

"You love me?" Displaying his shock. His lips unfolded into a smile as he repeated the fact he loved her. *'Back together?'* Each wanted the other to be sure. Reaching across and taking her hand into his as he drove, Bobby assured and she agreed that together they would be all right.

♪206♪
♪207♪
♪208♪

Being held close on the dance floor, whirling around beneath flickering lights and losing oneself in the rhythm of the music. Dancing was much like life, one minute fast, the next slow, sometimes unified and coordinated, sometimes what was calm seemed crazy. *'Loud or low?'* With her head resting on the broad shoulders of her booted and suited partner, she couldn't feel more relaxed if lay in amongst feather filled pillows on a king size bed, in love, happy and content. Watching eyes no longer matter and questioning glares were left unanswered, being together was what they were meant to be. From whirling beneath a single spotlight to moving along with and in-between flashing disco flickers. Jade adored being with her someone special. From artificial illumination to the brightness of natural sunlight, beneath her feet the hard, solid and highly polished dance floor turned to warm welcoming soft sand. From being pressed up against the fine material of his black designer suit jacket, she felt her cheek rub against the soft, smoothness of his naked skin. She wore her swimsuit and like always, Bobby looked comfortable in shorts. From a DJ to a steel drum band; from wedding to honeymoon. Lay beneath the high set moon, he came down on top of her, as his lips touched hers, her eyes closed, as his body lay upon hers she savoured his kiss.

♪209♪

"Jade!" Awoken by his kiss. "We're back." With his gentle touch Bobby brought his sleeping companion back to reality. If it were possible to dream in time to the music, Jade had dreamt along with each and every line of the continuing songs being played inside the car as they travelled the roads taking them back to the seaside village. From proposal to wedding and on to what she saw to be a wonderful honeymoon. When waking, Jade questioned dreams coming true. Apologising for not being good company, Bobby told her if the cassette of music brought sweet dreams, his time spent preparing what he played was worth it. *'Back together?'* Promising to call, they would write when his football took him away. Back together, Jade hoped with all hope this time wouldn't be spoiled by the events of the past.

♪210♪

A GEORGE

15: FAR

♫211♫

Looking through the Christening photographs to have arrived back from the printers while Jade was at work, her aunt sounded like a clucking hen, swooning over every other print. *'Maternal?'* Caring, considerate and always kind, those welcoming her back after her first shift of the week; called Jenna Rose beautiful.

"Look at you. I'm so proud." Why was it Jennifer and not Mama who made complementary comments? Why had Kevin and Jennifer never had children of their own when the two would make such wonderful parents? Since what had happened, Jade's head was filled with unanswerable questions. Why was it, after a long day, her entering the kitchen belonging to Jennifer and Kevin felt like she was home?

"I especially like the one of you and Bobby." Kevin said if she'd worn white, people would think it was her wedding and Jennifer told Jade she better not get married without she was invited.

"The two of you do make a lovely couple." Jade being told she could do worse than a semi professional footballer left her realising she already had. *'The worst of the worse?'* Would she ever tell them about Rojay?

"I doubt I'll get married." She sighed. "I don't think I'm the marrying type." She forced a smile.

"It is bound to happen one day." Jennifer told her not to be so down on herself.

"I doubt anyone would want me." Jade sighed when joining her elders at the table. *'Home for supper.'* Mealtimes were always accompanied by conversation.

"What's wrong with you? You're hard working, young, intelligent and beautiful." Kevin insisted his niece take a good look in the mirror. *'Looking in the mirror was something Jade hated having to do.'*

"Kevin is right, you're young. One day you'll get to wear the dress and carry the bouquet like every bride does."

"I guess." Jade felt obliged to agree. When with Jennifer and Kevin, Jade felt she was where she belonged. Home, she said she was, when asked if she was happy to be home. "Yes." She said they were, when asked if she and Bobby were back together?

♪212♪

Back at work, things seemed slow to pick up. Winter meant no outside tables and closed campsites equaled fewer visitors, opening an hour later and closing before dark. When the village was quiet of holidaymakers, local school children inhabited, used and invaded the places they saw belonging to them. Lunchtime menu's provided a choice of fillings with jacket potato's and sauces with pasta or rice. Flavoured hot chocolate drinks replaced the fizzy pop and ice-cream filled milkshakes. Providing snack boxes, wake me up coffee for the adults and warm vimto for the youngsters. Hot water for those who carried hot water bottles inside their coats. Those living in a village dependant on summer months, did all they could to make up for the money they missed when the weather turned harsher and the winds blew cold.

Joining locals in the church hall to watch whatever film was the top rental and sheltering from the rain inside the local bus shelter to eat takeaway fish and chips. Sometimes Bobby surprised Jade by turning up at work, bringing flowers, he never failed to be minus his handsome smile. *'Together?'* Shannon hugged those she said made a wonderful couple and Kevin was over the moon to receive VIP tickets to all local football games. *'Happy?'* Jade heard Jennifer telling her elder sister she should be ashamed for having stopped all parental support. *'Happy?'* The only time Jade felt sad was when she thought about those to have shown her nothing but their love; deserving to be told the truth.

♪213♪

Jade and Bobby, when together their sweet kisses went from being pecks to becoming long, meaningful, deep and sensuous. Managing to hold back the tears until he

I MAY PRETEND

was out of sight, each time his leaving was to play away or train with another team she assured him she'd be fine. Touching until the space between them prevented contact. *'Falling deeper in love.'* When Bobby's football meant his having to leave town, both agreed them being separated wouldn't split them up, not again. *'Older, wiser & stronger.'* Jade promised to wait. Wanting to be faithful, this time was different, because this time Jade was with Bobby and this time she knew it was Bobby she loved and wanted to be with.

♫214♫

"You okay love?" Uncle Kevin remained a constant tower of strength, there whenever he was needed, like a true father would, Kevin always knew the right thing to do and the correct things to say. Like Jennifer, Kevin was never too busy to check in with Jade.

"I'm fine." She sniffed. Accepting without hesitation the offered handkerchief he had on standby.

"I'm going to miss him too." He admitted.

"You are?"Jade questioned the male's statement.

"He's my hero." Her uncle smiled. Revealing the little known fact he'd always wanted to be like Bobby.

"You played football?" Jade gasped.

"I did." Kevin nodded. His stern and serious expression breaking into a sly smile as he admitted how unlike Bobbies his feet hadn't played the same game. "I played football for my country and scored the winning goal in the world cup." He winked. "In my head."He teased.

"Uncle Kevin."Jade accused her relative of being a fool, thanking him for his attempt to make her feel better. Back soon, soon never came around soon enough for the one who felt lost without her boyfriend by her side.

"Another letter."Shannon noticed how if Jade wasn't spending her break writing a letter, she could be found reading what appeared to arrive daily. "Will he be back for the summer?" Shannon teased upon joining her work colleague and friend having prepared a much welcomed coffee. April wasn't yet warm enough for the two to venture from what had become their usual table by the window inside. *'A place to sit when things got slow.'*

"Three weeks."Stopping what she was doing, Jade told Shannon she knew how long Bobby was away for. "It's another invitation." She handed over what she was examining. Gretchen and Greyson, two more of her friends were getting married. July the fourth, Gretchen wanted Jade to be bridesmaid and would be sending her the dress she wanted her to wear just as soon as she found it. An invitation and list of questions, her friend wanted to know her dress, shoe and hat size.

"A bit controlling."Shannon saw what she was given to read as being more a demand than a request. "A hat?" Both laughed at the prospect of Jade wearing a floppy sun hat to go with the floral flannelette floor length dress each saw coming her way.

♫215♫

Her dress size? Standing before her dress mirror up in her room, uncomfortable and unsure. A second, another bridesmaids dress? Would she ever be the one wearing white? Did she want to be a wife when being a wife was associated with becoming a mother?

Black leather shoes, white wool tights, a grey velvet dress and a bright white lace smock. Her shoulder length hair fell in curls and was tied back, taken off her face by a large white bow, she looked like a little madam as she walked around with her long legged rag doll draped over her right arm. Why was Jade remembering her being little; when looking at the young woman she'd become?

"Your aunt has no room for you in her life." Jade felt the statement delivered by an angry Mama should have been her saying aunt Jennifer was leaving to begin a new life. "You are staying here with your father and I." Jade may have been little, four years of age at the time, young, but old enough to remember Mama's stern and uncaring words. Recalling in detail her elders' matter of fact tone and closed body language. "Stop your crying."

The toddler was told to get over herself. "And give me that dam doll. You're my daughter now and no daughter of mine will be seen playing with cheap inferior tat." Questioning Mama using the word. *'Now?'*

Standing alone in what was her room, Jade wasn't sure what it was she was thinking when remembering how grannie said she should ask Jennifer. Unlike the woman she called Mama, her aunt had all the time in the world to spend playing, talking, or just being there.

Their nanny? *'Official, or unofficial?'* Jennifer had taken on the role of carer for Jade and her brother when residing under the same roof in a room to have felt mysterious and magical. Beaded curtains at the doors and windows, colour filled and shinny. Jade remembered the extra large scatter cushions arranged in the corner to form seating, cushions some of which were decorated with sequins and some embroidered with colourful silk thread. *'Handmade & bought.'* She remembered being allowed and encouraged to crawl amongst what were soft, square and round. Clapped for walking over the carpet and invited to play in amongst fur rugs and beanbags, watched over and cared for as she continued to grow. A room of multiple fabrics, magical colours and mysterious textures. Curtains hung from ceiling to floor were used to form the devisions needed to turn what had been one large room, into a small home. A sink, a worktop, a kettle, a fridge and a toaster, where other rooms in the house had fitted and walk through wardrobes, Jennifer had her wardrobe to one side and a mini kitchen to the other of what led through to her ensuite. Segregated, provided with what she needed to live within her personal space. Jade began struggling to remember her aunt ever coming out into what was the large multi room building Mr. and Mrs. Barris called home. A couch which doubled as a bed, Jade suddenly remembered the record player and realised how like her aunt, she too had left behind what they used to play their favourite music. Remembering, Jade recalled her and her aunt playing the music they danced and sang along to, together, everything from the clap, clap song to puff the magic dragon.

♪216♪
♪217♪
♪218♪

Tears, why was she crying, she and Bobby were together and two of their friends were getting married. *'Always the maid, never the fair maiden?'* Jade couldn't complain about the life Mama and Papa provided. Crying, it was when having to look at herself in the mirror she saw what was no longer there. Would Rojay have wanted what Bobby had been prepared to take on? *'Boy or girl?'* Would she have become a mother if her baby hadn't died? *'Nothing?'* No photographs, a plague she'd never see marking the place where what amounted to a hand full of ashes had been released into the earth. A spirit set free to roam, thankful for what Joe had shown and told her. Whenever she thought about her baby, Jade saw him, or her all alone. *'Only when with her aunt Jennifer did Jade feel she was where she belonged.'* Was it the guilt of not telling those she believed should know, causing her to cry? Kevin was her safety net and Jennifer her snuggle blanket. Bobby was again her boyfriend, but as she stood looking into the mirror contemplating her having to measure what was her unrecognisable body. Jade found herself wondering what and who she really was? Concerned about having heard Jade crying, when Jennifer told her husband she was worried. Kevin said there was something she should know. *'Happy?'* He hadn't wanted to upset what was working, but admitted he should have said something sooner. *'Sorry.'* Kevin told his wife, Jade had been at the hospital prior to her arrival. *'Something wrong?'* Kevin warned his wife to be cautious with her words, neither wanting to lose what they'd gained.

"Jade?" Jennifer had knocked before entering, but hadn't allowed the one inside the time to tell her to go away. "Jade what is it?" She fussed when finding her house guest upset and distressed.

"I can't do it." Jade sobbed. "I can't look at what I've done."

"What have you done?" Jennifer said Jade was scaring her. Believing her niece had hurt herself, the concerned elder asked if she needed medical assistance?

"Not anymore." Jade sniffed before saying she was sorry. Tablets? Jennifer scanned the room for evidence of what the maturing teen was talking about.

"What can I do to help?" The elder female said she would do anything?

"Mama needs to know." Jade said.

"Know what?" Jennifer asked.

"She is going to hate me."

"Jemima is a busy woman." Sisters' who rarely got along continued to stand up for one another whenever anyone outside their sibling conflict insulting the other. "I need Mama." Jade cried and she cried and she cried. Holding her in her arms, Jennifer agreed with Kevin's nod when he entered to see what was happening?

"I'm here." She said softly. "Your mum has always been here." Was she hearing correctly? Why was her aunt saying she was her mother?

"If there is something we should know, it can't, it won't be worse than what we need to tell you." Kevin suggested they go downstairs, assuring those there with him, he'd closed the shop. "We need to sort this." Jade didn't know what was happening, but agreed when asked if she wanted to go first and tell them what it was she'd done? Fearing the worst both adults were on standby to call for the assistance of an ambulance.

"I was pregnant." Shock. Jennifer was tearful but assured the one she was calling her daughter; she wasn't disappointed. Anger; Jade had expected her elders to be angry. "I was going to have an abortion."

"No," Jennifer shook her head. Kevin taking her hand and telling his wife they should listen.

"Bobby helped."

"Helped?" Next came Kevin's turn to be told to calm down and hear what was being said.

"My baby died inside me and after I delivered what was gone. I walked away. I didn't know what to do." Taking Jade into their arms, both Jennifer and Kevin agreed nature taking its' course the way she described, meant there was nothing anyone could do.

"I'm your mother?" Jennifer repeated. "I should have been there for you." She apologised for having waited so long to share what she was calling worse than anything anyone else could do.

"Is Kevin my dad?" It was a natural assumption, but Jade was told No. Kevin said he wished he was, telling Jade he had always seen her to be his daughter.

"What can't you look at?" Jennifer insisted Jade tell her if she needed medical help.

"Gretchen wants my measurements for the bridesmaid dress. I can't bare looking at myself. I can't measure myself." Relieved. Jennifer said she would help, both her and Kevin agreeing she could and should have come to them for help sooner. There for her, all agreed nothing could've been done to save what was gone. *'Sorry.'* Kevin said he should have paid more attention and questioned her sooner. *'Sorry,'* Both said they never meant to let her down, but now felt they'd let her down twice. Hugging and saying everything was fine. Jennifer said what she had to tell her would help her understand why she; more than most could relate to what she'd been through.

Embarrassed and guilt ridden, Jennifer said she was the keeper of the most scandalous of family secrets. Having told Jade she was her daughter, Jennifer said she'd given birth to her alone. *'A surrogate?'* Jade saw it as making sense for someone like Mama to hire another womb.

"No," Jennifer said she was ashamed to say she and Jerald had been lovers. *'A family scandal?'* Papa was daddy. Jade asked about Jeremy? Stepbrother, Jennifer said her being young wasn't an excuse, but her youth and naivety was why she agreed to hand her baby girl over to her older sister.

"Were you with Papa first?" Jade attempted to create her own explanation, but Jennifer shook her head.

"It took two." Kevin disagreed with his wife taking all of the blame. *'A family affair?'*

"Sorry." Jennifer said she understood if Jade had questions, needed space or hated her? *'Jade could never hate Jennifer.'* Shocked, the maturing female believed Jennifer did what she did because she saw it being for the best. It wasn't like she'd given her to strangers, or attempted to get rid of her baby. "Different times and circumstances." Jennifer said she could see why Jade saw abortion to be her only option. "You didn't want Mama to disown you." She admitted to not wanting to let her parents' down either. "The truth is, it's your parents' who have let you down." Stepping in when aware his wife was struggling, Kevin said them leaving her was because Jerald and Jemima wouldn't let them take her with them. *'A judge with the law on his side.'* Kevin said he would've gladly taken Jade into his home sooner if he could. Suddenly her aunt and uncle feeling more like mum and dad made sense. Suddenly the fact Jennifer was always there when Mama and Papa couldn't or chose not to be came with a plausible explanation. What a disorganised tangle of mixed up lies and misdirected deceit. *'The family secret?'* When Jennifer assisted with gaining the required measurements for what would be her second bridesmaids dress, Jade asked what she should call her? Told it was up to her, the younger female also asked that neither Jennifer or Kevin tell Mama and Papa what she'd disclosed. Agreeing it no longer mattered what others thought, Jade said she didn't want her secret being turned into gossip. Rushing out of the shop to prevent Kevin attacking Bobby, Jade realised her disclosing only part of what had happened, hid the fact Bobby hadn't been the father of her first child

"Not him!" She told Kevin he'd misunderstood when she spoke about Bobby assisting her. "Not his."She told Bobby she was sorry.

♪219♪

Fighting for her breath, unable to breath, her chest felt tight and her very being had become welded to the spot. *'Where was she?'* Wanting to walk forward, everything felt much too heavy, too stiff and too stubborn to move.

"Spirit!" She called, but there was no one there."I'm sorry." She said, but no one was listening. When it came to making her once in a lifetime mistake, Jade wished she hadn't made the mistake which continued to haunt her sleeping hours. "No!" Her not being able to prevent her baby from dying didn't prevent her from seeing what she saw when what was gone left her body. "I'm here to collect my scan." Those to have offered what was the only picture of her first child; told her she was too late, she'd said no. Told the choice had been her choice, she saw each shake their head in turn.

"No."Dr. Sutton said what was gone was gone.

"No."Ms Ford said she wasn't responsible.

"No."Dr. Jones said they didn't have the space to keep copies of unwanted scan photos.

"No."Nurse Louise shook her head.

"You should have taken it when offered." Joe said she missed her chance to have the only keepsake available.

"No."All said she wasn't permitted to visit what was private. A child's playroom and the final resting place for lost, unwanted souls. *'No.'* Jade would never stop being sorry.

♪220♪

16: AGAIN
♪221♪

Another journey she would rather not have to take, another celebration to attend. The village was her home, Jennifer and Kevin her family and Shannon the only one to tell it like it was. Happy with how things turned out, Jade wasn't comfortable having to return to the place she felt lucky to have escaped.

"Is that everything?" Bobby inquired as he and Kevin loaded his car. His sports car may not be spacious, but it was cosy, fast and practical for long journeys.

"Yes."Jade nodded.

"You sure you haven't forgotten anything important, Like the kitchen sink?" Her uncle teased when stretching out his back and making comment about getting old.

"That's it."Insisting she had everything, Jade rushed back inside to fetch her hairbrush, perfume and diary.

"Course it's not?" Both men smiled. Shaking their heads in unison when the one both adored eventually reappeared to announce she was ready.

"Yes."She assured them she was sure.

"Drive carefully." Why do people say what should be obvious? "Drive careful?" Jade and Bobby were told to watch the road and look after one another. It was a wonder those there to see them off weren't reminding them to breath.

"Take care." Both knew it was because others cared. Hugs and kisses, Kevin and Jennifer were reluctant to let go of the one promising she would be back. Handshakes and pats on the back, Kevin said he couldn't apologise enough for what had been his misunderstanding.

"Ready?" Switching on his cars engine, Bobby saw Jade nod as she sat in the passenger seat beside him, waving to those waving at them, their journey began.

♪222♪

July, so much had changed. *'July the fourth?'* Shannon was the first to point out how marrying on what in America was Independence Day seemed ironic, but that was the date Gretchen and Greyson would be tying the knot and the rehearsal was the reason why the chosen usher and bridesmaid were setting off three days early. *'Working, they avoided the hen & stag parties.'* Jennifer hadn't gone running to her sister when accepted by the one who was her true daughter, but grannie couldn't stop herself. The relief in her ageing voice when saying. *'At last.'* Revealing the fact she couldn't wait to inform her elder daughter of how her granddaughter was with the one she should never have been taken from. When talking to Jade, Loti told her no law could over rule what was right and should be. An adult, having turned eighteen, no one could stop Jade being where she wanted to be. *'Happy?'* Jade didn't want anything, or anybody spoiling her new life. *'Jennifer said she should call & promised she would join her if needed.'* Kevin assured the girls in his life he wouldn't let anyone, or anything hurt, or keep them apart, not anymore and not ever again.

♪223♪

"Back again." Arriving at his parents house Jade wondered if Jerald and Jemima had shared the news primed to be top of every gossip list for miles. Probably not, neither would willingly encourage what would bring embarrassment and awkward questions. *'Kept in house?'* Bobby had done nothing more than ask how she felt and said he would do whatever she wanted him to do to help, assuring Jade he would have her back should anyone say anything she didn't like. *'Friends with Kevin again.'* The men in her life had sorted and restored their relationship, both agreeing to respect what they saw to be her privacy. *'Her news, her business?'* Both understood the struggle Jade would have not to see everyone as talking about her? *'Tamara would tell someone about Spirit.'* When returning to what had been her hometown Jade was under no illusion that she, her life and her family would be being talked about. *'Back again?'* Back together, welcomed by Mrs. Hallas, them being given separate room at either end of the house spoke many more words than they knew those who cared ever would.

♪224♪

"Your friend Tarquin is a happily married man." Jade knew she shouldn't be listening and wasn't meant to overhear the father, son conversation taking place below the open window of her guest bedroom as Bobby and his father sat together in the garden below.

"So it would seem." Bobby agreed. Sat before the pine mirrored dressing table combing through her hair before retiring; she couldn't help but be interested in what she was able to hear. Making herself more comfortable on the cushions she placed on the floor below the open window, the lone female felt safe in the knowledge those below could neither see, or hear her.

"Am I to take it you will be next?" Mr. Hallas asked.

"I don't think I'll become a married man before Greyson." Bobby pointed out his reason for being home.

"You and Jade?" Tyler nudged his son. "We heard, or rather we knew."

"Pardon?" Confused Bobby was misunderstanding what Jade heard loud and clear.

"The tale of two mothers'"

"Dad."Bobby was use to his father saying it like it was, but found himself struggling to keep up with the meaning of what was being said.

"She's not who you thought she was."

"She's not who she thought she was." Bobby assured his elder his feelings for Jade hadn't changed. "I love Jennifer and Kevin." He reminded his old man of the many times he'd had reason to go to those to have always been there for him.

"Good people," Tyler nodded. "Your mother was beginning to worry she wouldn't get to buy a hat and she reckons she's putting me on a diet to get me back into my all occasion suit?" Enthusiastic and a little excited as he spoke, both men smiled when picturing the image set.

"We haven't discussed marriage." Bobby paused before shaking his head. "We haven't thought about it." He stuttered.

"Your mother and me will always stand by whatever you want to do son."

"But?" Bobby again questioned his fathers' words.

"We don't want to see you throw your career away."

"Why would I?" He asked.

"A wife won't want you playing football."

"Jade gets it." Wasn't that the truth, listening, Jade agreed she would never prevent or attempt to stop what was her boyfriends' career from progressing, willing to stand by her man. *'Would she marry him?'* Young and in love, neither she nor Bobby saw the urgency they noticed in others when it came to declaring how they felt and proving their commitment to anyone but one another Agreeing to knowing all they needed to know, Jade and Bobby said they would share with others how they felt when they were certain it was what they wanted to do.

"We'll manage whatever happens." Bobby assured his father both he and Jade respected and understood one another. *'How sweet?'* There were times Jade didn't understand herself. *'True.'* Bobby understood and knew her better than she knew herself. *'No more secrets?'* She accepted his demanding choice of career and a bitter experience meant she'd seen some of the problems they faced. *'Strong together.'* Sat listening, Jade wanted the two men to know and to hear her points of view, managing to refrain from throwing open the window and telling them she was there. *'Always there?'* Tyler spoke the truth when he said they were still young.

"Jade is a sweet girl, but I need you to promise you won't rush into, or do anything?"

"Is this conversation about to turn to the subject of the birds and the bee's?" Bobby blushed. Tyler rubbing his head and telling him, he wouldn't know where to start as both laughed together.

♫225♫

Standing side by side, the floppy hat and full length dress wasn't a million miles from what Jade and Shannon imagined. *'Different?'* Her work colleagues words sounded kind compared to what she and Tamara felt sure would be whispered; in amongst the giggles from the church pews. *'No real surprise.'* Tamara said the slightly ridicules outfits were so they didn't outshine the bride. The latest trend. Mrs. Gwen Garlock said what had been chosen for her daughters' wedding was in vogue while Tamara asked which century? *'Another wedding?'* Jade agreed others said it was nice to see her and Bobby back together, his checking she was all right before taking his place by the door of the church to direct the arriving guests described as being sweet by the bridesmaid whose husband was no where to be seen.

"Maybe you'll be next." Jade felt everyone other than herself and Bobby had their future planned.

"No rush."She hadn't meant her comment to relate to her companion being pregnant when she wed and immediately apologised.

"No worries." Tamara said she would've be glad of more time to shed the baby weight before having to stand as bridesmaid in a dress she accused of adding to her looking frumpy and Jade assured her, she looked fine as both agreed neither would outshine the bride whose chosen dress was stunningly beautiful. White, full length and delicately detailed with silk roses and tear drop pearls. Hair up, her bridesmaids had been asked to wear theirs down so the hats would sit right. A long, full length veil, when Gretchen arrived, Jade and Tamara assisted with what was her magnificent gown.

♪226♪

Waiting at the front of the church, Greyson Gaylord Pettson stood with his back to the large double entrance and his approaching bride. Decorated with wild flowers and yard upon yard of yellow ribbon speckled with gold glitter, that which shone in the sunlight reflected in the happy faces; causing smiling eyes to twinkle. Glancing to Jade, Tamara attempted to pull in her stomach as the two followed Gretchen's long lace train down the carpeted central isle. This was it, the event which indicated another of the three couples had matured enough to make an adult commitment.

♫227♫

"Dearly beloved, we are gathered here today." No one but Jade noticed how Bobby was listening. Tamara and Tarquin were married with a beautiful daughter and Gretchen and Greyson were about to exchange vows which would bind them forever, two couples. Married and together forever, Jade wished she knew what Bobby was thinking? *'Married.'* Man and wife. Mr. and Mrs. Pettson, following the hour long ceremony Gretchen and Greyson were joined together forever. From here comes the bride, to the couples happy ever after song.

♫228♫

Bells rang loud and confetti filled the air as each and every guest congratulated the newly weds. Pats on the back, shaking hands and the kissing of cheeks. Smiles brighter than the sun and two hearts flying higher than the clouds, two had become one. *'Standing alone.'* Jade couldn't feel sad when surrounded by so much joy. *'Always the bridesmaid?'* Standing back once the photographer completed the snaps in-which she was required, pleased life was again being kind. A big white wedding, the parents' of the bride had spared no expense and it appeared no one had been left off the guest list. Three hundred people, the parents of the groom appeared to know the world and most of the universe too, no one could blame those who were proud for wanting to share what was the happiest of happy days.

♫229♫

"Hello Jade." Turning, the one enjoying the sights and happy to absorb the atmosphere fell speechless. Stunned, the smile she was wearing with pride dissolved like snow melted by the sun. Was she dreaming? Unexpected, linking arms, why approach her?

"Hello." She gasped.

"How are you dear?" Now they asked? Now they wanted to know? They'd known where she was.

"Fine." What else should she tell them.

"Yes." Why answer what hadn't been a question?

"Is Jeremy with you?" Searching to find a shared topic of conversation when struggling to find common ground.

"At college." Of course, Jeremy was doing what they wanted him to do. Higher education, his choice meant him being closer to Gemma. Jeremy and Gemma would probably marry before Jade did.

"Jeremy is doing great." Jemima wanted to know if there was anywhere they could talk and Jade told her no. Not today, not now and maybe not ever because Jade had nothing she wanted to talk about.

"Dinner?" Jerald suggested as Bobby joined them to find himself greeted more warmly than the one they looked after since her birth.

"We have a hectic schedule." The busy footballer apologised for him and not being available.

"Another time." Jerald sighed. *'Why wasn't he saying he would visit his daughter soon?'*

"Thank you." Thanking Bobby for getting her out of what she saw turning into a sticky situation, she knew she would have to talk to them and said she wanted her aunt with her when she did.

"Anytime." Bobby smiled. Kissing her on the forehead as the groom requested his presence. More photographs, while a large wedding brought more gifts and less chance of anyone being on their own, the downside of a large crowd was the amount of time it took to keep everyone happy and move them from one place to another. *'Missing Jeremy.'* Catching up with Trevor waiting by the church gates to chauffeur Mr. and Mrs. Barris, Jade was reassured her stepbrother was well and told Jimmy and Sawyer were traveling in search of the ideal location for their business.

"We all miss you miss." Trevor promised to remember her to everyone and let them know she missed them too.

"You look nice." It took a moment for Jade to realise the older female was taking to her.

"Ratbag?" Her shock was obvious. Trust the one some called the biker mother to enter via what was the exit gate of the church. *'Why?'* Coming face to face with another she wasn't expecting to see, Jade didn't know what to say. *'What had happened?'*

"A friend of yours?" Dressed in her usual black, a loose leather waistcoat, silver grey blouse and almost full length, A-line leather skirt, the larger than life female appeared much more dominate when standing alone. Laced ankle boots and fish net tights, her long hair fell thick and heavy around her shoulders and down over her back. *'A funeral?'* Jade momentarily feared the worse. *'One of the bikers?'* "I'm guessing you're the bridesmaid." Ratbag commented before Jade had time to release her concerns.

"Gretchen," She nodded towards the bride struggling to escape those wanting more photographs.

"She looks good. Hope the vicar hasn't worn his voice out." Older, the one Jade had been introduced to when with Rojay; didn't appear to have changed her attitude or free thinking outlook. *'A bikers bride?'* Rough and ready, strong and powerful. Ratbag would never be the type of mistress to say, yes sir.

"Are you?"Jade inquired when noticing how like the female her long term partner arrive was also dressed smart for something?

"Getting hitched?" The loud female completed for her, her thought. "Not me," She laughed. "Could have been you." She smiled.

"Me?" Jade gasped. Her eyes looking but failing to see the next group of people arrive. *'Round the other side.'* When busy the church had one door in and another to exit. What at times became a conveyer belt of people weren't meant to meet, but Ratbag was refusing to take the longer route.

♫*230*♫

"Nice day for it."Stork asked if they should turn and walk around when realising they were at the wrong gate but Ratbag insisted they walk through.

"We'll mingle on the way." The females wink was a clear indication of her knowing what would happen as on her partners arm she walk towards the church, smiling at all to get out of their way. *'Why were they there?'* With the bestman insisting all get to the cars because it was time to go, Jade failed in her attempt to discover which ceremony Ratbag and Stork were there to attend.

"This one."Having found her, Bobby took her by the hand to escort her to the car waiting to take them where they needed to be. "We need to arrive before the new Mr. and Mrs." His smile was infective and his touch caused what she was thinking to fade away. *'Happy?'* A wedding or a funeral Jade didn't need to know why Rojay's friends were entering the church she was leaving. *'Did she?'*

♫*231*♫

Waving as Bobby dropped her back in the village, all inquired as to why he hadn't stopped to say hello? Relaying his apologies, Jade told how her chaperone and chauffeur had been called into his place of employment for an emergency meeting.

"Busy man?" Kevin took from her, her suitcase.

"Yeah."Jade agreed.

"Nice wedding?" Her uncle was the first to ask about the celebration as Jade nodded, entering the back kitchen to show him and Jennifer the photographs over coffee and cake.

Waving across to Jennifer as she wiped the outdoor tables, there was no hiding the way the morning rays of the rising sun caught the bright smile to have printed itself on her face since her return. *'Another day?'* Taking a deep breath, she felt pleased to see the return of the warmer weather. *'Busy.'* Day-trippers from the local area were again being outnumbered by those taking their annual vacations. The seventh day of July, busy. Told Bobby would be away for a two week retreat with his teammates, busy days would help time go by more quickly. Speaking on the telephone each evening at eight and writing her thoughts in her diary, Jade agreed when those around her said absence made the heart grow fonder. When attending the wedding of Gretchen and Greyson the two couldn't have been closer. Happy, Shannon said she hoped some of her joy, love and luck would rub off on her now the summer sun was back.

Working at the cafe and helping in the shop, engaging in telephone conversations, reading and writing, the two agreed to them being willing to do any and everything they could to keep what each called their special relationship alive. July, Bobby apologised for having to rush away so soon. *'Barely time to get her breath back.'* Bobby said he had a surprise he didn't want to give until they were able to have quality time together. *'Happy.'* Jade knew her being with her true biological mother would lead to Jennifer wanting to celebrate the fact she was truly home. *'A home baked cake.'* Jeremy called to say he would visit soon. Surrounded by people who cared, Jade realised she would have to get use to Bobby not always being where she would like him to be, when she wanted him to be there.

♫232♫

July, with the weather getting warmer, the village went from steady to hectic. *'Hectic & hot?'*

"Jade!" The tray almost fell from her hands as she spotted the person calling her name, feeling like her heart had stopped; when noticing the male wanting to gain her attention she froze.

"Do you know him?" Shannon nudged as she continued her work, turning and walking away; Jade knew he knew she'd seen him. Sitting at the outdoor table shaded by the large parasol; there were others for her to tend. *'People as far as the eye could see.'* Being full outside, meant the tables inside filling fast too.

"Jade we need to talk?" He again attempted to gain her attention as she told him she was working. "I need to tell you something." Rojay insisted.

"I don't need to hear." Continuing to ignore her pursuer. Jade asked Shannon to take care of the unexpected visitor. *'A customer sat at a table.'* Avoiding eye contact; Jade left Shannon to discover what the stranger wanted?

"The motorbike king, right?" If any sharper Shannon would cut herself. *'Was Rojay on holiday, or just passing through?'* He couldn't be there especially to see her, could he? Whilst not wanting anything to do with him, she couldn't help being curious. *'Rojay was history.'* She had a new life in a different place with people who made her happy, what was past was gone. *'Rojay & Stacey forever.'* Jade felt sure Stacey wouldn't let him go again. *'Where was Stacey?'*

"Are you all right?" Shannon assured her shaking friend, the one wanting to talk to her was gone.

"I need to get out of here." It being the end of the day meant Shannon agreeing to her colleagues' request, so long as she was back bright and early.

"You sure can pick em." The waitress preparing herself to do the work of two, assured Jade she could manage. "I thought Bobby was a dish, but that one is gorgeous with a capital G."

"Appearance isn't everything." Trust Shannon to put package ahead of content. *'Hadn't Jade made the same mistake?'*

♪233♪

Having admired him from afar, when approached by Roland Jackson, Jade Barris became besotted, allowing him to lead her into a world she had no experience of. *'He wasn't alone.'*

"Was that his girlfriend?" Shannon had noticed the one waiting by the motorbike in the carpark?

"Stacey," Jade nodded, relieved to hear the two were together. "Probably," She agreed.
"The school bully," Shannon sounded surprised.
"And the school hunk."Jade continued to nod. "The perfect couple." She sighed.
"I think I'd look better on his arm." Aware her friend wasn't in the mood for joking, Shannon apologised and offered to swop her day off. "Take tomorrow, that way if they're just passing through you can avoid them and I'll say you're visiting Papa, you never know, it could send them home."
"Tomorrow?" Jade questioned what Shannon was offering? The unexpected, unexplained appearance of those she never thought she'd see confusing and upsetting her just when she saw herself as being settled.
"See you Monday." Thanking Shannon for her thoughtful offer, Jade agreed she was right. *'Happy in her job.'* Both knew she wouldn't be able to work while worrying about who was watching.

Eight p.m. on the dot, within the same second when the large finger reached the twelve, the hallway telephone began to ring. Dark because it was the space which separated the front shop from the back kitchen and had no windows, it seemed the most practical place to put the downstairs telephone. Heard from the front and back of the building, Jade liked how when the shop was shut and everyone upstairs; she could hold a conversation without being listened to. Hesitating, should she tell him? *'Tell Bobby about Rojay?'* Would letting him know who was in the village help anyone?
"Hello."Should she?
"Hello."Could she?
"Jade?"
"Bobby."She smiled. Unable to see one another; she hoped her voice caused him to smile like his did her. *'Her boyfriend.'*
"Have you had a good day?" He asked.
"Yeah, you?" She fired his question back.

"Everything is going great." He said he was tired.

"Shannon and me are busy." She hoped he could hear the excitement in her words; even when her words were few. "I miss you." She told him.

"You too and I've been thinking." Bobby clearly had something to say. "My home is back with mum and dad."

"You're always welcome here. Kevin would love you to come visit." She panicked. Preparing herself for bad news, was he thinking of moving back home?

"I think I should start house hunting."

"House hunting?" She struggled to understand what it was she was hearing? What was he saying?

"The next time I have a few days off, we should get together and find a home." For him, or for both of them? What was Bobby asking?

"Where?" Agreeing, the stunned female didn't want to be left alone. Settled, she needed the people she saw to be supporting her, in her life her.

"In the village, I want to be where you want to be." Bobby said he wanted to include Jade in his future plans. Excited, Jade feared Bobby finding out about Rojay being where he was; would spoil everything. "I can't wait to see you." He told her.

"When will you be back?" She asked and was told he didn't know before the subject was changed by Bobby asking what was happening in the village?

"The camps are full and people are hungry." She said she'd barely stopped. "Sore feet," He promised they'd go for a pedicure together as soon as they could.

"Are you okay?" Should she tell him? How could she let him know his rival was closer to her than he was? *'Maybe Rojay had gone?'* What would be the point in worrying and upsetting Bobby if Rojay was merely passing through?

"Must be more tired than I thought. I wish you were here." She yawned

"And me," He agreed.

♪234♪

A GEORGE

Sat in the rear garden having said she wanted some time on her own, Jade felt surprised to be joined by Shannon telling her Kevin had let her through.

"Is something wrong?" The one given an unofficial day off prepared herself for having to go into work, but was told everything was fine. Tickets for a roadshow. "What?" Jade didn't understand. There was a national radio station and who knew how many pop, maybe rock acts hitting the local beach. Ticket only due to the beach being small. Shannon insisted Jade go with her.

"We can't miss this." Jade said she didn't have anything to wear, taking her friend by the hand; Shannon insisted she had a whole bedroom filled with things she was willing to share. "I will find you something." She promised.

♫235♫

The beach was full, packed to bursting with people everywhere. Young, younger and old, couples, families, singles and groups. Arriving as soon as they were ready Shannon and Jade found themselves surrounded by those eager to discover who was using the local beach as their personal stage. Loud, sun, sea, sand and sounds? What was there that didn't feel like it didn't belong together? Taking Jade by the hand to find a space where they could see everything which was happening Shannon told her friend to hold on tight and be prepared to have the best day of her life.

♫236♫

Watching, listening, singing and dancing to everything from what was classic to what was popular and everything which sounded like summer.

♫237♫
♫238♫

Fun and entertaining there was something for the younger, the young and the old alike.

♫239♫
♫240♫

Armed with the necessities for a day dancing, watching and relaxing in the sun, having fought, the two held onto what was the most suitable spot on the beach, unwilling to miss any of what was happening. Together in amongst

I MAY PRETEND

those soaking up the excitement and enjoying the incredible atmosphere; Jade hoped she would blend, disappearing within the crowd excited to be where she was.

♪241♪
♪242♪
♪243♪

Away from the pots and pans, giving their hands a break from the grease and the grime. Away from the constant flow of demanding customers, Shannon stood while Jade sat smiling at the way her friend became excitable, at times overly excited when encouraging her work colleague to jump up, sing along and dance. *'Fun in the sun?'* A roadshow:

♪244♪
♪245♪
♪246♪

Morning turned to afternoon and afternoon to early evening as the day and time moved on.

♪247♪
♪248♪
♪249♪

Getting cooler, pulling her thigh length baggy style, fluffy pink sweater on over what was a silver lamé tankini and long black lace shorts. *'Shannon said Jade looked hot.'* As the sun began to fade, Jade felt cold. Sitting, standing, singing and dancing, beneath their feet the cooling sand was becoming hard and damp. *'Fun in the sun?'* Having stayed to watch those to have played live from midday to midnight, Jade agreed to enjoying what had been a day and night of thrilling entertainment under the sun, the moon and as she looked up; the stars.

♪250♪

'A good time.' Shannon said she'd never experienced anything better. Having noticed a number of leather clad bikers within the crowd, Jade wondered if the roadshow was the reason Rojay and Stacey were in town? A good day, Shannon said it had been a great day when agreeing it was time for them to go home once the roadies came out to pack things up. Having swooned over the famous singers, groups and bands; Shannon said she didn't care

when Jade felt droplets to indicate it was starting to rain, allowing nothing to spoil her day.

"Don't be so soft." She insisted the dark walk home along the country lane wouldn't take long. "We will be fine." Her elder smiled when pulling an umbrella out from her beach bag and inviting Jade to join her.

♪251♪

Walking and talking, laughing and joking, it was late getting later and as they left the spaces where artificial illumination assisted ones sight, both agreed to not liking the road which was minus a pavement and hating the blind bends and pockets of space where it felt impossible to see ones hand in front of ones face. Walking and talking, singing and laughing. *'Happy?'* Jade was relieved not to have bumped into the two she saw as being her enemies. Yes, she agreed to being glad Shannon had insisted on taking her out, getting her out of herself felt good and Yes, she agreed to missing Bobby. *'Was it Bobby who almost didn't miss her?'* A roaring engine and speeding car going much too fast to stop, what past, knocked both females off their feet. Where had it come from? Why speed on a narrow, dark road known to be used by pedestrians? *'Bobby?'* When checking each was all right, Shannon said she was sure she recognised the dark coloured sports car as being the one owned by the footballer. No, Jade said Bobby was still away. No, if it had been him; he wouldn't have driven away. *'A motorcycle?'* As the roar of one faded into the distance the designative purr of the other filled the late night, early morning air.

"Are you okay?" While Jade shrugged off the one to have seen what happened and stopped to assist, Shannon allowed the leather clad male to assist her back up onto her feet. *'Rojay?'* What was he doing? "He should have his licence taken off him." The biker confirmed what Shannon suspected. "He shouldn't be driving and neither should he be overcrowding his car." Rojay had seen clearly what the two shocked, shaken and bruised females failed to notice. "I doubt he even realised you were there. Did he hit you?" He asked if either Shannon, or Jade were injured before offering to take them the rest of the way into the village.

"I'm fine." Jade said she would manage while Shannon couldn't wait to climb astride his waiting motorbike.

"I'll come back for you." Rojay insisted Jade step back off the road and wait for him to return. Shannon telling her to stop being so stubborn and do as she was told.

♫252♫

It couldn't have been Bobby, when Rojay returned, passing to her his spare helmet, Jade didn't want to do what she had no other choice in. Automatically, not intentionally; her arms wrapped around her riders torso as he sped her home. Ridding down the dark winding country lane, neither noticed the one who couldn't fail but see them through the dark windows of his black sports car. Parked on the grass verge by the village church, the driver to have almost taken from Jade her life; couldn't believe what he'd done, or what he was seeing. *'Not aware who?'* Bobby had returned to the scene of what could have so easily been his tragic crime having dropped his passengers, needing to see what he could see. *'An animal?'* He knew he'd gotten too close to something when driving at speed with too many people inside his little car. *'VIP tickets.'* Bobby had attended the musical event with teammates; instructed to escort the daughters of those their manager wanted to impress. Celebrities and paparazzi, there was bound to be photographs of the day to have ended in his near miss. *'He thought he'd almost killed an animal?'* Seeing Rojay, Bobby realised there was a beast in town.

Hidden by the darkness of the hour, the lone driver knew there would be no hiding from the morning newspapers. *'Why not tell Jade?'* He hadn't noticed her in the crowd and she failed to see him mixing with other guests of importance when posing with the celebrity DJ's and mixing with the pop, rock royalty. *'What had he done?'* Driving with too many people in a car barely able to carry four in comfort. Bobby hadn't realised where he was going when asked by his manager to join two of his teammates and three females who were the spoilt daughters of influential friends. He'd thought Jade and Shannon would be working and maybe his speed was so he wouldn't be seen? *'His day with another female meant nothing.'* A favour, a job, something he was asked to and felt he had to do. *'Why not tell told Jade?'* Why hadn't Jade told him Rojay was in town?

♫253♫

"Thank you." Arriving at their destination, Jade handed back the helmet to the one in no rush to leave as he removed his and gave her the beach bag placed on the luggage carrier to the rear of his cycles' seat.

"So, this is where you live?" He observed what looked small, dark closed and deserted. "Not as grand as the palace."He smirked.

"More homely."Jade liked where she was.

"Are you happy?" She assured him she was. "Are you sure you're okay?" She nodded.

"We should report him to the police." Rojay repeated the fact he knew who the reckless driver was. "Do the two of you see one another?" He asked. Jade telling him it was none of his business.

"I'm still struggling with you being a waitress." He quickly changed the subject. "What do Mama and Papa say about that?" Preventing her from going inside, Rojay continued to engage Jade in conversation.

"Papa and Jemima."She corrected his words. "A lot of things have changed." She sighed.

"Including you."Jade agreed to her being older.

"Are you okay?" Her companion repeated.

"I'll be fine." She nodded. A few bruises and the odd scratch, Jade felt sure she could tend to what could have been worse.

"Are you warm enough?" He asked. Aware she was shivering.

"Too much sun." She said.

"Or shock. Here, take my jacket." Before she could refuse; Rojay had removed and hung his thick, black leather jacket around and over her shoulders. "I still have the one you bought me, but I only wear it for best." He smiled.

"Glad it lasted." Unsure how she should feel, part of her was pleased they were being civil.

"Because it's quality, like you." Wishing he would stop with the compliments and niceties, Jade said she needed to go inside.

"Did you enjoy the show." He admitted to having seen her dancing.

"You were there."

"It was just Stacey and me." He interrupted what both knew she was asking. Struggling to hold her tongue there was so much she wanted to know, but knew her asking would sound like she cared.

"I need to go." She handed back his jacket and told him goodnight.

"We need to talk." He agreed when Jade reminded him it was late and said he would see her soon. *'Wishing he didn't know where she was.'* While Jade went inside without looking back, Bobby watched Rojay leave before driving back to his hotel room alone.

♫254♫

"Hi lover I'm home."

"In the kitchen," Chips, egg and beans, the evening meal was almost ready. One baby lay in his cot, another on her hip and a third on the way. *'The result of endless passion filled nights?'* A grease filled kitchen, a basic home, a council run high rise, or basement bedsit with minimal light and no outdoor space. Furnished on the cheap, her husband worked hard, but his wage was spent on cigarettes, ale and drugs to impress those whose patches he wore. *'Doing his bike clubs bidding.'* Rojay provided a home, but where was the love? Married to the man who said he loved her, what was she doing? Waking in a sweat, Jade felt relieved when aware it had all been a dream, glad she hadn't disturbed anyone. *'Jade & Rojay?'* Roland Jackson was with Stacey and Jade believed his being with Stacey was where he belonged. When settling back down to sleep, Jade shook her head; repeatedly telling herself Rojay wasn't who she wanted.

♫255♫

Ten tiny fingers and ten stubby toes with a cute button nose, soft flawless skin and big blue eyes. Cradling the sweetest of babies in her arms, content. Who wouldn't smile when holding something so perfect, who wouldn't feel protective when being responsible for something so small? She was beautiful, but Jenna Rose wasn't Jade's baby. Jade's baby had been Rojay's baby, boy or girl? Charming was the type of person their baby could have grown into. A baby, when looking down at the child in her arms; Jade saw Rojay's face looking up.

"No!" Waking for a second time from her dreams, Jade saw Rojay making a nightmare father.

♫256♫

Going about her work and day to day routine, Jade couldn't help wondering who she would see first? Bobby hadn't telephoned and two days on from Rojay having escorted her home; there was no sign of him either. *'What was happening?'* Shannon told her not to fret over what others may, or may not be thinking in the same breath as stating how she would be giving the footballer a piece of her mind when next she saw him. Serving customers and taking her own meals with Kevin and Jennifer. It was Kevin who said she should go see Bobby, revealing how his being a male meant him knowing males don't always know what to say in times of upset. Bobby had known what to say when he'd helped and been there for her, he'd known what to say when the two reunited to become more than friends. Having seen and read in the local and national newspapers how Bobby Hallas attended the roadshow with two of his teammates and three well to do females, Kevin assured Jade, Bobby would be coming to terms with his guilt, even if what he'd done was nothing wrong. Neither Kevin, or Jade were aware of the fact Bobby had seen her with Rojay.

♫257♫

A GEORGE

17: HOME

♪258♪

The grass smelt damp yet fresh. There he was, there playing, participating in his much loved chosen sport and promoting his chosen career. Playing in front of his fans. Bobby looked happy, like always he was calm, collective and completely comfortable with the bright white leather football between his controlled booted feet. Standing back, hiding in the shadows of others, Jade watched, her eyes observing the crowds, the families, friends and fans of both the game and skilful, dedicated players. All around people cheered, waved, whistled and called out words of encouragement to their favourite team member. Standing back, Jade watched on as Bobby floated over and across the smooth carpet like grass which held firm beneath his fast moving, precisely placed feet. There he was, the boy she loved and the one her young heart longed for. The maturing male she wanted and the one able to turn her knees to jelly with just one glance. The one able to cause her heart to skip a beat with one word. Knowing him for so long didn't stop it feeling like she was seeing him for the first time. Exciting and entertaining to the end, despite the crowds encouragement and Bobby's professional skill, friendly, or not, his team left the field defeated and he hadn't scored or gotten anywhere near the goal.

"Off his game." Kevin assured Jade she was doing the right thing by being where she was. *'Making the first move.'* They hadn't argued or fallen out. Bobby being photographed with another whose father was a celebrity wasn't the end of them, Jade knew more then most how a photograph didn't equal the reporting of a true story, Jade didn't believe Bobby had been untrue. Jade had spoken to Rojay, but she hadn't said or done anything she shouldn't. Having had enough of her brooding, Kevin insisted she join him when he went to watch their favourite footballer play. "He needs cheering up." Jade hoped her elder was right when telling her she was the right girl for the job. Moving out to the carpark, she waited by his freshly polished car, immediately disappearing out of sight when noticing him approach with another on his arm. Two teammates and a girl each, six smiling face's, he hadn't, or he pretended not to noticed she was there. Why hadn't he told her he'd found someone new?

♪259♪

"No," She replied when Kevin asked if she spoke to Bobby? She hadn't wanted to impose, watching as he climbed into his car with three of his companions. He looked happy when holding the door for the female invited to sit beside him. "No," She hadn't spoken, she watched when he and the girl he was with sped away. "It doesn't matter." She asked her uncle not to fuss.

"Come on love, it must be worth a try." Tears stung her blurring eyes as like metal to a magnet she felt drawn to follow the full, loud, speeding car, yet despite the hurt Jade knew she couldn't, she mustn't. "Can we just go home please."She asked.

"Of course." Noticing the car pulling out of the gate in front of them, Kevin saw what Jade had seen."Maybe she's a fans?" He suggested and Jade said maybe?

♪260♪

Waitressing, listening and watching as all around enjoyed themselves, kissing no one, but her teddybear goodnight.

"Join me at the camp disco?" Shannon pestered."It's no use you moping."

"I'm fine." Fine, or not. Jade knew it was no good her protesting when Shannon stepped in through the back entrance of the shop, make-up bag and clothes in hand. Asking for days, now she was telling. No longer advising, Shannon was demanding Jade join her. Up in her room, looking into the wall mounted mirror above her dressing table as Shannon began on her hair; Jade knew it was useless to resist.

I MAY PRETEND

"You're hard work you know." Her friend told her she wasn't use to someone being so stubborn.

"I am?" Jade questioned.

"You are." Was she? Even Jade gasped at the transformation, shocked by the stranger starring back at her. Curled hair, large earrings, a bright perfectly made up face. Standing, Jade felt surprisingly comfortable yet strange, very strange. Strapped black/silver sandals, the heel of which gave her an extra two inches in height, tight black smooth, shinning p.v.c trousers and silver belly top. Shannon placed chains of both silver and gold around Jade's hips, pinning them discretely to her pants. The black waistcoat was long in length and made of a floating fine lace cut in what fashion magazines called a handkerchief style, bangles and rings. Jade hoped she wasn't going to have to pass a forcefield; cos when wearing so much metal she could be sucked in. Dark nail vanish and deep heavy lipstick, revamped from top to toe; Shannon left no part not pampered.

"You look fantastic." Even the adults approved.

"A change will do you good." How could Kevin resist escorting two stunners, agreeing he would drive them to their destination and be there to pick them up. Shannon's choice for the evening was a tighter than tight, shorter than short deep red velvet dress with V back and no sleeves, being careful not to split the seams, she struggled to climb up into the front seat of Kevin's high, old yet trustworthy four by four without revealing her matching velvet knickers. *'Glad she was wearing some.'* No one could deny the two looked good, a fact most young males already inside the disco; soon picked up on.

♪261♪

"Time to grab ourselves some fun." Shannon smiled as they entered the somewhat crowded, music filled room. Fun? Fun was exactly what Shannon was in search of and exactly what she had, making a beeline for every half decent male in the dimly lit room, she danced and flirted the night away.

A GEORGE

♪262♪

"No, honestly I'm fine." Jade assured and reassured her flighty yet well meaning friend she was doing okay. Dancing, Jade enjoyed the company, blaming her not being use to heels on her needing to be a spectator for a while when finding and sitting herself on a stool by the bar.

"Beer? Wine? A short perhaps?"

"Pineapple juice, thanks." She smiled. Shannon had thanked but instructed Kevin not to collect them, telling him the walk home was all part of the fun. Jade still had the bruises to prove having ones wits about one was what was needed on the dark country lanes.

"You're friend appears to be enjoying herself." The young barman was dark in both hair and skin, handsome, Jade thought he was somewhat smooth as he handed to her, her requested refreshment complete with umbrella and cherry on a stick. "On the house." He refused her offer of payment, lingering to make conversation while she drank. "Have I seen you here before?" He apologised for being new and learning who was who?

"I'm old." Jade sighed.

"A local?" He asked.

"Yeah." She nodded.

"And your friend?" He questioned. Both watching as Shannon danced.

♪263♪

"The best friend anyone could have." Jade smiled.

"Would you like to dance. I'm Brent?" The young male introduced himself.

"Aren't you meant to be working?" Flattered, dark neatly kept hair, dark almost black eyes, smooth skin and perfect pearly white teeth. Jade knew his sweet talking the customer was all part of his bar tending skills. Born flirts, paid to keep the customer happy and there to help all feel special. Rumour was that he was more choosy than most, rumours ranged from him being married, to him being gay? No one knew for sure, the only fact was, Brent didn't seem to make a habit of what most working on the site enjoyed in relation to dancing and dating the ladies.

"I'm all finished." He announced. Stepping out from behind the bar. "Just a dance?" Jade also knew what it was like to be the butt of rumour, as with a nod he took her hand and led her onto the dance floor.

♫264♫
♫265♫
♫266♫
♫267♫
♫268♫
♫269♫
♫270♫
♫271♫
♫272♫
♫273♫

"How do you know Shannon?" The smile on his face gave away the fact his asking was out of personal interested?

"We work together." Jade smiled.

"No," Brent disagreed. "You don't look like a waitress." He shook his head.

"Tonight I don't look like myself." She blushed.

"No?" His shocked expression was because he'd noted her discomfort. Wearing too much make-up and alien clothes."You look lovely." He complimented.

"Thank you." As the music stopped and the brighter lights flicked on. Brent lifted Jade's hand to his lips and kissed it, noticing the friendship ring.

"All the best ones are taken. He's a lucky man." He said. "Or, do you wear it to keep others at bay?"

"Just a dance?" She reminded him and he apologised for having stepped over the mark before thanking her for the dance and bidding her goodnight.

"Goodnight."Like any true gentleman would. Brent pecked Jade on her cheek; his eyes looking to see if Shannon was watching before leaving to allow the two to join one another in readiness to leave.

"Nice."Shannon smiled.

"Okay." Jade nodded. "I enjoyed myself." She smiled, linking arm in arm with Shannon in readiness for the long stroll home.

"Better than starring at four walls all evening."
"Yes."Jade nodded.
"So, what's the story?" Being engrossed in her own party didn't mean Shannon missed a trick and wanted to know about Jade with Brent.
"No story."Jade shrugged.
"I don't know how you do it?" Her elder swooned.
"You landed the catch of the century, Bobby." She stated."Before him you rode around with the leather clad hunk known as Rojay and now Brent, hunks just fall at your feet you lucky witch." Shannon asked Jade share her spell.
"I don't encourage them." She shook her head.
"I saw the two of you dancing." Shannon nodded.
"It was just a dance." Jade blushed while knowing the dance had been innocent.
"More than any other girl's gotten, Brent rarely even talks to the opposite sex."
"He asked me about you."
"Me?" Shannon gasped.
"I think he's shy."Jade seemed to bring the introverts out of their shell, maybe because they recognised one of their own. Sure Brent wanted to get to know Shannon and not her, she was aware the walk home wasn't a time for either to be distracted by an in-depth conversation. "Let's just get home shall we." She suggested.
"You must come out with me more often." Shannon rambled. Staggering on sore feet as the two continued their walk along the main, dimly lit country lane, both laughing, both joking, both enjoying the gossip and one another's company. Company which was somewhat abruptly invaded, interrupted when another speeding car, roared by them, its head lights almost blinding the two, hurting their eyes as each stepped back only to be forced back further into the thick heavy, sharp hedgerows to avoid what would have been a head on collision. *'What?'* Jade said she was never walking home again. Not alone, the driver was again the one in-charge of a car bursting

at the seams. Perhaps he was smiling because he'd only barely missed them?

"You stupid bastard."Shannon couldn't stop herself from screaming out, her screams bringing the crowded car to a screeching halt as Jade wished she was anywhere but where she was. Perhaps he hadn't noticed them? Assisting her pal up onto her unsteady feet, both checked everything was intact, again feeling lucky to still be breathing. "I'm fine, but he won't be when I get my hands on him." Shannon fumed. Heading for the stationary car as followed by two somewhat scantily dressed females, Bobby made his way out to meet her.

"Are you all right?" He inquired. "Shannon?" He recognised the one walking towards him.

"Come back for a second try have you." She accused Bobby of being disappointed the first time he knocked them off the road. "Do you need your eyes testing?" She asked.

"Are you okay? Shaz I'm so sorry." He apologised.

"So you bloody well should be. Pro football star mows down two ex girlfriends in second attempt, sure wouldn't do your career any good should it be published. I can see the headlines now." She reminded him of this not being his first count of reckless driving.

"I'm sorry, I didn't see you."

"That was bloody obvious." She reminded him of the meaning of a blind bend. "Had your mind and your hands on other things?" She continued to make her accusations, allowing her mouth to run away with her and directing her glare beyond Bobby at his pathetic looking companions, plus another who she now saw to be male. "The papers would have a field day." Bobby suddenly becoming aware of who Shannon was with caused his whole Body to sink, lowering her head and wishing she could disappear. "Been drinking?" Shannon asked.

"You know I don't. I wouldn't." He shook his head.

"Perhaps it wasn't you doing the driving." Shannon looked to those who were with him as each lowered their head in turn.

"Neither do I allow anyone behind the wheel of my car." His being defensive did nothing to omit his guilt.

"You could have killed us." The upset and shaken female yelled.

"I said I'm sorry."

♫274♫

Feeling herself slipping deeper and deeper into the background, moving further and further away as Bobby and Shannon continued the heated discussion, Jade wanted to run.

"Are you all right Jade?" Why did he want to know? What did he care?

"See you tomorrow Shaz." It wasn't far to walk the remainder of the way home alone, neither was it easy to ignore Bobby, she still wore his ring, he still held her heart, but she didn't want to talk, not when he was the one staying away from her to be with someone else. Distressed and angry, shocked and on the brink of releasing the tears building behind her eyes. Shannon remained and Jade wondered what the two continued to talk about? Next morning at work the only information shared was that neither of the girls were with Bobby.

"A free agent," Shannon winked, as having removed his ring, Jade agreed so was she. *'Maybe?'*

♫275♫

"Free, but still lonely?" Brent it would seem had ignored her message about their encounter only being a dance and turned up at the cafe for lunch. His eyes searching to find Shannon, Jade smiled when realising her assumption had been correct, it was her friend he liked. Brent wanted Shannon to be the girl on his arm.

"May I take your order?" Jade asked.

"You look lovely." Blushing as he sat himself at a table for one, his taking her hand as she attempted to take his order was again accompanied by eyes straying to where Shannon stood. "What would you recommend?" He asked.

"I'm sure you'll enjoy whatever you choose." She smirked. Aware of what he was doing, Jade whispered the fact Shannon wasn't the jealous kind.

"I think I'll try your tuna and asparagus salad." It was his turn to blush as he released her hand.

"With or without chips?" She asked.

"With a glass of milk." He smiled.

"Won't be long." She also looked to see if Shannon was watching as he told her he was in no rush

"Are you both all right?" He asked. "The accident." It appeared others had passed only to join in what had been Shannon's dispute with the local footballer. "Incident." Brent had observed the absence of the ring when releasing her hand.

"We're Fine." Jade had to stop herself from saying they were getting use to the near misses, instead excusing herself to fetch his and other orders.

♪276♪
♪277♪

Remaining for what seemed to hours, Brent ate his lunch, ordered more drinks and watched Shannon flirt with all except him.

"She's clever, but she can't read minds." Jade told the male sat torturing himself; he should say something, but he said he didn't know what? "Shannon." Jade called her friend over, her actions leaving the one she saw as being shy, no choice but to talk.

"Will you be at the disco tonight?" He asked. His eyes looking to Jade who immediately looked to Shannon.

"Won't you be working?" Shannon took Jade's nod as meaning she should be the one to answer.

"I get off at ten thirty." Brent smiled.

"What about you Jade?" Shannon was confused

"I'm washing my hair." Jade said she was busy.

"And your hair takes all evening to dry?" Shannon questioned what it was her friend was doing?

"Sometimes." She nodded.

"Then maybe I'll see you when it's dry?" Brent attempted to stand as Jade pushed him back down.

"Jade?" Shannon questioned her friend doing what she did? "You cant treat a customer like that." Shannon apologised for what she saw Jade do.

"He isn't asking me." With another nod of her head Jade attempted to tell Shannon, Brent was there for her.

"I'll be there, I'm employed to October." Standing and leaving fast, his shyness swamped his courage.

"She'll see you before you go." Jade called."You cracked it there girl." She nudged Shannon as both watched Brent climb into his bright, white Suzuki jeep and drive away. "Told you he was shy. You do like him don't you?" She questioned Shannon's puzzled expression which turned to a smile when realising what had happened. "Go girl!" Jade smiled as both high fived one another.

♪278♪

18: YOUNG HEARTS
♪279♪

Knocking when everywhere was closed, Kevin was use to a local or two seeing him as open all hours should they run out of milk for their coco

"Could I speak to Jade?" Not who anyone expected?

"I don't think so son." Kevin shook his head as from her bedroom window, having washed her hair like she said she would; Jade watched. A bunch of flowers? While her heart fluttered like an excited out of control butterfly, her head agreed with Kevin. Surely he wasn't so blind as to believe a simple bunch of flowers would put everything right? Maybe they weren't for her? No, Bobby was more than likely just double checking he hadn't caused any lasting injuries while on his way to date another admirer. *'Clearing his conscious?'*

"Is she all right?" He asked.

"Depends on your version of all right?" Remaining behind her partly drawn curtains, staying out of sight, with the window ajar Jade heard the words being exchanged by those below.

"Did she mention what happened?" Bobby asked

"Is there something I should know?" Kevin expressed his concern.

"Would you give her these." Flowers? Flowers for the sick, the injured, the recovering, the retiring. Flowers for those in love and the deceased. Flowers for the broken hearted didn't work? No, for such a reason Jade felt flowers were wrong.

"I don't like seeing my step daughter hurt." Kevin growled at the male preparing to leave.

"I would never hurt her." Bobby shook his lowered head.

"You don't call breaking her heart, hurt?"Kevin asked.

"A broken heart?" Bobby it seemed was just covering his back.The fact Kevin was calling Jade his step daughter was what brought a tear to her eye and caused a lump to form inside her throat. Why was Bobby being so uncaring? Why had his attitude changed? *'Should she rush down to speak to him?'* She knew she shouldn't be listening, she shouldn't be living in hope or longing for what was; to return. Perhaps she should realise they were all the same. *'Out for themselves unless married?'*

♪280♪

Blonde hair, brown hair, brown eyes, blue eyes, reliable, unpredictable. Mr. Nasty and Mr. Nice, Bobby and Rojay? Different, Jade now saw the one thing they had in common, their one and only similarity, the thing they shared was the worse thing, they were both male. Both boys maturing into men, the only man a girl could and should rely on; was her father. *'Not Papa?'* Her having two to call dad caused Jade to realise what it took to be a true father. *'Could she call Kevin dad?'* She would if he allowed it. Strong and protective without being controlling or judgmental, Kevin was within his rights to tell Bobby she didn't want to see him and right when he said she didn't want to be hurt any more.

♪281♪

Flowers? Why flowers? Because of the accident? The incident? Shannon would appreciate flowers.

"Flowers?" Having joined Jennifer in the kitchen Shannon admired what the elder female had seen fit to place in the centre of the table.

"There's a card, but she hasn't read it." Jennifer's intention was to be heard by Jade as she entered. Morning, Jade hadn't come out of her room to see what Kevin had accepted on her behalf. *'Not interested.'*

"Beautiful," Both elder females commented on what Jade was seeing for the first time.

"Am I late?" Surprised to see her work colleague; she asked Shannon if there was something wrong?

"No, we have the day off." She smiled. "Mum and dad said we earned it."

"Well, if they insist." Jade nodded, happy to turn around and go back to her bed.

"Coffee and toast?" Kevin offered. "Would you like to join us Shannon?" He invited their early morning visitor before Jade had chance to decline.

"Thanks." Simple but filling, Shannon said toasted bread always tasted better when she didn't have to make it. Sitting around what stood in the centre of the pine kitchen table, the afore mentioned flowers had been beautifully arranged by Jennifer who despite Jade's disinterest said; to bin them would be a waste.

"Bobby?" Shannon confirmed her knowing who the floral gift was from.

"Yeah."Jade nodded.

"They're lovely. Does this mean you have made up?"

"Didn't he send you flowers?"Jade asked

"Why would Bobby send me flowers?" Shannon shook her head.

"Because of what happened." Explaining, Jade saw what Bobby delivered as being a way of easing his guilt and checking they hadn't gone to the papers.

"Mine must've gotten lost in the post. What does the card say?"

"I haven't read it."

"Why not?" Shannon questioned her reluctance?

"I'm not interested." Telling Jade to stop lying to herself, Shannon said she should take a look at the words written to accompany what were colour and fragrant filled, before the suspense killed someone.

"Read it." Both Jennifer and Shannon insisted she see what Bobby had to say.

"I don't want to." What was she afraid of? Rejection? Was she scared of her assumptions being correct? Afraid the beautiful, sweet smelling bouquet was nothing more than a simple apology? What more did she want?

"What are you girls going to do with yourselves?" Kevin asked when placing the coffee and toast down on to the table. "Shannon?" He asked.

"It's a days shopping for me. Jade?" She repeated the line of inquiry.

A GEORGE

"I reckon I'll stay home, help out here."

"Read the card." All told her to put herself out of her misery.

♪282♪

Entering the kitchen to put on the kettle Shannon's words echoed around the otherwise deserted room. The card still sealed, still in place at the left hand corner of the arrangement, that which wasn't natural jumped out from the array of bright colour like a skyscraper in a jungle, its' bright whiteness appearing misplaced, its' square shape unwanted and somewhat unattractive amongst the mini garden of beauty.

"Read the card." Shannon, Jennifer and even Kevin advised it would put her mind at rest. Filling the silver jug kettle from the tap, Jade knew they were right, but returned to the shop having resisted temptation.

A day of helping out in the shop meant her offering to take out the bins when the day was done. Dark, she hadn't realised it had gotten so late. She wanted to throw the flowers too, but promised Jennifer they could stay to help brighten the kitchen. *'The card?'* In her pocket because she knew someone would give in to temptation before she did. *'Should, could she throw it?'*

"Something you don't want?" Shocked by the one walking towards her from out of the shadows, it wasn't so dark she couldn't see, but she hadn't expected anyone to be there. *'Placing the card back into her pocket.'* She asked what it was her unexpected visitor wanted and he told her they needed to talk.

"Somewhere private."His eyes told her there was something he needed to say they might not want others to hear.

"Do you have your bike?" She asked. Saying she needed to let her mum and Kevin know where she was. "We can go to the beach." Jade told those she lived with she wouldn't be out long. Kevin watching as he heard the motorbike leaving with Jade onboard.

♪283♪

Two years? It had been two years. Why now? What did he want? Wasn't he happy with Stacey?

"I didn't believe it when they said you moved here." Walking ahead; Jade led her companion around and over to what was an arched entrance to something no longer there. A cave entrance, a large shaped rock in-amongst other rocks. A seat to sit on, dark, but safe so long as they watched for the tide coming in."A true local." He praised her knowledge of the area. "I never saw you being a waitress."

"No."She agreed. Sitting, as he sat beside her. Whilst enjoying what she did, all knew the old Jade would never clear tables or wash pots.

"I didn't come looking for you." He continued. "But I'd be lying if I said I wasn't hoping to bump into you."

"Why?" She asked

"I want to know what happened?" The look in his eyes told her, he knew nothing.

"When?" Her questioning reply was quick and sharp as she told him, he must know because he was there. Watching as Rojay shook his head; Jade struggled to believe what was his take on events and her wanting to get away from the situation. Shrugging her shoulders; Jade told Rojay it didn't matter, what was past was gone.

"I can't help the way I feel." Listening to what he wanted to say, why was she preparing to give him the benefit of the doubt? "Aren't you sorry?" He asked. Shocked, she failed to know what she had to be sorry for?

"Your friends' told me where you were."

"What friends?" She questioned who?

"Tamara," Why was she not surprised? Tamara wasn't one to refuse when her opinion and knowledge was called upon. Jade hoped with all hope the one she saw to be her friend hadn't revealed everything. "Bobby boy really wanted to punch my lights out." Rojay smirked. Not wanting her companion to say anything she wasn't prepared to hear, Jade repeated the fact the past was in the past. "Why didn't you tell me?" He asked as she listened. "Why didn't you let me know? I realise I've never so much as pretended to be a gentleman, but the least you could have done was told me."

"I need to go." Attempting to stand and get by, Jade was blocked by the male who wanted answers to his billion questions.

"Why did you leave me?" He asked as she stepped back, his nod indicating they should resit. *'Why was this happening?'* "What happened?" He questioned.

"Tamara shouldn't have told you where I was."

"No, you should have." Rojay told her. Lowering her glance, Jade shook her head. "Why?" Unable to answer, the lone female fell silent. "I need to know."

"I have nothing to say." She told him.

"I deserve an explanation." Rojay insisted she tell why she left without saying anything. "Why run away?"

"Why lock me up?" She answered his questions with a question.

"I never."He shook his head.

"You locked me inside." Jade reminded him.

"Because I wanted to keep you safe."

"I" Jade stuttered.

"Didn't you think I had a right to know where you were?" He repeated.

"You hurt me." She told him.

"It was you who walked out on me." Rojay had clearly misunderstood what she meant by her being hurt.

"I couldn't stay." Relieved his inquiries weren't heading in the direction wanted was avoiding, Jade told him things couldn't continue. "We were over." She said. "You took my money." She said without trust they couldn't be together.

"We both made mistakes, I needed it, I was going to pay you back." His playing the victim caused Jade to realise her leaving him had been the right thing to do.

"You should have asked." She said he could pay her back whenever he had what he owed.

"I needed the money to"

"It doesn't matter." Interrupting what she saw as being a poor excuse for stealing, Jade shook her head and told him to forget it. "If it's gone, it's gone." She shrugged.

"I didn't know if you were alive or died." Why was he blaming her?

"I had go." She insisted.

"You could have gone home." Without words, the look she gave Rojay told him there was no going back to Mama and Papa.

"No." She disagreed with her having a choice as to where she went when she left him. "You hurt me." She repeated. "It was over. It is over." She asked he allow her to pass so she could go home. *'Would he hit her again?'* Struggling to hold back the tears swelling behind her eyes, Jade felt a mix of anger and confusion. *'Would what had happened ever go away?'* Would the hurt, pain and upset ever stop? Feeling Rojay's hand grip the top of her arm, taking a hold which stopped her from leaving as she stood, she asked if he wanted to hurt her again?

"No, I don't fight girls." Looking to the hand which was keeping her where she was, there was no need for her to say what she was thinking. *'Why squeeze so hard?'* Releasing his grip, he told her he was where he was because he needed the truth.

"No." She disagreed.

"We would have worked things out." There it was. The side only she was permitted to see, the side proving the male rock had feelings and was capable of caring.

"No." With tears beginning to sting behind her eyes Jade fought not to release their flow. Weak, Jade knew she needed to stay strong.

"I love you Jade. I loved you." He told her.

"I never loved you." She said. Having experienced what she had, Jade now knew the only thing she had fallen in love with was the idea. *'Not real?'* In Rojay she'd seen a freedom she could only dream of, what she'd forgotten was how fast a dream can turn into a nightmare. Like, admire and envy, Jade had never been in love with Rojay.

"Never?" He asked.

"Never."Unsure why she was allowing him to pull her towards him, she admitted to being sorry. Holding her close, both realised this was bound to happened sooner or later. This was them saying goodbye to what was gone

"I wish I'd known where you were so I could have gotten to you sooner." He sighed.

"There was nothing you could have done to change anything." Taking and keeping hold of her hands as she stepped back from his embrace, Rojay continued to reveal his kind and caring nature. *'Understanding?'* It was clear neither truly understood the hidden meaning behind what each was trying to say.

"I could have turned on the charm." He smirked his cheeky, charming smirk. A smirk the like of which was unique to him.

"It wouldn't have made a difference." She wanted to tell him her mind had been made up, the truth included much more than what he was thinking and she didn't see any reason to say more.

"I would have married you." He said.

"I couldn't be your wife." In a much gentler way than intended, Jade told Rojay what had happened wasn't all about him. His action and reactions confirming the fact she had no need to say anything more. *'She never loved him.'* With her tears being restrained; she smiled a smile which faded when noticing Stacey stood watching and waiting, a smile which turned to a look of dread as she noticed the tail lights of Bobby's car leaving. *'What?'* This couldn't be happening? Surely she was dreaming and about to wake to find herself lay beneath the midday sun? Not Rojay, Jade saw herself slipping, taking a fall and knocking herself unconscious when putting out the rubbish. Slipping in her attempt to follow the one leaving, there was no getting away from the fact Rojay and his strong arms stopped her from falling in amongst the sand and rocks. No mistaking the message in their eyes as their eyes met, both were sorry both misinterpreting the sorrow each saw them-self as forever holding onto.

Rushing, moving as fast as she was able over and between the rocks, rushing across the sand, going as fast as her feet would carry her, the smug grin crawling across Stacey's face; like her having been caught in Rojays arms; told Jade this wasn't a dream.
"What?" She needed to know? "What?" Jade questioned. "What?" She needed to know what had been said.
"No need for words, he saw." Stacey had allowed Bobby to believe the worst. Neither onlooker had heard anything, but that didn't stop them thinking a lot.
"Jump on the bike, we'll catch him up." Rojay offered, but Jade said there was no point.
"Are you together?" Did Stacey really have to ask?
"I'll explain." Rojay assured Jade he would sort things as he questioned what Stacey said.
"Nothing." She shrugged. Unable to hear; Bobby had seen Jade in Rojay's arms and watched as the two held hands before parting.
"Stacey?" Rojay demanded she tell what she knew.
"He asked what the two of you were doing." She shrugged.
"And?" Rojay demanded.
"I said you were talking." Stacey asked Rojay to trust her while Jade realised her school bully had gotten the ultimate revenge.
"I, we never meant." Unsure who and what to believe as Rojay attempted to apologise; Jade said she was going home and asked they leave her alone.
"I'll take you." Taking a second hold of her arm, Rojay insisted on making sure she got home safe.
"I can walk." Pulling away; she told him not to fuss.
"One last ride." He offered.

"She said she could manage." Not happy, Stacey was told the exercise would do her good as she walked after the one following. "It's dark." Telling Stacey it was dark because it was night, Rojay pointed the bemused female in the right direction and said he would join her soon. "You told me you didn't love her." She complained. The two catching up to Jade as they reached the road between the camp and beach. "You married me." Stacey screamed.

"I'll see you at the van." Rojay continued to insist Jade join him while walking away from the one calling herself his wife. *'Married?'* Jade wasn't sure what to say?

Married? Both had kept to themselves the things they didn't want one another to know. *'One last ride?'* Arriving back in the village; Jade said Rojay dropping her around the corner and across the street was fine. *'Not wanting to wake Kevin & Jennifer.'* Jade realised it was Kevin who contacted Bobby to ask if he knew who she was with. *'Thoughtful?'* She could and would forgive those getting use to being parents'.

"Married?" The word escaped her lips as she removed and passed to Rojay his spare helmet. "Congratulations."

"Our honeymoon," He stuttered. "We got tickets to the roadshow as a wedding gift." Forcing a smile; Jade was relieved he hadn't come looking for her.

"From Tamara by any chance," She joked, but if honest she wouldn't put such a stunt past the friend who never saw her doing the right thing; being wrong. "Roland Jackson a married man." She wanted to ask who proposed? *'Was she jealous?'*

"You were at the wedding." His words took Jade back to when she bumped into Ratbag and Stork outside the church on Gretchen and Greyson's big day.

"I thought it was a funeral." She said as with a smirk he said maybe it was.

"She could well be the death of me." He sighed.

"You love her?" She asked. His lowering his gaze confirming his marrying Stacey to be more out of duty.

I MAY PRETEND

'Pregnant?' Regaining her breath and steadying her stance; Jade felt numb upon realising Rojay was going to be a father."Congratulations again." She gasped.

"I would have stayed with you?" He said.

"If I hadn't left." She looked for confirmation, watching as Rojay nodded. "I would have married you." He told her he wished things had been different.

"Yeah," Jade felt the same for different reasons. *'She wished she hadn't had to go for the reason she had.'*

"I can talk to Bobby." He offered.

"No."Jade said things would workout."You talking to him won't help." She shook her head. "A husband and father?" She called him all grown up and he said he would never let his baby down.

"No."She agreed. No, she realised. No, she wished he hadn't said what he did."No, best not." She shook her head when he asked if he could kiss her goodbye. No! Bidding her goodnight; Rojay left Jade standing in what was the deserted and silent village street. *'Rain?'* Jade could hold back her tears no longer when watching Rojay ride away and hearing the hum of his motorcycle disappear into the silent darkness of the night. *'A married man?'* Rojay being married to Stacey should make her happy. *'On honeymoon?'* Relieved neither had come looking for her. Switching the blame, she now knew he would see it as being her who left him and not him who hurt and drove her away. *'A dad?'* How could she tell him what had happened; having learned how he saw being a father as something he refused to fail at? *'His & Stacey's baby?'* Jades' baby hadn't been strong enough to live. *'Spirit.'* Should she tell him? Having to walk the length of the street and cross the road to reach home, her rushing into the bus shelter was to avoid what turned from drizzle into a sudden downpour. She needed her tears to dry before going inside. Tears, crying because she was on her own. *'No telephone call.'* Pushing her hand into her pocket, she pulled out the card to have been attached to the flowers from Bobby. *'Should she read it?'* What would be the point? Kevin was doing his best to prevent her seeing the daily news article telling of a budding romance between the up and coming footballers and those they'd accompanied to the beach roadshow. More than enough photographs to fill an album. Kevin said reporters would invent anything to sell tabloids, calling what had been printed a good relations exercise. A way of gaining investment, Kevin and Jennifer said the purpose of a newspaper was to promote and advertise. Made up scandal to attract the vulnerable and untrue stories to entertain the gullible.

'Sad & confused.' Jade felt both gullible and vulnerable, wet getter wetter, as she stepped out from under the shelter, tears stained her face alongside the falling raindrops. *'Why hadn't Bobby contacted her?'* Why had she given Rojay the time of day? *'Upset.'* Her tears felt colder than what was making her wet. Wet getting wetter, the rain which was fast, thick and heavy hit her shivering, shaky form like a thousand tiny stones. Rain, it raining seemed the perfect end to a day she would rather forget as she decided to continue to make her way home. Crying, when stepping into the road; a set of bright headlights suddenly illuminated her form. *'From nowhere?'* Why hadn't she seen or heard anything? Headlights, stepping forward and falling back as the car came roaring, before screeching to a halt. *'What happened?'* Dropping to the ground, the driver dashed over to where she lay. *'Please let him be all right.'* Why was she lay worrying about him?

"Bobby!" Her vision blurred by tears and the falling rain, the night was cold and dark, looking towards the stationary black car. "Bobby?" She whispered. *'Was it him?'* The shinny, slippery black road and the thick, dark, heavy rain. *'Who?'* Dressed in black, an eye witness said the hooded figure checked what had been hit before abandoning the car and running away. A motorcycle? Jade was sure she heard a bike. Lay, not

I MAY PRETEND

moving, not knowing what it was she was seeing, Jade saw nothing as everything went black.
♫284♫

"Third time lucky."Shannon was only saying what was true, two near misses and a hit. When opening her eyes Jade felt shocked to find herself propped up by white starched pillows; tucked into a hospital bed. *'What happened?'* "He could have killed you." Who was Shannon talking to? Blurred images, able to hear her friends' words, Jade struggled to see what she made out to be the busy fussing female arranging and rearranging flowers and cards on a window shelf dressed with blinds. "It is a wonder there are any flowers left in the florist." Shannon continued. "If you don't wake up soon there won't be." She sighed. Was Jade sleeping? "Guilty as sin if you ask me."

"Ask you what?" Jade questioned what Shannon was talking about, but the chatting female didn't react to her words.

"You need to wake?" Jade was able to hear but unable to reply. "Wake up soon Princess." Shannon told her friend she was still alive.

"Yes," Jade agreed by repeating the positive word inside her mind. Confused, stiff and sore but alive. "Yes," She was alive. *'Had she almost died?'* Was she in hospital? A private room paid for by Papa and insisted upon by Mama. Told the patient needed rest, Shannon and others who rose to leave; told Jade they would be back soon.

"I will let you know if anything changes." The nurse was male with a voice Jade recognised. Why was he there? Having her questions answered as he tucked in the covers of her bed, Jade questioned why Joe was there with her? Why was Mr. Joe Holt the nurse looking after her? What had happened?

Sleeping, when first closing her eyes Jade didn't want everything to go black again. Not a hit and run, she felt sure she hadn't seen the car until it was too late. Unsure, she couldn't say whether or not she'd looked before crossing the quiet road. *'Third time lucky?'* Kevin wanted to know why no one mentioned the other two near misses and Bobby sending flowers by the bucket load was because he was told to stay away. *'A pink & blue teddybear.'* The note said get well soon from Mr. and Mrs. Jackson. Why would Rojay and Stacey wish her well? *'Six days?'* When her eyes again opened; Joe said her not waking for almost a week was expected. No head injury or internal bleeding.Yes, Papa had paid for all medical care needed, but it had been Jennifer and not Jemima who insisted their daughter have the best care his money could buy. Joe was the best private nurse her true parents could find. *'Sorry,'* Why was everyone sorry for what she saw as being her own fault? Eyes filled with a mix of rain and teardrops equaled next to no vision and her listening to what was going on inside her heart resulted in her hearing nothing inside her head.

Late, visiting time would most definitely be over, more flowers, Jade said thank you for the delivery arriving before she saw who carried what she could see. Bobby?

"Am I glad to see you." He gasped as she asked if he was all right. "Not really."He shook his lowered head.

"I'm so sorry." She said. *'Why was she apologising when he had things to apologies for?'* "Sit." She invited him to take a seat in the armchair beside her bed. Civil, Jade didn't have the strength to be angry. Late, with the room being dimly lit she knew it was dark outside.

"We thought we'd lost you" He said. "I thought I had lost you." He told her.

"No," She assured Bobby she was alive.

"I was jealous." He apologised for not getting over himself sooner.

"So you ran me down." Jade half smiled, but Bobby wasn't finding any of what had happened funny. He said there weren't words to say how much he regretted what happened.

I MAY PRETEND

"Don't lie." Jade ask him to be honest when asking why he left her for someone else?

"I didn't." He shook his head. "I should have told you about me and the boys escorting Di and her friends. It was a favour, not a date." He said he was only doing what he was told and then he saw Rojay. "Your hero." He said he didn't blame the biker helping when he couldn't. "There for you while I was being kept busy." Bobby said what he saw made him remember when she ran into the leather clad arms of the motorbike king.

"Rojay is married." Jade assured Bobby that even if he were available; she'd promised herself never to make the same mistake twice, the truth being she was sorry she had made her mistake once. "Interested in where I was." She told him Tamara had said more than she should and the new Mr. and Mrs. Jackson were where they were on honeymoon at the village campsite. Before leaving Bobby placed the card she hadn't yet read into her hand. *'Someone had sent it back to him.'*

♪285♪
♪286♪

Pitta patter rain drops on her window pane, the daylight coming in through open curtains meant she was able to see out and the curtains caused her to realise she wasn't in a private hospital ward, home. Back in her bedroom over the post office/general store, Jade was in the village. A hospital bed, medical equipment and a private nurse, Jennifer said her daughter needed to be where she could keep an eye on her.

"It's raining." She didn't remember falling asleep. "Hope it brightens up. I brought me bathers." Was it morning, or another day? Another week? Had she dreamt what felt like she was dreaming? If yes, what was true? What was real and where was she? The fall down the school steps, that was when her life began to change, becoming surreal, could it be one dying before they are ready; means them going on to experience the life they should have had? *'Alive or dead?'* The pipe over the stream? Had she slipped and fallen into the deep, fast moving water, dying because she drowned? It didn't take a huge drop in body temperature for one to succumb to hypothermia. Had her life become more lost than she had when living through the winter in a trailer? Had Rojay killed her in the attack? Had the train crashed? Had her escape been in vein? Jade recalled waking up in hospital, but found herself questioning whether or not her eyes had ever reopened. *'Was she not there?'* Had she been swallowed by the ocean waves from which Bobby saved her? *'Was Bobby dead too?'* The burial playroom? Had she joined Spirit? The wet cold road? Where? Which had been her true ending? How could she still be alive having faced so very many ends?

"Jimmy?" She questioned the presence of someone she missed. "Am I dying?" Was this her life flashing before her eyes? Having spoken to grannie and Sam on the telephone, Papa sent a telegram and when answering; Jimmy told her he was there with Sawyer and Jeremy. Shannon, Jennifer and Kevin had all been by her hospital bed. She read the card from Rojay and Stacey. *'Had she sat talking to Bobby?'* Joe was a good nurse. Was it time for her to go?

"Dad sends his love and Mavis baked you a cake." Where was she? "Are you okay? I could go run you a warm bath or something." Caring, "Sawyer loves his hot bubbles when he's suffering his aches and pains after ridding." What she was hearing made sense, where she was, was familiar, but how she was feeling felt wrong.

"Jimmy, Am I dying?" Entering the room to sit beside her on the bed, the pinch Jeremy inflicted was to prove she was neither dying, dead or dreaming.

"Scaring us half to death is what you do best." Her brother asked she stop doing what he was sure would make him grey before he reached twenty.

"Memory loss?" She questioned.

"No."Jeremy told her she hadn't been in hospital, but she had, had a fever following her being hit by the car.

"Bobby?" She asked and was told No, Bobby wasn't the one driving, the black car left at the scene was a hire car stolen from the camp. "Five cars were stolen in the local area that week." Stollen cars and umpteen break-ins, Jade had been the only hit and run. Bikers, locals blamed an influx of those preferring two wheels to four. No one they knew, someone saw a figure dressed head to foot in black, but there was no one awaiting their time in court.

"One day and two nights."Joined by Sawyer, those she saw to be true family reminded her of the fact they'd rented grannie's house for the week."On holiday." The trip had been planned and as Jade began to regain what she felt to be herself, she realised she'd dreamt about all the things she wanted, not what had actually happened.

"Here to get you back on your feet." Sawyer said he was in-charge of exercise, Jeremy was there for talking to, and Jimmy had tagged along for fun. Smiling, Jade said she never felt better as all hugged a welcome back hello.

♫287♫

Fun in the sun, sometimes she joined in and sometimes she sat back to watch as her brother and friends swam, surfed and sunbathed.

"Call him." Kevin advised. Taking breakfast into Jade to find her looking at the card she hadn't opened. "Or read it." The male said they all needed putting out of their misery. What did she want it to say? As they entered to tell her of the day they had planned, Jimmy asked Jade what it was she was looking at.

"An envelope."She said what was obvious.

"An envelope containing a card the flowers for which had found the bottom of the bin weeks ago. From Bobby."Kevin asked the boys if they could get her to see sense and make sure she ate something before going out.

"Bobby?" Jeremy questioned? "He's back playing with some of his old team this Saturday. Why don't we go watch, give you chance to talk to him."Jade told her well meaning brother she tried that and was still dressing her wounds having seen him with another girl

"Ouch." Sawyer winced.

"So read the card." Jimmy asked what it would cost her to see what he had to say.

"That would depend what it said." She smiled and he promised to be there to hold her hand.

"Open it." As those around her repeated the word over and over, Jade gave in to peer pressure, her eyes filling with tears as she read and passed the card to Jimmy.

"How long have you had this?" He asked.

"Kevin said weeks." Jeremy answered on his sisters behalf as Sawyer handed her a tissue.

"Marry me?" He gasped having glimpsed what was written on what his partner was holding.

"And you've kept him waiting?" Knowing the last time she saw Bobby was when she was with Rojay. *'A proposal?'* Jade doubted he was still waiting for her answer.

"Only one way to find out." Rushing her downstairs and through the shop; all stopped when finding Bobby stood by his car outside.

"Kevin."Jade should have known someone would be keeping him up to date with what was going on.

"No, Bobby."Jimmy advised she get his name right before she told him her answer. Stepping back and allowing her to walk forward, Jade asked Bobby if Kevin had asked him to call round.

"Yeah," Smiling as he looked up before looking into her eyes. "He said you had something to tell me."

"He knew?" Shaking her head; Jade couldn't believe no one said anything.

"I had to ask him and your mum for your hand first." Bobby asked if he had done the right thing.

"I guess." Jade took a deep breath as she stood before the one waiting for her to answer his question.

"Shall we do this in the car."He opened for her the passenger door as she agreed and stepped inside, sitting side by side, both smiled nervously.

"Open the glove compartment." Expecting to find a ring box, Jade was puzzled to find an envelope. "That is how much I love you, how well I know you." Her baby scan and a silver bracelet inscribed with the word Spirit. "I collect it. I knew you would change your mind. I missed being there by a matter of minutes." Both knew nothing either had done would or could have changed anything.

"Yes."Jade sniffed. "Yes."She told him. Placing what she'd opened back into the glove compartment for safe keeping, Jade got out of the car; went around to his door open it and told him. "Yes," Her acceptance causing everyone to cheer as Bobby got out of the car. "If you still want me to marry you." Taking her into his arms. Bobby told Jade there was nothing he wanted more.

♪*288*♪

Ringing bells and a singing choir, friends and family, flowers and balloons, doves and a harpist, press and photographers, anyone who was anyone and everyone they wanted, was there.

"Always the bridesmaid, never the bride?" Jade kept her promise to have Shannon as her bridesmaid and her bridesmaid smiled over to her plus one Brent whose wink told her she looked fine. Tamara and Gretchen, white, not everything was traditional. Yes, the father of the bride paid, but it was those she called mum and dad who walked with the blushing bride down the aisle. Mrs. Suzann Hallas got to wear her big hat and Joe was where he was with his colleague Louise because the two medical professionals were considering a change in career. Jimmy and Sawyer made the most handsome of ushers alongside Greyson and Tarquin while Jeremy took his place as bestman. *'A true family affair.'*

"I do." In the bright, warm month of August. No bride ever looked happier, no parents could be prouder, no step mother ever looked more awkward and friends more relieved. An outdoor setting, standing as ushers Jimmy and Sawyer couldn't ask for more than the vast amount of publicity the event being held in the grounds of their new venture would bring. *'Man & wife?'* How friends got to use the marriage of a footballer to promote their hotel dedicated to cyclist and sightseers and how many brides got to spend their honeymoon cheering from the football terraces at Wembley football Stadium.

♪*289*♪

THE END

A BOOK WITH ITS' OWN PLAYLIST

*Many different artist
have recorded & released
some of the songs listed
The ones in the authors collection
are from 60s 70s 80s & 90s
A families collection of songs
creating the sound tracks of a childhood
#playlist*

A BOOK WITH ITS' OWN PLAYLIST

1: Black is Black
2: Ob La Di Ob La Da *(Mum's fav)*
3: The Happening
4: Rose Garden
5: Happy Birthday to you
6: Remember the days *of the old school yard*
7: Lonely this Christmas
8: Happy Birthday
9: Under the Boardwalk
10: Pretend
11: Leader of the Pack
12: La Bamba
13: Days of Pearly Spencer

14: Oliver's Army
15: Only the Lonely
16: Another Brick in the wall
17: The Boys are back in town
18: Love's Unkind
19: The Tide is High
20: Rag Doll
21: Senses Working overtime
22: Dreaming
23: Cool for Cat's
24: Swords of a thousand men
25: Goody two shoes
26: Don't Stop
27: More than a number *in my little red book*
28: It's your life
29: The Wild One
30: Generals & Majors
31: Born to be Wild
32: Substitute
33: Drowning in Berlin
34: The Model
35: Pop Muzik

36: Save the last Dance
37: Hold me close
38: Rebel Yell
39: Give a Little Love
40: Girls, Girls, Girls
41: Si Si Je Suis un *Rock Star*
42: Video killed the *Radio Star*
43: Automatic Lover
44: Rich Kids
45: Let it snow, let it snow
46: He's a Rebel
47: I'll meet you at *Midnight*
48: Ever fallen in love
(With someone you shouldn't have fallen in love with)
49: Kissing in the back row
50: Dancing with Myself
51: Apache
52: Summer in the city
53: Mr Blue Sky
54: Red Light Spells *Danger*
55: Shoop Shoop Song
56: Road to nowhere
57: Two Princes
58: A Thing called love
59: Day dream Believer
60: Love is like Oxygen
61: I want you to want me
62: Sweet Sixteen
63: It's my Party
64: Sweets for my sweet
65: All of me loves all of you
66: The Locomotion
67: Wig-wam bam
68: Little Willy
69: Duke Of Earl
70: Black Night

A GEORGE

71: Ball Park Incident
72: The Six teens
73: Perfect
74: Love the one your with
75: Picture This
76: Teenage Rampage
77: Ca plane pour moi
78: Cruel to be Kind
79: You Spin me Round
80: Sunday Girl
81: Heart of Glass
82: Lies
83: The Boys of Summer
84: Tell Him
85: Girls just wanna have fun
86: D.I.S.C.O
87: Come Dancing
88: The Safety Dance
89: Homely Girl
90: Cotton eye Joe
91: Take Me Home Country Rd
92: Some Girls
93: Rock me Amadeus
94: Say Hello Wave Goodbye
95: Love & Pride
96: Wild World
97: Crush
98: Secret
99: The Animal Song
100: Will You
101: Free Falling
102: The Look of Love
103: Living in the Plastic age
104: Devil Gate drive
105: Ma Baker
106: You take me Up
107: Because the Night
108: I wanna be free
109: Let your Love Flow
110: If you think you know How to love me
111: Forever Live or die

112: Boys don't Cry
113: Forever & ever
114: Terry
115: Moonlight Shadow
116: Seasons in the sun
117: Mississippi
118: I cant stand up for falling down
119: Money for nothing
120: I wish it could be Christmas
121: Stop the Cavalry
122: Glass of Champagne
123: Soldier Boy
124: Merry Christmas everyone
125: Little Saint Nick
126: Fairytale of New York
127: I won't back Down
128: All or Nothing
129: Fade to Grey
130: Have I the Right
131: Leave in Silence
132: Master & Servant
133: Eight Day
134: They don't know
135: Public image
136: On my Radio
137: King of the wild frontier
138: Gypsies Tramps & Thieves
139: Dance yourself Dizzy
140: Hourglass
141: Way Down
142: Runaway
143: Watching the Detectives
144: Silly Games
145: Tainted Love
146: White Wedding
147: Do you really want to hurt me
148: Go your own way
149: Dear John
150: Into the Valley
151: Are Friends Electric

152: Fade away & Radiate

474

I MAY PRETEND

153: A New England
154: Once Bitten Twice Shy
155: This House *Is where your love stands*
156: 7 Teen
157: Bang Bang
158: No more Heroes
159 Cruel Summer
160: Holiday
161: Smoke gets in your eyes
62: Just Like Jessie James
163: Messages
164: Don't let me be *misunderstood*
165: Karma Chameleon
166: Silence is Golden
167: Runaway (DJ)
168: Going to the Chapel
169: Diamond Smiles:
170: Third finger, left hand
171: Y.m.c.a
172: Oops upside your head
173: My Boy Lollipop
174: Do the Hucklebuck
175: Hold Me
176: I can't help *falling in love with you*
177: Cars
178: Maybe Tomorrow
179: Bang Bang *my baby shot me down*
180: Knocking on heavens door
181: Locomotion (OMD)
182: Do it all over Again
183: Don't turn around
184: Its raining
185: Dreams
186: It started with a kiss
187: Cupid
188: Dr. Love
189: Poison Arrow
190: Another Nail for my heart

191: Chirpy Chirpy Cheep *Cheep*
192: January
193: Please Mr. Postman
194: Sorrow
195: One Way Ticket
196: The Lion Sleeps tonight
197: Gonna make you a star
198: Joan of Arc
199: Nah Nah Hey, *Hey kiss him, goodbye*
200: Talking Loud & Clear
201: Funky Town
202: Antmusic
203: This town ain't big *for both of us*
204: Einstein a go go
205: We gotta get *out of this place*
206: Labelled with Love
207: Just what I needed
208: Down Under
209: Don't worry Be Happy
210: Lightening
211: Walking Back *to happiness*
212: Far, Far Away
213: Happy Hour
214: Your kiss is sweet
215: Bad to me
216: Church of the poison mind
217: The Clapping Song
218: A Windmill in *old Amsterdam*
219: Puff the magic Dragon
220: Theres a ghost *in my house*
221: Toy Soldiers
222: So you win again
223: I'll take you there
224: Ring my Bell
225: Three Steps to Heaven
226: Wedding Bells
227: Lets jump the broomstick
228: Something old *Something new*

A GEORGE

229: Lets stick together
230: Its a mystery
231: My Co ca Choo
232: Prince Charming
233: Thats what love will do
234: Always on my mind
235: Eyes without a face
236: I only wanna be *with you*
237: It ain't what you do
238: Puss in Boots
239: Itsy bitsy teeny *weeny yellow polka do bikini*
240: Snoopy v the Red *Baron*
241: Baby come Back
242: from New York to LA
243: Nice legs *shame about the face*
244: Sit Down
245: Tarzan Boy
246: Summer of 69
247: Jimmy Jimmy
248: Running Bear
249: Teenage Kicks
250: Bad Moon Rising
251: Blinded by the Light
252: Should I stay *or should I go*
253: Hot in the city
254: Ball & Chain
255: Take these *chains from my heart*
256: 9 to 5
257: Nutbush City limits
258: No place like Home
259: Girlie Girlie
260: I Knew I Loved You
261: Juke Box Jive
262: The Bump
263: Keep on Dancin
264: Trojan Horse
265: Agadoo
266: Let's Twist Again
267: The Time Warp
268: What I got in mind
269: Jimmy Mack
270: Tease Me
271: The birdie Song
272: The Floral Dance
273: Saturday Night
274: Breaking the law
275: Good Girls Don't
276: Drop the Pilot
277: Dizzy
278: Drummer man
279: Young Hearts run Free
280: I could be Happy
281: Telegraph
282: Things
283: Silver Dream machine
284: Mad World
285: Wide Boy
286: I can't stand the rain
287: Shang-a-lang
288: Summer love sensation
289: You ain't seen *nothing yet*
  The End
290: We're not gonna take it
291: The Ballroom Blitz
292: If the kids were United
293: I'm a Believer
294: Touch Me
295: Rasputin
296: Top of the pops
297: Relax
298: I don't like Mondays
299: Kung Fu Fighting
300: Bye Bye Baby

Some songs may offend the author would like to remind you this is their playlist you are in no way obliged to seek out & listen. If you do, it could be fun to listen to something different, or remember what you use to hear.

A BOOK WITH ITS' OWN PLAYLIST
ADD YOUR PLAYLIST

A GEORGE

YOU MAY ALSO LIKE
STARRY
STARRY

Who from Where

**A story of not belonging
Magic Mystery & Witchcraft
Not from the planet Earth**

I MAY PRETEND

THERE IS ALWAYS A FIRST TIME
We all grow up
SOME THINGS SHOULD NEVER HAPPEN
TRUST
Should never end in
BETRAYAL

What a tangled web we leave
When those we love are the ones we deceive.

Fifteen and not yet kissed. Fifteen years of age and not included on anyones party list, never permitted to go where everyone else goes. How was one to learn about the world if never allowed to go out and experience what the world holds? Fifteen, a mature teenager for who being fifteen meant she would be sixteen soon, all she wanted was to fit in where being a straight 'A' student equalled being the odd one out. Protected from the world by rich influential parents for who embarrassment was the worst crime imaginable.

Seventeen, he was the local bad boy who rode around on his motorbike. Eighteen, he was the good guy with everything going for him, the super fit sportsman with the world at his feet, she just wanted to fit in and be like everyone else.

Growing up isn't always easy & when one steps outside what is boundaried they face having to explore what is bad, alongside the fun filled adventure. Growing up is exciting up to the time when it becomes complicated.

Nothing in her protected life failed until everyone in it let her down. When Jade Jennifer Barris experiences things for the first time, she discovers how some firsts can quickly escape ones control, creating a confusing tangled web of white lies & behavioural deceit. Having done what she was told she shouldn't, Jade believes her tragic secret is the biggest secret of all, but all is never as it seems when everyone attempts to keep what is personal hidden beneath a cloak of deceit and lies.

Printed in Great Britain
by Amazon